BALTHASAR'S VOICE SOUNDED THROUGH HER EARPIECE. "YOU HAVE CONTROL, SILENCE."

All around them, the keelsong changed. It deepened, and at the same time gained a whole new range of sound. The dome of the hull quivered, then quietly faded to translucence. The stars shone through.

The yoke moved smoothly under Silence's hand. She smiled, allowing herself a brief moment to savor the experience of flying a new ship, then turned her attention to her course. She took a deep breath and sought her voidmarks.

Almost immediately, the Carter's Road took shadowy form before her: first the curve of the great wheel's rim, the fire-edged ghost of the spoke, then the entire shape of the cartwheel, turning lazily against a purpled starfield splotched with the gaudy coronae of uncountable suns. Silence marked her course with a practiced eye: over the top, onto the rim and then down it, moving with its spin, then out through the white-hot hub. *Sun-Treader* seemed to float on a river of fire, beneath a sky of fiery cloud.

FIVE-TWELFTHS OF HEAVEN

MELISSA SCOTT

BAEN
science fiction
BOOKS

FIVE-TWELFTHS OF HEAVEN

This is a work of fiction. All the characters and events portrayed in this book are fictional, and any resemblance to real people or incidents is purely coincidental.

A Baen Book

Baen Enterprises
8-10 W. 36th Street
New York, N.Y. 10018

First printing, April 1985

ISBN: 0-671-55952-4

Cover art by Kevin Johnson

Printed in the United States of America

Distributed by
SIMON & SCHUSTER
MASS MERCHANDISE SALES COMPANY
1230 Avenue of the Americas
New York, N.Y. 10020

FIVE-TWELFTHS OF HEAVEN

Chapter 1

The court complex was crowded as it always was, jammed with contentious Secasian natives babbling away in the local variant of the Hegemony's official coine. Silence Leigh edged her way through the crowd toward the entrance of the Probate Court hall, trying not to draw too much attention to herself. For all that she was decorously veiled, the stark mourning cloth drawn so tight across her face that she could barely stand to breathe the stifling air of the corridors, she had neither man nor homunculus to escort her, and an unaccompanied woman was fair game at any time. Almost as if conjured by the thought, a bearded man jostled against her, trying to see her face beneath the veil. Silence turned slightly, so they met shoulder to shoulder, refusing to let herself be pushed aside. The man grinned down at her, then was lost in the crowd. Silence felt a surge of pure, screaming fury. In the three weeks since her grandfather had died, stranding her on Secasia until his affairs could be settled, she had had to put up with that sort of harassment almost daily.

Then her anger was drowned by the numb misery that seemed to follow any thought of her grandfather's death. It had been so unexpected, had given her no time to spot the warnings of ill health or sheer old age, no time to prepare herself for the unthinkable. There had been only the call from the planetary police, then the chill, sterile hall where she had identified the body, and finally the search for her uncle, the third member of the crew, whose signature was required before the police could release the body. She still could not fully understand what had happened. Bodua Leigh had been an old man, true enough, but not that old. Certainly he himself had felt no warnings of impending doom: he had left his business in its usual state of inspired confusion. Silence shook her head. Her grandfather had been a brilliant businessman in his way—it had been his talent for profitable improvisation that had made him the chief man of business for the richest oligarch on Cap Bel. But that had been ten years before, before the Hegemony had conquered the Rusadir worlds, and in passing ruined the oligarchs of Cap Bel. Bodua Leigh's methods were less suited for managing the affairs of a single starship, trading along the fringes of the Hegemony. But he had refused to change, and now she was paying the price of his stubbornness.

Two men were waiting at the door of the Probate Court, both in the dark red livery of the court's staff. The older of the two held out a hand to bar her from entering.

"This is the Probate Court, miss. Women's Court is two floors down."

"Yes, I know," Silence answered.

"You're a litigant, then?" The guard's expression made it quite clear that he found that hard to believe but, given the Hegemony's laws, there was no other plausible explanation.

"Yes, I am."

This time, the off-world cadence of her speech betrayed her, and the two guards exchanged glances. The older said, "This way, miss. You're familiar with Hegemonic law? You know you need a guardian—a male guardian—to speak for you in court."

"Yes," Silence said, and was unable to keep the bitterness out of her voice. "I'm meeting him here."

"I see, miss." The guard's expression showed only too clearly what he thought of a guardian who would allow a woman to travel alone to the court complex, but he said nothing. He escorted her to the benches reserved for the litigants, handed her to a seat, and then returned to his post. Silence loosened her veil slightly, letting in some of the cooler air of the courtroom, then glanced nervously around the long hall. The Probate Court was even more crowded than the corridors, the benches on the floor of the hall filled to capacity with both local notables and off-worlders who thought they might have an interest in one of the many wills to be proved today. The gallery was equally crowded, filled with idlers from the port come to see the show. They were in a holiday mood, she thought sourly, and why not? There was a special attraction today: it was not often that an off-worlder died so magnificently intestate, or with a woman as his sole heir. She scanned the hall again, looking for the pudgy figure of her maternal uncle. There was no sign of him in the sea of unfamiliar faces. Where are you, Uncle Otto? she thought desperately. I can't do anything without you to sanction it.

Then her lips thinned slightly. She could guess

where her uncle had gone. There were only two choices. Either he was drugged in one of the many smokehouses around the port, or he was being swindled by a dealer in curiosities, feeding his obsession with lost Earth. No, she corrected herself, it hardly qualified as an obsession. The explorers and magi who sought Earth simply because the true roads had been lost during the Millennial Wars, or for the lost knowledge, or because Earth was mankind's proper home were obsessed. Otto Razil was interested only in the profits involved. The last time he had tried to persuade her grandfather to make a search, Razil had quoted a possible profit of over five million Delian pounds. The old man had laughed at him, and Razil had stalked out, muttering something about going where he would be appreciated. Silence's eyes filled with tears she could not afford.

The group talking softly in front of the judge's high bench broke apart, and the clerk-of-court consulted his sheaf of printouts.

"The case of Bodua Kesar Leigh," he announced, his voice carried to the corridors and waiting rooms by the microphones embedded in the heavy torque of his office. "Will the interested parties come before the face of justice?"

Silence hesitated, hoping against hope to see her uncle's stocky figure appear at one of the doors. There was movement at the farthest door, someone shoving his way into the hall, and she sighed her relief. Then the figure came clear, and a merchant in long robes shifted sideways along a rear bench to make room for his colleague. Silence whispered a curse.

"The case of Bodua Kesar Leigh," the clerk announced again, and Silence shook herself. She gathered her full, ankle-length coat around her, and edged her way out into the open space before the judge's bench. The old man peered down at her, his wrinkled brown face not unfriendly.

"Is there no one else?" he asked the clerk, who shrugged. "Call again."

The clerk repeated his call, but there was no response except for an appreciative chuckling from the gallery.

"No one at all?" the judge repeated, frowning. "Young woman, come here."

Silence did as she was told, staring up through the narrow slit in her veil.

"Now, what's this all about, girl?" the judge asked. "Surely you know the Hegemony's laws."

"Yes, your Honor," Silence said carefully. "I've been told that I cannot speak for myself, but must be represented by a male guardian, and I had made arrangements for my uncle to be here. But he isn't, and I'm from Cap Bel, in the Rusadir. I don't know anyone else who'd be able to speak for me."

"Your uncle's name?" the judge asked.

"Otto Razil."

The judge gestured to the clerk. "Call Otto Razil."

The clerk nodded, and adjusted his transmitters to reach every area of the court complex. "Otto Razil! On pain of fine and forfeit, answer to the Court of Probate. Otto Razil!"

Silence held her breath, but refused to look at the open doors of the hall. Razil wasn't coming, that much seemed clear; he was as useless as he'd always been, and she was stuck with the consequences yet again. . . .

The judge cleared his throat and leaned forward. "We can't wait all day, girl. You can either hire an advocate—" One withered hand swept out, indicating a bench of shaven-headed lawyers toward the front of the hall. "—or the court will appoint a guardian for you. Which will it be?"

"My money is tied up in my grandfather's estate," Silence said, forcing herself to think constructively. "Unless I can draw on that, the court will have to appoint a guardian."

"Since it is the court's responsibility to decide the rightful owner of the estate," the judge said dryly, "you could hardly be permitted access. The court will appoint a guardian. Your name?"

"Silence Leigh."

The judge raised an eyebrow at the old-fashioned name. "And your relation to—" he glanced at his printout "—Bodua Kesar Leigh?"

"My grandfather," Silence answered, then corrected herself, remembering the Hegemony's laws. "My father's father."

The judge nodded. "The uncle you mentioned, he's not of agnate kindred?"

Silence hesitated. "He's my mother's brother."

"Not the agnate line," the judge murmured, noting that on his printout, then signaled to the clerk. "There's quite a bit of property involved, young lady."

The clerk rose to his feet. "Is there any free man, citizen of Secasia or other world of the Asterion Hegemony, who will, under the provisions of the Tabiran Laws and the decree of the Hegemon, act as guardian for this woman, Silence Leigh, granddaughter and heir of Bodua Kesar Leigh, provided thereby that guardianship is not taken away from any legal guardian? A fee of three solas is offered for the service."

There was an excited stirring in the gallery—three solas was a day's wage on Secasia—and some quick exchanges among the merchants on the floor of the hall, the latter prompted by the preliminary assessment of Bodua Leigh's estate, now displayed on the viewscreens that ringed the hall. The sound died away in a disappointed mumble as a man rose to his feet in the front row, lifting his hand to attract the judge's attention.

"May it please the court, I'm willing to act as Miss Leigh's guardian."

The judge nodded gravely. "Come forward, and give your name."

The man stepped out from the row of merchants, his hands folded politely in the sleeves of his crimson coat. Prominent on one sleeve was the mark of Secasia's largest trading house. "My name is Tohon Champuy, merchant-master and freeholder of this world. I have often had dealings with the young lady's grandfather, and know something of his business."

"No!" Silence bit back the rest of her startled exclamation. Champuy knew her grandfather's business, all right, but only because he'd been trying to cheat the old man for the past five years. "Sir, your Honor, rather, can I refuse?"

The judge frowned. "On what grounds?"

"Merchant Champuy's been trying for five years to buy *Black Dolphin*, or to get Grandfather under contract," Silence said. "And at scrap prices, too, for a starship with a new keel and engines—" She broke off, realizing that she was babbling, and Champuy spoke quickly into the silence.

"I don't like to contradict a lady, your Honor, but the *Black Dolphin* isn't worth much more than the scrap price. In fact, that was one of the reasons I offered Bodua Leigh a contract, in hopes that he'd be able to repair the ship properly. I'm sure the strain of handling so battered a ship hastened his death."

"That's not true," Silence said.

The judge glanced dubiously at her, then touched buttons on the control pad embedded in the surface of the bench. Screens slid across the upper windows of the hall, dimming the light considerably. A display globe descended slowly from the ceiling, a scale replica of *Black Dolphin* coalescing in its center. Silence's eyes filled with tears at the sight, and she shook them away angrily. There was no time for that now, she told herself. If she wanted to keep the ship that was rightfully hers, she would have to fight for it, and she could not afford emotion.

"What was your position aboard the *Black Dolphin*, young lady?" the judge asked.

"I am the pilot, your Honor."

"The pilot?" the judge repeated incredulously, and a murmur of surprise rippled through the hall.

Silence ignored it, used to being an oddity. "Yes, your Honor."

"A pilot has very little to do with the maintenance of the ship," Champuy said quickly. "I am certain that Bodua would not have burdened a woman—"

"Wait, please." Silence clasped her hands in supplication, playing for time. She had been thinking like a man, in terms of ships and cargos, the economics of a star-traveller's life, but that wouldn't help her in the Hegemony. Only the Hegemony's peculiar customs could rescue her—if she could make them work for her. "Sir, I don't want him as my guardian because—there's another reason he wanted the ship, battered as it may be. He wanted not only the ship, but her pilot—myself." She bowed her head as if in shame, scanning the surrounding faces from under the protection of her veil. "My grandfather, all honor to his name, wouldn't sell."

For a moment, she thought she had overdone it, that the judge and the staring spectators would catch her lie, but then there was a swelling mutter of voices from hall and gallery, angry and indignant.

The judge glared at Champuy, who spread his hands wide.

"Your Honor, the young lady is distraught. I assure you, my offer was genuine, and my concern for her merely fatherly, prompted by my long association with her grandfather. I will state, in open court and under binding oath, the terms I offer. I will purchase *Black Dolphin* from her—at the assessors' price, even though I believe it to be an inflated figure—and I will keep Miss Leigh on as pilot, if she should choose to stay." He turned and spoke directly to the pilot. "You will not find a better offer, young lady."

I know a threat when I hear one, Silence thought. To the judge, she said, "Your Honor, I do not want him for my guardian."

The judge glanced from her to the merchant and shrugged irritably. "Very well. Merchant Champuy, the young woman has declined your services as guardian, and I will uphold her refusal. Please stand aside."

Champuy bowed, expressionless. "As your Honor pleases."

The judge nodded to his clerk, who rose to his feet. "Is there any free man, citizen of Secasia or other world of the Asterion Hegemony, who will, under the provisions of the Tibiran Laws and the decree of the Hegemon, act as guardian for this woman, Silence Leigh, granddaughter and heir to Bodua Kesar Leigh, provided thereby that guardianship is not taken away from any legal guardian? A fee of three solas is offered for the service. This is the second time of asking."

There were a few stirrings among the lesser merchants toward the back of the hall—after all, there were potential profits to be made from the guardianship of a woman who was heir to a starship—but Champuy turned to look blandly at them and the noises subsided. Silence winced. Champuy was one of the most powerful merchants on Secasia by virtue of his combine directorship—certainly he was the most powerful in the hall. If he had some scheme, none of the others would risk interfering in it.

The judge leaned forward, scowling first at the more solvent audience on the floor of the hall, then up at the galleries. "This is absurd," he exclaimed. "Is no one willing to fulfill his obligations—even for three solas?"

There was a burst of conversation in the gallery then, as the unemployed men seated there realized that they were being given the chance to earn a day's pay, and to have some fun in the process. She had outsmarted herself, Silence realized, and her stomach twisted. She had avoided the Champuy's direct guardianship, but a guardian chosen from the gallery would have no reason to try to protect her interests, as one of Champuy's rivals might. In fact, to avoid offending Champuy, and to buy favor and perhaps a job, anyone from the gallery would cheerfully sell *Black Dolphin*, regardless of her wishes. Under the Hegemony's laws, there was nothing she could do to stop it. If only the Rusadir hadn't resisted its absorption by the Hegemony ten years ago, she thought greyly. The Hegemon might have let us keep a few of our old rights. . . . But there was no use wishing. She was going to lose the *Dolphin*, and with it her only chance to lead a star-traveller's life. Oh, she would get enough money for ship and cargo to take her back to Cap Bel in style, to let her live without a husband, or provide her with a highly respectable dowry, as she chose. But without a ship, she would have no way of proving herself as a pilot. It had been hard enough to get her license for the Rusadir, and to have it extended to cover the Hegemony, when she was twenty and her family had influence with the Commercial Boards. Now, with the Hegemony in complete control of the Rusadir, and threatening to expand into the Fringe, there wasn't a captain alive who would make trouble for himself by hiring a woman pilot. Silence closed her eyes, momentarily grateful for the veil that hid her despair.

"Excuse me, most honorable. May I speak?"

The call came not from the gallery but from the back of the hall. Silence looked up quickly, but could see only an arm, encased in star-traveller's leather rather than Secasian rosilk, waving above the heads of the men standing behind the last row of benches. Then the arm's owner worked himself free of the crush, stumbling over someone's leg as he stepped out into the aisle.

"I beg your pardon, sir, but I believe I can help."

The speaker was not a particularly impressive man, of average height, hawk-faced and greying, but he was a star-traveller—a captain, from the medallion slung around his neck. Silence held her breath as the judge glanced from her to Champuy, who was frowning openly. The latter seemed to decide the judge.

"Come forward, Captain."

"Thank you, sir." At the head of the aisle, the star-traveller bowed twice, first to Silence and then to the judge. "If the court allows it, I'm willing to act as the lady's guardian—given her consent, of course."

"Your name and status?" the clerk asked.

"Denis Balthasar, owner-captain of the Delian ship *Sun-Treader*." He held up a hand to forestall Champuy's immediate protest. "I am a citizen of Delos, but I have commercial rights—citizen status in the courts—as granted under the Johannine Law to persons doing a significant amount of business in the Hegemony." He reached into a pocket of his jacket and produced a thin metal disk slightly smaller than his palm. The clerk took it and fed it into one of his machines.

"Your identification disk?"

Balthasar slipped his medallion from around his neck and handed it over. The clerk consulted his machines again, then returned both disks.

"Your status is confirmed."

"One moment," Champuy exclaimed. "Your Honor, you cannot uphold the right of a mere Delian, even one with commercial rights, and give him precedence over Secasians born and bred."

The judge looked at him with undisguised distaste. "Merchant-master Champuy, the majority of Secasians present today show no desire to do their civic duty. Captain Balthasar is a star-traveller, and therefore the young lady's kin by association. If Miss Leigh has no objection, I am willing to appoint Captain Balthasar to represent her interests."

Silence hesitated only momentarily. While the men had argued, she had had time to think. Balthasar was an unknown quantity, and it was certain that no man would offer to take on the duties of a guardian unless he thought there was some advantage in it for him. But he was also a star-traveller, part of a world she understood and could manipulate, and a Delian—and a far better choice than anyone else she had seen. She could worry about his motives later. "Your Honor, I accept Captain Balthasar as my guardian."

The judge nodded. "See to it," he said, and the clerk rose to pronounce the formulae. When he was done, and both parties had set their thumbprints to the agreement, Balthasar drew her aside, smiling a vague apology to the judge.

"Quick, was any of that true?" he murmured, still smiling.

"Which?" Silence whispered back.

"What you told them," Balthasar answered.

Silence hesitated, then admitted, "Champuy's never wanted me, just my ship."

"Well, then—"

"No, hold on," Silence said. "Why're you doing this?"

"I suppose you wouldn't believe mere benevolence?" Balthasar asked.

"No," Silence said flatly, old fears stirring. There were worse things than ending up back on Cap Bel—but the man was a fellow star-traveller, she reminded herself, and would follow those codes. At least this way, there was a chance of keeping the ship.

"I need a pilot," Balthasar said quietly, suddenly serious, "and for reasons I can't explain here, it's worth a lot to me to get a woman pilot. You're the first one I've found."

Or at least the first one who was desperate enough to take the job, Silence thought. Sure, there were no female pilots in the Hegemony or, any more, in the Rusadir—it was not explicitly illegal for a woman to hold a pilot's license, but the legal and customary restrictions, particularly the veil, that kept women under some man's tutelage throughout their lives, made it impossible for a woman to meet the licensing requirements. But there were no legal bars to women on the Fringe Worlds and, if custom kept them out of piloting, there was always Misthia. Women ruled on Misthia; women flew Misthia's starships, and no star-traveller was averse to money. If the price were right, he could always hire one of their pilots—though, to be fair, no Misthian liked working for a man. Still, she thought, I don't like the sound of this.

"You'll have to tell me more than that," she said.

Balthasar looked pained. "I can't tell you now, not here," he said. "Look, I don't blame you for not trusting me. I'll do whatever you say I should about your ship, about your grandfather's things. But look what I'm offering. I'll give you a pilot's job, passage from here to Delos guaranteed even if you turn down my other offer, and you can leave the ship there without any other obligation. On Delos, you're bound to find work."

Delos. *Black Dolphin* had never traded there; the ships that plied the Delian lanes were owned by richer men than Bodua Leigh. But Silence had heard tales of Delos. It was the richest of the non-aligned Fringe Worlds, their unofficial leader—richer even than much of the Hegemony. And Delos was free. She would not have to resort to fictions there. Silence shook her head, an almost unacknowledged dream dying stillborn. She had thought, in the first days after her grandfather's death, of trying to run *Dolphin* herself, as pilot and owner. But she would never find a crew willing to serve under a woman, especially not on Secasia. She had no choice worth making, except to accept Balthasar's offer.

"All right," she said slowly. "I'll do it."

"Thank you." Balthasar looked over his shoulder at the display globe, and the ship's image frozen in its center. "What do you want done?"

Silence took a last look at the ship she had piloted for nine years, then resolutely looked away. "Sell it—the assessors' price is the absolute minimum, but I doubt you can get much more. The cargo's included in the assessment, so we can forget that. There'll be some debts—field fees and the like—but the money in Grandfather's accounts should cover them."

Balthasar nodded and turned back to the judge. "I beg your pardon, sir. We're ready to proceed."

"I'm glad to hear it, Captain." The judge glanced at his printouts again. "You're prepared to take possession of Bodua Leigh's property—the standard freighter *Black Dolphin*, her cargo, and the assets currently in accounts held under that name—and to assume responsibility, within the limits of those assets, for any debts legally incurred by Bodua Leigh, all this in the name of Captain Leigh's heir, Silence?"

"Yes, your Honor," Balthasar said.

Silence touched his shoulder. "The debts first."

The captain nodded. "Sir, it's Miss Leigh's—and my wish that the money in Captain Leigh's accounts should go to pay off his legal debts. Any surplus, of course, should go to Miss Leigh."

"I beg your pardon, Captain," the clerk interjected, "but Captain Leigh's debts were substantial. Even applying the total amount available, over half the debt remains unpaid."

"Let me see that," Silence snapped.

Balthasar caught the printout as it emerged from the clerk's console, and held it while Silence scanned the columns of numbers. There were half a dozen entries of which she knew nothing, repairs and modifications that had never been made, supply purchases that made no sense, contracts that suddenly showed losses instead of profits. . . . Even her grandfather's haphazard methods should not have produced such strange results. Her confusion was replaced by anger as she read the list of creditors' names. Herlich and Wak; Chandlers; Adelphi Yards; Swirka Company: they were all part of the combine Champuy headed. Champuy's own name was even on the list, and according to the faint printing Bodua Leigh had owed him more than he owed any other single creditor. Silence frowned. She actually remembered that contract, a cargo of rosilk, to be sold on Akra Leuke. They had indeed bought on credit, but had made a decent profit, and had paid off the debt on the return trip. It would have been easy enough for Champuy to change his own records, and the other companies' as well, but the ship's data bank should have shown payments to Champuy, and should have proved that Bodua Leigh never bought any of the other things—

"Uncle Otto," she said aloud.

"What?" Balthasar turned to look at her.

"Uncle Otto. He could sign for Grandfather; he's the one who ran up these debts."

"Can you prove it?" Balthasar asked calmly, too calmly for her liking.

Silence took a deep breath, fought back the urge to strike out at him and at Champuy, to shriek her fury. "No, of course not." It was clear now why Champuy had tried to get himself made her guardian, and why her uncle had failed to appear at the court. Champuy might be owed the largest amount of money, but that did not give him clear title to *Black Dolphin* if she were sold to pay the creditors. And it would be the ship he was interested in, not just the money—no, she realized, not the ship so much as the ship's fittings, her charts, and most especially the star-books, the collections of pilots' instructions that took the ships from sun to sun. Rusadir star-travellers, free until the absorption from the Hegemony's strict regulations, had always kept better books than the Hegemony's star-travellers were allowed to own. Or was there more to it than that? she wondered suddenly, remembering port gossip. Champuy, it was said, was interested in Earth—interested in the same mercenary way as was her uncle. It looked as though Razil had finally found himself a backer, though she

could not tell why the merchant would be willing
to go to so much trouble when he could afford to
buy another ship for Razil and leave her stranded. . . . She put that train of thought aside as
unprofitable: he was doing it. Well, the joke's on
you, Tohon Champuy, she thought. You may get
the charts as part of the ship, if I can't get it
broken up and that price split among the creditors,
but I know there's nothing you can use in them.
The star-books are my own property—they're the
tools of my office, and that makes them dower-
property, and even Hegemonic law can't take them
away from me.

"What's the total I owe?" she asked.

"Here." Balthasar pointed to a figure at the bottom of the sheet.

Silence winced. The scrap price she would get if
the ship's value were divided among the various
creditors would hardly cover that. She would have
to sell.

"What's Champuy after?" Balthasar asked. "Your
books?"

Silence looked up in surprise. "How—?"

The captain shrugged. "I've seen this kind of
trick before. What do you want to do?"

"I don't have much choice, do I?" Silence said
bitterly. "See if he'll buy it—but by God he'd better pay the assessors' price—and claim my books
as dower property. I'll have to let him have the
charts."

"All right." Balthasar turned to the judge. "Your
honor, since Captain Leigh turns out to have owed
such an unexpectedly large amount, Miss Leigh
has asked me to sell the ship, and use that money
to pay the various creditors. Her personal—dower—
property, which wasn't included in the assessors'
survey, of course isn't included in the offer of sale."
He glanced at Champuy, his grey eyes suddenly

mischievous. "Merchant Champuy had already said he would buy the *Dolphin*, at yard price. Do I hear a better offer?"

Behind her veil, Silence smiled for the first time that day. It was a petty revenge, but it was a beginning.

"My offer was made under other circumstances," Champuy said warily.

The judge cleared his throat. "Merchant Champuy, your offer was made in open court, and I am compelled to hold you to it. Is there a counteroffer?"

There was an echoing silence in the hall. Clearly, no one was prepared either to challenge the merchant, or to get him out of his current position. The judge's eyebrows twitched, though Silence could not tell if that were a sign of annoyance or amusement. "Very well, the ship is sold. Draw up the papers."

Silence waited while the clerk tapped at his keys, and the machine spat sheet after sheet of paper. Both Balthasar and Champuy signed, then Silence added her thumbprint and accepted Champuy's voucher for the pitiful four hundred Secasian solas that remained after all debts were paid. It would be less that half that amount in the more usual currencies, Delian pound or Asteriona marks, but she made no outward protest. It would be one more item on Champuy's account, if ever she had the chance for revenge.

"The case of Sumi aBrand," the clerk announced, and Silence started.

"What now?" she asked.

Balthasar made a face. "Let's get out of here," he said roughly. "Then to *Dolphin*, to get your books. You don't want to have to fight with Champuy after he's already taken possession."

"No," Silence agreed, and followed him from the court.

The Secasian streets were drowning in an afternoon sunlight that bleached all color from the world. The buildings and the people alike had faded to a uniform sandy shade. Only the few women, shrouded as law and custom required in black or dark blue veiling, provided any break in the uniform pale brown. Sweat pearled on Blathasar's harsh-boned face, one drop running down a curious bleached patch of skin on one cheek. Silence reached automatically to push aside her veil, wipe the sweat from her own face, but realized in time where she was. She brushed feebly at the weighted cloth, feeling like a fool, then jammed her hands into the pockets of her coat.

At the edge of the court plaza, a line of cabs was waiting, their domes on the reflective setting to drive off some of the heat. Balthasar tapped on the window of the leader and was rewarded by a sudden clearing of the shell. A mechanical voice spoke from the driver's compartment.

"You wish transport."

A homunculus, Silence thought, and barely restrained a shiver. She had spent most of her adult life in space, where heavy work was done almost exclusively by the homunculi, but she still could not be comfortable in the presence of the quasi-living specimens of a magus's art. They were little more than crudely shaped pseudo-flesh slapped onto a metal skeleton, given rudimentary intelligence and volition, and turned loose to do the dirty jobs no human being wanted. She knew they were useful—necessary, even—but today more than ever, the thought of the caricatured face, like a child's drawing, made her cringe, and she was glad that the part of the dome that covered the driver's section remained reflective.

Balthasar did not seem in the least affected. "Yes, to the port—to the assessors' dock."

"Enter," the homunculus said, and the rear canopy rose slowly. Balthasar scrambled in, and Silence followed more carefully, gathering the skirts of her coat about her. The canopy slid closed again, and the interior fans whined, sending a stronger jet of cooled air into the compartment. Balthasar sighed and leaned back against the seat cushions, eyes closed.

The homunculus droned on. "The meter will run at a standard rate of two bazai each kilometer. Luggage is carried at the rate of three bazai per piece, one las per large parcel or crate. . . ." There was more, but it was dulled by the thrum of the motors as the cab lurched away from the plaza. Silence sighed and loosened the uncomfortable veil, folding back the piece that had covered her nose and mouth. The touch of the air was deliciously cold on her sweating skin.

"So that's what you look like," Balthasar remarked. Silence looked at him, and he quickly changed the subject. "You really think this uncle of yours made a deal with Champuy?"

Silence shrugged, wondering again what the Delian wanted and what price she'd have to pay for this much help. But there was no reason yet not to answer the question honestly. "If Champuy wanted the books, there's plenty he could offer Otto—my uncle's not picky. And that could cause me trouble later, since he's still my legal guardian."

"I forgot that," Balthasar muttered.

Silence said, "The Tabiran law only allows the courts to appoint a temporary guardian in the absence of a male relative. It doesn't give you any permanent rights."

"I see," Balthasar said. There was a speculative look in his eyes, but he did not pursue whatever thought had occurred to him.

Silence watched him out of the corner of her

eye, trying to guess what had caught the other's attention. But after that one brief, calculating glance, Balthasar's face closed up, discouraging questions and giving nothing away. Silence looked away again, nervous and dissatisfied. *The sooner I find out what's really going on, and what his real price is, the happier I'll be,* she thought. *And the sooner I have some real bargaining power—however I can get it, even if I have to use my starbooks somehow—the safer I'll feel. But it'll have to be an awfully good offer before I'll take his second job.*

The cab slowed then, and they passed through the massive arch that was the gate to the port area. Peering through the darkened dome, Silence could make out the delicate spire of the main control tower, the customs house, and the other administrative buildings clustered at its feet. To either side of them ran rows of the long, low barns that were the docks and tuning sheds and mechanics' workshops. It was remarkable how little those buildings varied from world to world. Only the control tower and its associated complex was ever different.

Beyond the docks was the field itself, a flat expanse of fused earth, linked to the docks by a network of taxiways. A cradled ship waited at the far end of the field, its tow scurrying away toward the bunkers at the edge of the fused strip. As soon as the tow had vanished inside, the ship's harmonium whined to lifting pitch—even two kilometers away, Silence could feel the vibration in the walls of the cab. The ship trembled once, a great shudder that racked it from nose to tail. Then it lifted, rising at first quite slowly, then faster and faster, the gleaming silver of the sounding keel lifting it toward heaven. Silence watched it dwindle until the cab turned into the tunnel that led to the assessors' buildings, and the walls cut off her view.

The cab stopped outside the double doors of the assessors' dock, and Balthasar fed local banknotes into the meter to pop the canopy. The docking bay was almost empty, only two of the twelve spaces surrounded by the durafelt baffles that marked the presence of a ship. There was a small glassed-in cubby just inside the door, and Balthasar approached it confidently.

"Excuse me," he said, tapping on the glass, and a gnomish little man appeared as if by conjuration.

"Yes?"

"We're here to get some things off the *Black Dolphin*," Balthasar said. "She's been sold, so you won't have her hanging around her much longer."

The watchman looked suspiciously at him. "I'll have to see the papers."

Balthasar handed over the paper authorizing his temporary guardianship, and Silence produced the bill of sale, pointing out the provision that exempted her own belongings. The little man examined each page with excruciating care, but finally nodded.

"All right, I'll let you aboard—but I'll have to come with you. And you can only take things from your cabin, miss. Otherwise I can't know what's yours."

"Fair enough," Silence said, when Balthasar didn't answer.

The watchman led them down the row of empty cradles, past the first baffled ship, whose bow curtain hung open enough to reveal the sharply raked nose of a customs lighter. The unprotected sounding keel showed silver, not the oiled lead of a true keel: it was a local ship, not capable of interstellar travel. There would only be enough Philosopher's Tincture in the metal of the keel to take the ship away from the elemental earth of Secasia's core, not enough to reach purgatory and the stars.

"Silence?" Balthasar called softly, striking a whispery echo from the two keels. "Are you coming?"

Somehow the other two had gotten ahead of her, were already standing on the catwalk that ran along the top of the *Dolphin*'s cradle. Silence hurried to join them, her feet on the rattling stairway drawing a new low thrumming from the keel as she passed. The watchman was waiting at the now-open stern hatch, a rainbow-glittering key in his hand.

"Which is your cabin, miss?"

"This way."

Silence took them down the main corridor that ran the length of the ship to her cabin across the common room from the ladder leading to the lower bridge. The latch clicked open at her touch, and the door slid back. There was not much for her to take: clothes, tapes, trinkets, and jewelry, and finally, from the locked strongbox beneath the mattress in the platform of her bunk, her star-books. They were real books, bound in thin metal, the paper edged with metal as well, to help protect the fragile contents. Charged locks bound covers and pages tightly together, a pinpoint light winking red in the center of each touchplate. She lifted them out of their hiding place, the *New Aquarius* and the ninety-first edition of the *Speculum Astronomi*, written in the bastard Latin that had been the magi's first language; then the fussy, much-abused *Star-Follower's Handbook*, and her copy of the Hegemonic Navy's *Topoi*. One was missing. She frowned, and looked around the cabin again, wondering if she could have left it out on the shelves. But she remembered putting it with the others and locking the box over it.

Balthasar glanced at her and said in an undertone, "What's wrong?"

"My *Gilded Stairs*. It's not here." Silence frowned

more deeply. Only the captain had the master key that would unlock the cabin strongboxes, and she had seen it among her grandfather's effects; Razil could not have stolen it. "Unless Grandfather borrowed it, and left it in his cabin?"

Balthasar nodded once, then cleared his throat. "Was that your bell, watchman?"

"Hm?" The man frowned suspiciously—as well he might, Silence thought disgustedly, that was one of the oldest tricks in the book—but then sighed "I didn't hear it. You'll have to come with me while I check. I can't leave you aboard alone, you know."

"I'm ready anyway," Silence said.

Balthasar hoisted the larger bag, the one containing the rest of her belongings, to one shoulder. "Is this everything?" he asked. Face and voice were still expressionless, but there was a new tension in his stance.

"All except the books, and I have those," Silence said, and let him precede her from the cabin. The watchman glanced back, but saw only an incompetent woman fumbling with the latch of her carryall. Balthasar was with him, and that was what mattered. Silence held her breath, timing her steps carefully. When the watchman reached the hatch, she was beside her grandfather's cabin, her hand, concealed behind the carryall, fumbling with the latch buttons. She pressed them in the proper sequence, upper left, lower right, lower left and upper right, and then, as the watchman leaned out of the ship to listen, she kicked the opening panel. The door popped open, and she slipped inside. There was no time to look around; the familiar grey binding of the *Gilded Stairs* stood on the shelves beside the door, and she seized it and swept it into the carryall in one motion. Then she was outside again, the door closing behind her, consumed by the nightmare fear that she had gotten the wrong book after all.

"Sieura Leigh?" That was Balthasar, calling from the hatch. She looked up and saw both men staring at her, the watchman not bothering to hide his annoyance. "The men are here to claim the ship," Balthasar went on.

"Oh?" Silence said, trying to keep her voice level. She glanced down into the carryall, saw the proper title, and hid her sigh of relief. "Then I suppose I'd better hurry." She left the carryall unlatched and walked on to the hatch. Balthasar was still staring at her, one eyebrow slightly raised in question, and she nodded as discreetly as she could.

The captain nodded back. "We'll be off," he said. "You needn't see us all the way out, watchman, we'll be going by the tunnels."

The other man hesitated at the head of the cradle stairs, but shrugged. "Go ahead, Captain. Good voyage."

Balthasar nodded his thanks, then took Silence's arm and hurried her down the cradle stairs and toward the dimly lit tunnel entrance at the far end of the dock. She quickly matched his pace, glancing once over her shoulder toward the main entrance. Sure enough, a group of men were waiting there, their dull coveralls badged with an insignia she could not quite read, but was certainly the mark of Champuy's combine. Champuy himself did not seem to be with them.

"Do you think they'll start trouble?" Silence asked.

"I doubt it," Balthasar said, hauling back the door to the tunnels. "No profit in it—I hope." Despite his words, he glanced nervously over his shoulder at the approaching figures.

Wishing that she knew how to interpret that look—and that her ten-shot heylin were not buried at the very bottom of the carryall—Silence hiked her coat to her knees and hurried down the narrow stairs. Balthasar followed more slowly, his free hand deep in the pocket of his jacket. The fabric bulged with more than just his fist. At the first landing, he paused to listen.

"Well?" Silence asked, after a moment.

"We're clear, I guess. Come on."

The pilot shrugged, biting back her anger, and followed him down the winding stairs.

The area beneath the dock buildings was honeycombed with tunnels, originally intended to give the dock workers some sort of protection from Secasia's baking heat. The star-travellers had taken it over almost immediately, turning it into Secasia's version of the transients' Pale, and expanded the network of tunnels and caverns to include hotels and apartments, recreation areas catering to every conceivable taste, shops and local offices for the giant combines, mechanics' workshops, and even a minor magus's laboratory. Stepping from the secondary tunnels into the main concourse was like stepping into another world, a world far more hospitable than Secasia.

Silence pulled off her veil, stuffing it deep into a pocket, then slipped loose the fastenings of her coat and let it swirl back over the short tunic and sober grey tights she wore beneath it. The cool, machine-scented air of the Pale flowed past her, and she threw back her head to let it stir her close-cropped hair, washing away some of the misery of the past hours. The sight of the colorfully dressed crowd, Oued Tessaans, Rhosoi, Castagi, even a Numluli youth sporting festival ribbons, and the rise and fall of the pure coine of the star lanes calmed her a little. She had lost her ship, but her dream of being pilot-owner of a starship had never been more than that, and an impractical dream besides. She had escaped working for Champuy, or being forced back to Cap Bel—and with a minimum of harassment, despite her sex. She had passage to Delos even without accepting Balthasar's second, dubious offer, and some chance of finding more work. Things could have been worse—

"Silence!" The voice came from one of the hole-in-the-wall bars that filled the shorter side tunnels, and stopped her in her tracks.

"It's my uncle," Silence said involuntarily.

Balthasar made a face. "You can't ignore him now."

"Silence, wait!" The tubby man pushed open the shutters that gave onto the main concourse and clambered out through the empty window frame, ignoring the curses of patrons and passersby.

"Don't you know enough to use the door?" Silence asked.

"I was afraid you'd get away," Otto Razil panted, straightening a jacket that tended to ride up over his paunch. "When is the hearing with Probate?"

"This morning, and you damn well knew it," Silence snapped. Razil was flushed, and the faint, cloying scent of iore, the most expensive of the Ariassan narcotics, clung to his beard. He could rarely afford even the cheap taio on his share of *Dolphin*'s profits, and Silence's anger flared again.

"I'm so sorry," Razil said, slurring his words only a little. "What happened? Did you have to sell the ship?"

Silence took a deep breath. "Yes, I sold *Dolphin*. It turned out there were some very interesting purchases made on the ship's account that I never saw results of. Do you know how that happened?"

"Your grandfather was always spendthrift," Razil blustered. "I never wanted to trouble you with the financial problems he had—"

"Troubles, hell," Silence said. "You did all the buying, and you altered our records. How much did Champuy pay you for it?"

Razil hesitated, then drew himself up in an attempt at dignity. "If I choose to work for him, that's my business. If you're too stupid to know a good offer—well, I'm not going to let you drag me down with you. Especially when I should be a captain in my own right."

"That's what he offered you? To be *Dolphin*'s captain? Or to go to Earth?"

Razil abandoned all pretense. "Yes, by God, and I'll make it to Earth, now that I've got the backing I need, and there'll be no sharing with some chit of a girl pilot." His expression was momentarily clever. "You're still legally under my power, Silence. I could refuse to let you sign a contract with anyone else, make you come back and pilot for me, let you drool over the five millions and never give you a penny—"

"Shut up," Silence said. She was suddenly consumed with fury, not just at Razil, but at the entire situation. "Listen to me. Law or no law, if you ever try to act as my guardian, if you ever interfere with my life again, I will kill you. Here and now, with my bare hands if I have to. Do you understand me?"

The pudgy man took a step backwards. "Silence, dear girl, no need to be hasty. It's a good job I'm offering."

"No. Now go." Silence reached for the bag Balthasar was carrying, but the captain stepped out of her reach. In the instant her attention was distracted, Razil vanished into the crowd. "Goddamn it, I will kill him!"

"I don't blame you," Balthasar said, "but not here." He nodded at the curious faces around them, the beginning of a crowd of witnesses, and Silence sighed. Her anger faded almost as quickly as it had flared up; she was shaking now with the reaction.

"All right," she said. "But I meant it."

"I know," Balthasar said. "Let's go."

Balthasar's ship was cradled in the fifteenth dock, a long low barn nearly at the end of the row of port buildings. These were the cheaper docks, far from the tuning sheds and the central offices, and were consequently crowded. All but two of the thirty-odd berths were full, and workers were busy preparing those two for new arrivals. It was hot in the dock, especially after the cool of the Pale, and Silence slipped out of the heavy coat. It was the designer's fault for building windows in a dock, she decided, no matter how much it saved the Port Authority on lights. The narrow row of windows that ran around the entire perimeter of the dock, just below the roof beams, showed nothing but Secasia's white-hot sky.

Sun-Treader's cradle was in a berth in the middle of the row. Balthasar lifted a corner of the baffle curtain to let them through, then carefully secured it behind them, shutting out the extraneous noises that might upset the tuning of the keel. Silence stared at the ship. She had been expecting another ship like *Black Dolphin*, a rounded, fractionally ungainly hull bulging over the edges of a narrow keel. *Sun-Treader*'s hull was long and sleek, not as narrow as a Navy three or four, but still very slim, a streamlined bump on the arrow of the keel. She was clearly build for speed and maneuverability, and Silence's fingers itched for the feel of the controls.

"She's Delian built," Balthasar said casually, but there was a calculating expression in his eyes. "A half-and-half, the yards call that design. She'll only carry about seventy-five mass units—but she's twice as fast as an ordinary freighter."

Silence nodded, following him up the catwalk that clung to the cradle's side. That said a lot about Balthasar, whether he had intended to reveal it or not. A half-and-half just might be a respectable ship on Delos and in the Fringe, but in the Rusadir it was a pirate's ship, at best a smuggler's ship. The cargo space might be limited, but the most valuable illegal cargos tended to be small, and a half-and-half could outrun anything smaller than a Navy five. Just what do you do for a living, Denis Balthasar? she thought, but said nothing, watching Balthasar work the hatch controls.

"Yo, Julie?" Balthasar stepped into the narrow corridor, peered around and upward. "I'm aboard, with a pilot."

"Oh?" A temporary ladder rattled sharply, and a heavily built man dropped through a maintenance hatch into the corridor in front of them. Packing fluid streaked his hands and a few droplets were caught in his untidy beard. He looked momentarily startled to see a woman, but recovered quickly. He removed most of the fluid by dragging his hands across the thighs of his trousers and held out a hand in greeting. "Welcome aboard, pilot."

Silence took his hand speechlessly, overwhelmed by the sheer size of the man. He towered over her by nearly half a meter, his bulk filling the passageway.

"Silence Leigh, Julian Chase Mago, my engineer," Balthasar said. "Silence has signed on at least to Delos."

"Oh?" Chase Mago looked down at his captain, over Silence's head. "So she's going to—"

"We haven't discussed that," Balthasar cut in quickly. The engineer shook his head.

"That reminds me," Silence said. "What was this deal you couldn't talk about at the court?"

"Let's drop your things in the pilot's cabin," Balthasar said. "Then we'll talk."

The half-and-half's construction was very different from that of a standard freighter, and the differences made Silence wonder again just what kind of cargos Balthasar carried. The main hatch opened not onto the main deck but into a short length of corridor running between the two main holds. A ladder led up to the crew deck, directly into a common room that was little more than a broader section of corridor fitted with a few battered pieces of furniture. A bank of automatic kitchen machines stood against one bulkhead, separated from the rest of the common area by a woven metal partition. Silence could see grooves in the floor where other partitions could be fitted to create at least two more cabins.

The pilot's cabin was right up in the bow, at the base of the ladder that led to the double bridge. It was oddly shaped, almost triangular, but the fittings were fairly standard. Bunk and monitor console were built into opposite bulkheads, and a shower compartment was tucked into the apex of the triangle.

"I know it looks like you're right over the keel," Chase Mago said, "but you've got about a meter of packing in between. You shouldn't feel a thing."

Silence nodded and tossed the smaller carryall onto the bare mattress of the bunk. Balthasar set the larger bag just inside the door and turned to go.

"I'm fixing tea," he said. "Do you want some, Silence?"

"Please."

The door slid shut automatically behind him, and Silence stared at the empty cabin. Bare walls, bare bunk, darkened console . . . suddenly all the practical difficulties of starting over, of imposing her will on a new ship and fitting into a new unit, threatened to overwhelm her.

"Is there anything I can do to help?" Chase Mago asked.

"No, thanks, I'll settle things later," Silence answered. Then at last the cadence of his speech registered. "You're from the Rusadir, aren't you?"

The engineer hesitated briefly, then said, "Yes, from Kesse."

Silence looked up quickly, the trivial question of mutual acquaintance dying on her lips. Kesse—renamed Tarraco by the Hegemony in an attempt to wipe out the memory of the planet's resistance—had been the last of the Rusadir worlds to fall to the invaders. It had lasted for a year under siege, had turned back all the tricks the magi had thrown against it. Only the treachery of a splinter faction of its oligarchs had forced the planet to surrender. The survivors had been forcibly relocated and subjected to harsh sanctions—among which, if she remembered correctly, was a ban on star travel.

Chase Mago shrugged, reading the question in her eyes. "Lots of things are possible if you pay off the right people. And we don't go very deep into the Hegemony if we can help it. . . . I think the tea's ready now."

Silence nodded, oddly embarrassed, and followed the engineer out of the cabin. The smoky aroma of the tea filled the commons. Chase Mago sniffed at it, then dropped heavily into a folded cushion chair that bore the permanent imprint of his huge frame. A hammock chair stood by the dented table, the paint worn from its metal frame by constant use; it was obviously Balthasar's favorite. There was a third chair as well, an oil-inflated armchair whose undented cushion proved it had only recently been taken from storage. Silence drew it closer to the table and settled herself cautiously against the still, chill padding. Balthasar emerged from the galley cubicle with three large mugs balanced on a tray, and Silence accepted one blindly, sipping at the steaming liquid. For the first time in days, in the weeks since her grandfather's death, she had the time to think of her own feelings, and she winced, expecting the familiar tide of grief and anger. But there was only exhaustion, a numbing fatigue and a sense of being out of place. There had been so much fighting, and not much to show for it, really—only this strange ship and its equally strange crew.

"Do you want to talk?" Balthasar asked.

"No," Silence said, rising so quickly that she almost spilled her tea. "Not now. I'm dead tired, and I want some sleep before I have to make any decisions."

"Sure," Balthasar said, and Chase Mago nodded. Their eyes flickered toward each other in almost subliminal conversation, but Silence had no interest in reading it. She retreated to her cabin, closed and latched the door behind her. She stooped for the bag that held her bedding, but lost her balance and stumbled back against the bunk. The mattress was positively seductive in its Spartan comfort, and she let herself lean back against the pillow. In just a minute, she promised herself, in just a minute I'll get up, make the bed. In just a minute. And then she slept.

Chapter 2

Silence woke stiff from sleeping curled on the unmade bunk, her coat dragged loosely over her. She had dreamed, she knew, but already the thread of it was fading, leaving her with a vague memory of her grandfather's face and an odd sense of release. She groped for the substance of the dream, and it was gone. She sighed and stretched, muscles protesting a little. At least she had slept, and slept soundly, for the first time in weeks. She smiled wryly to herself. I think I can even face this offer of Balthasar's.

The ship was very quiet, only the hissing of the ventilators proving that the ship was alive. She got up, wincing—the lights faded on automatically with her movement—and searched the monitor for the chronometer display. She found it at last and keyed it on: the little screen declared it to be 0941 hours. She checked the abbreviated notation beneath the numbers. That was local time, but the

34

arbitrary ship's time matched it fairly well, at 0652. She bathed and dressed and, thus fortified, pushed open the cabin door.

The common area was dark and empty. Past the closed doors of the men's cabins, a guard light burned orange in the entrance to the engine room, but there was no other sign of life. Even the ladders to the other decks were only just outlined by the blue pinpoints of safety lights. Chastened, she retreated, closing the door behind her.

So they're late risers, she told herself. Let them sleep. You can use the time to put this place to rights. Determinedly, she flung back the straps to release the mattress, exposing the strongbox beneath. Unlocking the smaller carryall, she put the starbooks away, and adjusted the strongbox's lock to respond to her palmprint. Then she pushed the mattress back into place and began unpacking the rest of her things. She was stacking the last filmbook in its place when someone tapped gently on her door. There had been noises in the common room for some time, she realized, as she moved to unlock the door, but she hadn't noticed them until now.

"Yes?"

"Breakfast is ready," Chase Mago announced. "And Denis wants to talk to you."

"Thanks. I'm sorry I—about last night," Silence amended, following the engineer through the commons into the kitchen area. She drew a mug of coffee from the huge urn mounted on one bulkhead, but refused a slice of the sweet, heavy daybread. Balthasar, already sitting at the table, raised a hand in greeting.

"Good morning," he called. "Pull up a chair. How are you feeling?"

"Better," Silence said, taking her place at the table. "And curious."

At her elbow, Chase Mago grinned briefly.

"All right, I owe you an explanation, I know." Balthasar made an odd face: seemingly the thought of explanations caused him physical pain. "Did Julie mention he's from Kesse?"

"Yes." Silence stole a glance at the engineer. His bearded face was grim, and one hand slowly contracted on his mug, as though he would shatter it.

Balthasar went on as if he hadn't noticed. "You know the restrictions that were imposed. Relocation, confiscations, restrictions—it's the restrictions that're important. The Kessemen can't travel except with special documents, controlled from the capital, and Julie doesn't have—can't get—those papers. You can't really forge them," he added quickly, forestalling Silence's question. "Asterion handles them directly, and the Hegemon himself has to approve each one. So far, we've gotten by with some pretty crude Lachesan papers and a lot of bribe money. But we can't go very deep into the Hegemony that way, and it's getting more expensive every trip."

"And so?" Silence asked.

"I'm a Delian citizen," Balthasar said. "You know the citizenship laws there?"

Silence frowned, wondering when the connection would be made, but answered willingly enough. She felt almost as if she were in school again, when the quickest way to get the information she wanted was to humor the teachers. "They don't allow immigration. Population control, I think, since it's a crowded world."

"Right. But it's less a question of population than that they want to restrict the number of people with citizen status, to make it hard for offworlders to get it. Being a Delian citizen has a lot of advantages . . . and there are only two ways to get it: be born on planet to two full citizens, or marry a Delian. Now, Julie would be free of the restrictions if he had Delian citizenship. You see the problem?"

"Delos doesn't recognize one-sex marriages?"

Chase Mago said, "That would make things too easy."

"They don't bring full citizenship," Balthasar said.

"I'm still not sure I see—" Silence began warily, and Balthasar cut in.

"But they do recognize multiple marriage."

"Oh." Silence looked from one to the other. "So you want me to marry both of you?"

"That's the idea," Balthasar said.

Chase Mago frowned at him. "There wouldn't be any—physical obligation on your part, I promise. It would be a marriage of name only."

"Delian law lets all parties keep citizen status only if the marriage lasts a year or longer," Balthasar added. He made an apologetic gesture. "They don't want it to be easy."

"So if I did this, I'd have to wait a year to get out of it if I discovered I couldn't stand the two of you?" Silence shook her head. "Why couldn't you just marry a Delian woman?"

Chase Mago stared into the depths of his mug. "I do not know many women—many people at all—on Delos. And the laws against marriages of convenience are strict. . . ."

His voice trailed off, and Balthasar said practically, "It's just not to their advantage. There's nothing he—or I, or we—can offer that a Delian doesn't have already. Even on Delos, or anywhere in the Fringe, there aren't a lot of women who become star-travellers. The ones that do are all supercargos, or stewards, things like that. You're the first woman pilot I've met, except for Misthians. I don't have any use for a supercargo—Sun-Treader's too small to need a separate person to handle cargo—but I do need a pilot. Anyway, most of those woman are already married, and I guess I don't have to tell you why."

Silence nodded. The Hegemony was the largest political entity in known space; all star-travellers had to deal with it and its laws at some point. Marriage was probably the easiest way for most women to gain legal existence under the Hegemon's code. "So why not marry a planetsider?"

"We couldn't prove the marriage," Balthasar said. "Delian law defines marriage as cohabitation over a set period of time. I can't spare Julie, and there isn't room aboard for anyone who doesn't work." He smiled winningly. "This isn't a one-sided deal. You'll get citizenship, too, and pilot's work. And you won't have to worry about your uncle."

"Let me think!" The words came out more sharply than Silence had intended, and she gestured an apology. "I don't know."

"Just think about it," Balthasar said. "The rest of my offer holds."

"How can I tell if I can work with you?" Silence asked. "I've known you less than a standard day."

"The flight to Delos," Balthasar said. "We'll take a long road. That'll show up any incompatibilities." He grinned, delighted by his own inspiration.

Chase Mago's eyebrows rose, but then he smiled faintly. "It's a thought."

Silence looked at them again, at Chase Mago's broad, bearded face, Balthasar's face all angles, with the patch of pale skin beneath one eye. Chase Mago was at least a Rusadir man, Kesse-born and Kesse-bred; she and the engineer shared a common culture. Balthasar was another matter, closed in and secretive, giving so little of himself that even his apparent benevolence was unsettling. . . . Both of them were unknown quantities, with unknown strengths and weaknesses . . . she was not ready to commit herself to anything, especially not to a new ship, not yet. Still, it was the best offer yet, and who could know what things would be like on Delos? Even a Delian might hesitate to hire a woman pilot. And she would gain her freedom. She shook her head again. The marriage was nothing, less than nothing if Balthasar kept Chase Mago's promise and it remained a marriage of name. Love was less intimate a relationship than the trust that had to exist between the members of a starship's crew.

She sighed. Balthasar's idea was a good one. A long road, lasting six hours or longer in subjective time, was usually reserved for the superfreighters with their ten-man crews—but if the three of them could take *Sun-Treader* through, the difficulties of the passage would either weld them into a functional crew or prove the attempt to be pointless. Either way, it would be quick. Against her better judgment, she nodded.

"I'm not stupid," she said. "I can see how it's to my advantage. I'll work out a long-road course to Delos, captain, and I'll give you my answer when we're cradled there."

"Fair enough," Balthasar said. He gulped the last of his coffee and stood up quickly. "Julie, I've got business in the port. Why don't you show Silence the ship, let her get the feel of the controls?"

"Right," Chase Mago answered, and Balthasar was gone, disappearing down the ladder to the main hatch. The engineer shook his head, sighed. Silence took a last sip of her coffee.

"Shall we start?" she asked.

"There's no hurry," Chase Mago said. "Look, Denis makes up these plans as he goes along. He doesn't have some great controlling scheme in mind, even if he'd like to make you think he does. This marriage—he was going to try and find a supercargo, and worry about those problems later, but then he saw you at the court, and figured you were what we really needed. He—don't let him push you, that's all."

"Oh, I won't," Silence said, more grimly than she had intended.

Chase Mago looked down at his plate as though he were surprised to find it empty. "Then I guess we might as well get started," he said. He swept up his own plate and utensils, caught both their mugs in his free hand, and dumped the lot into the cleaning slot as he passed the kitchen console. Silence did the same with Balthasar's dishes, then wondered if she should have left them. Before she could ask, Chase Mago had begun his tour.

"This is the cabin space," he said, gesturing to the two doors beyond the commons. One—Balthasar's, Silence thought—was open a crack, revealing an unmade bunk and bare walls. "We can fit in two more cabins by breaking down the common area—three cabins if we eliminate commons all together," Chase Mago went on. "Engineering's through here."

Silence stepped over the raised coaming, through the warning barrier of orange light, and blinked at the sudden sterile brightness of her surroundings. There were two main consoles, and half a dozen smaller monitors, mostly dark and silent. The smaller of the two consoles hummed and clicked softly to itself. Chase Mago glanced once at it, then turned his attention to the other, his eyes caressing the few pale lights flickering among the darkened gauges. He touched keys on the double board and watched the readings shift, before turning his attention back to the pilot.

"We're Delos built," he said, "but we tune to the Numluli scale." He touched a glowing key set apart from the others and the harmonium spoke, a low chord that was no known harmony, no human music. The sheer beauty of it shivered to her bones.

Into the silence that followed, Chase Mago said, "We reach five-twelfths of heaven."

Silence tried to convert that to velocity and failed. Considered as a measure of time, it was easier to see what that would mean. Compared to *Black Dolphin*, whose harmonium would only make a sixth of heaven, *Sun-Treader* would spend less subjective time in purgatory. Or so she thought. Frowning, she reviewed what she knew of the engineer's art. The essential parts of a starship were the sounding keel and the harmonium. The keel was made of a base metal impregnated with the Philosopher's Tincture, the only celestial substance that could exist in the mundane world. The tincture in the keel always sought to return to the transcendant, nonmaterial world—heaven—beyond apparent reality, but was bound down by the material substances with which it was surrounded. Only under stimulus from the harmonium, which was tuned to as close an approximation of the music which ruled heaven as was humanly possible, could the tincture rise toward heaven, first fleeing the elemental earth of a planet's core, then rushing faster and faster into the void between the stars, where the barriers between the mundane and the celestial were thinnest. The rest of the ship, riding on the keel, was drawn up with it. Because most of the ship was made of material substances, gross matter, it could never reach heaven—but the harmonium could bring it to the crucial point, the twelfth of heaven that was purgatory. Time and space twisted, doors opened, and the ships passed between the stars in minutes rather than in hundreds of years. And that was where the ranking of fractions came in. The closer a ship came to heaven, the less time it seemed to take to pass through purgatory.

Chase Mago was still talking. ". . . biggest problem has been the cargo space. The holds are right over the keel, not on the top deck like on a freighter, and none of the baffles has worked quite right. We have to be really careful about the stowage."

"What kind of cargo do you carry?" Silence asked.

The engineer hesitated. "All kinds. Denis is under contract to a group, and we run a lot of their light stuff."

The explanation did not ring quite true—for one thing, if *Sun-Treader* were a contract ship, where were her employers' markings?—but Silence said nothing.

"You'll see what I mean when Denis gets back," Chase Mago said. "Do you want to see the control room now?"

"Sure."

They walked back toward the bow, then Chase Mago waved her up the ladder ahead of him. The lower control room was about what Silence had expected, twin consoles for captain and pilot, twin acceleration couches that could be tilted back to form almost-comfortable bunks, the triple viewscreen dominating the forward bulkhead. She gave it a cursory glance and pulled herself up to the pilot's bridge.

The dome was starkly functional, empty except for the massive control yoke, shaped rather like the wheel of one of the legendary sea-ships of old Earth. Rudimentary status lights glowed on its hub and along one of the thick spokes, but the well-worn metal was otherwise unadorned. Nothing more was needed: In purgatory, control was maintained as much through symbolic effects as through any sophisticated mechanical linkage. Silence stepped onto the platform before it, slipping her feet into the waiting hollows. The clingfoam covering wrapped itself around her ankles. She took hold of the wheel itself—it swung freely to her touch, disengaged from its systems—and her eyes narrowed as she tried to imagine the ship in purgatory. The hull would go transparent, the voidmarks glittering through. . . .

In the compartment below, Chase Mago cleared his throat, and she came back to reality with a start. Sliding down the short ladder, she asked, "What happened to your old pilot? You can't have run this ship with just two people."

"Actually, we have been," the engineer answered. "Denis is a licensed pilot—can tune a ship, too, if you can believe him—and when Alex was offered a better post, Denis took over until we could find someone to replace him."

"It looks like it's taken you quite a while," Silence commented. If they had been running short-handed, that would explain the surprisingly spartan commons: there would have been no time to arrange more than minimal comfort.

Chase Mago shrugged. "It's hard to find a good pilot, and Denis believes in leaving our options open."

Silence's lips tightened in spite of herself, but she could think of no safe response. Then there was a clattering from the hatchway, and Balthasar's voice echoed up from the lower deck.

"Yo, Julie?"

Chase Mago leaned into the ladder well. "Topside."

Feet rattled on the ladder rungs below him, and Balthasar appeared in the opening, looking up with a quizzical expression. "There wasn't much after all. Come help me manage the homunculi."

"I'll be right down." The engineer dropped through the hole without a backward glance. Silence hesitated, not sure if she were included in the order, of if she wanted to be, but then Balthasar's voice floated up over the rattling of the ladders.

"Where's Silence?"

"Coming," she called, and dropped down after them.

The homunculi were waiting at the base of the cradle, three short, stunted, vaguely humanoid creatures, each with a metal-bound crate nested in the frame embedded in its shoulders. Balthasar, at the top of the catwalk, raised their control disk, and the crude faces turned toward him, dull glass eyes full of a false awareness. He adjusted the settings, and the homunculi shambled forward, apelike arms taking part of the weight off their forward-leaning torsos. Silence shrank back in spite of herself as they started up the stairway.

"Silence?" Chase Mago pulled a key box from his pocket and tossed it in her direction. Startled, she batted at it, and knocked it clattering to the deck plates.

"That's to the forward hold," Chase Mago said. "Go on ahead and unlock it, would you?"

Silence nodded, scooping up the key, and ducked back into the ship. The lock responded willingly, and she folded back the stiff leaves of the hatch. The lights came on in the hold as she did so.

"Watch yourself," Chase Mago called.

Silence turned, and found her path blocked by the column of homunculi. Rather than risk their touch, she stepped into the hold, retreating up the slight incline toward the bow. The plates underfoot were soft and spongy, made of the same combination of elements as the baffles that surrounded the ship.

The first homunculus loomed in the hatchway, levering itself over the low coaming with clumsy

movements of its arms. Silence stepped to one
side, almost tripping over one of the low, soft ridges
that crisscrossed the stowage space. It shambled
past her and the next one lifted itself stiffly into
the hold. It was followed by a third, and then by
Balthasar, who positioned himself to one side of
the hatch, watching their progress with an anxious eye. Chase Mago, standing stooped to peer
into the hold, gnawed on a thumbnail, guessing
distances.

"That looks all right," he said at last. His voice
was without resonance in the padded compartment.

Balthasar nodded and adjusted the disk again.
The homunculi froze in their tracks. "Unload?" he
asked, and Chase Mago shrugged.

"Why not? We'll have to do most of the shifting
by hand anyway."

Balthasar moved the disk. Each homunculus
reached over its shoulder, massive three-fingered
paws closing surely over the crates on their backs.
With surprising grace, they lifted the crates over
their heads and set them on the floor-plates in
front of them.

"Is there more?" Chase Mago asked.

"No, this is it." Balthasar looked up as the engineer edged cautiously into the hold. "Where do
you want these?"

Chase Mago consulted a chart laminated to the
bulkhead behind him. Then he pulled a small,
thick notebook from his pocket and began flipping
through the pages, mumbling to himself. "What is
this, anyway?"

"The usual," Balthasar answered airily.

"Right." Chase Mago tucked the notebook away
again and slid back the cover that protected the
field controls. "Clear."

Hastily, Silence stepped out of the stowage into
the narrow corridor that ran between the two

spaces. Behind her, light—the outward manifestation of a Newtonian field that would confine the cargo—flared briefly along the ridges, then coalesced to outline three widely spaced squares, two to her left, one to her right. Chase Mago cut the field, frowning.

"The crates are light," Balthasar interposed. "It might be easier for us to move them than to try and tell the homunculi where to put them."

Chase Mago sighed. "All right. You see where they have to go."

"Sure," Balthasar said, and reached for the first of the crates, lifting it with apparent ease.

Silence copied him, carefully staying out of the nearest homunculus's reach. It would not move without an express command and she knew it, but her skin crawled at the thought of its touch. The crate itself was lighter than it looked, but heavier than she had expected from Balthasar's attitude. She could barely raise it, and settled for shoving it along the decking, tipping it over the ridges into its proper place. Chase Mago did the same, and Silence was meanly gratified when she spotted the captain rubbing his back muscles. Balthasar was stronger than he looked, but not as strong as he pretended to be.

Chase Mago straightened. "I can handle it from here," he said. He pulled a small, egg-shaped object from his pocket and tapped it against his palm, then set it to his lips and sounded a single note. Silence winced—even a pilot, not trained to listen for the fractional variations in pitch that concerned an engineer, could tell that the cargo was positioned out of tune. Chase Mago had a long, niggling job ahead of him, shifting the crates by millimeters until the ship was in tune again.

"I'll get the homunculi back to the agency," Balthasar said quickly, and picked up the control disk, bringing the homunculi back to life. They straightened to their walking stance and turned slowly toward the hatch. Silence scrambled out of the way, then turned to the engineer, trying to pretend unconcern.

"Do you need my help?"

"No." Chase Mago's attention was on the problem in front of him, but he looked up long enough to smile at her. "Surely a pilot's not interested in tuning?"

"Not quite," Silence said, and fled before he could accept her offer.

Once in the commons, she drew herself another mug of coffee, less because she wanted it than to give herself an excuse for sitting at the table. God, she thought, I hate beginnings. And I'm not at all sure I want to make a beginning here. A three-way marriage. . . . Three-way marriage was considered, at best, peculiar in the Rusadir, even among the avowedly eccentric star-travellers. She knew of only one such triple among the ships that travelled *Black Dolphin*'s roads, and the three—it had been two women, both of whom took care of the passengers on the tiny mail liner, and a man, the captain— had claimed that the arrangement existed only to guarantee rights if one of them died. But there had been something between them, something in the glances that passed between them, that gave the lie to their simple explanation. There had been a lot of gossip about them among the star-travellers, gossip and a sly exchange of looks and words every time the triple came into a bar. No, she had no desire to end up like that, the object of snide remarks and speculative glances. Better to begin again on Delos, no matter how hard that might be.

That decision made, she felt a little less lost. Balthasar had suggested a long flight to Delos; she might as well begin plotting that course. She stuffed her mug into the cleaning slot and was already at the door of her cabin when Balthasar appeared on the ladder.

"Silence?" he called. "You starting the course plot?"

"I was going to."

"How long do you think it will take?"

"I don't know," Silence answered. "Are you taking on more cargo?"

"No, this is it," Balthasar answered.

Silence waited for a further explanation, but the captain smiled cheerfully at her and swung himself off the ladder. You could be a very irritating man to work for, Silence thought. I know perfectly well the only cargos as small as this one that pay expenses—never mind making a profit—are the illegal ones. "I think," she said carefully, "that if you want me to consider this scheme of yours seriously, you owe me an explanation."

Chase Mago, stepping off the ladder behind Balthasar, gave a short bark of laughter. "She's right, Denis, you owe her."

The captain made an odd gesture that was not quite a shrug. "All right. The cargo isn't precisely illegal—I've got genuine papers for it, it's going to its rightful owners, it isn't restricted—but it is, well, sensitive. My employers pay very well to see that it arrives on Delos within certain time limits, without anyone asking awkward questions."

Balthasar was a master of the art of talking without giving anything away, Silence thought sourly. He didn't say a thing I couldn't have figured out on my own. "And who are these employers?"

Chase Mago cut in irritably. "It's a laundering operation, Silence. Loot fenced on Enkomi and Astapa buys iore on Ariassus and spring spice from the Madakh. That buys gems on Tartessos, and gems buy credit on Delos. And Delian credit buys anything, anywhere. We're just the couriers on the last leg."

"And who pays you?" Silence asked, even though she suspected the answer.

It was Balthasar who answered, with a grimace almost of pain. "Wrath-of-God."

Silence shivered. Wrath-of-God was the greatest of the pirate combines that had dominated the starways from the Millennial Wars to the reformation of the Hegemony, and the only one to survive the police raids that had earned the Hegemon Adeben II his title of the Scourge. Wrath-of-God's power had been diminished since those days, when its squadrons had raided even Asterion with impunity, but its ships still roamed the Fringe, snapping up unwary, or unlucky, freighters. *Black Dolphin* had sighted one, once, or what they had thought was a Wrath-of-God ship: a sleek longship, barely more than a collection of weapons-turrets balanced on an outsized keel, travelling unmarked and with its identity beacon silenced. *Dolphin* had turned and run, back toward Tell Sukhas and its patrols, and when they had taken time to look, the unknown ship had faded from their screens. Bodua Leigh had refused to travel that route again, even after the Tell Sukhan patrols had made a sweep and claimed to have destroyed the pirate. Silence looked at Balthasar, at last able to identify the bleached patch of skin on his right cheek. The senior captains who ruled Wrath-of-God marked their men; that scar was the mark where their tattoo of a fire-eyed skull had been hidden or removed.

Balthasar raised one hand to his cheek, rubbing two fingers over the mark as though her stare had made it hurt again. "We're not pirates," he said. "A half-and-half isn't really good enough any more, not to take the profitable cargos. Those travel in convoy anyway. We just handle the business end."

"I see," Silence said. But I don't have to like it, she added to herself. No wonder they didn't tell me who they worked for. They knew I wouldn't even consider their scheme if I did. Well, they were right. I'll get this ship to Delos, and then I'll leave it—so long as Balthasar keeps his part of the bargain. She shivered again at that thought.

Balthasar had taken her silence for assent. "Can you have the course ready by tomorrow morning?"

"Yes."

"Good." Balthasar disappeared into the galley, returning a moment later with a mug of coffee. "Then I'll try to arrange a morning liftoff."

Silence swallowed her protest. She could work out a course in six or seven hours, one that would bring the ship through in one piece. And if it wasn't a particularly easy passage—that would be one more reason for Balthasar to let her go once they reached Delos. "I'll get right on it," she said meekly, and stepped into her cabin.

Latching the door behind her, she crossed to her bunk and pulled out the starbooks, then settled herself at the console, pulling out the tiny writing board to give herself more space in which to work. The *Gilded Stairs* had the best tables for this part of space and she flipped to them only to stare in surprise at a set of unfamiliar symbols. The treated paper felt odd beneath her fingers, far older than any of her own books. . . . She paged back quickly to the frontispiece, sought the date of imprint among the tangle of decoration. It read 781 N.A. Prewar, she realized wonderingly, touching the pages with more respect, but she could not remember the formula for changing the old "New Age" dates to the Standard Years of Rusadir and Hege-

mony. So how had a starbook printed before the
Millennial War gotten into Bodua Leigh's cabin?
It was not as though he shared his nephew's interest in things prewar that might lead to Earth. She
turned back to the blank pages at the very front,
hoping to find a bill of sale or some indication of
ownership and found instead a small slip of paper,
closely covered with her grandfather's spidery
writing.

"Silence," it began, "one of Otto's dealers came
looking for him, wanted to sell this for the usual
exorbitant price. I'd have sent him away, but for
the initials in the beginning. Of course, he claims
this was Gregor Mosi's very starbook and, well, I
can't disprove it. In any case, I'd rather you had it
than Otto. Happy early (or late) name-day, with
love from your grandfather." There was no date.

Silence looked automatically for the initials, but
her sight was blurred by tears. She blinked them
away, and found the tiny, intertwined G and M
that might stand for Gregor Mosi, legendary pilot
of the prewar era. Mosi had been her hero from
the time she had first decided to become a pilot;
he had discovered a dozen new worlds, made and
lost a hundred fortunes—always in the most romantic fashion possible—and had finally disappeared while attempting to find an utterly alien
planet, his ship presumably torn apart by the bizarre tuning of his harmonium. She stroked the
pages reverently. This edition would no longer be
of much use in travelling from star to star, but she
could think of no better talisman for a pilot. Clearly,
Bodua Leigh had thought so as well.

After a moment, she sniffed and wiped her eyes
hard. It was a good present, she told herself sternly,
but of no practical use. You have a job to do, pilot.
Get on with it. For a moment, she wished for her
own up-to-date *Gilded Stairs*, but the *Topoi*'s tables

were almost as good. She turned to them, jotting down the relevant hieroglyphics and cross-referencing them. There was only one long route from Secasia to Delos, though there was a cluster of linked shorter routes that would have been her first choice under other circumstances. But Balthasar wanted a long route, and a long route he would get. She checked her notes again, and slid one hand down the column listing duration until she reached the proper time. Then she searched across the top of the table for the hieroglyph indicating the physical route, Secasia to Delos, and found the point of intersection. The sign indicated the Way of the Carts. The *Topoi* had better tables, but the *Speculum Astronomi* used a better system for noting the voidmarks. She flipped through the pages until she found the proper place, then propped her feet on the edge of her bunk, scanning the half-page of cryptic text and the accompanying symbols. But the picture, the dog-headed man who capered awkwardly atop a wheel turned by a blindfolded woman, the second woman who crouched in a corner shielding a fretted lamp, remained obstinately only a drawing. Nothing came to her but the sterile, common knowledge that was within the grasp of anyone who had read a standard hieroglyphica. The Carter's Road, as the *Speculum* named it, was a tricky route—that was the meaning of the crouching woman—and shielding the lamp suggested that the pilot should conserve strength and ship's power. The wheel stood for a random vortex, a twisted knot in heaven, reflecting the presence of some massive object existing on the material or submaterial planes.

Silence sighed and closed the book, keeping a finger between the pages to mark her place. She took a deep breath and tried to relax, to reach the calm she needed if she was to read the voidmarks accurately. She was looking for a gate that was not a gate. . . . It was an old riddle, but it focused her mind admirably: true understanding was the key to true perception, her first teacher had said. The gates of which the pilots spoke were not really gates in the sense of being fixed locations in space and time. Rather, they were methods, ways of getting from one place to another in a set amount of time. Some—like the Carter's Road—needed certain physical features in the space through which they passed, so that the ship could benefit from the ghostly, nonmaterial reflections of those objects. Others required nothing more than the pilot's understanding of the signs that marked them. Metaphysicists said that any place, if such a word could be used, in purgatory was exactly the same as all places, that all things existed there and that star travel was as much a matter of laying departure point and destination side by side as it was a matter of following rules and voidmarks.

She opened the starbook again, and this time the meaning leaped out of the picture at her. The Carter's Road was a random vortex, with a blind spin clockwise and a nasty twist to it at the end. The way to get through it was to drive into the current, to ride with it, nursing the ship along just as the woman nursed her lamp, until the distorted reflection of a sun that was the center of the vortex, the hub of the wheel, came clear. And then you dove straight through. Silence blinked, and the vision faded slightly. The passage through purgatory would, in itself, be fairly simple, now that she had a coherent picture of the route.

There was a tentative knock at the door. Silence glanced up at the chronometer as she reached for the button that would release the latch, and was surprised to realize that four hours had passed.

The door slid open, and Chase Mago stood framed in the doorway, a dinner tray weighting his hands.

"I thought you might be hungry by now," he said.

"Oh, thank you." Silence had been so caught up in her work that it took a moment for the contents of the tray to register. Chase Mago grinned as her expression reflected sudden hunger.

"Shall I set it on your desk?"

"Please." Silence swept aside the starbooks and a sheet of paper covered with obscure symbols, and the engineer slid the tray onto the smooth surface, lifting the cover with something of a flourish.

"It's the last real food we'll have for a couple of days," he said. "I didn't think you should miss out on it."

"Thank you," Silence said again. It was an unexpected courtesy, on a new ship and from a couple of men who were little better than pirates, and she asked impulsively, "Why do you work for Denis?" Instantly, she wished she had said nothing. She had not meant to ask, and she was not sure she wanted to hear the answer. But Chase Mago only frowned momentarily.

"You mean, why do I work for Wrath-of-God," he corrected without anger.

"I suppose—" She hesitated, then answered honestly, "Yes."

"Because they fight the Hegemony." Chasc Mago was suddenly very serious. "They raid Hegemonic ships, and that hurts the Hegemon in a way the Rusadir could never manage. And, of course, Denis hates the Hegemony, too." He hesitated in his turn, absurdly unable to find a place for the tray cover. "I was supposed to tell you, we lift just before dawn, 0430 our time."

Silence nodded, the moment in which she might

have asked more questions clearly past. "I'll set my alarm."

"Then I'll let you eat in peace. . . ." The engineer's voice was lost in the hiss of the closing door.

Silence stared after him. It made sense when she thought about it, and fit in better with her first impressions of the big engineer. Kesse had fallen, the Rusadir had lost, but the pirates still raided, and Chase Mago could turn that into a continuation of his own war. As long as the Hegemony suffered, he could accept the cost to the innocent. In spite of herself, her longstanding fear of politics, and her resolution to leave *Sun-Treader* as soon as she could, she found herself sympathizing with him. She pushed the thought away, and turned her attention to the dinner he had brought. She would put in another hour or two studying the marks, and then go to bed.

She woke a few minutes before the alarm sounded, roused by her own internal time sense, and reached automatically to shut off the mechanism. Already, she could hear the others moving around in the common room—Chase Mago, probably, since the engineer had more to do to prepare for lift-off than either captain or pilot. But if he was up and about, it was more than time for her to go to work. She threw back the light coverlet and headed for the shower. The stinging water woke her fully, and she felt almost confident enough, when she emerged from the cloud of spray, to skip the ritual last minute review of the voidmarks. But not quite confident enough: the *Speculum* lay open on the console where she had left it the night before, and she glanced quickly over text and picture even as she wrestled herself into the clinging shipsuit and fastened the multiple seals. There was really nothing new to be learned, but the brief glance focused her mind, and put her into the proper mood for her art.

The chronometer display read 0321. It was high time that she was on her way. Hastily, she dropped the starbooks back into the strongbox, then drew the security netting over the unmade bunk and swept a few loose baubles into the nearest drawer. Then she caught up the gloves and hood that matched her suit and stepped out into the common room.

As she had expected, Balthasar was there, hunched over his mug of coffee, but Chase Mago had already disappeared into the engine room. The heavily baffled hatch was closed across the entrance, but a faint something, not sound but more than mere vibration, leaked out through it. Silence felt the familiar excitement rising in her belly, but she fought it down, and drew herself coffee and a bar of nutritional concentrate. Balthasar regarded her blearily, dark circles prominent under his eyes.

"Did you have trouble getting clearance?" Silence asked.

"Not exactly. Just the usual red tape and nuisance." Balthasar sighed, and seemed to see her for the first time. "You could have real food if you wanted it. The tow doesn't come for half an hour."

Silence shook her head. "I'd rather not. I don't like to eat first thing in the morning."

Balthasar grunted and returned to the morose contemplation of his coffee. Silence stared—she had not expected to find anything that could subdue the captain, least of all something so trivial as lack of sleep—then forced herself to pay attention to her own meal. The Carter's Road was five full minutes long, real time, which would translate to about five hours' subjective passage, and even if Balthasar could spell her in the early stages, she would need all her strength.

"Oh, captain?"

"Um?"

"Do you want to go over the route now, or later?"

Balthasar sighed, rubbing his eyes. "Now, I suppose. How are we going?"

"By the Carter's Road," Silence answered.

Balthasar looked at her blankly.

"The Way of the Carts?" she added.

The captain nodded. "I know it. A wheel-road, right? Over and around, then through and out?"

"That's right. I'd forgotten you were a pilot."

Balthasar grinned, looking more like himself. "Of sorts. I can take some of the first leg, I think, once you've got us lined up."

"That's what I was thinking," Silence agreed.

"All right—" Balthasar's next words were cut off by a buzz from the wall monitor. With a glance of apology, he reached across the compartment for the response switch. "*Sun-Treader.*"

"Captain Balthasar? This is Kardal, your tow boss."

"Yes. Are you ready to bring us out now?" Balthasar's irritated glance at the chronometer made it clear that the tow had arrived early. Silence hid her grin.

"We're ready whenever you are," Kardal answered. Even through the distorting speakers, his voice was appallingly cheerful.

Balthasar glared at the monitor. "I'll be in the control room in two minutes to unlock the cradle." He switched from the exterior channel to the inside speaker without waiting for Kardal's answer, but turned to Silence before calling the engine room.

"Would you mind making sure things are secured here?"

Silence sighed, even though she knew that this was always the newcomer's job. "No."

"Thanks." Balthasar turned his attention back to the monitor. "Julie?"

The acknowledgement was indistinct, distorted by the rising wail of the harmonium.

"The tow's here—yes, already. I'll want systems power in three minutes. Can you do it?"

Silence didn't wait for the engineer's answer, or for Balthasar's grumbled acknowledgement. She collected the breakfast mugs and shoved them into the cleaning chute—they would be safe there for the flight—and then gave the common room a quick inspection, making sure that all the furniture was fastened to the decking and that the cabin doors were securely latched. Satisfied that nothing was likely to come loose and start wandering—a pseudo-animation, the result of the stimulation of the tiny amounts of spiritual substance present in every ordinary material object as the ship came closer to heaven, was one of the most disconcerting effects of purgatory—she followed Balthasar to the lower bridge.

The captain was already strapped into his chair, his hands moving quickly across his controls, instruments coming alive at his touch. He nodded to Silence as she slipped into her place and settled her headpiece, featherweight earphones and microphone, as comfortably as possible. In the middle of the blinking confusion of newly activated instruments, the triple viewscreen flashed to life, two screens showing only the dull grey folds of the baffle curtains. The third showed the tow, an ugly rounded thing squatting on its treads in a narrow opening in the curtains. The top hatch was open and a man in Port Authority badges—Kardal—sat on the edge, a massive control wand in one hand. At the bottom of the screen, Silence could just see one of the homunculi that responded to that wand. It was better articulated than the carriers, thinner limbed and quicker moving, with outsized hands for attaching the two hooks to the cradle.

"Is everything clear below, Julie?" Balthasar asked.

"Everything's fine," Chase Mago answered.

"Then I'm releasing the cradle lock," Balthasar said. He threw a series of switches, leaving a trail of orange warning lights in his wake, then touched a control stud. "Kardal?"

In the screen, the tow boss raised his free hand to his earphones. "Here."

"I've released the lock," Balthasar said. "You can make the link."

"Right." Kardal answered and his image in the viewscreen gestured sweepingly with the control rod. The ship shuddered faintly as a homunculus jostled the cradle.

Silence leaned back in her couch, deliberately divorcing herself from the liftoff preparations. None of this was her responsibility—her job only started when they reached the twelfth of heaven, and crossed into purgatory. She watched idly as the link was made and tested, then braced herself against the first jostling as the tow got underway. The cradle was well stabilized, however, and the motion quickly settled to a rhythmic swing.

The massive doors at the far end of the dock stood open to the half light of the hour before dawn. Cradle and tow moved between the last pair of tightly baffled freighters, and then the ship lurched sharply as the cradle passed from the smooth floor of the dock to the rougher pavement of the taxiway. The forward-focused viewscreens showed the tow and the long wedge of runway picked out by its lights. The third screen showed the port tower, black against the greying sky, the lights of the tracking room giving it a starlike crown. The stars themselves were hidden by a thin wash of cloud.

In the screens, the tow bounced once, and then the cradle jerked again as it was dragged onto the launch table. Balthasar opened a line to the tow toss, reeling off a string of coordinates given him by the astrologers in the port tower. Kardal repeated them, and began edging the cradle around, so that the ship's bow was directed away from the sunrise, onto the most favorable line away from the planet, the line freest of solar and planetary influence. Balthasar watched his instruments intently. At last the ship was positioned to his satisfaction; he signaled Kardal, and waited with some impatience while one of the homunculi detached the tow link. The the tow moved away, the homunculi clinging to the retracted link platform, and vanished into the bunker beside the taxiway. The heavily baffled gate slid shut behind it.

"All set below, Julie?" Balthasar asked.

"Whenever you're ready," the engineer answered.

Balthasar reached across to the astrogation console set between the two couches and fiddled with the controls. In the tiny projection globe, a Ficinan model of Secasia's system sprang into existence, the five planets and their sun positioned accurately in relation to each other, the lines of harmony and dissonance, the *musica mundana*, visible as a ghostly flush of color ringing each of the worlds. *Sun-Treader*'s course appeared as a vivid blue line, following what Silence recognized as the path of least resistance. She took a deep breath as Balthasar read off the last harmonium setting, unable to control her small excited smile. Balthasar grinned back at her as he activated the primary control board, posing his left hand delicately above the keys, the same eagerness in his eyes.

"Secasia Control, *Sun-Treader* is ready to lift."

The port tower answered promptly. "Acknowledged, *Sun-Treader*. You may lift when ready."

"There must not be much traffic," Silence murmured.

"Not this early," Balthasar agreed. His hand was trembling slightly above the keys; he stilled it with an effort. "Julie, give me the first sequence."

"Coming up." Chase Mago's voice was swallowed in the sudden surge of music as he opened the stops of the harmonium. The ship shuddered throughout its length and pulled free of the cradle. There was a second of fierce pressure, a massive weight on chest and stomach, and then Silence felt the familiar tingling deep in her bones as the harmonium's influence brought the entire ship into tune. In the screens, Secasia's surface fell away, the pull of the planet's elemental core cheated by the protective sphere of the music.

The viewscreens flickered briefly as *Sun-Treader* burst through the veil of clouds, and Silence looked away, dizzied by the shifting images. The astrogation console showed that *Sun-Treader* was drifting slightly away from the planned course, attracted by some affinity between the ship's tuning and the music of one of Secasia's sister-worlds. She opened her mouth to point it out, but Balthasar's hand was already moving on his keyboard. In the chaotic music of the harmonium, a single note changed, and the pinpoint that was the ship steadied to its course.

"*Sun-Treader*, this is Secasia Control. We confirm a successful liftoff, and that you're running true to your projection. You should be clear of planetary and solar influences in four hours. Good voyage!"

Silence glanced at the captain, but his attention was still wholly on his instruments. "This is *Sun-Treader*," she said, keying on her own headset. "We copy your projection, and thanks for the good wishes."

There was a faint burble of static, and then Secasia Control faded with its planet. Balthasar seemed to relax a little, though he still held his hands ready to correct the ship's flight.

"Almost," he whispered. "Almost—there."

Silence felt it too, the sudden steadying as *Sun-Treader* reached its true flight line, the point at which the celestial harmonies were first discernible, not blocked by the noise of the planets. The sound of the harmonium faded, the affinity between its sound and the music of heaven easing the passage. At the same time, the meaningless velocity reading winked out.

Balthasar sighed. "That does it. Now it's just a pleasure cruise 'til we get out of the system. Thanks for dealing with Secasia Control, by the way."

"No problem," Silence said, and tilted her chair back to its farthest position. The captain nodded approvingly.

"Good idea."

"Thanks," Silence said, and closed her eyes.

As always, she did not mean to sleep, but the distant sound of the harmonium half hypnotized her, seeming perpetually on the verge of forming itself into a recognizable tune. Neither listening nor ignoring it would exorcise it; she lay back in the couch and let the music sweep through her. In no time at all, there was a hand on her shoulder.

"Silence."

She sat up, rubbing her eyes. The viewscreens showed the black of deep space, Secasia's sun a reddish pinpoint in one, the other stars faded and remote. They did not yet show the garish corona that marked the twelfth of heaven, but it was very close. "Time?"

"Twenty minutes," Balthasar answered. "We'll be switching over to the upper register in ten."

"Right." Silence unclasped her harness, stretching. "I'll go up now."

For some reason, sleeping shipboard was twice as restful as any other sleep, and drowsiness never seemed to linger afterward. She stretched again, and was fully awake, ready to face the passage through purgatory. Underfoot, the decking and then the rungs of the ladder felt faintly sticky, as though she had stepped in glue. It was another effect of the harmonium, and she noticed it only as one more indication that everything was working properly. In the upper control room, she settled her feet in the recesses before the wheel and methodically set about activating all the control systems, first locking the yoke so that it could not move. Then she opened her intercom link and announced, "I'm ready to take the con."

"All right," Balthasar said. "Julie, we're ready to go to the upper register."

"Switching over," Chase Mago answered.

All around them, the keelsong changed. It deepened, and at the same time gained a whole new range of sound, floating above the first notes. The dome of the hull quivered, a trembling beginning at the base, then running up the walls to meet above Silence's head, and then quietly fading to translucence. The stars shone through, ringed by unmoving halos of fire. She took a deep breath, setting her hands on the yoke in front of her, and saw without surprise the bones gleaming beneath her skin, webbed by a ruby lace of veins and arteries. They had entered purgatory.

"You have control, Silence." Balthasar's voice sounded in her ears, and her hand had already reached for the lock, snapping it aside, before she answered properly.

The yoke moved smoothly under her hand, as smoothly as she had expected, with the hint of resistance that meant all the controls were working properly. She smiled, allowing herself a brief moment to savor the experience of flying a new ship, then turned her attention to her course. The stars were fading as their coronae brightened: they had passed the first twelfth long ago. She took a deep breath and sought her voidmarks.

Almost immediately, the Carter's Road took shadowy form before her, first the curve of the great wheel's rim, the fire-edged ghost of the spoke, then the entire shape of the cart wheel, turning lazily against a purple starfield splotched with the gaudy coronae of uncountable suns. Silence marked her course with a practiced eye: over the top, onto the rim and then down it, moving with its spin, then down the center of a lower spoke and out through the white-hot hub. The wheel grew larger and larger as the ship approached, and Silence adjusted her course to bring the ship in over the top of the monstrous image. She brought *Sun-Treader* down slowly, turning it to lay the keel against the apparently molten surface of the rim. The ship sank into it, shuddering. Silence clung to her bucking controls, blinking and unable to spare a hand to shield her eyes from the fierce glare that enveloped her. Then the ship struck the stability she had known would be there, and the light faded to a bearable glow. Cautiously, she lifted one hand from the control yoke and, when the shuddering did not begin again, rubbed at her watering eyes.

This was the easy part of the passage, now that the ship was positioned properly. *Sun-Treader* could be relied upon to stay on this course without much attention from her, until the time came to turn into the spoke—in fact, if she never touched the yoke, *Sun-Treader* would simply circle the cart wheel until the elemental water that powered the harmonium was utterly exhausted. She relaxed, her hands loose on the controls, and watched the shifting lights around her. *Sun-Treader* seemed to float on a river of fire, beneath a sky of fiery cloud. All around her, the hull had faded to nothing, except underfoot, where the specially compounded metal resisted the translucence of purgatory. The cloth of her shipsuit contained traces of the same compound, spun fine by witchwomen on Castax and Akra-Leuke, decently veiling bone and blood and organs.

After a time she could not define, there was a hand on her shoulder. She turned, and met Balthasar's eyes, twin points of green light glowing in a face that was as much skull and brain as flesh. Wrath-of-God's skull tattoo was sketched ghostly on his cheek.

"The clock's ticked once, so I figure we're about halfway," he said. "I'll spell you, if you like."

"Thanks," Silence said. She leaned away from the controls, allowing Balthasar to slip in front of her, then relinquished her grip on the yoke. Around her, the voidmarks faded, becoming insubstantial shadows of what they had been. She reached for the ladder, a transparent shimmering in the air, and carefully felt her way to the lower control room. The fittings there were made of the resistant metal; the consoles appeared perfectly solid, though the screens and readouts were dark, the chronometer frozen at the instant in which they had entered purgatory. Or not quite at that: Balthasar had said it had clicked once since then.

She dropped down the second ladder to the oddly quiet common room, her feet clinging to the soft tiles of the deck. There was fruit juice in the galley's ready box, and she drove a straw into the soft pack, but set it aside after the first sip. She would not need the distraction of a full bladder when it came time to make the turn from the rim to the spoke. Spurred by that thought, she went into her own cabin to relieve herself, then stretched slowly to work out the stiffness of the first half of the trip. Then she returned to the lower control room.

The chronometer had changed again—she had not been in the commons for very long, she thought, but then real time passed irregularly in purgatory. She climbed to the next level and stood frowning for a moment, willing the voidmarks into existence again. They resisted at first, obstinately refusing to come clear, but then the pattern formed. The spoke loomed overhead—Balthasar had turned the ship onto its back, sparing her the chore and making the course change that much easier.

"Thanks," she said again. "I can take it now."

"You timed it perfectly," Balthasar answered, and slid out of her way gracefully.

She nodded, and instantly forgot him as she began to line up the ship for the turn down the spoke. Amid the tongues of fire, she could see the line of least resistance, marked by the eddies that curled to either side. She eased the ship toward it, nudging the control yoke. The ship bucked, protesting. At last she had *Sun-Treader* aligned with the current she wanted, and she leaned hard into the wheel, forcing the ship into the turn. It came around sluggishly at first, and then the current caught it, sweeping it forward down the spoke toward the glowing line that marked the hub. The controls leaped in her hands, struggling to get free, as the ship's apparent speed increased, so that *Sun-Treader* seemed to be pulled toward certain annihilation at the center of the wheel. The hub changed shape, too, as they approached, going from a line to a disk, the celestial reflection of a star. In spite of long experience, Silence tensed, bracing herself for the collision—and then the ship burst through,

like a Gresham's tiger through a flaming hoop.
She was suddenly aware of a change of pitch, and
the quick conversation in her earphones as the
ship went from purgatory to the mundane universe.
The ship had been falling out of purgatory even as
she flew down the spoke, she realized, the approach to the material somehow translating to an
apparent increase in speed. Automatically, she
reached to secure the yoke, turning control back to
Balthasar.

"—respond, please. Delos Approach One, this is
DRV *Sun-Treader*, respond, please."

That was Balthasar's voice in her ears, quick
and mechanical as he concentrated on the dozens
of readouts suddenly alive on the boards below.
The deck shuddered delicately underfoot as *Sun-
Treader* passed the invisible border of the Delian
system, and that faint motion released Silence from
her near-trance. She would be needed below, if
only to handle the initial conversations with Delos Approach, and Customs, and whoever else might
be interested in their arrival. She stepped onto the
ladder, then kicked free and slid the rest of the
way to the control room deck. Strapping herself
into her couch with one hand, she reached for the
communications switches with the other.

"I can take that now," she said.

Balthasar nodded, his eyes fixed on the projections in the screens before him. One was a two-
dimensional copy of the Ficinan model in the
projection globe, the others were representations
of Delos itself, each webbed with the lines repre-
senting the standard approach roads. "See if you
can get through," he said, without taking his attention from the readouts. Around them, the ship
shuddered and leaped, the harmonium quavering
as he fought toward a harmonious bearing. "I need
to know which Roads they want us to come in by."

Silence adjusted the frequency knobs. "Delos Approach One, this is DRV *Sun-Treader*, respond, please."

"*Sun-Treader*, this is Delos Primary Approach." The voice in her earphones was a woman's, cheerful beneath the competence. "We have you on our scopes, and we suggest you funnel into the Saefrin Roads, with descent to St. Harbin's field controlled by their speaker."

Silence reached for the navigation plot, keyed in the information she had been given. Balthasar's nod was a mere formality. "Agreed, Primary Approach. The Saefrin Roads, and then a landing on St. Harbin's field. Would you bespeak a berth there for us?" She glanced at Balthasar before adding, "Class four."

"Done, *Sun-Treader*," Approach answered promptly.

"In the Roads," Balthasar said quietly. The vibration slackened perceptibly.

"We are in the Roads, Approach One," Silence said.

"Confirmed by our musonar," Approach answered. "You will switch to St. Harbin's beam at the planetary perimeter."

Silence glanced at the navigation projection and found the pale halo of blue surrounding the pinpoint world, marking the edge of planetary influence. Balthasar had already set up a course, a simple curve skirting the influence of Delos's single sister-world.

"ETA to transfer is five hours, twenty-three minutes," Approach went on. Remain in the Roads, and you'll have no trouble with local traffic. Delos Primary Approach out."

"Thank you, Primary Approach," Silence said, but there was no answer.

Balthasar nodded to her. "I can handle it from here, if you want to rest. That was a long flight."

Silence's answer was choked by a yawn that caught her unaware. "It was that."

"Take a rest," Balthasar urged. "I'll wake you well before the final approach."

"All right, thanks." She had tilted the couch to its most comfortable position before she realized that he had read her real hesitation about sleeping now: she did not want to miss her first landing on Delos. He had been good about other things, too, she thought, her mind dulled by the subjective hours at the wheel. He's different in space. He had showed up when she needed him to take over, let her handle the secondary control room jobs—no, he had simply assumed that she would do them, as any pilot would, then done his own part without fuss or bother. It could be good to work for a man like that, no matter who paid for his cargos. . . . Hold on, now, she told herself sharply. This is no time to make your decision. Wait til we land, til you've had a good night's sleep, and then you can decide.

Chapter 3

"Silence."

There was a hand on her shoulder, too. She gasped and tried to sit up, but the protective webbing held her back.

"Sorry," Balthasar said, "but I didn't think you'd want to miss this."

"No," Silence said slowly, and pulled her couch upright. All three screens were filled with the disk of Delos, a perfect grey-black circle defined by the diamond-ring effect of Delos's sun, thrown into artificial eclipse by their angle of approach. The planet itself was not entirely dark, however. The surface was webbed with light, the pattern broken by banks of cloud that could not completely hide the reflection of the cities' lights. No, not cities, Silence thought. All of Delos was a city, or so the books and films said, a single vast urban area that filled every available meter of solid land and spilled out into the ocean which they farmed so assiduously.

That single city made it beautiful, too, glittering and spangled like one of the festival balls that dove and swooped above the midsummer crowds on Cap Bel.

The voice of the planetary approach controller sounded in her ears, making her jump again. "*Sun-Treader*, this is Saefrin Local. Everything looks good from here. You'll enter atmosphere in twenty-eight minutes; switch over to St. Harbin's Field Control now."

"Thanks, Saefrin," Balthasar answered, before Silence could recover enough to respond. "We'll take it from here."

A new voice cut in immediately, young and brisk and male. "*Sun-Treader*, this is St. Harbin's Field Control. We'll transmit a tuning beam whenever you're ready."

Balthasar flipped an intercom switch. "Julie?"

"I'm ready to record," Chase Mago answered promptly.

Silence glanced at the captain, who nodded. "Field Control, this is *Sun-Treader*," she said. "We're ready for the tuning beam."

"Transmitting," Field Control answered, and a moment later Chase Mago announced, "Transmission received and recorded."

Silence passed that on to Field Control, received his updated estimate of the time to atmosphere, then relaxed against her cushions to watch Balthasar work. Liftoff and landing were properly the captain's responsibilities, but on *Black Dolphin*, as her grandfather aged and his touch on the controls became less sure, she had taken over more and more of his technical duties. It felt very good, not to have to feel out the approach line on a world as crowded as Delos. . . . As though to emphasize her relief, a tiny speck of light, the bronze reflection from some in-systems ship's keel, drifted across the central screen, well down and ahead of their flight path. The musonar screen showed even more ships around them, the specks of light swarming like a cloud of gnats.

Balthasar was obviously used to the difficulties of the descent. His eyes flickering from musonar to the course plot, now replacing the picture of Delos in the left-hand screen, he brought the ship into line, then, as the St. Harbin's beam came on, brought her down into the atmosphere, laying the keel against the beam, using it to cheat the shattering dissonance of Delos's core. *Sun-Treader* shivered, passing through the layers of air, but the trembling never threatened his easy control. They sank rapidly toward St. Harbin's field, flashing through the cloud layer, and Balthasar's hands tensed over his keys. The course plot showed a plan of the field, their cradle drawn in flashing red.

"Stand by for breaking harmony, Julie," he murmured.

"Ready," Chase Mago answered.

Balthasar did not answer. He watched the screen intently, and Silence found herself tensing. This was the trickiest part of landing, when the ship was riding the field beam down toward its cradle. That beam had to be interrupted, its hold on the ship broken, before the ship smashed full speed into the field harmonium. Judging the right moment to switch the ship's harmonium to a dissonant chord was a knack she had never had; her landings tended to be rough, cutting the beam too soon. But Balthasar was waiting too long; the field buildings were distinct in the screen. She thought she could see a laggard vehicle disappearing into a bunker. . . . Her hands closed on the couch arms, and she bit her tongue to keep from shouting to Chase Mago.

"Now, Julie!" Balthasar cried.

The pitch of the harmonium split painfully, re-forming with a grating shriek that set Silence's teeth on edge. The sudden change racked her guts, but the ship slowed perceptibly. Inertia carried it down further, slowing all the way, until it settled easily into the cradle. Instantly, padded clamps reached for the hull, and a new bank of lights sparked green along the top of the captain's board.

"Cut power," Balthasar ordered. He wore a small, satisfied smile.

"Power's off," Chase Mago answered. The song of the harmonium faded, leaving a quiet that was almost tangible.

A new voice spoke into the stillness. "*Sun-Treader*, we're ready to bring you in. There's another ship on your tail, so we need to get moving."

Balthasar stopped trying to loosen his webbing and looked up at the face reflected in the screen above him. The lights from the main tower made the field as bright as day. "Tage Rolin, isn't it?"

"Yes, Captain Balthasar. I hope your trip was fortunate?"

"Decent," Balthasar answered. "All my locks show green. Go ahead and hook us up." He waited until the harshly lit image in the screen had given orders to the team of homunculi before he asked, "Is all well with you?"

"Tolerable, captain, tolerable," Rolin answered. His voice became suddenly formal. "Hookup is complete."

"I show that green," Balthasar answered.

"Stand by for the tow," Rolin said.

"Ready when you are," Balthasar answered, and a moment later the ship and cradle lurched forward together.

There were more docks on this field than on the Rusadir worlds where *Black Dolphin* had traded, a triple rank to either side of the main control complex, and Silence could not begin to count the tuner's sheds and other supporting buildings. Like any newcomer, she switched from camera to camera, staring eagerly at each new perspective.

The cradle turned a corner then, off the taxiway to the broad road that ran along the perimeter of the field, then turned again to pass between the dock buildings. The door of one, almost in the center of the row, was open, and in spite of herself, Silence breathed a sigh of relief. She had not thought to confirm that Primary Approach had found a dock space for them; on some worlds, that failure would guarantee delays, bad docking, and inflated prices. But then, Delos lived on the starships. It would not pay to cheat them.

The tow nudged ship and cradle into the empty berth between two tightly baffled superfreighters, carefully avoiding the customs team that was already waiting beside the smaller, pedestrians' entrance, their sensor pack resting on the back of a patient homunculus. As soon as the cradle was in place, Balthasar bolted from his couch to secure the curtains, leaving Silence to make her way more slowly down the ladder to the common room. Chase Mago, emerging from the engine room, had the desperately alert expression of a man trying to keep from falling asleep on his feet. Silence drew him a cup of coffee, then, at his despairing grimace, found the bottle of wake-up pills behind the spice dispenser. The engineer swallowed them dry, then reached for the coffee with a little more spirit.

Balthasar returned with the customs team then, calling from the bottom of the ladder for the ship's papers. Chase Mago set his coffee aside and went to fetch them from Balthasar's cabin, along with the two sets of identification papers. Silence collected her own documents from the strongbox and followed Chase Mago to the cargo deck.

The customs team had split up, one man probing the forward cargo compartment with a bell-mouthed sensor, a second directing a slender wand at the bulkheads around him, the third conferring with Balthasar over the bills of lading. The captain accepted the ship's registry documents with a quick nod of thanks, then turned back to the customs man's questions. The second officer finished his examination of the lower level and vanished up the ladder to the crew deck. Silence leaned against the bulkhead, out of the way of the man with the bell-mouthed machine. She would be the last, as the least senior, to have her papers checked. The customs man got around to her at last, asking the routine questions—name, birthplace, planet of origin, citizenship—in a voice that was neither bored nor particularly interested. Silence answered, handed over her papers, and waited while they were photoflashed and the important information circled on the copies.

"Good enough," the customs man said. He flipped through the sheets of photoflash paper. "Denis Balthasar, captain; Julian Chase Mago, engineer; Silence Leigh, pilot. That's your full crew?"

Balthasar nodded.

"Permanent, or will anyone be leaving here?" the customs man went on.

"Julie and I are permanent," Balthasar answered, and glanced at Silence.

"I'll be staying on, too," Silence answered, then looked quickly at Balthasar. "If you're willing."

"It was your choice," Balthasar murmured. "Sieur Anane, I believe I'm required to file intent papers if I plan to marry an off-worlder. Can that be done through you, or do I have to visit the licensing bureau?"

Anane gave the pilot a sidelong glance, and Silence felt herself blushing fiercely. No, I'm not like that, I'm only marrying him for convenience's sake, she wanted to say, but it was too late now. The customs man was droning on about the various legal requirements, forms to be filed and medical scans to be completed, and Balthasar was nodding attentively at every pause. Oh, why did I ever say I was permanent crew? she wailed silently. I could've found other work here, found another ship—one that doesn't fly for Wrath-of-God. But it would have been another beginning, she reminded herself, and these two are good to work with, a smooth, quick-working crew. I work well with them, and they haven't hassled me at all. And besides, she added firmly, it's too late to back out now.

"—and for Sieur Chase Mago," Balthasar finished, and Silence brought herself back to reality with a start.

The customs man, filling out registration forms, looked from pilot to engineer with a startled, disapproving expression on his face. "A triple?"

"Good God above," Silence began, and Balthasar gestured for her to be quiet.

"That's right," he said, with perfect equanimity.

Anane had the grace to blush. "I beg your pardon, sieura, sieurs." He finished stamping the three forms, using the homunculus's casing as a writing board, then passed them back to Balthasar. "Captain, since you're a citizen, I don't need to remind you of local regulations. Information on trading combines, markets, currency exchange, and so on is available in the Port Authority library for a nominal fee. The librarians there can give you a more exhaustive catalog if you're interested." The customs man who had been investigating the crew deck slithered down the ladder again, giving Anane the slightest of nods as he did so. Anane nodded back. "Well, captain, it seems everything's in order.

You're free to do as you please. I hope your stay is pleasant."

"I'm sure it will be," Balthasar answered, and the customs team disappeared out the hatch. He looked at Silence then, obviously somewhat at a loss for words. "Well—"

"Thank you, Silence," Chase Mago interrupted. The stimulant was working; he looked almost awake now. "I am glad you decided to stay."

"Yes, thank you," Balthasar added gratefully. "How are you feeling, Julie? Awake enough for a ride into the city center?"

"Yes, I suppose," Chase Mago answered. "Why?"

"It'll take a while for the papers to be processed," Balthasar answered. "I figured we'd be here at least two weeks, so why stay shipboard? I got us a suite at the Parsley Vine."

The name meant nothing to Silence, but Chase Mago raised an eyebrow. "Let's hope the factor has more work, then."

"He will," Balthasar said. "You're sure you feel up to going in now?"

"Oh, yes. But I've got packing to do, if we're staying." Frowning vaguely, Chase Mago hauled himself back up the ladder to his own cabin.

"Two weeks, you said?" Silence asked.

"About that." Balthasar shrugged. "The factor tends to take his own time finding us work, and I thought you might like to see a little of Delos."

"Thanks." Silence stumbled a little over the word, surprised by the sudden, casual kindness. "Then I guess I've got some packing to do, too."

There was not that much she needed to take with her. The starbooks would have to come, of course—she could not risk losing them—and her good clothes, but that would hardly fill a carryall. Shoes, toilet kit, jewelry box.... From what she had read of Delos, she would look drab indeed compared to the flamboyant star-travellers, merchant captains and adventurers all, who populated this world. She hesitated a moment, then switched on the section of her monitor that was tied in to the standard local-conditions channel. The narrow screen flashed white, then settled down again. Silence contemplated the list of options—transit schedules, library codes, a list of advertising tapes coded by service. . . . Among the last was a list of major banking houses and commercial institutions with offices on Delos, and she wondered briefly if Denis's factor, Wrath-of-God's business representative on this planet, would be listed among them.

There was no time for that sort of speculation, she told herself sternly, and pressed the keys that called up the local weather forecast. The screen filled momentarily with stars, then the stars moved off the screen and words crowded on after them.

"Current conditions, St. Harbin's Field and St. Harbin's mainurb. Time, 0449 hours of twenty-five. Temperature, twelve point four degrees centigrade. Precipitation, none; humidity, low. Probability of precipitation negligible. Two-day prediction—"

Chill then, and dry, Silence thought, turning away from the screen. The next days' weather didn't matter to her, nor did the local season: she was bringing all of her shore clothes with her anyway. She fumbled momentarily in her carryall, then brought out a rich blue tunic and the tights that matched it. She unsealed the shipsuit, fighting the clinging material down over her hips, then pulled on the tights and the loose tunic, adjusting the waist tabs without a glance at the reflective panel on the back of the cabin door. The sleeves were very full, and the tight cuffs turned them into more than adequate pockets. She slipped her passport folder into the left sleeve, along with a thin book of universal cash slips and the card with her starbank access code, then zipped closed the cuff. Then she fitted the clear plastic shields over her feet, wriggling her toes to make sure that the treated substances would cling securely to each other. She glanced quickly at her reflection: she was very pale, but the pallor was in striking contrast to her black hair and the rich blue of her clothes. In any case, there was no time to spare for makeup. She tossed the shipsuit hastily into a drawer, caught up the carryall, and hurried from the cabin.

The other two were waiting by the main hatch, each with a carryall slung across his shoulder. Silence was glad to see that they had changed clothes, too, and for a wonder, neither remarked on her tardiness. Chase Mago wore the plain trousers and high-collared shirt common in the Rusadir; the colors were dull, but the fabric was expensive and the three buttons that closed the collar and the off-center opening of the shirt were carved from glowing, semi-precious stones. As she had half expected, Balthasar was more eleborately dressed, in a loose, wide-sleeved coat that hung open over a full shirt and tight trousers, but it was a style that gave no clue to his origins. He turned to meet her, and the coat swung open further, revealing the low-slung belt that carried his heylin.

"Do you think we'll need that?" she asked.

Balthasar frowned momentarily, then touched the gun butt gently. "This? I doubt it. But it's better to be prepared." He swung the coat closed again, the heavily brocaded facings holding it shut, concealing the weapon. "The Watchers will register it, of course, but they won't report it unless I have to use it, in which case I'm sure I'll want their intervention. Are you ready?"

Watchers? Silence thought, but nodded anyway. "Whenever."

They caught the tubetrain from the St. Harbin's Field station to the mainurb, carefully avoiding the lower levels where the cross-continental trains came and went. There were a surprising number of people in the car, but except for that, Silence could see no difference between Delos and half a hundred other worlds. They left the train at Anagra Market, Balthasar leading them through the crowd with practiced ease, and rose the long stairwalk to the surface. There was light above them, Silence realized abruptly, a strong orange light that mimicked sunlight. Or perhaps it was sunlight, though she could think of no sun that would produce such odd, harsh colors. And then the stairs rose above the surface, and she stumbled forward, staring onto the hard-glazed tiles of the market plaza.

There was no night on Delos. The sky overhead was black and shiny as enamel, but stars and even moons were drowned by the thousands of lights that played on the streets of the mainurb. Twin ranks of trees flanked the plaza, and each tree was filled with lights, each twig seeming to sprout a bulb of fire. The reason for the glaring brilliance was instantly obvious. The market was alive with merchants even at this hour, from mere peddlers who sold their gaudy wares from trays in the middle of the pedestrian walkways to vendors with carts to the brightly lit storefronts that surrounded the plaza. Hundreds—thousands—of potential buyers made their way past the carts and squatting peddlers. Some—usually young men and women in the too-smart clothes that marked clerks from Athos Maria to Tartessos—rushed past without looking at the goods spread out before them. More paused to look or to buy or to exchange banter with one or another of the sellers. Silence shook her head, almost overcome by a feeling like vertigo. It was night, there should be quiet—

Balthasar caught her arm, pulling her out of the way of a hurrying knot of men in factory-hands' coveralls. "You can shop tomorrow afternoon," he said. "But for now, I think we'd better be getting to the Vine."

"Of course," Silence answered automatically, glad he hadn't guessed the real reason for her hesitation. "It'll be good to get in."

Their path to the Parsley Vine—Silence was still not sure if it was a hotel or a transients' apartment house, or indeed, why Balthasar had not found them rooms in the Palc—took them along the edge of the market, in the broad walk between the shopfronts and the first rank of carts. At the end of the plaza, Balthasar darted to his left, onto a broad street less crowded but as brightly lit as the plaza. The sudden change of course took even Chase Mago by surprise. Trying to follow, Silence was first separated from the engineer, then pushed by the crowd toward the massive statue that stood squarely in the center of the intersection of street and plaza. Trying to avoid a collision, she slipped and nearly fell. Glancing down, she saw she had stepped onto a ring of bright red tile that surrounded the statue's pedestal. There was a grating sound above her, and she looked up to find the statue staring down at her, its deep-carved eyes suddenly alive and glowing. Frightened, she stepped back quickly, off the tiles. Instantly the eyes closed, and the massive, leonine head swiveled stiffly back to its original position.

"Silence!" Balthasar waved to her from the side of the avenue and, shaken, she worked her way through the crowd to join him.

"What is that thing?"

"A Watcher," Balthasar answered, a note of pride in his voice. "There's one at most of the important intersections. They're controlled by a magus, who sees through their eyes, hears through their ears. Usually he just moves from one to another at random, but if you step over the ring it alerts him, and he checks on the particular Watcher that called."

"I see." Silence glanced back over her shoulder. The statue once again crouched unmoving on its base, empty eyes half-lidded. It was just another application of the principles that created homunculi, she told herself—but she disliked the homunculi as well. It was one thing to deal with the ordinary low magi, who helped tuners, handled communications, and generally worked with star-travellers and mechanics to make life easier. It was another thing to deal with the high magi, who manipulated not only matter but the sub- and supermaterial planes as well, or with their creations. She shivered and turned away, following Balthasar up the long street.

The Parsley Vine was not what she had expected at all, neither a hotel nor an apartment complex but closer to the travellers' inns usually found only in the Pale. It was a tall building, the base taking up almost the entire block, the upper stories set back, so that the building resembled a stair-stepped glass pyramid topped by a glass obelisk. The obelisk was darkened except for a ring of warning lights, and she craned her head to see better. Balthasar nudged her and pointed saying, "Greenhouse."

Silence nodded, and followed him through the thick archway of the main doors. While Balthasar paused at the concierge's desk, Chase Mago handed his carryall to a youth in sober building livery. Silence stared at the lobby, entranced. There were shops and a cafe against the walls, and the open atrium was dominated by a broad pool, where water rippled down the channeled sides of a central pyramid. In opposite corners, stairwalks coiled together like snail shells, or the double helix so important to the ancients. Fountain and stairwalks alike were mechanical; when they reached their suite, one wall of the main room was filled with monitor screens and controls for the room's various elaborate systems. No other planet Silence had visited had been so lavish in the use of mechanical devices—most worlds were forced to restrict them to protect the magi and their Art from the mechanical interference that could disrupt even the best-shielded harmonics. But then, Delos was crowded enough to need these systems, and, more importantly, it was not a great center for the Art. Merchants could live with minor interference as the magi could not.

There was no time to consider the subject further. Chase Mago had already claimed the first bedroom, dropping the painted curtain behind him without a word spoken. Balthasar shrugged, and pointed to the ladder set against one wall.

"There're two more bedrooms up there. Take your pick."

"Aren't you coming up?" Silence asked, and immediately regretted it.

Balthasar smiled. "I'm flattered. But I've got some calls to make—let the factor know I'm here, and where here is, for a start." He dropped his bag in one corner and pulled a chair up to the communications board.

Silence shrugged to herself and, slinging her bag more securely across her shoulders, climbed to the loft. There was little more there than the two bedrooms, each containing a bed and a storage chest that would double as a chair. The entire suite was much smaller than it looked at first glance, she realized suddenly—another triumph of mechanical design. Above her, the glass wall of the building slanted up and back, the sky growing grey behind it. She frowned. In a few hours, the sun would be up, and the thin painted-paper curtain would be no protection from the glaring light. . . . As if he had read her mind, Balthasar leaned out of his chair, stretching to reach the window controls. The glass darkened abruptly, cutting off all sight of the outside world. Silence sighed and went on into the bedroom, dropping the curtain behind her.

The first week on Delos passed in a whirl. The unending activity of the Delians—nearly all the businesses operated on a twenty-five hour schedule to accommodate the star-travellers—unnerved Silence at first, and she was disoriented by Balthasar's determination to keep to ship-time, so that their day was planetary night. At Chase Mago's insistence, however, the captain shifted their sleep-wake cycle until it coincided with planetary night and day, and Silence found herself more at ease among the hurrying crowds. But the starless, moonless sky still bothered her, and after dark she would not look up, demanding that the windows be blanked as soon as night fell. As her sense of time steadied, she began to find the patterns amid the confusion, learning to find her way through the maze of streets and markets that surrounded the Parsley Vine. With Balthasar and Chase Mago, she filled out an endless number of applications and depositions for the marriage, and each flimsy sheet and scrawled set of signatures made it a little easier to contemplate. The more papers she signed, the harder it would be to back out. As it became more difficult to stop the process, she thought less about it, accepting the marriage as merely the price of having work and a good crew to work with. Her doubts surfaced only in her dreams and, with a pilot's stubborn discipline, she contrived to forget those nightmares in the daylight.

Mornings were usually spent in one or another of the offices that dominated the mainurb's center, filling out forms. In the afternoons, Chase Mago disappeared to the Field, where he apparently closeted himself with the magi who were specialists in shipbuilding and tuning, officially pricing repairs and overhaul, but actually catching up on the gossip of his art. Balthasar slept or left message after message for his factor, who obstinately refused to answer. It seemed that this was not unheard of, as the captain did not seem particularly concerned, and Silence did not pry. There were other offers of work as well, and Balthasar provisionally accepted two, but primarily he waited.

Silence, not needed by either man, made the expected visit to the Charthouse, hoping to catch up on the pilots' gossip. But though the workers at the Charthouse grudgingly agreed to update her starbooks—as they were required to do for any licensed pilot—she was still a stranger, and no citizen. The traditional channels of rumor remained obstinately closed to her.

Rather than admit she was at loose ends, Silence played tourist, visiting the nearby pre-War sites, and generally exploring St. Harbin's mainurb. Most of the pre-War sites were fortresses, of the kind she had seen a dozen times on as many other worlds. However, the center of the mainurb boasted an installation she had never seen before: a pre-War data center, one of the last to be built before the magi forced the closing of all such institutions. She paid her two-pounds admission fee and stepped into the gloom of the central lobby feeling her skin tingle from the shield that kept the residue of mechanical energies from affecting the buildings that surrounded it. Like any tourist, she gaped at the retrieval terminals, row upon row of cubicles, each with its tiny screen-and-keyboard, and a slot in the wall where, according to the bored guide, information was copied instantly for each user. The upper floors were filled with similar cubicles. Some were elaborately appointed, designed for scholars, but most were simple, accessible to anyone. On the lowest floor, she peered through thick glass at the dead heart of the installation, the massive computers that had stored the information. Seeing them, Silence could not repress a shiver of amazement. No one built machines that large any more. Most worlds, in fact, restricted size by law; but even where there were no regulations, practical considerations—and the influence of the magi—kept them small. And computers were among the worst of all mechanical creations. Their peculiar function—a parody of human thought—produced a parody of the powers controlled by the magi, a sort of anti-thought that completely disrupted any work of the Art brought into contact with it. They were still necessary for certain kinds of work, but inconvenient; none was larger than the small machines that handled the port's information service.

But it was the final exhibit that Silence found the most disturbing of all. A single reader was still functional—though the guide was quick to assure them that it was no longer connected to the main banks—and a copy of the Library's catalogue had been placed within it. Scanning the topics, Silence could understand why the magi had crusaded against such banks as dangerous institutions. Mixed in with ordinary information—fiction, common references, other entertainment—were listings for starbooks, advanced alchemical works, even a guild handbook on starship construction and tuning. And anyone, anyone at all, the guide assured her, had been allowed to read those books. Silence shivered again, thinking this time of craft secrets, and of laymen reading her starbooks. It was a good thing such places had been closed.

She was very glad, that night, of Balthasar's habit of waiting each evening for the rest of his crew in a windowless star-travellers' bar called Bangum the Boar's. It was a battered, comfortable place, and the drinks were strong. Silence was grateful for the last, and did not ask either about its name or the odd group of star-travellers who congregated there. Balthasar seemed to know most of them; many were employed by Wrath-of-God, or were free-lance raiders, and those who were not were professional explorers, gaudy, hard-bitten men who were either richer than Croesus or too poor to pay their Field fees.

On the ninth day since landing, Silence arrived at the Boar to find only Chase Mago waiting for her. In the end, Balthasar was nearly an hour late, but when he did arrive, he brought word that the marriage contract had come through at last, and that they would sign it the next morning.

"Then we pick up the citizenship papers," he went on, "and we're all set. *If* Nnamdi ever calls."

"He hasn't gotten in touch with you either?" a stocky, balding captain asked, frowning.

"He's been late before." That was Tasarla, captain of the *Ostinato*. She was a Misthian, something of a renegade in the eyes of the other star-travellers from that caste-proud, matriarchal world, who had done courier work for Wrath-of-God for seven standard years. "Give him time." She leaned forward, setting one elbow carefully on the unsteady table. Her bracelets chimed, falling from wrist to elbow. "When is the wedding, Denis? And are we invited?"

"Times and mores, Tasarla," Balthasar said uncomfortably. "It's just a contract."

"So?" The Misthian captain raised one eyebrow, a kohl-darkened line on her bronzed face. She was not of the highest caste—her hair was too light, brown rather than true black, she was too tall, and her skin was space-darkened rather than naturally brown—but she had learned the gestures somewhere. "It's a rather important contract, isn't it? And one that should be started in good fortune, not tempting fate?" Surprisingly, she grinned. "Besides, we always need an excuse for a party."

Chase Mago nodded, his face completely serious. "You're right about tempting fate, though. We should do something."

Balthasar looked from one to the other, a hint of annoyance in his smile. "Silence? What do you think?"

The pilot looked up quickly. It was on the tip of her tongue to say that she agreed with Balthasar, but the faces around her made her hesitate. The Delian's face had closed up again, with the habitual secretiveness that Silence found infuriating. Chase Mago's expression was as grave as always behind his beard. And Tasarla was simply cheerful, ready to give a party, and sincerely wishing them well. It was the last that decided her. She smiled and shrugged. "It might be fun."

"You're outvoted, Denis," Chase Mago said.

The captain spread his hands. "All right, a party it is. At noon, say?"

"Noon?" Tasarla's eyes widened. "That's dawn for me, Denis."

"Our appointment's in the morning," Balthasar answered.

"All right, I'll shift my schedule," Tasarla said, rising. "And now, if you'll excuse me, I'll start collecting for your fountain."

Balthasar moaned and put his head down on his folded arms.

"Tasarla—" Chase Mago began, but the Misthian was already out of hearing.

"Not a fountain," Balthasar said, his voice muffled against the table.

"What's a fountain?" Silence asked.

"It's a drink," Balthasar answered, without raising his head. "It's a tradition at the Boar—it's a party all by itself."

Silence looked at Chase Mago, but for once the engineer did not seem inclined to modify his captain's statement.

The marriage itself was very straightforward. They arrived at Sisika House, the section of the mainurb's primary administrative complex that handled marriages, and made a final, formal statement before a minor official. Then all three signed the statement of intent, the contract itself, and an application for citizenship for Silence and Chase Mago. The papers were duly witnessed, and they were sent next door to the records office, where the citizenship application was officially accepted, and pilot and engineer were issued new papers. The entire process took less than half an hour. The trip back to the East End and the Boar's was longer, and Silence could not help feeling a distinct sense of anticlimax.

But the party at the Boar raised her spirits immediately. The fountain was all Balthasar had said. She did not know the name of the ruby liquor that coursed through the nesting spiral tubes of the fountain machine and splashed in the silverwashed catchbasin, but it was sweet and thick and spread a warm glow through her body. Startravellers, mostly friends of Balthasar's—the captain seemed to be both well-known and well-liked despite the core of silence beneath his outgoing manner— crowded around to congratulate her, and to give ritual approval to her new papers. The level of liquor in the catchbasin dropped slightly, then rose again when Tasarla spoke quietly to the bar's owner. The room grew noisy, and the talk freer.

"—lucky man, Denis." The voice carried clearly over a sudden lull in the conversations. Silence glanced up to meet the leering gaze of one of the explorers. "But I wouldn't want to share her."

A burst of laughter from the group at the fountain swallowed Balthasar's reply, but Silence could feel her cheeks burning. She rose, intending to demand an apology, to explain that this was nothing but a convenience, but instead pushed her way out of the group to find a place at a side table. The man was drunk, she told herself, you'll get no apology from him. And you can't explain the contract without annulling the marriage itself. My freedom—instinctively, she touched the new papers in her pocket, reassuring herself that they were still there—is worth a little humiliation. It's worth more than that if necessary.

"Silence?" Tasarla slid a plate of treats, miniature cheeses and tiny loaves of bread, onto the table in front of her. "May I join you?"

"Sure."

"Look," Tasarla said, settling herself comfortably, "I heard what Istavan said."

"So, I think, did everyone else," Silence snapped.

"Yes. He's a fool, though. Everybody knows that." Tasarla hesitated, Misthian frankness warring with caste-pride, but then frankness won out. "What's troubling you? You did marry them. Surely you thought about what people would say."

Silence hesitated in her turn, then said, "I thought. But—the marriage isn't a real one, it's just to get the citizenship." Why did I say that?

she wondered instantly. It must be the wine talking. As unobtrusively as possible, she pushed her half-filled glass away from her.

Tasarla raised an eyebrow, but then slowly nodded. "I do see."

"They promised it would be a marriage in name only," Silence said. She could not bring herself to match the proverbial Misthian bluntness.

"And you're worrying about that?" Tasarla's tone made it only half a question.

"Yes. Hell, Tasarla, I hardly know them."

The Misthian nodded, her expression suddenly gentle. "But I know them. They're good men, Silence—honorable men, honest as a woman." She made a wry face at the Misthian phrase, and Silence laughed in spite of herself.

"Truth," Tasarla said. "They wouldn't—" Silence winced in anticipation, and the captain obligingly rephrased it. "They won't force you to do anything you don't want."

"I believe you," Silence said. "I really do—I wouldn't've agreed to the contract if I didn't. But I can't help worrying a little."

Tasarla nodded and started to say something, but her words were cut off by the slamming of the street door. Heads turned across the room, and a woman's voice said, into the silence, "Tasarla neAda?"

Tasarla raised a beckoning arm. "Over here."

The other woman—also a Misthian, small and slight, with an expression of utter contempt for the perversity of the rest of the galaxy—shouldered her way through the crush to plant herself beside the table. She said something in Misthia's peculiar dialect, deliberately ignoring Silence. Tasarla frowned, listening, and then her expression changed from annoyance to concern. When the other woman had finished, she snapped a brief question, and received an equally short answer. Tasarla rose quickly.

"I am sorry, but I must go," she said to Silence. She seemed to have lost all command of coine. "There is a thing, an emergency happened—"

The other Misthian turned and stalked away, tossing a sentence over her shoulder, and Tasarla broke off to follow her. Silence stared after them, wondering.

"What did Cyrilla want?" Chase Mago asked, looming suddenly over the table.

"I don't know," Silence answered slowly. "An emergency, Tasarla said—but I don't know Misthian."

"Who does?" The engineer looked rather forlorn, standing there with a half-empty glass forgotten in his hand, but before Silence could say anything, Chase Mago asked abruptly, "May I join you?"

"Of course." Silence had expected him to say something about Tasarla's emergency, but the big man stared into his glass, apparently oblivious to her presence. At last she nerved herself to ask, "Is anything wrong?"

"I suppose not." Chase Mago sighed. "I don't know what's the matter, it all went very well. But—there's something missing. And, Silence, I don't even know what it is I want."

A romantic, Silence thought, and could not repress a bemused smile. Who would have expected the big engineer to have that in him? "I don't know either," she said gently. Her eyes fell on the other's glass and she stood up. "But I do know what you need. Another drink."

Chase Mago did not protest when she slipped his glass from under his nose, and he reached for it automatically when she returned with the refills. Silence caught his wrist.

"No, wait." She lifted her glass. "I propose a toast, for us. No regrets."

"No regrets," Chase Mago echoed dutifully, and then he smiled, his mood lifting. "You're right, there's no reason to regret anything. I'm a free man now." His smile turned suddenly shy. "And you are a good friend, Silence."

Silence blinked, pleased in spite of herself, and reached for her glass to hide her embarrassment.

Balthasar joined them then, three more drinks precariously balanced in his hands. They were the first of too many. Silence grew giggly, a state she despised, and Balthasar got the hiccups; in the end it was Chase Mago, as drunk as they but steady-footed, who got them both back to the Parsley Vine and into their respective beds. Pale and shaky, they ministered to each other's hangovers, sharing the suite's tiny pharmacopia as well as exotic remedies culled from a dozen different planets. Despite the latter, they recovered.

Two days later, the factor called.

The taped transmission was double-coded, and Balthasar spent a quarter of an hour adjusting his machines before the tape would run. Silence retreated to the far side of the suite's living room, trying not to watch. The tape ended, but Balthasar played it through again before switching off the machines and coming to join her.

"Well?" Chase Mago said, appearing in the doorway of his room as if on cue.

"Well, indeed," Balthasar answered. "It's very weird, that's all. It was taped, all the codes right, check signs in order—but I tried to get back to him and his house won't accept the call. He wants me to come out there. He lives in one of the suburbs, I forget which one—"

Chase Mago ducked back into his bedroom. "Go on."

"And he'll give me instructions then," Balthasar finished. "I wish to hell I knew what was going on."

"Fen Micheas," Chase Mago said, reemerging.

"What?" Balthasar asked.

"Fen Micheas. That's where Nnamdi lives." The engineer held up a small pamphlet. "According to this, it's about thirty kilometers outside the Rota mainurb. On the Rota-Mavrides Port line."

"When are you supposed to go there?" Silence asked.

"Now." Balthasar went back to the console, sliding back the figured screen that covered the tourist information board. "And I think it might be a good idea if you people came, too. Safety in numbers."

"Do you think this has anything to do with Tasarla's emergency?" Chase Mago asked. "She and Cyrilla lifted off yesterday, in a hurry."

"I don't know," Balthasar answered.

Silence looked from one to the other. "I don't like to be an alarmist," she said slowly, "but would I be wise to bring my heylin?"

She had hoped Balthasar would laugh, but he considered her words quite seriously for a moment. "Probably. You, too, Julie."

"What else did Nnamdi say?" Chase Mago asked.

"I told you everything." Balthasar hit a final set of keys and straightened up. A miniature printer, cleverly concealed in an apparently ornamental carving, clattered and spat a set of ticket foils.

Chase Mago scowled, and Silence asked hastily, "When do we leave?"

"Now. We've got tickets on an express leaving in half an hour," Balthasar said. "Better get your heylin."

They made it to the train with perhaps ten minutes to spare, Balthasar leading them easily through the crowds. There was a Watcher at the gate, a diminutive copy of the massive statues decorating the streets, and Silence slowed in spite of herself, suddenly conscious of the heylin in her shoulder bag. Balthasar frowned at her, and handed their tickets to the guard. He checked them, verifying the reservations, then waved them through onto the platform. As Balthasar passed beneath the delicate archway, the Watcher sprang suddenly to life, tilting its head so that its open, beady eyes could scan all of his body. The captain ignored it, and it settled back to its perch. It reacted the same way when Chase Mago passed through, and as Silence stepped past, holding her breath, she was eerily aware of its eyes at her back. It had seen the heylins, she knew, and as she walked toward the open doors of the train she was tensed for the call of police whistles. But the magus controlling the little Watcher did nothing more than note the presence of the guns. They were allowed aboard the train without trouble, and ushered to seats in one of the desirable middle cars.

The warning signs began to flash, and Silence automatically checked the crashwebbing. Then the train's harmonium sounded, a low hum that quickly rose to a metallic scream, and she was thrown violently against the back of her seat as the train jerked forward. A moment later, the pressure eased, and the noise faded to a more bearable level, though it was still loud enough to make conversation difficult. Apparently the other passengers had been expecting that: the group of merchants who occupied the expensive cluster of seats in the middle of the car pulled out thick ear guards and the latest news sheets. Balthasar, too, produced a set of ear guards and set them in place, then closed his eyes, instantly asleep.

Silence glared at him. It was typical, she thought.

He could've mentioned this, warned us what to expect—but he's incapable of telling us anything without a direct question. She turned to Chase Mago, but he was deep in concentration, listening to the sound with the abstracted intensity of an engineer. Silence grimaced, and leaned back in her seat, trying to relax. The noise of the train's harmonium was wearing, always on the edge of dissonance, and at last she leaned over to touch the engineer's shoulder.

"Why do they have to do this?" she said, raising her voice to carry over the wailing.

"That's what happens when you try to tune a harmonium to a core harmony," Chase Mago shouted back, leaning so close that his beard tickled Silence's ear. "And then they never can cast elemental earth properly—"

"No, that's not what I meant," Silence said. "I know perfectly well how these systems work. I just don't understand why they don't use something mechanical instead. I mean, Delos doesn't seem to put much restriction on mechanics in general. . . ."

Chase Mago was shaking his head. "Something mechanical on a world-wide scale? Think of the interference."

"I would've thought you could keep the individual components small enough for safety," Silence screamed, more to distract herself from the wearing noise than because she was seriously interested in the subject.

"The sheer volume would be enough to distort everything," Chase Mago said. "And think of the chaos a mechanical system would produce near the port. I suppose discomfort's just the price we pay for progress."

"Discomfort," Silence muttered, but could not muster the energy to continue the conversation.

By the time the train pulled into the Rota

mainurb station, Silence was sure she had been permanently deafened. But in fact when they pushed their way up from the platform to the huge lobby, the noisy crowd gathered there proved that she had lost none of her hearing. The vast space, dimly lit by cool-light globes that floated uneasily near the vaulted ceiling, was filled with people, some scurrying between shops and ticketing counters, more resting on the stone benches that dotted the area, or relaxing in the coffee houses.

Like all crowds she had seen on Delos, every individual dressed with a lavish disregard for conformity or common fashion—but there was a common factor here. She glanced up at the massive glowing map that dominated one wall of the station, directly above the ticketing machines. Rota was marked by a single, multi-faceted jewel; the other mainurbs, linked by threads of light, were marked by different, smaller stones. With difficulty, she identified St. Harbin's, traced their route south and farther south, to Rota. As if to confirm her thoughts, a door swung open at the far end of the station, admitting a miniature tow and a sled full of cleaning apparatus. With the tow came a wedge of glaring light, and a sudden breath of air like the blast from a furnace. Balthasar had known, of course, having visited the factor before, but hadn't bothered to tell the others. Silence glanced down at her heavy tunic and swore to herself.

Chase Mago had come to the same conclusion as she had. Glaring down at Balthasar, he said, "Rota's equatorial, isn't it?"

The captain shrugged, undisturbed. "Yes, but drier than you'd think." He gestured vaguely to a number of small shops clumped together by the entrance to the public lavatories. "You could pick up some light clothes there."

"Thanks," the engineer said sourly, but made no

move in their direction. "You might've told us, Denis."

Silence glanced from the stores and the cheap, gauzy things displayed in the archways that served as doorway and walls, to the now-closed entrance. "Well, I will," she said, and stalked off toward the shops.

The clothes were both cheaply made and overpriced. In the end, she simply removed her heavy tights and pinned back the full sleeves of her tunic. Just outside the lavatories, an adolescent in the glossy white robes of a magus's apprentice squatted beside a tiny burner, offering instant sandals. Silence let him paint the warm, sticky liquid heavily across the soles of her feet, and add a lighter layer across the tops of her toes. It dried almost instantly, leaving only a faint tingling that faded to a mere reminder of something on her body, no more annoying than the feeling of clothing. She paid him, and hurried to join the others.

Despite his complaints, Chase Mago had made some concession to the heat, removing his shirt and twisting it into a complicated turban. He glared at her as she approached, and Silence, wisely, said nothing.

"Are you coming?" Balthasar asked. He had removed his coat and loosened the neck of his shirt, but that was all.

"I'm ready," Silence said hastily. The engineer grunted something, which Balthasar ignored.

"Let's go, then."

Pedestrians left the station through a double revolving lock, designed to keep the cool air in. The glare on the white-painted towers and pale grey streets was nearly blinding, and Silence blinked hard, tears starting. Before she could clear them, Balthasar caught her arm, and steered her toward a waiting cab, pushing her gently down and into the passenger section. Chase Mago was already inside; she was jammed against him as Balthasar climbed in beside her. The engineer shifted slightly, but seemed quite content to let her lean against him. For the first time, she was fully, physically aware of him—of his height, of the bands of hard muscles beneath his sun-browned skin. . . .

"Where to?" The driver's voice shattered the spell, and Silence drew a shaken breath, edging away toward Balthasar.

"Fen Micheas," Balthasar answered. "Bellman's House?"

Through the half-darkened canopy, Silence could see a human hand moving on the map console. Not a homunculus, then—but she had learned, in her short stay on Delos, that the planet was too crowded to allow a creation to usurp any job a human being could or would perform.

"Right, Captain, Bellman's House it is." The driver's hands moved again. The overhead canopy lightened a little, enough to let them see out without allowing in too much of the heat, and the cab edged out into the traffic.

Rota mainurb was much like St. Harbins, except for the small details of window size and the inelegant solar towers decorating every roof. Tall buildings vied with low, enclosed markets for space. There were fewer pedestrians but many more bubble cars, and everywhere the signs of flourishing commerce. The cab darted through the crowded streets for perhaps a quarter of an hour, and then, with startling suddenness, turned a corner into another world. Two tall buildings, apartment complexes of the kind common in St. Harbins as well as Rota, stood to either side of the street, but directly ahead was a bridge, arching over a stream too straight to be natural. Across the canal was an expanse of green, broken by a line of trees in the middle distance. Beyond the trees, a roof showed coyly.

"What the hell?" Silence murmured in spite of herself.

"That's a suburb," Balthasar grinned. "The rich live there."

The very rich, Silence amended, as they crossed the bridge and passed twin Watchers. The lawns to either side were immaculately tended, not a blade of grass out of place; the hedges sprouted flowers from half a hundred worlds—not merely Fringe Worlds, either, but from as far into the Rusadir as Athos Maria and Reshef. The houses were hidden by stands of trees or casually placed sculpture, but even the tilt of a roof or the single visible corner was enough to betray the amount of money spent.

"Not all of them," Chase Mago said mildly. "Quite a few of the shipping magnates live in the mainurbs, with their folk."

"And our factor lives out here," Balthasar muttered, but before Silence could decide if that was criticism or compliment, the cab pulled up at a private gate.

"Here you are, Captain, Bellman's House."

"Thanks." Balthasar popped the canopy and slithered out into the glaring sun, pausing only to hand the driver a thin sheaf of Delian pounds. Silence followed, cautiously, and was surprised to find the air cooler than in the mainurb. From within the hedge-shielded compound came the sound of a fountain.

"Yes, sieurs, sieura?"

The man who had emerged through a discreet break in the hedge carried gardener's shears slung at his waist, but his loose trousers and shirt were of a mottled green fabric, perfect camouflage against the cool greens of the lawn. A tiny, monkey-like creature clung to one shoulder, chattering in his ear: no gardener, then, but a guard, and an expensive mercenary from the look of him, Silence decided.

Balthasar stepped forward. "My name's Denis Balthasar. I've business with Nnamdi—he should be expecting me."

The creature on the guard's shoulder chittered discreetly, and the guard said, "Yes, Sieur Nnamdi is expecting *you*—but these others?"

"My crew," Balthasar said. "I wasn't sure of—conditions here. Nnamdi's request was unusual."

The creature tugged gently at the guard's ear, spoke urgently in a low monotone. The guard nodded, and the thing clambered down his body, skittering off through the hedge toward the house. The guard said, "Sieur Nnamdi says you are all welcome, though he wasn't expecting Sieur Chase Mago and Sieura Leigh. Won't you come in?" He gestured to the hedge and the branches shrank back on either side, revealing a respectable opening.

"Thank you," Balthasar said again, and stepped through the gap. Following him, Silence noticed three-inch thorns hidden in the foliage, saw too the pale flowers of a camisado vine winding through the branches. Clearly Nnamdi—or Wrath-of-God—was willing to pay dearly for his privacy.

Once inside the shelter of the hedge, the temperature dropped dramatically, becoming almost springlike. Magus's work, Silence thought—shaping elemental air into an enclosure, and then creating the gentle weather pattern that prevailed inside. The expense must have been astronomical.

Nnamdi's house sat atop a gentle rise, windows and doors apparently open to the soft breezes, though Silence was sure that security considerations made that an illusion. Trees placed at artfully chosen intervals spread a network of shade across the immaculate turf; a black-plumed merry widow bird clung to a lower bough in the nearest one, its trilling like well-bred laughter.

"This way, please." The guard led them up the winding path toward the house, leaving the pavement only once to skirt a basking vipera. The chunky lizard lifted its head as they passed, and hissed without lifting its neck frill.

They were met at the door by two more mercenaries in typical house-servant's livery, and by another of the monkey-like creatures. Nnamdi was well guarded, Silence thought. *I wonder if it's just for show, or if he needs them?* She glanced around discreetly, but could see no further signs of security measures, or of any recent attack which might have prompted new causation.

"Sieurs, sieura," the older of the guards said quietly. He had a faint Rusadir accent. "If you would please leave your weapons here . . . ?" He let his voice trail off, implying that he was merely asking a favor, but Silence had no doubt that any refusal would be swiftly dealt with. She handed her bag to the younger guard, and Balthasar and Chase Mago passed across their heylins. The young man locked them away in a cabinet, and the first guard bowed deeply.

"Captain Balthasar," he said. "Sieur Nnamdi will see you in the library. If Sieur Chase Mago and Sieura Leigh will accompany Edmon, he will see that they are made comfortable on the terrace."

"Lead on," Balthasar said. The monkey-like creature followed him out. It was some kind of familiar, Silence decided—a magus's eyes and ears—but she could not tell if it were some responsive species or, like a homunculus, the creation of a laboratory.

"If you'd come with me, please?" Edmon asked. He seemed less comfortable in his role as house-servant than the others had been; his military bearing betrayed him as a soldier.

The house had not seemed particularly impressive from the outside, especially when set against the lush grounds. Within the walls, however, its true size and luxury were glaringly apparent. The hallway through which they passed was decorated with art that even Silence could recognize as expensive, and the floor was covered with copper-highlighted blackwood from Oued Tessaa. Half-open doors provided glimpses of yet more spectacular wealth—a table set with gilded dishes, resting on a cloth of spider-lace from the Madakh; a sun-bright room filled with expensive gymnastic equipment; a hothouse room apparently stocked only with Sareptan orchids. Then Edmon slid open a final door, and gestured for them to precede him onto the terrace.

A table was waiting for them, and twin chairs, looking out over a huge fountain and a stretch of lawn as immaculate as the first. A young woman in a loose white shift was adjusting the thin canopy covering the entire terrace. A gentle breeze stirred the plants on the terrace, and died at the edge of the canopy.

"Lisele," Edmon called. "The sieuri are here."

The girl secured the canopy cord and came forward. Her arms and legs were as hard-muscled as a dancer's, and Silence could not help wondering if she, too, were part of the guard force. But the Rusadir mercenaries never hired women.

"Sieur, sieura," Lisele said, bowing. "Please make yourselves comfortable. Sieur Nnamdi tells me that he should not detain your captain for long, so I brought only drink, but if you should wish for anything else, you have only to tell me."

"Thank you, this will do nicely," Chase Mago said.

The girl bowed again and backed away, disappearing behind the drooping edge of the canopy. Silence could just make out her shadow against the thin material; she would remain there, ostensibly to serve them, but equally to report anything of interest that might be said. Silence touched the engineer's shoulder and nodded toward the corner.

Chase Mago murmured, "Yes, I know." He handed her to a seat with unexpected grace, and poured the thin, cold wine into the crystal glasses that stood ready.

Silence lifted hers gingerly, afraid that even the lightest pressure would shatter the fragile things. The wine was the best she had ever tasted, with a flavor that hinted at a dozen different things but in the end was something unique. "What is this?" she asked at last.

"Sanguis Auri," Chase Mago answered without hesitation. "Blood-of-gold." He lapsed into silence again, staring into the pale depths of his glass.

Silence regarded him and the wine with equal admiration. Blood-of-gold—Sanguis Auri, she corrected herself—was one of the rarest wines in the galaxy, produced only in a single province of a single world. Once it had been reserved for the table of the Hegemon. Now magi's aid made it possible for some, at least, to be sold on other worlds. That she had been served it was remarkable; that Chase Mago had recognized it was incredible. Certainly the engineer did not seem at all intimidated by his surroundings, though Balthasar had been fractionally ill-at-ease. She had seen that in his very refusal to be impressed. But Chase Mago seemed very much at home.

She glanced sidelong at him, realizing once again how little she knew about him. He was from Kesse, a rich planet—and on some of Rusadir worlds, a double name marked an oligarch. But would an oligarch ever have allowed his son to become an engineer? The oligarchs of Cap Bel, for all their mercantile connections, would have considered that a waste of a child. Yet how else could he have become familiar with such surroundings? She could not ask here and now, but she filed the questions for later. Perhaps she would ask Balthasar, although she was far from certain that he would know. . . .

"I don't know how to thank you for this, Nnamdi." That was Balthasar, appearing suddenly at the right side of the terrace. He held back the canopy for Nnamdi, a small, slim, dark-skinned man with close-cropped grey hair. The factor wore an unornamented, tightly cut coat and equally plain trousers. Only as he approached did Silence see the quality of the material and the expertise of the tailoring.

"I have my orders, Denis," the factor said. "As you do."

"I don't have to like them," Balthasar answered. "The least you could do is pay me for my cargo now."

Nnamdi spread his hands. "Again, orders, Denis. Besides, our mutual employer wishes to be certain that all his captains are present. You will be paid on arrival." He held up one finger to stop Balthasar's protest. "I am authorized to advance you the money to pay your expenses here, and for the trip. In fact, the money has already been transferred."

Balthasar hissed softly. "So that's why you let me make those arrangements."

Nnamdi bowed slightly. "But of course."

"Damn you," the captain said, without heat. "What about transport?"

Nnamdi gestured to the lawn. Beyond the fountain, one of the low hills split open, revealing the mouth of an underground hangar. A slim needle of a local transport plane emerged, rolled by a crew of mechanics in Nnamdi's livery. "All settled."

Chase Mago stood up, setting aside his empty glass, and Silence imitated him.

"What's up, Denis?" the engineer asked.

"A change of plan," Balthasar said grimly. "We've been ordered back to Wrath-of-God for a captain's council, no further details."

"This minute?" Silence asked, and Chase Mago said, "Is there an emergency, Nnamdi?"

"I do not know," Nnamdi said. "Really, Sieur Chase Mago, I do not. But I don't think so."

"Let's go," Balthasar said.

Chapter 4

Nnamdi and Wrath-of-God spared no expense for transport, either. The little ship was capable of sub-orbital flight, riding her silver keel up toward the break between celestial and mundane, then gliding back to the planet's surface. They would make the flight to St. Harbin's in less than two hours. After Nnamdi had said his farewells, and had moved back out of range, they took they places. One of the mercenaries handed their heylins aboard and the pilot lifted off in a thunder of sound. As the transport gained its cruising altitude, harmonium flickering on and off to maintain them, the noise steadied to a sound no worse than wind.

"All right," said Chase Mago. "What's going on, Denis?"

"I told you," the captain snapped. "We've been ordered back to Wrath-of-God for a captains' council."

"That's all?" The engineer plainly did not believe him.

"That's all." Balthasar glared at him. "We leave immediately—our things are being sent directly from the hotel to the ship. This flight lands at St. Harbin's Field, and we go straight aboard *Sun-Treader*. Nnamdi's orders."

"He said it wasn't an emergency?" Silence asked.

"Ha." The captain leaned back in his seat.

"Nnamdi doesn't usually lie outright," Chase Mago said thoughtfully.

Balthasar sighed, somewhat mollified. "No, he doesn't. And I think that's what worries me most of all."

They landed at St. Harbin's Field on schedule, and found a low-slung car waiting for them, ready to take them to the dock. The Parsley Vine had done its work well—they were probably used to that sort of thing, Silence thought—and their baggage, packed for star travel, was waiting at the foot of the cradle. They hauled it aboard, and then Chase Mago switched on the coffee brewer in the commons.

"We don't have time for that," Balthasar said.

"Yes, we do," Chase Mago said. "Silence still has to learn the voidmarks."

"Hell." Balthasar scowled, and Silence winced. "How long will it take you?"

"Will they be completely unfamiliar?" Silence asked.

"Not completely," Balthasar answered. "You should know the notation."

"Let me see them."

Balthasar hesitated, then shrugged, unlatching his cabin door. "Come on in."

The room was spartan—bare walls, plain dark blanket on the bunk, the book rack half-empty, with only a couple of the most trivial popular nov-

els tucked between manuals and a general hieroglyphica. The disordered clothing had been put
away. There was nothing to give her any clues to
the captain's personality. Then, tossed aside on his
writing board, half-fallen between that and the
monitor console, she saw a glint of silver. She
reached for it automatically, to set it right, and
pulled out a tiny model of a ship. It was a Navy
six, only one class below a dreadnought, but there
were no markings on it that she could identify.

"Do you want to see the marks?" Balthasar asked
abruptly. He left his mattress standing on its edge,
but closed the lid of the strongbox over whatever
else was left inside. He held out a single folded
sheet of paper, obviously torn from a pilot's manual.

"Yes, please." Silence set the model ship carefully on the writing board. "Is that a Wrath-of-God
ship?"

"Yes. I served on it." Balthasar swept it aside,
and unfolded the sheet of paper. There was something about his very indifference that made Silence certain there was something important involved, but there was no opportunity to question
him further. She focused her attention on the page
displayed before her.

The voidmarks were not at all what she had
expected. The tiny, handwritten notation at the
top of the page said "The Path of Small Restraint,"
and added, cryptically, "dense clouds, no rain."
Silence groaned to herself. As Balthasar had promised, she recognized the notation: the page had been
taken from the *Tiger's Book*, the most obscure and
least useful of all the starbooks she had ever studied.
But at least she had studied it.

"It'll take me a couple of hours to relearn Tiger's
system," she said, "and another couple to get comfortable with the road. Five or six hours, say."

"Make it five, if you can," Balthasar said. "I'd like to find out what's going on."

"I'll do my best," Silence said, staring at the unfamiliar drawing, where demons and dragons and completely unrecognizable figures crawled through clouds that hung low over a parched and barren plain. "May I take this?"

"Feel free."

It took her a little more than six hours to learn the voidmarks, but Balthasar was able to arrange for an immediate clearance. Silence suspected Nnamdi's hand in that. As soon as *Sun-Treader* settled into the line of least resistance, Silence freed herself from her couch and reached for the ladder to the upper bridge. Balthasar shot her a questioning look, but did not speak. It was not unusual for a pilot to want time alone before an unfamiliar passage through purgatory, and Silence did not bother to offer that explanation. On the upper bridge, she settled herself against the bulkhead, and rested her forehead against her drawn-up knees. The voidmarks for Wrath-of-God, for the "Path of Small Restraint," were still unfamiliar, the symbols less than comfortable. She took a deep breath, using the tricks of memory taught her as an apprentice to conjure up an exact mental image of the page of the *Tiger's Book*. Painstakingly, she began to identify each individual symbol, murmuring the name of each one out loud.

"Silence."

She looked up with a start, saw the bulkheads cloudy-clear around her, Delos's distant sun showing a ring of green flame. "Yes?"

"Are you ready?" Balthasar's voice was beginning to show strain.

Silence hurried toward the control yoke, wiggling her feet into the clinging surface of the platform, then locked the yoke and activated its systems. "I'm ready."

"All right, Julie, ready for the upper register."

"Switching over," Chase Mago answered, and the song of the harmonium split again, bringing in a whole new range of notes.

"You have control, Silence," Balthasar said.

Silence slapped off the lock in a panic, swearing to herself. The ship was surrounded by clouds, thick, impossibly solid clouds that rolled slowly toward her, lightning flashing in their depths. She had never seen voidmarks come clear so quickly—she had been too concerned with them, had had them too firmly in mind ... With an effort, she looked away, letting the ship take its own path for a moment before looking again. The clouds seemed fractionally less threatening—they no longer seemed to be advancing on the ship—but there was still no indication of a path. And then, at the point where the horizon would have been if there had been land beneath her instead of a mirror-image of the clouds above, a line of calm showed clear.

The ship was shivering a little, the shaking growing worse with every heartbeat. Cautiously, she edged the nose down, lining herself up with the distant horizon. It stayed as distant as before, but the shuddering eased away. The clouds stayed where they were, but hung ominously close, above and below, lightning sparking now and then in their depths. Dense clouds, she thought, but no rain. Then this is the path, and I don't need to do anything more. The Path of Small Restraint indeed.

The apparent horizon came closer at last, growing brighter as it came until it gleamed like a white-hot gash against the clouds. The harmonium's note changed again, and there was the familiar rush of speed as the ship fell out of purgatory. Then there was a sharp change of pitch, and the bulkheads were solid around her. She hurried to lock the control yoke and switch off the systems, her eyes filled with the scene she thought she had glimpsed in the split second before the bulkheads firmed up. She slid down the ladder to the control room, anxious to get a look at the viewscreens. The sight took her breath away.

Two massive waves of dust rose up, frozen in the instant before breaking, starkly limned against a sky scaled with gold fire. The light tipped each billow of dust with gilded spume. A cluster of suns hung against that brilliant curtain, so bright that she could only count three of them before her eyes were dazzled and she had to look away. Green shadows blinded her, almost obscuring the chain of lights that hung just below the right-hand wave. If that wave ever broke—and the chance formation of dust mimicked water so closely that it seemed impossible for it not to fall—the tiny lights would be engulfed. Balthasar freed a hand to tap the screen gently, just above the lights.

"Wrath-of-God."

I can see why, Silence thought. Aloud she said, "That's a space station, not a planet."

"That's right," Balthasar said. "Actually, it's a group of linked stations—hollowed asteroids, really—" He broke off as a light winked on in the communications board.

"Wrath-of-God, this is Balthasar 70219, *Sun-Treader*. I repeat, this is Balthasar 70219, *Sun-Treader*. Acknowledge, please."

The response, when it came, was alarmingly sharp. "Balthasar 70219, *Sun-Treader*, this is Yoshiko 75851, *Raksha*. We identify you. Follow me in; the local approach tugs will take you in tow when we reach Mageara." Silence glanced quickly at the musonar. A ship was visible on the screen, well within shooting range of *Sun-Treader*.

"Yoshiko 75851, *Raksha*, there's no need to take us in tow. I've mated to Mageara dock before."

"Sorry, Balthasar 70219, *Sun-Treader*," the escort ship answered. "That's orders, from the Council. Things are a bit crowded around the docks now. No one wants to take any chances."

"I don't want those damned flame-throwers near my ship," Balthasar muttered, but Silence saw that his transmitter was switched off.

There was nothing to do but follow the escort ship in. It travelled at a maddeningly slow pace, and Balthasar's scowl grew deeper. As they approached the string of stations, Silence began to pick out more details, the instrument towers and the docking rings sticking out from the three large units that made up the station.

"Three separate stations?" she said aloud, more in hopes of distracting Balthasar than because she really wanted to know.

"Mm." Balthasar roused himself from his black mood with an effort. "Five, actually. You just can't see the other two, they're beyond Alecto. The three main units—they were the first built—they're Megeara, Tisiphone, and Alecto." He grinned sourly. "We're lucky they've lasted. Phobos and Demos— they're the new stations, the ones you can't see— have needed repairs since the day they were put into position. But the great magi, and most of the merely competent, don't work for us. We get the same kind of magi that we get pilots and captains."

Raksha cut in again with a comment about their tuning, and Balthasar's attention was instantly elsewhere, leaving Silence to puzzle over his last remark. Of course, most of the magi gravitated toward the established, legitimate worlds; there, at least, they could be assured of some security. These days, more and more were taking service with the Hegemon, who could promise much more than security. The only price was that those magi worked first for the Hegemon's glory, not their own knowledge. Which meant, Silence thought, that Wrath-of-God would get two kinds of magi, those who hated the Hegemon and wouldn't accept his service, and those whom the Hegemon wouldn't accept. And, with the Fringe full of worlds that welcomed magi, there would be more of the latter.

"It was Zeheb Omena who built the first three units," Balthasar said.

Silence looked up, startled. She had thought Omena was more than half legendary.

Balthasar saw her expression and smiled again. "Truth, he did. I can show you his forging-mark, on Alecto. He brought the asteroids here, set up his engines and shaped them, hollowed them out and made them habitable, all in a standard week. The little creation, they called the scale he used to shape them. That's lost, if anyone else ever knew it."

"Why did he work for Wrath-of-God?" Silence asked. The stories all say he was a good man, she added to herself, but did not quite dare voice the words.

Balthasar's expression twisted as though he guessed her thought. "It was a challenge, something no one had ever done. And Wrath-of-God could always pay well. Omena wanted to go looking for aliens." He broke off, glancing at the musonar. "There's the tug."

That made sense, Silence thought, scanning the viewscreen until she too had found the flickering dot that was the tug. A magus's good and evil were traditionally fluid: if an act brought new knowledge, any price, even a blood price, was worth paying.

Balthasar muttered something to himself, and Silence's attention snapped back to the screen. As the tugs got closer, she could see why the Delian had objected to them. They were primitive things, powered by chemical fuel, shooting jets of flame across the intervening distance. Despite the tug pilots' obvious skill, she held her breath as the tiny ships worked themselves into position on either side of *Sun-Treader*. The grapples fired—Balthasar winced, and Silence heard a heavy sigh from the engine room as Chase Mago contemplated what that new force would do to his delicately tuned keel—and the tugs began to work their way down to the dock. The waiting dock seemed much like a standard cradle—but then the tugs deftly rotated the ship, bringing it in so that the top of the ship, not the keel, was against the dock.

The cradle lock monitors flashed green, and at the same time the right-hand viewscreen showed a flexible tube snaking up from the dock to fasten onto the airlock. Balthasar waited until a small indicator faded from yellow to green, then touched a speaker button.

"Cargo team?"

"That's right," a voice said cheerfully. Silence could just see the man's shadow on the screen, bulky in an old-fashioned spacesuit.

"Come on aboard," Balthasar said, and worked the hatch controls.

Customs formalities were nonexistent on Wrath-of-God. From Balthasar's offhand comments, Silence gathered that one was either expected, and therefore already cleared, or dead. Their cargo was removed—Balthasar asked for, but did not get, the voucher for his pay—and they were quickly assigned rooms and a table in one of the dining halls. Wrath-of-God was unusually crowded, filled to capacity with the crews of the ships whose captains had been summoned to Council; they were lucky to be given three tiny cubicles, set across the hall from a lavatory that they would share with the seventeen other people billeted on that hallway. The rooms contained only a bunk and a set of shelves, and Silence could not avoid thinking that they were hastily converted storage cells.

Conditions in their dining hall were somewhat better. They were assigned to a table with eight strangers, but already a brisk exchange of seats was in progress. Silence was whirled from table to table in Balthasar's wake, Chase Mago running interference for them both. After involved negotiations, they took their seats at a long table occupied by Tasarla and her crew, and another captain whom Balthasar introduced as Lenno.

Conversation turned wholly on the purposes of the Council. Rumor ran wild: the Hegemon had declared secret war, Lenno whispered, but Tasarla's pilot contradicted him. The opposite was true, she said; the Hegemon and the Council were ready to sign a secret truce. When one of Lenno's men suggested that someone had finally found Earth, and the Council was planning a raid on the ancient world, Silence stopped listening. I'm sick of hearing about Earth, she thought, stabbing viciously at her food. Earth was gone, destroyed, or if it wasn't it was staying hidden in the Rose-World's unbroken trade ring, refusing all contact with the planets of Hegemony, Fringe, and Rusadir. But that sort of common sense was unappealing, especially to people like Otto Razil, and expeditions were launched almost every year to find the lost road to Earth. Most of those ships simply vanished, though occasionally a broken exploring vessel would limp back to an outlying port, with a half-starved crew and a cargo of wild tales. Silence sighed. That time and sacrifice would be better spent on the search for alien worlds, she thought. At least we know they have to exist, even if the magi haven't been able to construct a harmonium that would play an alien enough scale. She sighed again, and put aside those thoughts.

They were hustled out of the dining hall by serving homunculi, making room for the next shift of diners, but no one wanted to return to their cheerless rooms. *Sun-Treader*'s crew stood with Tasarla in the crowded corridor until a harassed-looking man with an official armband told them to return to their assigned rooms.

"Hell with that," Tasarla said, as soon as the man was out of earshot. "Let's try the observatory."

Chase Mago glanced at Balthasar, who shrugged. "Why not?"

The three followed Tasarla through the gently curving corridors to a central stairwalk, rising and falling treads coiled together, then up two levels to the tube connecting Mageara to Tisiphone. Tisiphone seemed almost identical to Mageara, except that a different set of directional symbols marked the walls. It was only when they passed through a second opaque transfer tube into Alecto that things changed. The corridors were wider in this, the central unit of Wrath-of-God, and there seemed to be fewer people moving about. At first Silence thought this was only an illusion brought on by the greater space, but then she noticed that nearly all the passersby bore Wrath-of-God's skull on cheek or hand. Tasarla was careful to keep out of their way, and Silence wondered just what the tattoo meant. Tasarla didn't have one, and plainly never had, but Balthasar. . . . She glanced surreptitiously at him, and saw him rubbing at the patch where his mark had been, a pained scowl distorting his features.

Like the other two stations, Alecto had a central stairwalk, but it was wider, and bathed in a cooler, bluer light. Tasarla stepped on, judging the speed perfectly, and Silence followed, stumbling. As the stairwalk rose, she could see a part of the level that had been hidden by the curve of the stair. Heavily armed guards stood outside a massive door that was spattered with warning hieroglyphics.

"What's down there?" Silence asked, reaching to touch Tasarla's elbow.

"Library," the Misthian answered, without looking back. "Off-limits, of course, unless you're captain of at least a five."

"Oh." Tasarla was hugging the right-hand rail, Silence saw, leaving room for people to pass. The pilot imitated her, and a moment later was glad she had done so, as a gang of laborants—failed apprentices or impoverished mechanics bound to a magus's service—rushed by, carrying unidentifiable equipment.

They rode the stairwalk to its end, where the treads flattened and vanished beneath the spongy flooring. The stairhead was empty except for a stairway, marked with the domed tower that had symbolized an observatory since long before the Millennial Wars, and with the red-slashed circle denying admittance. Two more doors leading off the stairhead were marked with the same symbol. Tasarla crossed to the third door and fiddled with its stiff lock.

Balthasar touched Silence's shoulder. "Look up." Obediently, Silence tilted her head back—and saw, set into the ceiling, a woman's face, distorted in fury. For a moment, she thought it was real, somehow preserved by magi's art, but then she realized it was only stone, carved from a rock lighter than the rest of Alecto. Beneath it, gold letters spelled a brief message: *Omena me fecit.* Omena made me.

"Are you coming, Silence?" Tasarla called.

Silence shook herself, and stepped through the now-open doorway onto a platform that circled the base of the observatory tower, protected from space by a single layer of mage-cast glass. Silence stepped gingerly onto a black floor so highly polished that it reflected the stars, and then, when it did not break, and she did not slip and fall out into the starfield, she walked carefully around the curve of the instrument tower, toward a glow in the sky.

From this angle, the wave of dust reared over the station, doubly black against the flaming brilliance beyond, light tipping each of the billows. Silence took a step backward, ready for it to fall and crush her. Chase Mago caught her shoulder, keeping her from running into him.

"My God, that's—incredible," Silence said, and felt a fool for using such an inadequate word.

The engineer nodded, releasing her. "I know," he said. "It's always so. . . ." He, too, let his voice trail off in defeat.

Tasarla said, "Now that I've got you here, Denis, there's a thing or two I want to ask you."

Silence glanced over her shoulder in time to see the Misthian pull Balthasar back to the other side of the circular platform. In the glaring light, the Delian looked ill, his shoulders slumping, his face haunted. But then he was gone, and Silence wondered if she had imagined it all. Shrugging to herself, she turned back to the nebulae.

It took an effort of will to look away from that terrible splendor and examine the station spread out below her. Beyond Alecto lay two more stations, clearly newer than the others, hollowed from a different kind of rock. Each of those stations had two docking wheels, and every space was full, but she could see none of the large raiding ships, the navy-built fives and sixes she knew Wrath-of-God owned.

"That's Phobos and Demos," Chase Mago said.

"They're mostly for the magi, and for anybody else who's staying long-term."

"Where are the big ships?" Silence asked. "I didn't see any when we docked."

"They dock here, to Alecto," Chase Mago answered. "Around here." He led her along the platform, back around the observatory, until its dark bulk blocked half the nebula. "If you look almost straight down, I think you can see them."

Silence pressed herself against the glass, staring down between her feet, and could just glimpse a docking wheel far more massive than any of the others, and the immense keel of a six.

"All the warcraft dock to Alecto," Chase Mago went on. "Alecto's the biggest dock, and the tracking center's here—most of that's done by this observatory—plus the master controls for the stations' harmonia, and the Admiral keeps station from here."

"I see," Silence said. The dark quiet of the observatory platform seemed to loosen the engineer's tongue, and Silence willed him to keep talking. "What do the tattoos mean?"

Chase Mago hesitated, then said, shortly, "Crewman from a fighting ship."

"Then Denis was on one of the raiders?"

"I suppose he must've been." The engineer shrugged. "He doesn't talk about it, in any case."

That was a clear warning, and Silence gave up her questions, taking a few more steps along the platform. She was almost back to where they had started; Tasarla and Balthasar, leaning against the observatory wall, looked up from their conversation in surprise. Silence hardly noticed them. To the side of Tisiphone, swelling out from the station's lower quadrant, was a billowing cloud of material, shimmering from rich blue to white as it moved.

"What the hell is that?"

Chase Mago moved to join her, stared entranced.
"An airtight bubble? I don't know."

Balthasar pulled himself away from the wall.
"That's the assembly hall," he said. "They can't fit
all the captains into any of the rooms on the station,
so we meet out there." He shivered slightly. "Everyone must be here."

Stragglers from Wrath-of-God's fleet arrived over
the next few sleep/wake periods, a number of couriers and two rather battered fours, for which there
was no room on Alecto's docking wheel. In the
end, they were tethered to a makeshift dock off the
axis of Demos, and the crews were ferried back to
Alecto for quartering. Silence and Chase Mago
watched their arrival from the observatory deck,
then moved around the platform to look again at
the blue-white sphere of the assembly hall. It looked
like nothing so much as a giant balloon, but that
illusion was spoiled by the tiny human shapes that
could be seen moving around on the inner surfaces.
Stringing guideropes and seating nets, someone
had said. The magus who had created the hall had
not brought it into the field of the station's harmonium, though he had given it an atmosphere:
the captains would have to float weightless throughout their meeting.

Now, as she leaned against the slick cold glass,
staring down at the hall, a three-toned chime
sounded overhead, and all motion stopped. For a
brief second the quiet was so deep that she could
feel the low hum of the harmonium buried in the
depths of Alecto. Then a woman spoke.

"This is the Voice of the Council," she announced,
her voice cool and faintly menacing. "The Admiral
and senior captains summon all the captains of
Wrath-of-God to Council. Council will begin in one
local hour. Failure to attend will result in loss of

privileges and status. The Voice of the Council has spoken."

"Who or what is the Voice of the Council?" Silence whispered, but Chase Mago shook his head, frowning.

"Later."

Throughout the station, the summoned captains streamed toward the temporary tube that connected the assembly hall to the side of Tisiphone. The two captains who had been on the observatory deck hauled open the door to the stairhead, nearly knocking over a laborant unlucky enough to get in their way, and hurried out. Below, Silence could seen the first arrivals filing into the transfer tube. She watched in fascination as the hall filled, the surface of the sphere darkening as more and more men took their places in the maze of rope.

"So what happens now?" she asked.

"I don't know for sure," Chase Mago answered. "Presumably the Council tells everyone why they've been summoned, and then they put the question to a vote."

"How long do you think it'll take?" Silence asked.

Chase Mago snorted. "The Committee stage-manages things as well as any clutch of oligarchs. An hour or two, no longer."

"You know a lot about politics," Silence said, and did not add, *and about the sort of life Nnamdi leads*. The words hung unspoken in the air between them, and for a second she wondered if she had gone too far. Then Chase Mago ducked his head in embarrassment.

"My father was an oligarch—a new man, the first new man to break into the Circle of Families on Kesse in a hundred years, but still an oligarch. I just absorbed a lot of things, growing up in his house."

"And he let you become an engineer?"

Chase Mago shrugged. "I had brothers, and my father thought I'd be happiest and most useful if I could help run the family fleet. That was how I escaped when the Hegemony put Kesse to the sack." A spasm of pain crossed his bearded face, and Silence did not need to ask what had happened to his family.

"I'm sorry," she murmured. For a long moment, neither said anything. Then Silence smiled, wistfully. "My family always wanted me to marry an oligarch, but I don't think this is what they had in mind."

Chase Mago looked down at her, his face breaking into the first real smile she had seen from him. "But you're not first-family yourself."

"No, my kin are merchants, clients of one of our oligarchs," Silence answered. "But when I was nineteen, the third son of Vald Kiollr—he was one of the most powerful men in the senate at that time—asked me to marry him. He was everything a girl could want—handsome, clever, only twelve years older than I. My parents didn't believe I was serious about becoming a pilot until I refused him the third time. The next year, my grandfather got his patron to sponsor me for my license."

"Kiollr." Chase Mago was frowning, oblivious to the rest of her story. "The Kiollr are on Cap Bel, aren't they?"

"Yes. I'm from there."

"And a Kiollr arranged the general surrender, didn't he?"

"Yes," Silence said again. Chase Mago's face darkened with an old anger, and the pilot hurried on. "Not all of Cap Bel supported him, not even all the oligarchs. That's how my grandfather lost his fortune, reinstating Avaras—that was his patron—when the Hegemony despoiled him. And not all the Rusadir's as defensible as Kesse. We don't have the fleets or the moon stations to fight from."

Chase Mago's expression eased a little. "I know. I'm sorry."

"It's all right," Silence said, vaguely. She could still remember when Avaras had been ruined, the second year she had had her license. She had been flying one of Avaras's smaller ships, and had brought it home only to see her captain forced to hand over ship and cargo to the Hegemon's men. There had been nothing left for her, she had thought, and she had gone home, numb, to find her female kin in tears and her grandfather at the computers, calmly turning assets into cash. Of all Avaras's clients, only three had stood by him, turning over their own funds to help him buy back his properties. Bodua Leigh had given more than any—he had received most, he said, in Avaras's good days—and bankrupted himself in the process.

The observatory had emptied while they stood talking. The stars and the half-hidden fire of the nebula had become faintly menacing, and the air seemed suddenly cold. "Let's go below," she said.

Despite Chase Mago's confident prediction, the Council lasted seven hours. Silence sat cross-legged on her uncomfortable bunk, trying without much success to concentrate on a Misthian novel borrowed from one of Tasarla's crew. The conventions of the plot were peculiar, and her attention kept straying to the hallway beyond her half-open door. At last there was a stirring in the air, a muttering that began below the level of hearing and swelled rapidly to full-scale shouting. Silence stepped to the door, pushing it fully open, and leaned out into the hall.

"What's happened?"

"Council's over," a stranger in a patched shipsuit shouted eagerly. "War's declared."

"On who?" she cried after him, but he had disappeared down the hallway.

Chase Mago looked at her from his door, his expression grim. "No use listening to rumors yet," he said, as much to himself as to her. "We have to wait for Denis." Balthasar appeared at last, following a gang of be-ribboned Numlulians. He looked very tired, the skin of his face dragged tight over his harsh bones, and he walked as though his back hurt.

"Well," he said, when he came close enough to be heard over the babble of talk filling the hall.

Chase Mago raised an eyebrow. "Well?" he repeated. "That's it?"

"Hardly," Balthasar said, with a bitter smile. "Let's talk."

The captain's cubicle was as cheerless as any of the others, more so because Balthasar had made no effort to personalize the space. The captain kicked his carryall beneath the bunk, clearing a square of floor, and hoisted himself onto the mattress, pushing back against the wall to make room for the others. Silence settled herself on the very foot of the bunk; Chase Mago lowered himself to the floor.

For a while no one spoke, until Silence nerved herself to say, "I heard war's been declared."

Balthasar sighed and sat forward. "Yeah, well. Apparently the Hegemon's decided to start cracking down on Wrath-of-God's connections inside the Hegemony. The Council might've known he wouldn't tolerate that forever. And this crackdown's neither subtle nor discriminating, from all accounts."

Silence remembered one battered ship she had seen in the Mageara wheel, remembered too Tasarla saying the crew was being kept in quarantine.

"Was *Skrymir* involved in that?"

Balthasar grinned. "And how. The Navy's caught two others—squadron mates to the twin fours that came in last—and the crews just vanished. They're either dead, or the Hegemon's magi have them, and I, for one, hope they're dead. *Skrymir* got real lucky, that's all. She carries Delian markings, and that made the Hegemon's people just wary enough. You saw the damage she took anyway."

Silence nodded, remembering the scored paint and the dulled, off-color look of *Skrymir*'s keel.

"And that's not all," Balthasar continued, with a sort of grim relish. "They've arrested two of our factors in the Rusadir, executed one with all his family, and are ready to do the same to the other one. Not to mention that they publicly flogged the satrap of Inarime—and him an aristocrat, one of the Thousand—for not keeping a closer eye on his customs officers."

"And the customs officers?" Silence asked, after a moment.

"Dead."

"That would explain why it's been harder to bribe the customs people lately," Chase Mago said. The captain grunted, and the engineer went on, "I didn't think we did that much business through the Hegemony. Not enough for this to hurt too much."

"We don't," Balthasar said. "We mostly live off their ships, but we still need contact. But there's also talk on Asterion that when the Navy has dealt with the Rusadir—secured them, that is—they'll move into the Fringe."

Silence shivered. The Fringe Worlds, unprotected by any league of planets, would be even less of a match for the Hegemony than the Rusadir had been. And with the Fringe gone, Wrath-of-God would have no place left to sell its plunder. "So what did they propose?" she asked.

"A raid on Arganthonios," Balthasar said.

"The water world?" Chase Mago looked up. "That would hurt the Hegemony, all right."

So it would, Silence thought, but it might hurt us, too. Arganthonios was an anomalous world, a thin skin of ordinary ice concealing a core of elemental water—and it was elemental water that powered a starship's harmonium. Arganthonios was the single largest source of the substance in the known galaxy; control of that was one of the cornerstones of the Hegemon's power. It was not a world to take lightly.

"Arganthonios must have a substantial garrison," she said cautiously.

Balthasar grimaced. Silence thought the expression might have started as a smile. "It does. But the Council has decided to throw all our ships against it."

"All?" Silence could not keep the protest from her voice.

Even Chase Mago looked startled. "The couriers can't be of much use, surely."

"Oh, but the raid's practical, too," Balthasar answered. "The Hegemon is talking about refusing to sell water from Arganthonios to outsiders. So the captains plan to take enough of it to fill all our tanks, enough to last two or three years."

"How?" Chase Mago asked.

"The big ships—the fives and sixes, and anything else with enough guns to be useful—will swoop in first and secure the planet. Then the rest of us will land and load up with the water." Balthasar added quickly, "Don't worry, Julie, the shipwrights will make the modifications to the holds."

"And retune when they're done?"

"Of course," Balthasar said.

"They'd better," the engineer said, but without

heat. Some of the worry was smoothed from his face as he contemplated the attack, and the damage to the Hegemony. Silence shook her head.

"I suppose there's no way out of this," she said.

Balthasar smiled wryly. "None."

The next week was spent planning for the raid. *Sun-Treader* was assigned a place in the third wave of couriers—*Ostinato* was part of the same group, to Silence's relief—and given the road to follow between Wrath-of-God and Arganthonios. She had flown the Lion-Road before, but she spent hours with her starbooks anyway, defeating uneasiness with the familiar symbols. She saw little of the others. Balthasar was occupied by almost constant captains' councils, and Chase Mago spent his waking hours at the docks, supervising the shipwrights. The day's routine was set by the Voice of the Council, her perfectly modulated tones issuing new orders at regular intervals. Silence asked again about her, wondering how even Wrath-of-God could give so much power to a woman, and Balthasar explained, looking over his shoulder as he spoke. The Voice was a revenant, he said, an idiot or a criminal bought by a magus, who then destroyed the existing personality and replaced it with a matrix only slightly more complex than that given to a homunculus. The Voice was capable of repeating the most complex instructions, and of making very simple decisions, but she could never use her power as the Council's representative to create a policy of her own.

The use of a revenant was only too typical of Wrath-of-God; a black carelessness filled the station, and Silence found her thoughts slowly deadened by it. The raid was a gamble, but unreal—the couriers grumbled a little, but were solaced by the thought of the profits to be made. The warships' crews were frankly ecstatic—but none of it affected

her. She knew she should be afraid, and was not;
only the unreality of it all raised a nagging worry.
Sitting on her bunk in the badly lit room, she
opened the *Speculum* to the pages showing the
Lion-Road, but could not concentrate on the over-
familiar symbols. Sighing, she set it aside, and
reached for the *Gilded Stairs*. The odd texture of
the treated paper reminded her that this was not
her copy. She turned the pages anyway, glancing
idly at the unfamiliar tables and strange roads.

While the number of roads known to the com-
piler of this version of the *Gilded Stairs* was limited,
the number of planets he had known was far greater
than she had imagined. The major worlds of Hegemony and Rusadir were listed in the tables, and a
few of the Fringe planets, but there were also listings for planets that had been destroyed in the
Millennial Wars. There were worlds she had never
heard of, and she assumed that they, like Latmos
and Vahalis, were among the planets shattered by
the war. Then she recognized, among a table full
of unfamiliar names, Sicyon, and then Aja. Those
were Rose Worlds, prohibited worlds, and she wondered if the other names in the table could be
variants of the other planets of the ring. Lemirey
might be Limyre, she thought, and el Mersa could
be Mersaa Maia. That was easily enough checked,
and she turned quickly to the *New Aquarius*, comparing the listings for the roads between Asterion,
listed in both books, and Mersaa. The books gave
the same roads, and she turned back to the *Gilded
Stairs* with a feeling of satisfaction. It was rather
amusing to think that she now shared the vaunted
secrets of the Rose-Worlder pilots. No one knew
precisely what they had to hide, though there was
much speculation. The majority, like Otto Razil,
said that the Rose Worlds knew how to reach
Earth. . . . Silence drew a sharp breath. Was it

possible that this book might really hold the key Razil had been looking for?

There was no index. Instead, the entries in the tables that made up the first third of the book were arranged according to an unfamiliar system. She could not work out the key, and was finally reduced to going through it page by page. And then, among the mix of symbols and oddly misspelled planetary names, she saw it: the circle surrounding a cross that stood for Earth. The cross-referenced worlds, the originating planets, were ones she did not recognize, though at least one of the roads was a familiar one. Perhaps that was why no one had noticed the value of this copy, she thought. The listed worlds were mostly unknown or unreachable, so the Earth symbol, if anyone had noticed it, had been ignored because the roads were useless. But probably not completely so, she thought. I imagine that, with patience, I could trace those worlds, and from there I could reach Earth— I wonder why Grandfather never noticed this? Probably because he never looked, she told herself. He had bought it only a few days before his death, if he had bought it for her name-day— and that day had come and gone, she realized suddenly, without her noticing—and even if he had bought it earlier, he was not particularly interested in the arcana of the pilot's art. It would have been like him to buy it without ever looking beyond Gregor Mosi's initials.

She pulled herself up off the bunk, wondering if Balthasar were in his room. Then she hesitated. If she told the Delian what she had found, the Council would inevitably hear about it—she was sure their surveillance was more than adequate. And that's something I don't want to risk, she thought. If Wrath-of-God had the Earth-Road ... I don't know what they'd do, how they'd handle it, but I'd almost rather see Otto find Earth first. She closed and locked her *Gilded Stairs*, then buried it at the bottom of her carryall, pulling a shirt over it. She could not even think of looking for the worlds that had been the departure points for Earth until she was well clear of Wrath-of-God—and probably not even then, she admitted. But at least *I can always sell the book, if I need money. If we survive this raid.* For the first time, the possibility of death seemed real, and she wished she could spend what might be her last days on any world but Wrath-of-God.

Twenty-four hours after her discovery, the warships lifted from their docks; six hours after that, the couriers followed. *Sun-Treader* did not so much lift from her cradle as fall from it, her harmonium tuned low, barely giving her steerage way. Sweating, Balthasar took the ship through the confusion of traffic, dodging other formations and ships under tow. *Sun-Treader* was sluggish in the interference from the other harmonia, and the captain took his time working her into her assigned spot behind *Ostinato*. Chase Mago lowered the pitch of the harmonium even further then, waiting for the signal from the fleet commander.

Finally, the formation was complete. At the head of the long column of starships, the fleet commander gave a signal, which was reflected back along the line of ships. Silence saw Balthasar's face pale as *Ostinato* repeated the brief transmission and opened the stops of her harmonium. The captain's eyes were fixed on the twin pitch recorders, one tuned to *Ostinato*, the other to his own harmonium. To keep station, he and Chase Mago would have to keep *Sun-Treader*'s harmonium tuned a full step below *Ostinato*'s primary note.

"Now," Balthasar said quietly.

Silence reached for the transmitter switch, sent

the prepared signal to the ships behind them. At the same moment, Chase Mago opened the stops, and the music rose glorious, only to waver instantly into dissonance. Balthasar winced and touched his keys, bringing the ship back into line. The interference eased, but did not disappear entirely, and Silence glanced nervously at the strain gauges. The needles were flickering, but only at the edge of the yellow area. They had a long way to go before they reached the red danger mark.

"Acceptable?" Balthasar asked, without taking his eyes from the pitch indicators.

"Looks fine to me," Silence answered.

"Good."

When the pitch indicators showed *Sun-Treader* to be less than twenty minutes from the twelfth of heaven, Silence climbed to the pilot's bridge. It took every exercise she had learned in apprenticeship to put herself in the proper state of receptivity, but at last she was able to look at the fading bulkheads with some confidence. She knew the Lion-Road well enough, but had never flown any road in company with so many other ships. She could not entirely quell the fear that she would lose control of *Sun-Treader* in the eddies and backwash set up by other ships.

"Are you ready, Silence?" Balthasar asked. In the background, Silence could hear Chase Mago's monotonous chant, counting off the fractions as they approached the twelfth. Balthasar would be paying more attention to the readings from *Ostinato*, keeping *Sun-Treader* half a step behind.

"Ready," she said softly, and did not expect an acknowledgement. She rested her hands on the control yoke, fingers on the lock, and waited as the metal surrounding her grew nebulous and vanished all together.

"You have control, Silence."

The pilot snapped off the lock and searched quickly for her bearing. To her surprise, the marks were palely visible already, the snarling cats setting the path that curved gently down to a gate that seemed to be shaped both like a prison portcullis and the mouth of a lion. She shook her head, trying to make the lion's head come clear, but the dual image persisted. It was the other pilots' doing, she realized. The standard texts disagreed on the symbol for the end of the path, and purgatory was doing its best to accommodate both visions.

Sun-Treader fell into the proper path almost without her help, its path eased rather than hindered by the starships that had preceded it. Seeing that, Silence relaxed a little, staring at the chain of ships. *Ostinato* rode ahead of her, her keel shining rainbow bright, and beyond her was the slimmer arrow of *Micah*, half transparent and glowing. Beyond *Micah* was *Freya's Witch*, and beyond her more ships whose names Silence did not know, strung out like beads on a string. They were all in the road, not a ripple of dissonance to mark a deviation.

. As the lead ships approached the distorted image of the gate, the first dissonance appeared. It was harder to control the ships as they fell out of purgatory; captains lost control of their harmonia, setting up new distortion. The needles of the new strain gauges set into the yoke jumped sharply, hung just at the edge of the red zone. *Sun-Treader* shivered, and Silence tightened her hold on the control yoke.

The disturbance grew worse as *Sun-Treader* came up on the gate, apparent speed increasing as they fell away from five-twelfths of heaven. The ship bucked, then swerved crazily as a new eddy manifested itself as a tiny tiger crouched to spring.

Silence brought them back into line, but not before the harmonium shrieked wildly. She heard Chase Mago swear, and realized that he had lost control of the tuning. The end of the path loomed ahead of them, *Ostinato* framed against the teeth of the half-lowered bars. Or were those a lion's teeth? Silence's head swam as she tried to take in the double picture. With an effort, she banished the lion's head.

They were gaining on *Ostinato*. She was sure of that despite the difficulty of judging relative distance, with only illusion to measure it against. She bit her lip, hesitating. Should she wait, take the chance that both ships would make it out before they collided, or should she risk the dissonances that bordered the path and sheer off now?

"Julie, watch the pitch," Balthasar snapped in her ears. "Watch it, we're climbing their tail."

Chase Mago's only response was an inarticulate growl. He'd lost it, Silence realized, was no longer a fraction ahead of things. *Sun-Treader* seemed to leap forward suddenly, and she no longer had a choice.

To either side loomed the stone pillars of the gate, terribly solid even as the illusion faded. Below was indeterminate, a nothingness she avoided without knowing why she did it. Even before she was completely aware of her reasoning, she leaned back against the control yoke, hauling the protesting ship up and out of the path. The illusory world around her spun crazily as she twisted the yoke against the stuff of purgatory, dissonance that was the gate-image, momentarily bit into and through it. A ghost of sound passed through the pilot's bridge, and then they were through, falling rapidly away from purgatory.

Silence clung to the yoke, retching, then gathered enough strength to lock her controls. That touch of celestial stuff had very nearly been too much for her material self.

"Are you all right?" Balthasar demanded. "Silence? Are you all right? God, that was completely off the scale. Silence?"

The pilot swallowed carefully. "I think I'm all right," she whispered. "I will be, anyway."

"You don't sound it," Balthasar said. "Julie, lock things down and get up there—"

"I'm fine," Silence said, and almost meant it. "I'm better already."

"I—" Balthasar broke off as the interships channel crackled to life.

"Balthasar 70219, *Sun-Treader*, you are off station."

Silence did not bother to smother her weak giggle, and Balthasar snarled, "Tell me something I don't know. Ayaz 59982, *Mesmer*, we were overrunning *Ostinato*."

Ayaz, the fleet commander, seemed unruffled by Balthasar's tone. "Report any damage, Balthasar 70219, *Sun-Treader*."

"Well, Julie?" Balthasar asked.

"We need to retune," the engineer answered. Listening, Silence could almost hear something different, something not quite right, perhaps a single note a half-step higher, that changed the harmonium's song from pleasant to faintly wearing.

"Right away?" Balthasar asked.

"As soon as possible," Chase Mago answered. "But we could go another gate or two. If we have to."

"Ayaz 59982, *Mesmer*, this is Balthasar 70219, *Sun-Treader*. We need to retune, but it's not quite desperate."

"Received. Tasarla 68035, *Ostinato*, report your condition," Ayaz said.

Tasarla's answer was quick and cheerful. "Ayaz

59982, *Mesmer*, this is Tasarla 68035, *Ostinato*. We're all right, nothing more than a shaking. Nice piloting, Silence."

"Thanks," Silence murmured, though she was certain the transmitter was off.

"No gossip, Tasarla 68035, *Ostinato*," Ayaz said. "Change places with Balthasar 70219, *Sun-Treader*."

"Acknowledged," Balthasar said, and Tasarla echoed him.

Slowly, Silence pulled herself upright. She still felt shaky, but not as sick as before. Carefully, she let herself down the ladder, rung by rung, then dropped heavily into her couch. Even that limited activity left her dizzy, and she had to close her eyes for a moment before she could summon the strength to secure the safety webbing.

"Are you sure you're all right?"

Silence nodded. "I really am. I'm better already."

The captain looked dubious, but the shift to approach formation demanded his attention. "The warships have secured the orbits, and things seem to be going well on the ground—channel four, if you want to listen."

Silence shook her head, staring at the screens. Visual and musonar showed Arganthonios and its sun, forever circling an invisible point like a pair of wary wrestlers. They were bound together by limited Newtonian forces, pushed apart by the mutually exclusive elements, fire and water. The *musica mundana*, reflected in the Ficinan model, showed the contrasting forces interwoven, each distorting the other, achieving only a precarious harmony. On the visual screen, Arganthonios showed almost as bright as its elderly sun. *Sun-Treader* was still too far out for the scanners to be able to distinguish the picket ships, but the musonar showed them clearly, two rings of bright dots, one banding the planet at the equator, the other circling it from pole to pole. A cluster of lights hovered around Arganthonios' irregular moon: the garrison was fighting back.

"So we're going in," Balthasar finished grimly.

Chapter 5

The descent to Arganthonios was unexpectedly easy. The fleet of couriers fanned out into landing formation, designed to minimize the impact of any attack from the planet, and met nothing except the guidance signals from the orbiting warships and the beacons planted beneath the temporary fields. There had even been time to set up field harmonia, so Balthasar did not have to make an unassisted landing, balancing the keel against the song of the planet's core. *Sun-Treader* rode the beam down as she would onto any world, onto padded skids rather than a cradle, and was dragged to one side by a team of heavy-duty homunculi. Balthasar and Chase Mago saw to the fitting of baffles around the already stressed keel, and adjusted the chocks that held the ship upright, ready for a quick liftoff.

Silence waited for them just within the hatchway, an unfamiliar projectile rifle cradled in her arms, her heylin slung at her waist. Cold settled over the ship, chilling her in spite of the thickly quilted jacket and trousers provided by the quartermasters on Wrath-of-God. With the cold came the quiet, doubly unnatural on a planet just taken by storm. There was no noise, no shouting, not even the nearly soundless popping of heylins or the flat crack of the projectile rifles. Across the steaming metal of the temporary field, she could just make out a cannon emplacement, half-hidden by the last ship in the parking line. It took much more effort to find the white-garbed troops who manned it, but when she finally picked them out of the snow, they were drinking coffee, very much at their ease.

When the men returned, they brought the cold with them, an invisible cloud about their bodies. Chase Mago headed immediately for the engine room to set up collectors to power the secondary plant. Balthasar and Silence remained behind to set up the security devices—monitors that would sound alarms if anything moved too close to the ship—then retreated to the commons.

"Isn't there something we should be doing?" Silence asked.

Chase Mago passed her a mug of coffee from the giant urn, and she sipped at it cautiously. The engineer had left his jacket on her chair, and she lifted it off, noting as she did how the cold still clung to it. Her own clothes were chill, too, and she worked her way out of them, precariously balancing the mug.

"Like what?" Balthasar asked. He, too, accepted a cup of coffee, and drank half of it in a single gulp, before beginning to strip off his cold-weather gear. "We aren't heavily armed enough to help in securing the main installation, and the field guards don't need our help. All we can do is wait for the order to start loading the water."

"And be ready to lift," Chase Mago interjected

quietly. "Where do we go, Denis, if things go wrong?"

"There's nothing in the plan," Balthasar said. "It's too late for things to go wrong."

I don't like the sound of that, Silence thought, and saw Chase Mago surreptitiously make a gesture to avert bad luck.

"All right, so what's your plan?" the engineer asked.

Balthasar shrugged. "The Madakh, I suppose. Or would Ariassus be better?" He took a deep breath and, with a great effort, focused his attention on the idea. "Yes, I think Ariassus. Bigger population, more ships calling there, and the governor doesn't ask questions even if the Hegemon does pay his salary. Silence, go ahead and set up a course for us, Arganthonios to Ariassus—plot a backup, too. Arganthonios to the Madakh." He glared at Chase Mago. "Does that satisfy you?"

The engineer, staring into his coffee, said nothing. Silence rose and went into her cabin to collect her starbooks. I didn't think Julie was being that unreasonable, she thought, lifting the mattress and unlocking the strongbox. It seems only reasonable to want to have a disaster plan. But then, Balthasar had a point, too. It was too late for things to go wrong. If they were attacked now, there would be nothing to do but run. Or be blasted on the ground. . . . She shied away from that thought, flipping quickly through the tables in the *New Aquarius*, but the planet's chill quiet had crept into her cabin. She was uneasily aware of the slightest creaking of cold metal, of the occasional scuff of a footstep outside her door. In the end, she swept up her books and returned to the commons.

The others were sitting as she had left them, but Balthasar had lit the wall screen, which showed a picture taken by a camera placed just above the main hatch—the row of parked ships, the snow beyond them, and the spindly drilling towers. She squinted at it, and thought she could just make out the cannon emplacement at the edge of the temporary field.

"Nothing yet?" she asked, and Chase Mago answered, "Nothing."

Silence sighed, and spread her books across the table, pulling up a chair so she could work in comfort. The tables in the *New Aquarius* listed only three routes between Arganthonios and Ariassus, and none between Arganthonios and the Madakh, but the *Topoi*'s tables listed seven for each. Two of those were familiar roads, ones so common she had lost count of the number of times she had flown them. She could take *Sun-Treader* through to either the Madakh or Ariassus, even if the ship were falling apart around her, or if she herself were hurt. And it spared her the effort—likely to be unsuccessful—of trying to memorize voidmarks when her mind was on other things.

She closed her books and put them away in her cabin, then returned to the commons. Balthasar had a fresh cup of coffee, but nothing else had changed. In the screen, night was falling on Arganthonios, grey-white fading into the blues and violets of twilight. In the distance, she could just see a sliver of moon rising behind the drilling towers, casting the faintest ripple of light across the gently mounded snow.

Suddenly, lights blazed from the top of the drilling towers and from the roofs of the other buildings. She jumped, reaching instinctively for the heylin she had discarded with her heavy jacket and, in the screen, the cannon's crew jumped for their weapons and fired hastily. The blazing ball of energy blasted away the darkness, nearly shorting out the camera and blinding the three watchers in *Sun-Treader*'s commons. When Silence's eyesight returned to normal, she saw that that was all the damage it had done. A great puddle was slowly refreezing on the hill beyond the towers, but nothing else had changed.

"Attention, attention," a voice blared over both loudspeakers and the internal communications channel. "Kesin 453, ground forces commander, speaking. There is no attack. Repeat, there is no attack. All troops, cease fire at once."

"An automatic switch," Chase Mago said, and drew a shaky breath.

"Damn stupid of them not to warn us," Balthasar growled, but before he could go on, the speakers crackled again.

"Attention, all personnel, this is Haldan 309, operations coordinator. Stand by for fleet orders. All commanders check in."

"This is it," Balthasar said, and reached to touch a single button set beneath the screen. The snow-covered landscape faded, and was replaced by a man's face. In one corner of the screen, numbers flickered rapidly, froze, then disappeared before Silence could read the total.

"Attention, all personnel, this is Haldan 309, operations coordinator," the man repeated. "Stand by for new orders. Orbital control was achieved at 1428 hours, local; ground control at 1450. However, the amount of elemental water in the storage tanks was considerably less than projected, threatening the second half of the Council's objective. Therefore, the senior captains have decided that the fleet will remain on Arganthonios until enough water can be pumped to fill our tanks back on Wrath-of-God. The resident magi have agreed to operate the mining machinery in exchange for interviews with selected captains and crewmen, on the usual terms."

Silence could not help shaking her head in

wonder. A magus would sell his soul for new knowledge. These magi, despite their presumed oaths of loyalty to the Hegemon, were prepared to give active aid to his enemies, in exchange for the right to ask questions. They were even willing to keep the answers secret—those were the usual terms.

"Garrison troops will be held on the lunar station," Haldan went on. "Transport captains will be detailed to ferry prisoners up there, and those selected for interview will also be notified within the hour. Haldan 309, operations coordinator, ending transmission."

"They're crazy," Balthasar said. "They're totally insane. What makes them think the alert hasn't already gone out, and that we won't have a whole task force down on us within the day?"

"Maybe it's worth the chance," Chase Mago said. "The water will last for years, even at the rate the fleet uses it—"

The speaker buzzed again, and Silence reached for it quickly. "*Sun-Treader*."

"Mikos 949, speaking for Haldan 309, operations coordinator. You're the pilot?"

"Yes," Silence said.

"Right. I need to speak to Balthasar 70219."

The captain spoke without turning, raising his voice to carry to the pickups. "What the hell do you want, Mikos?"

The coordinator's representative did not seem disturbed by the obvious hostility. "Official orders, Balthasar 70219, *Sun-Treader*. Your pilot is required by the magi—seems they've never heard of a woman pilot before, at least one that wasn't a Misthian. She's to take up residence in the main compound. You can come with her or not, as you choose."

Balthasar ground his teeth, swung to face the screen. "I protest."

"Protest denied." Mikos's face softened a little. "You can bring it before the Council when we get back, but I can tell you now you won't get very far."

"Very well." Balthasar took a deep breath, fighting to control his anger. "We'll all move to the main compound."

"Thank you, Balthasar 70219, *Sun-Treader*. A sled will be by for you in one local hour." The transmission ended abruptly, leaving Balthasar staring at the blank screen.

"They're determined to kill us all," he said at last, quite calmly, then turned on his heel and vanished into his cabin.

Silence stared at the table top, a lost feeling settling in her stomach. It had been so good, the past few weeks, being treated not as something strange or exotic, but merely as one of the crew. It hurt to be an oddity again, to be reminded that she was a woman, without status—and, worse than that, to be treated as a commodity, something to be traded to the magi in exchange for their help and silence.

"Don't blame Denis," Chase Mago said, after a moment. "There's nothing he can do, if they won't allow a protest until we get back to the Wrath." He hesitated, then added, "I'm sorry."

Silence waved a hand in negation. "It's all right." She could not quite bring herself to say she was used to it, or that she was glad to help, and compromised on, "It's not a difficult thing."

The sled arrived promptly an hour later, setting off the alarms that ringed the ship. Balthasar made them wait while Chase Mago set a trip lock at the hatch, so that opening it would also snap on the ship's power and start the harmonium, then tossed their bags into the cargo well behind the seats and climbed aboard, extending a hand to help Silence

up. The pilot followed cautiously, stepping over
the ice-coated running board directly onto the floor
of the cabin. Chase Mago climbed in next, followed by a guard in white cold-weather gear heavily trimmed with ice-colored fur. The sled jerked
forward, its tiny wheels awkward on the rough
surface of the field, then slid off into the deep
snow. The wheels came up into their recesses, and
the machine shot forward, throwing Silence against
the back of the seat. The cabin was unheated, and
she was grateful for the warm bodies to either
side.

The trip from the field to the main compound
was short, and the glaring spotlights turned the
snowfield into an indistinct expanse of glittering
white and coal-black shadow. It was impossible to
see details, and Silence was glad when the sled
slid to a stop in front of one of the buildings. An
airlock door was just visible, set back into the
thick walls, a waist-high retaining wall curving
beside it, presumably to protect it from the drifting snow. Silence collected her bag, probing automatically through the thin sides for the shape of
her starbook, and pushed through the door into a
pleasantly lit hallway. The air inside was so cold it
took her breath away; she gasped and tightened
the collar of her jacket.

A mercenary from the assault team was waiting
for them, his head tilted to one side as he listened
to the chatter from a tiny mechanical box clipped
to his collar. The words were gibberish to Silence,
though she thought she recognized the language as
the solider's guild's private tradetalk, but the mercenary muttered something in response, and came
forward.

"Come with me, Captain, sieuri?"
The three followed silently down the white-walled
corridor, then into another identical hallway, then

down a short flight of stairs and through a corridor that grew suddenly low-ceilinged as they passed from one building to another. The air was warmer in the second building, and there were guards posted unobtrusively at the top of the stairs from the connecting tunnel, manning a small cannon. Their escort tossed them a salute, and the gun crew returned it silently.

There were signs of fighting here, the first Silence had seen since the landing. The walls were stained, a door had been blasted away, and she caught a quick glimpse of charred furniture and ruined machinery. Guards were posted at many of the doorways, and the men who moved through the halls were either soldiers from the landing team or bore the tattoos of the warship's crews. For a moment, Silence wondered why this part of the installation was so important, but then they passed a board filled with directional hieroglyphics. Main power plant controls to the left, communications and astrology one flight up, drill monitoring and map . . . of course the assault commanders would concentrate their men here.

Their escort led them down another short flight of stairs, past yet another cannon emplacement, and into a third building. There was heat here, too, but very little else to provide comfort. Furniture was piled in the hall outside office doors; one was open a crack, and Silence could see a very young soldier asleep on a thin mat, one arm thrown up against the light.

"What is this area normally?" Balthasar asked.

"Magi's quarters, laborants' hall, and workrooms," the soldier answered. He glanced at Balthasar, saw more questions in the captain's eyes, and sighed. "We kicked the magi out of their regular quarters and have them under guard in one corner of the buliding. We took the laborants up to

the lunar station with the garrison, just in case.
You get one of the workrooms." He stopped in
front of an unmarked door, and kicked the lower
right-hand corner. The door slid back, revealing a
stack of folded cots and a tiny portable heater.
"Heat goes down at 2200. Follow the signs for
dining hall and lavatories. And don't go wandering around. There's no heat in any of the other
buildings, and you could freeze to death."

"Thank you," Balthasar said bitterly, but the
man was already out of earshot.

Chase Mago sighed, tossed his bag into a corner,
and began methodically unfolding the cots.

"Are the ground troops always this friendly?"
Silence asked.

To her surprise, Balthasar managed a wry grin.
"They aren't usually this bad, no. But I'm sure
they aren't happy about the change of plans, either."

Chase Mago had finished unfolding the cots, and
knelt by the heater. After a brief examination, he
pushed it away in disgust. "That thing's no good.
The power cell is nearly drained."

"Wonderful," Silence muttered. Raising her voice,
she added, "How cold does it get when the heat
goes down?"

The engineer shrugged, and Balthasar said,
"Cold."

"Very funny." Silence glared at the others a
moment, then, with an effort, controlled her anger.
"Should we try and get some food?"

"Sounds good to me," Chase Mago said, accepting her implicit apology, but Balthasar held up his
hand.

"No, I brought rations from the ship. We're better off staying here, out of the troops' way, and
besides, I want to talk to you." He settled himself
on one of the bare mattresses. Pilot and engineer
exchanged glances, then copied him.

"Look, if the Hegemony comes back, we're going to need a plan of action," Balthasar began. He lowered his voice. "And I don't mean the official, fight-to-the-last kind, either. If we're attacked, we head for the ship, above-ground."

"What if they've brought siege engines?" Chase Mago asked.

"If they do, then we try to get to the tunnel to the drill towers, and take our chances in the open from there," Balthasar answered. "But I doubt they will. It would be too tricky, with all the elemental water just below the crust—the engines would be more likely to break the planet open than to disrupt us."

The engineer nodded, and Balthasar went on. "There's a lock to the surface two cross-corridors back." He searched briefly in his pockets and, after a moment, Chase Mago handed him a tiny notebook and pen. The captain tore a sheet from the back pages and scribbled on it for a minute, then held up a crude diagram.

"Turn left from this door, down two corridors, then left again, and you'll see stairs and an emergency lock. From there, you can see the fields, so just head straight for the ship."

Silence took the sheet of paper, studied it for a moment without speaking, then handed it to Chase Mago. They could make it out of the building, she thought, but there wasn't much chance they could make it across the open snowfields to the ship. But then, Balthasar had never promised that.

"Any questions?" the captain said, after a moment.

Silence shook her head, and the engineer said, "I can't think of any."

"Then let's eat," Balthasar said, reaching for his bag.

The meal was a quiet one, and shortly after they had finished, the heat began to fade. Each cot was equipped with a heavy sleepsack, and Silence crawled into hers fully dressed. Feeling like a fool, she wrestled with buttons and ties, and finally freed herself of her outer layer of clothing, setting it on the floor beneath the cot. Chase Mago did the same, folding himself to fit into a too-short bag, but Balthasar stripped without regard for an audience. Silence watched in sleepy fascination— the captain was leanly muscled, brown-skinned and fit, belying the grey in his hair—but Chase Mago yawned loudly. Balthasar glanced at him, his expression unreadable, then reached to dim the lights.

Silence woke shivering, her body contracted to a tight knot beneath the layers of the sleepsack. Wincing, she tried to straighten her legs against the painful stiffness of her muscles, whistling softly at a cramp in one calf. The fabric was icy beneath her feet, and her toes were beginning to ache from the cold. The heater's broken down completely, she thought, but a quick glance showed a pinpoint of red light in the far corner. Theoretically, at least, it was functioning. Still shivering, she worked one arm out of the sleepsack, and rummaged beneath the cot frame for the clothes she had discarded earlier, heaping them on top of the sack. They stopped the shivering, but she did not dare uncurl from her fetal position for fear of dislodging them.

"Silence?" That was Balthasar, whispering across darkness and the intervening cot. "Are you awake?"

"Yes."

"Julie?"

The engineer mumbled something inarticulate, but Silence, shifting uneasily beneath the piled clothes, could see his eyes wide open through the darkness.

"Are you as cold as I am?" Balthasar went on.

"Frozen," Silence answered.

"It'd be warmer if we put all the sacks together," Balthasar said.

For a moment, no one said anything, and then Silence shrugged. "Anything to get warm again," she said.

"I'll agree with that," Chase Mago mumbled.

In the end, they simply piled the cot frames one on top of the other, then, shivering, fastened the sleepsacks together and climbed in. Silence huddled in the middle sack, wondering miserably if she would ever be warm again. To either side, captain and engineer shifted restlessly, each trying to avoid the others' cold feet. For some reason, the situation reminded her of nothing so much as the outings sponsored by her grandfather's patron for the offspring of his clients, and she smothered a laugh at the memory. While the boys went camping, the girls were taken to one of the summer compounds on the Garumnan coast, where they spent the days swimming and sunbathing, and learning the traditional female crafts. At night, they took the mattresses from the beds and spread them together on the floor, so they could huddle together and share secrets in the dark. But that had been a long time ago, and the secrets they had shared had had to do with dreams and ghosts and whispers of boys. The memory was comforting and, as she grew slowly warmer, she slept.

Silence woke to find herself curled tightly against Balthasar's side, her cheek on his shoulder. Chase Mago was nowhere in sight. Silence lay frozen for a moment, wondering what to do. If she moved, she would wake him, and in pulling away would look like the stereotypical homebred girl whose virginity was her only property. On the other hand, she had no particular desire to have him wake up to find her in his arms. Maybe if I stretched, she thought, that would wake him, and I could pretend I'd just wakened myself. At that moment, Balthasar opened his eyes. He blinked twice, as though disconcerted, and then his lips curved in a knowing smile. Silence glared and sat up quickly to hide her blush.

"Good morning," Balthasar said, and the smile turned into a grin.

Pig, Silence thought, and felt her face freeze automatically into that stony incomprehension that had been her best defense against all men, from oligarch's sons to fellow star-travellers. "Do you want breakfast?"

She pulled on her quilted trousers and reached for the ration packs discarded next to the heater. One had been broken open, and Chase Mago had scrawled a short note on the inner wrapping: "Gone to see about quick-tuning *Sun-Treader*. Back when I can."

"What's up?" Balthasar asked. Coming up behind her, he rested his hands very lightly on her shoulders, a touch at once tentative and apologetic. "I suppose I ruined my chances," he added.

Words and tone were at odds with his cautious hands. Silence glanced over her shoulder, not knowing how to answer. A flat agreement would sound petty, and anything else would sound flirtatious; she settled on naïveté.

"Chances?" Without waiting for his answer, she went on, "Julie's gone to see about the keel."

The captain's hands lifted from her shoulders. "Maybe not utterly," he murmured, but his expression, when she glanced again at him, was oddly wistful. He saw her look, and his manner changed abruptly. "So Julie thinks he can quick-tune?"

Silence shrugged. "It looks as though he's going to try," she said.

"I doubt he can do it," Balthasar mused.

Privately, Silence agreed with him, Quick-tuning—forcing a stressed keel temporarily back to its original pitch—had to be done in the confined space of a tuner's shed, or else the beneficial harmonies dissipated before any good could be done. She shrugged again, and changed the subject. "What about the magi? Will they send for me, or what?"

"I don't know," Balthasar said, and reached for a ration pack. Silence copied him, seating herself precariously on the edge of the bottommost cot. The captain sat on the floor. "I am sorry about this," he said presently. "I intend to file a protest at the next captains' council."

"It's not worth it on my account."

Balthasar looked up with a quirky smile. "Oh, I'm not just doing it for you, I admit it. There's a matter of my rights as captain and freeholder to be considered. My crew shouldn't be dragged off without their first consulting me and getting my consent."

"I see." Silence busied herself with her ration pack, wondering as she nibbled at the flat, faintly bitter drybread whether she should be flattered at once again being treated as just another crew member. She put that question aside with the rations, and began to return the room to its original condition. After a moment, Balthasar moved to help her.

She had just set her own sleepsack back on its cot frame when someone knocked at the door. Balthasar moved to open it, one hand in his jacket pocket.

The young man who stood in the doorway was wearing star-traveller's clothes rather than a mercenary's uniform, and Wrath-of-God's mark was dark on the back of one hand. "Denis? The magi are ready to talk to your pilot now."

"Tell her yourself," Balthasar growled.

"Sieura?" the messenger began, and Silence said, "I heard." She reached into her carryall for her heylin, checking to make sure the touchplate was warm beneath her thumb, then tucked it into her pocket. "I'm ready."

"I protest, Kirkja," Balthasar said wearily.

"I know." The messenger grimaced. "What can I do? They know you're not happy."

Balthasar made a gesture of disgust, and Kirkja sighed. "Sieura? If you'd come with me?"

"Of course," Silence said.

The magi were comfortably imprisoned in a room on the top level of the building, watched only by a single guard from the assault team. He checked their credentials, then unlocked the door.

Three men who had been sitting on a low couch rose to their feet; the others, already standing, nodded with old-fashioned courtesy.

Silence froze. These weren't the mere technicians she had been subconsciously expecting, men whose talents confined them to the simpler arts one step above a mechanic's skill, men who inquired into anomalies like herself merely out of a sense of duty. These were high magi, men who manipulated heaven and submaterial hell with ease, as one small part of their greater work. *Dangerous men.*

But the magi were also honest, she reminded herself, at least in the sense that they kept their given word. They were too powerful, too dangerous, and at the same time too few and too individualistic, and therefore vulnerable, not to have to guard jealously their reputation as honorable, disinterested men. If they pledged her safety, she was safe. Even so, she walked very warily into the room.

She was at once conscious of the stares. The magi were eating her with their eyes, stripping not her clothes but every thread of information that she possessed that might help them to understand the workings of the universe. Theirs was not a physical lust—indeed, they seemed unaware of her as a woman—but an intellectual one, far more frightening than the stares of men on the street because it denied her even the reality of a body.

Behind her, Kirkja cleared his throat. "Sieura Leigh, I present the Masters of Art Omanisa Boldisar and Rahab Magire; the Master in Fire Adem Girault; the Doctors Grantham Axtell, Saskska Alassid, Haram Ubald. Sieuri, Silence Leigh."

The oldest of them all—Silence thought it was Alassid, but the introductions had gone too quickly for her to be certain—cleared his throat and said, "Thank you, Kirkja. That will be all."

Kirkja bowed and left, closing the door behind him. At the same time, the Master in Fire said, "Won't you sit down, Sieura Leigh?"

He gestured to a chair standing next to the low table that held an elegant silver coffee service. Silence sat carefully, marveling that Wrath-of-God's troops had not robbed them of all these riches. Besides the coffee service, worth five hundred Delian pounds at the least, she saw statuary in highly polished electrum, and a dome beneath which an immensely fragile dancing doll stood frozen in midstep. But then, magi were considered neutrals throughout the galaxy. And no one could afford to earn their enmity; though they would not unite to oppose an enemy, their refusal to work for any state was tantamount to passing a sentence of death.

"Coffee?" one of the masters of arts asked. Silence nodded, and he held a fragile-looking cup beneath the spigot of the immense silver urn. The pilot took it, murmuring her thanks, and sipped cautiously. It was hot and heavily spiced, sweeter than she liked.

Alassid cleared his throat again. "Ah, Sieura Leigh. You do understand the terms of our agreement?"

"Yes, I think so."

"Nevertheless, I would like to go over them, just to make certain." Alassid steepled his fingers. "We have agreed to supervise the extraction and distillation of elemental water for your employers, in return for your answers to our questions. Do you agree to answer everything as fully and honestly as possible?"

"I do." Silence set aside her cup, the coffee barely tasted, and one of the other doctors waved a hand at her.

"Oh, please, my dear lady, make yourself comfortable. This shouldn't be painful at all."

"Magire," Alassid said softly. "Get the boy."

The master of arts sitting on the far side of the room, a grim man who looked older than his actual years, rose silently and disappeared behind a painted screen that half concealed one corner of the room. When he returned to the circle of chairs, he propelled before him a boy about ten years old, who walked with slow, faltering steps. There was something odd about the child, Silence thought and, as though he had read her mind, Magire said, "My son, Nial. He was born—defective. But one makes use of what one has." He sat down again, and with the gentle pressure of his hand on the boy's shoulder compelled him to sit also. The child was a revenant, Silence realized with a start, as mindless as the Voice of the Council. She stared at him, trying to keep her revulsion from showing, and the boy stared back at her with luminous, empty eyes.

"Sieura Leigh." Alassid sat forward on the couch. "Shall we begin?"

"Go ahead," Silence said, bracing herself. The boy was still staring at her; she shivered to think of him later repeating her exact words, his voice and expression a parody of her own.

"Your given name is Silence?" Alassid continued. If he was aware of her discomfort, he gave no sign of it.

"Yes."

"That's a very old style of naming," Boldisar said. "Were your parents aware of the symbolic significance of the realist tradition?"

"I doubt it," Silence said. "Virtue names are common in the Rusadir."

"You're from the Rusadir? What world?" That was Ubald, leaning plumply forward.

"Have you found that a virtue name, as you call it, has any effect on your piloting?" Boldisar demanded, riding over Ubald's reedy voice.

"Gentlemen, please," Alassid snapped. "One at a time, and please allow the others to finish a line of questioning. You will all have your turn."

Ubald drew himself up. "I am not accustomed to sharing a subject under investigation, nor am I accustomed to take a second place to a mere Master of Art—"

"Do you wish to leave?" Alassid demanded sharply. "No? Then we will proceed as agreed. Sieura, you will answer Master Boldisar, if you please."

Silence collected herself hastily. "I don't think it's had any active effect. Having a symbolic name may have made me more sensitive to symbols in general, but that's about all."

Boldisar gestured politely to Ubald, and the plump man, still glaring, said, "Where are you from in the Rusadir?"

"And what is the status of your family?" the hitherto silent doctor—Axtell—interjected.

Silence answered those questions, and the others that followed, ranging from questions about her family to the circumstances of her apprenticeship to a minute description of the voidmarks on several common roads. She felt as though she were being dissected, the magi following some invisible checklist. It was late afternoon by the time they were finished; Silence was tired, and twitchy from too many cups of coffee with too little food. Each of the magi thanked her politely, and then Kirkja escorted her back through the installation to the room she shared with the rest of *Sun-Treader's* crew.

Balthasar and Chase Mago were crouched by the heater, the engineer making some sort of adjustment to the mechanism, Balthasar staring dubiously at it, his hands full of tools. They both looked up as the door opened, and Chase Mago slammed shut the cover of the heater. He took his tools back from Balthasar and said, "How are you?"

"Starved," Silence answered.

"I traded for some new rations," Balthasar said. "And some juice-packs."

"Fantastic," Silence said. She ate and drank ravenously, focusing all her attention on the mundane act of feeding herself. The other two watched without speaking.

They resisted the temptation admirably, Silence thought, as she slipped out of her trousers and overshirt in the combined sleepsack, trying not to disturb the engineer drowsing beside her. Balthasar dimmed the lights and crawled into the sleepsack.

Only then, perhaps feeling himself protected by the darkness, did the captain ask, "So what did they want?"

Silence groaned and pushed herself down into

the sleepsack, hiding her face beneath the upper lining. Chase Mago laughed softly, and Balthasar said, "Don't ask?"

"Don't ask."

A screaming woke her. A noise like the wailing of a banshee rose and thickened to a shriek that clawed at her bones. Silence jerked upright, screaming herself at the pain that knifed through her. Balthasar was on his feet, slapping on the lights, his face contorted with the effort. Seeing her, he shouted something, but his words were drowned in the din. Then the screaming faded a little, the pitch dropping to a less piercing level, and Balthasar's hoarse shout came clear.

"I knew it! I fucking well knew it!"

Silence was already out of the sleepsack, fumbling into her cold-weather gear. Now that the worst of the noise had passed, she was able to recognize it; the Hegemony had returned to Arganthonios.

The noise again—a less painful sound—peaked, and fell away again. Chase Mago, fastening the collar of his jacket, paused momentarily to listen.

"That's another ship," he said. "About five miles off."

"They're buzzing the planet, they can't risk siege," Balthasar said impatiently. "Come on, before the lights go."

Even as he spoke, the overhead panel flickered and died. Silence gasped and clutched at Chase Mago's arm, totally disoriented. Then the weak emergency lights faded on, casting a pale blue light on the room.

"Move," Balthasar said again, and kicked open the door.

They hurried into the corridor, Silence clutching the bag which held her starbooks. They were halfway to the emergency exit before she realized she had forgotten her heylin. She slowed, and Balthasar caught her wrist, dragging her forward.

"My heylin," she cried.

"You can pick up another," Balthasar shouted. His words were swallowed in a new wave of sound, the screeching interference of a ship's keel, tuned to celestial harmonies, skimming along the edge of a planet's atmosphere, clashing with the harmonies of air and earth. Chase Mago caught at Silence's other hand, and pressed something into it. She looked down with a gasp, and saw her heylin.

The emergency exit was unguarded. Balthasar waited until the starship passed overhead and the noise eased, then slammed back the door. The frigid air rushed in, taking Silence's breath away. Balthasar dragged her forward, choking.

It was not yet dawn, but the sky had already grown light, the snow taking on a newly luminous hue. The spotlights were dead, but the landscape was full of bobbing handlights as the assault teams ran to their defensive positions. There were lights on the landing field as well, and a rising cacophony from that direction revealed a number of the couriers were preparing to abandon the planet. Even as she watched, a starship shot up from its blocks, its keel gleaming against the dark sky. It rose steadily, and then, when its keel was barely more than a fleck of gold, it burst apart in a shower of sparks. Automatically, Silence counted to five before she heard the first rumble of the explosion.

The rest of it was swallowed in a new screaming, flattening them against the wall of the installation. In spite of herself, Silence looked up, hands pressed to her ears in a futile gesture. Far above, a slim bronze arrow moved majestically across the stars, red interference flickering like lightning along its sides. As it swept past, the Doppler effect modulated the noise, and Balthasar waved them forward.

They plunged into the snow, Silence sinking nearly to her knees before she found solid footing. She reached instinctively for Balthasar to steady herself, but the captain lost his balance too, and both went sprawling. Chase Mago, taller and heavier than either of the others, was less hampered; he pulled them both to their feet, and the three staggered forward.

A new sound rose overhead, a thin keening that was like a needle striking through the ears to the brain. On the field ahead of them, a courier caught at the moment of liftoff reeled out of control, crashing just beyond their line of sight. Elemental water erupted where it had fallen, a frozen spray roaring up beyond the snow, carrying with it the crumpled pieces of the hull. Squinting up at the sky, Silence could just make out the narrow outline of a naval fifty, the slim and deadly lines of the short-range attack ship barely visible against the fading stars. A second courier rose from the field, and the fifty dove at it, cannons blazing. Balls of brilliant flame exploded to either side, but the captain held the ship steady. Then a shot exploded beneath the courier's belly, and the keel darkened perceptibly. Chase Mago caught at Silence's arm.

"That's Cyrilla, and *Maxixe*."

"Come on, woman, pull up," Balthasar growled. "Pull her up."

The damaged ship nosed down slightly, then steadied, the keel dimming even further. Silence held her breath, willing the Misthian to recover. The fifty's shot had shocked the keel, disrupted the tuning. If the engineer was competent, and the ship lucky, the harmonium could be modulated, the pitch recovered. The fifty dove again, and from the field came the throaty roar of a harmonium forced to lifting pitch before fully warmed.

"Tasarla?" Silence cried, and then the ship lurched drunkenly into the air, rolling to reveal the Misthian's distinctive markings. *Ostinato* rolled again, not toward the horizon and away, but back toward the fighting, spiraling up toward the circling fifty. Gun ports opened along the stubby control wings, and *Ostinato*'s tiny cannon spat defiance. Most of the shots fell short, but one exploded just behind the fifty's silver keel. Lazily, the Navy ship turned, sliding down a harmonic line to meet its attacker. *Ostinato* dove away, scrambling for room to run, but the planetary core was interfering with her tuning. The fifty caught her with ease, waiting for the optimum shot before firing. The balls of light exploded against *Ostinato*'s keel. The metal went dark, and the little ship tilted down, burying its nose deep into the snow just beyond the drilling towers. A moment after the impact, the ice crust gave way, and the nearly-elemental water beneath the surface gushed out, carrying the wreckage with it. The mundane metal of the hull dissolved, but the keel remained whole, caught in the center of the column of ice that formed as the water mixed with and was further contaminated by common air.

"Tasarla!" Silence cried again, and tears stung her eyes, freezing on her cheeks beneath her thin scarf.

"Cyrilla's got away," Chase Mago shouted.

Overhead the fifty circled back to finish its original victim, but the brief respite had been all the time *Maxixe*'s engineer had needed. The courier was already well out of range; the fifty tilted up momentarily, but then its captain seemed to think better of it and abandoned the pursuit. The bronze fleck of *Maxixe*'s keel dwindled still further, and vanished.

"Come on," Balthasar said again, through clenched teeth.

Somehow, they made it through the snow to the field, driven to their knees each time one of the Hegemony's warships passed overhead, dragging its keel along the interference line. A few of the cannon emplacements fired at the great ships, and at the fifty circling contemptuously above them, but the range was far too long. At the edge of the field, they were greeted by the shriek of a courier's liftoff. Balthasar waited, cursing, until it was well away, then hauled himself up onto the warm, ice-free platform. Burdened as she was by starbooks and heylin, Silence was glad of his helping hand. She struggled to her feet, only to be knocked aside by the sudden burst of sound as a courier five ships away started its harmonium. She pressed her hands to her ears, knowing it would do no good, then curled into a tight ball as the pitch rose higher still. The noise struck through her flesh to jar her bones, was reflected by the field coverings; she fought to pull herself upright, away from the vibrating metal, and was slammed down again by the almost palpable sound. Through a haze of tears, she could see Balthasar twisting in pain, arms wrapped around his head.

Then the noise eased a little as the ship lifted, the field no longer thrumming in sympathy with the harmonium. Balthasar rolled over, shouting after the rapidly fading ship, but Silence heard his words only as a thread of sound.

"You son of a bitch, I'll get you for this!"

Silence shook her head, trying desperately to clear the cottony deadness that had settled in her body. She could barely hear Balthasar's shout, could see only dimly, as though through a layer of gauze. Even her fear came slowly, as though it belonged to someone else. I'll never be able to pilot now, she thought, but it was a remote sensation. She became aware then that Chase Mago was shouting at her, his face reflecting the same disorientation that she felt. She shook her head again, and could hear, but her sight remained blurred, her sense of balance askew.

"—all right?"

Silence frowned, digested the question. It took an effort to remember the meanings of the words. No, I'm not all right, she thought, I doubt I can pilot, and I know you can't manage the harmonium—

"We've got to get to the ship," Balthasar shouted again. He was swaying as though he had lost all sensation in his feet. There was blood on his mouth, and he wiped impatiently at it with one gloved hand.

Chase Mago shook his head, still on hands and knees. "Can't."

Balthasar reached for him, almost falling himself. "We have to—"

There was a change in the air around them, and Silence looked up quickly. Three points of white light showed on the horizon, rising rapidly above the low buildings of the original landing field. She could feel the sound of their keel, but could not hear it. She touched Balthasar's arm and pointed.

"Too late."

The captain swung around, stumbling, and she saw the intensity drain from his face. "Marines," he said, so quietly that she barely heard him. She could almost read the agonized calculations in his eyes: ten minutes to the landings, and at least twice that before they could raise *Sun-Treader*, and five more minutes before they were out of range of even the lightest ground-based cannon. There was no place to run, on or off the planet.

The white ships swept closer, changing from mere points of light to the broad-winged silhouette that even Silence recognized as the famous houri-class transports that served the Thousand, the elite troops of the Hegemon's personal army. Two banked away, one to each side of the installation, the crown and galaxy of the Hegemony vivid on the white wings. The cannon fired at them, but the gunners' aim had been destroyed by the constant barrage of sound, the shots falling far behind and to the sides. The third ship kept coming, dropping lower and lower as it came on. Silence stared at it in utter fascination, unable to raise the strength to move out of its path. She could hear the song of its keel now, a fiendish shrieking that cut through the cotton that seemed to close her off from the world. It swept low over the main compound, interference flickering faintly along the edges of its keel, the vibration of its keel shattering the ice that had gathered on the buildings' roofs. She realized her danger then, but could not seem to move. Then Balthasar shoved her forward into the abandoned cannon emplacement, and she fell hard against the gun mount. Chase Mago pulled her out of the captain's way as he dropped beside them, reaching hastily for the gunners' screen. The houri's keel-song struck like a hammer, and Silence lost consciousness.

Someone was shaking her, not gently. Reluctantly, Silence opened her eyes, her body responding as though it belonged to someone else. She was no longer in the protected gun emplacement, but lay sprawled on the warm metal of the field, Chase Mago bending over her. Balthasar crouched beside them, head hanging, in someone's shadow. Silence looked up with a gasp. A slim figure in white cold-world camouflage stood over him, a heylin held negligently in one hand. He had an officer's crescent pinned to his collar. To either side stood two more of the Thousand, projectile rifles trained on them.

"Who are you?" the officer asked, his voice conversational, almost polite.

Balthasar looked up. "Balthasar, captain of the half-and-half *Sun-Treader*."

"And these are your crew?" The officer's voice remained blandly courteous.

Balthasar nodded warily. "Also my wife and co-husband."

"You may surrender, captain," the officer said.

Balthsar hesitated, and the officer smiled. "You were expecting terms, captain?" he asked lightly. "Come now, pirates are lucky to be allowed to surrender—and some of you aren't getting that much." He nodded toward the edge of the field, where bodies lay in an untidy heap, their white cold-weather gear stained red and black. "Do you surrender?"

"Yes." Balthasar dragged himself to his feet, reached down to help Silence. The pilot rose slowly, her carryall banging at her hip.

"Freeze!" one of the troopers ordered sharply. "What's in that?"

"My starbooks," Silence stammered.

"Hand it over," the trooper said. "Slowly, now."

Very carefully, Silence lifted the carryall over her head, held it out to the trooper. He slapped it from her hand, then kicked the lock expertly, spilling the books into the snow. Silence winced as he ripped at the lining, making sure no weapons were concealed inside. When he was finished, he prodded at the books with the toe of his boot.

"What do I do with these, sir?"

The officer looked from the spilled volumes to Silence, then back again. "You're the pilot, woman?"

"Yes."

He sighed. "Keep them for now. If we can't use you, I'm sure they'll be of interest."

The trooper tossed the mutilated carryall at her. Silence caught it automatically, then bent to collect the books. She scooped them up hastily, noting with relief that the bottom of the carryall was intact. The strap was broken, however, and she tucked it under her arm, hugging it tight to her body.

"Let's go," the officer said, and one of the troopers prodded her with the muzzle of his rifle. She pulled herself upright, Chase Mago steadying her, and they began the long march back toward the main installation.

Chapter 6

The Thousand gathered their prisoners in the largest docking shed. There were perhaps fifty men, Silence thought, squinting through the gloom that was increased by the column of sunlight pouring through the single skylight—the Misthian ships had escaped or had been destroyed. The survivors were mostly crews from the couriers that hadn't made it off the landing fields, though once the doors had opened to admit a batch of men captured in space and brought back to the planet for whatever the Hegemony chose to do with them. One crouched against the wall near her, a young man in his teens, who held a bloody rag to his face where his tattoo had been. His wound was the most serious she could see—the Thousand had not bothered with injured prisoners.

"What happens now?" she asked softly.

Balthasar ignored her, staring blindly into the column of sunlight.

"The Hegemony needs star-travellers," Chase Mago said. "It happened on Kesse, when they took it. They interned all the star-travellers they could catch, and bound them to the Hegemon's service—not the warships, of course, but all the support ships, supply, transport, everything. That freed the aristocrats for the fighting."

It made sense, of a sort, Silence thought. The Hegemony was only moderately well-populated, and its aristocracy was tiny. When Jairus III had begun his program of conquest, he had relied on the only trained military men he had, his nobles. The aristocracy in turn had demanded and received the monopoly of military positions in subsequent generations, even though the pressures of war had forced Jairus's successors to allow certain bourgeois into lower level positions, and to draft prisoners into the support ships.

"We might have a chance, then," she said, lowering her voice even further.

Chase Mago shook his head. "I said bound. Under geas."

Silence sat very still, feeling the hope run out of her. A geas was a mental bond, a set of compulsions created by a magus to produce desired behavior; it was unbreakable, and permanent unless a magus removed the restriction. Once so bound, she would serve the Hegemon in spite of herself. "No," she whispered, and that seemed to rouse Balthasar.

"Would you rather be dead?" he asked.

"I'm not sure," Silence retorted.

Chase Mago sighed. "Nor am I," he murmured. "Nor am I."

A final batch of prisoners was brought in around noon, when the last of the smaller warships landed, but it was not until midafternoon that anything further happened. From outside came the wail of a heavy ship making an unassisted landing, balancing itself against the planetary harmonies. The noise was clear despite the baffling of the shed, and heads turned quickly toward it.

"That's a transport," Chase Mago said, listening intently. "Military—a Beacon-class, maybe?"

Balthasar shrugged. "Your ear's better than mine."

There was more noise from outside, as the sound of the harmonium stopped, and there was heavy scuffling around the main entrance to the shed. That was punctuated by the harsh clang of metal against metal, and then there was a sudden, oppressive quiet. Silence rose to her feet, unable to wait passively any longer. The others stood as well, across the shed; most of the couriers' men were on their feet, watching the door.

It slid open at last, not onto sunlight but onto the dulled light of a transfer tube. A detachment of troops, these in the gorgeous dress uniforms of the Thousand, braid sparkling from shoulders and sleeves, stood there, ten troopers with leveled rifles, and a cluster of officers. Among the officers, conspicuous in his drab robes, stood a single magus.

The most senior of the officers, the crimson fabric of his coat almost invisible beneath braid and decorations, lifted a hand. "Attention," he called, his voice carrying easily without amplification. "Under the laws of the Hegemon, the officer corps of a ship of the Thousand may act as a tribunal, and has done so. You have surrendered to mercy; prisoners, hear the sentence."

Silence shivered, saw Chase Mago's face go bleak and bitter. Balthasar's hands twisted together, but then, with an effort, he jammed them into his pockets.

"Because of the necessities of war and through no merit of your own," the officer went on, "the

Hegemon will accept you into the lesser branches of his service, if you accept his geas." A shudder ran through the group of prisoners, a whisper of protest that the officer ignored. He gestured to the sergeant, standing deferentially one pace to the rear of the group of officers. "Line them up."

There were more troops than the ten she had counted, Silence realized. A full detachment, perhaps twenty in all, poured out of the transfer tube, began prodding the prisoners into a straggling line. As they approached, Silence looked around wildly, but there was no place to run. She was not yet ready to give up all hope; she allowed herself to be pushed into place, Balthasar and Chase Mago behind her. At the head of the line was a man she recognized as the engineer of *Freya's Witch*, one of the ships assigned to her formation. The officer beckoned him forward; the engineer moved slowly, like a man in a dream, and the magus lifted a hand to make a complex gesture in the air before him. His words were inaudible, but the engineer shuddered suddenly, shaking his head as though he had been struck. A trooper pulled him aside, shoving him toward the transfer tube and the waiting ship.

The procedure was repeated twice more, the former pirates dragged off toward the transport, but at the fourth man the magus hesitated, frowning. He said something to the officer, and the prisoner laughed.

"No, you can't bind me," he said, raising his voice to be heard throughout the shed. "I spit on you all—"

The officer made a sharp gesture, and the nearest trooper dragged him out of the line, flinging him toward the far wall. Before the pirate could recover his balance, two troopers fired quickly, and he fell. Silence shuddered and looked away, but could not shut her ears against the whip-crack of the coup de grace, and the gentle scuffing of the body being dragged away.

The line seemed to move even more slowly after that, Silence's fear giving everything a nightmarish clarity. Ten times more the magus frowned, and troopers stepped forward to kill a man who could not be bound. The last was the man standing directly in front of Silence, a stolid, stocky man who had served on one of the larger couriers. At the magus's frown, he cried out sharply, but to no avail. His body joined the others stacked against the wall.

Before she had fully realized what had happened, there was a hand on her shoulder, shoving her forward. The magus stared at her impassively, seemingly unaffected by his work, but the officer cleared his throat.

"A woman, Gerik?"

The magus lowered his hand. "As you wish, Colonel, but she is a pilot."

The officer pursed his lips, considering, then shrugged. "Very well. We do need competent pilots."

Silence held herself rigid, suppressing a shudder of fear. He would have killed her, without reason, just for being born female. . . . The magus lifted his hand, drew an elaborate figure in the air. His hand seemed to leave a trail of shadow in the air, a disturbance in the fabric of reality, the submaterial chaos of hell, from which the magi drew much of their power, showing through. In spite of herself, she stared, fascinated, and then the magus spoke. His voice was low, almost conversational, but the words struck like physical blows, beating against her ears like the tolling of massive leaden bells. The force of the geas drowned the meaning; she fought it, grasping frantically for the sense of the words, a knowledge of what bound her.

". . . to obey . . ." She heard those words clearly, understood them with an effort, but in puzzling them out missed exactly what it was she was to obey.

". . . forbidden to think of escape . . ." That she could understand without effort, the words searing across the surface of her mind. To be told not to think of something always had the opposite effect, and the word "escape" struck echoes of resistance deep within her soul. I will think of it, she cried silently, I will free— Pain lanced through her body, worse than anything she had ever felt. She doubled over, moaning, and the next words snapped her upright. She stood quivering, sick with pain, held suspended by the heavy words that finished the geas. Abruptly, the flow of speech ended. Silence sagged forward, tears filling her eyes, and was caught by one of the troopers. He slung her casually toward the transfer tube; she struck hard against the metal connecting plate, and was promptly sick. Another trooper, with an exclamation of disgust, shoved her on toward the waiting ship.

She staggered up the gently slanting tube, leaning against the ribbed fabric, trying to bring herself under control. Her body still ached from the memory of pain—at the thought of it, her stomach heaved—and her mind felt as though someone had woven wires through her brain. She could almost see their reflections, ghostly lines splintering her vision. Then she stumbled over the raised coaming of the entry hatch, fell, and was sick again.

She was lifted by surprisingly gentle hands. "You'll be all right, girl," a voice said.

Silence straightened slowly. The pain had eased somewhat now that her body had vented its outrage, and she was learning to see in spite of her fractured sight. "I don't feel it," she said, and was remotely surprised that she could still speak.

"Brave girl." The speaker was a young lieutenant, barely past his majority, with almond-fair skin and a delicately aristocratic face. But that at least was no surprise, Silence thought. He was one of the Thousand, and the Thousand were the elite of the elite. Each trooper was a gentleman and the son of a gentleman; each officer could prove at least three generations of nobility.

"You." The lieutenant snapped his fingers at a small figure crumpled against the nearest bulkhead. It lifted its head, and with a glad start Silence recognized the boy from the warship, who still clutched a bloody rag to his cheek.

"Come here," the officer continued, still gently. "Help the—" He hesitated briefly, then chose the foreign, noncommittal term. "—sieura."

The boy did look steadier than she felt, Silence thought. I suppose it's because he's so young, he can take this better than the rest of us. That thought sparked a new fear, one she had almost forgotten in her own pain. "My husbands."

"You're married?" the lieutenant asked, looking down at her ringless hands.

Silence ignored him, twisting against his steadying arm to face the hatchway. For a long moment, she saw nothing except the trooper on guard duty, his sonic pistol held negligently at his side, and she felt a wail of loss and fear rising in her throat. She choked it with an effort, shook away tears. I will not cry in front of them, she told herself, I will not— Then she heard staggering footsteps in the transfer tube, and tensed, afraid even to hope it might be one of them. Chase Mago hated the Hegemony too much, Balthasar was born stubborn, resenting any control. . . . The feet stumbled at the hatchway, and she looked up with a gasp.

"Julie!"

The engineer lifted his head, his face chalk white beneath the beard. His eyes were glazed, barely able to focus, and he moved with aching precision. Silence pulled away from the lieutenant, desperately ignoring her own pains, and stumbled forward to catch Chase Mago's arms. They leaned together, each supporting the other, and Silence could no longer restrain her tears. Chase Mago rested his head against her shoulder momentarily, then forced himself upright.

"Denis," he whispered. "They took him—"

Silence's face paled again with fear, and the engineer shook his head violently, almost unbalancing both of them. "No, they bound him, he's alive. They're bringing him."

Even as she spoke, there were more footsteps in the tube, and a pair of troopers appeared in the doorway, a limp form held between them. With a shudder that mingled new fear and a relief Silence had not known she could feel, she recognized it as Balthasar.

"Lieutenant Marcinik?" one of the troopers called. "This one's marginal, but the colonel said to try it anyway." They dropped the body unceremoniously onto the decking.

The lieutenant frowned, but said nothing, and knelt beside Balthasar. "You may go."

The troopers saluted as one, and headed back toward the docking shed. Silence gently freed herself from Chase Mago's grasp—the big engineer was wavering badly, and she herself could feel a new dizziness sweeping over her—and knelt beside the lieutenant.

"Will he be all right?"

Marcinik looked up. "I don't know," he said simply. "There are those who can be bound, but will not live under geas. He may be one of those."

"No." Silence shook her head, fighting a fresh wave of nausea that threatened to overwhelm her. "What can I do?"

"Nothing," Marcinik answered. He beckoned to the boy, who still hovered uncertainly, and both caught hold of one of Balthasar's arms. "I'm sorry," he added, as they dragged the captain toward a protected corner. Silence followed, and collapsed at Balthasar's side. The captain was pale beneath his tan, and he breathed raggedly, as though caught in a nightmare. She shook him, tentatively, but he did not seem to feel it.

"Let him be," Marcinik said. "Do you understand the geas, how it works?"

Silence shook her head, and saw the lines that speared through her vision crackle and reform. Her stomach twisted at the sight, and she tasted bile.

"Listen, then." Marcinik squatted beside her. "A geas is a compulsion, shackles on the mind. You're bound to obey all our orders—the orders of any of the Hegemon's lawful officers—and not to think of freedom or escape."

Silence shied away from the words. They touched raw places in her mind, places that she already avoided. Marcinik was watching her closely.

"You see? It's already taking hold, you're already adjusting to it. But some people fight harder— Wrath-of-God lays its own geas on its higher officers, for one thing. This one—" He gestured to Balthasar. "All you can do is leave him alone, let him fight through it. Give him water, if you want." He stood up, dusting off his hands.

Silence stared blearily after him. "Will that help?"

The lieutenant did not answer, already moving toward another knot of prisoners. Silence tried to pull herself to her feet, but the walls of the compartment were padded, and she could not get a grip on them. She slid slowly to the decking, and then, not knowing exactly why she did it, wrapped her arms around Balthasar's motionless body. She closed her eyes, and the sickness faded a little. A moment later, there was a new presence beside her, and she felt Chase Mago reaching blindly for her. They clung together, Silence huddled between the two, comforted and comforting, until, mercifully, sleep or unconsciousness overcame her.

She woke slowly, becoming aware of pains in her head and back. She shifted her position, then sat up, and the stabbing pain in her back vanished. The headache remained, dull like an old bruise, but at least the lines that had run crazily across her vision had disappeared. She glanced automatically to either side, saw Chase Mago stirring uneasily. Balthasar, however, lay very still. She caught her breath, reaching for his wrist, and then saw his chest move, his breathing quick and shallow. Water, she thought. The lieutenant said to give him water.

She looked around cautiously. They were in a cargo hold, she realized, or perhaps in a regular transport hold from which all bunk fittings had been removed. Bulkheads and deck were thickly padded, and the surviving prisoners were scattered throughout the compartment, about thirty in all. She recognized some of them—Niko Minda'a, the engineer from *Freya's Witch*; a pilot named Yacesen from one of the armed couriers; another pilot known as Fynn; *Grenadier*'s captain, Audan Verney—knew more by sight as people she had seen around the docking wheels. Minda'a was at the back of a line that had formed at an installation set into the far bulkhead.

"Silence?" he said. His voice was hoarse and croaking; he swallowed hard and tried to clear his throat, but it did no good. "How—?" He nodded toward the corner, where Chase Mago had managed to sit up.

Silence shrugged. "I don't know. Denis—it doesn't look very good."

The engineer nodded sadly. "Arne's going," he said. "There's nothing I can do."

Arne was the captain of the *Witch*. Silence opened her mouth to protest that, but then she saw the misery in the other's eyes. She said, "No. I'm sorry."

The man ahead of them moved away from the machine, and the engineer stepped to the keyboard. Looking over his shoulder, Silence could see that it was a fairly standard model, dispensing ration packets and clear drinking bubbles at the touch of a button. There was a sign above the keyboard, but it was printed in the unfamiliar Hegemonic script. She puzzled over it, then realized that it was simply coine transliterated: "This machine is set for one pack per man per half-day. Do not exceed your share."

Three packs, then, she thought, glancing back to make sure that Chase Mago had not joined the line. The engineer was still huddled against the bulkhead, forehead resting against his drawn-up knees. The machine beeped softly, and deposited three square packets and an equal number of the clear plastic bubbles on its shelf. The *Witch*'s engineer collected them and stepped aside. Silence took her place in front of the keyboard and typed in her request. The machine flashed a message—once again, transliterated coine, gone so quickly that she had no time to work it out—and considered her request. She glanced nervously at *Witch*'s engineer, wondering if something had gone wrong, but he nodded reassuringly. The machine beeped, and produced the rations; she swept them up without looking, her attention caught by a hatch she had not noticed before, set into the bulkhead just beyond the food dispenser. She wondered how many guards were stationed there—

The shooting pain caught her off-guard, stabbing through her belly, then tearing up to heart and lungs. She doubled over, dropping the rations, all thought of freedom driven from her mind. For an interminable moment, her thoughts swam crazily, unable to focus on anything, yet equally unable to free themselves from the topics of escape and freedom. Then, with an effort that was almost physical, she tore herself free.

"One, and it is two," she murmured, forcing herself to concentrate on each word, each apparent contradiction of the formula that described the Philosopher's Tincture. "Two, and it is three; three, and it is four." One was the Stone, from which the Tincture was made. Two exhalations, three principles, four elements. . . . The pain eased further, and she pulled herself to her knees, suddenly aware of the circle of prisoners gathered around her, and of the smashed bubble beneath one hand.

"Oh, no," she said, and *Witch*'s engineer handed her an unbroken package.

"Here," he said, "Arne doesn't need it."

Silence looked up, managed to murmur her thanks, then collected the other packets. The other two water bubbles were unbroken, and the rations, though cracked, were still edible—though she, for one, could hardly think of food without nausea.

"Are you all right?" a new voice asked, and someone else said, "What happened?"

The second question sent her mind perilously close to the danger area. With an effort, she blocked the answer before it was fully formulated—a warning twinge rolled through her body, but the pain was not incapacitating—and shook her head.

"I can't tell you," she gasped. "Think about it—"

She fled, but not before she saw her questioner double up in agony.

Chase Mago was waiting anxiously for her. "Are—"

"Don't ask," she said quickly, and this time the pain was only a reminder. "The geas—"

The engineer nodded. "I understand," he said, and grimaced briefly.

"I brought water," Silence said quickly, "and food, if you're hungry." She was relieved to see the abstracted expression from the other's face.

"Thank you." Chase Mago took one of the water bubbles, sucked greedily at the corner, but waved away the ration pack. "Maybe later."

Silence bit into the corner of one pack, drank her fill, then, her needs met, stared at Balthasar's limp body, wondering how to give him water. He obviously could not suck it from the package. . . .

"Bite it open, then dribble a little on his lips?" Chase Mago suggested dubiously.

Silence followed his suggestion awkwardly. Most of the water ran down the captain's chin, but she thought a little got between his lips. Then Balthasar swallowed convulsively and opened his eyes.

"Denis?" Silence said tentatively, but there seemed to be little recognition in the captain's expression. He reached blindly for the water, and she set the bubble to his lips. Balthasar sucked at it, drained the package, then pushed it away, sinking back with his eyes closed. Silence and Chase Mago exchanged glances.

"I think it's a good sign," he said, after a moment, and Silence could not bring herself to disagree. But she stared dubiously at the captain's still form, hoping that he was sleeping now, not in the trance-like state from which he had just awakened. She glanced over her shoulder, and saw that Chase Mago's attention was elsewhere. Cautiously, she shook Balthasar's shoulder. There was no response, and involuntarily her eyes filled with tears. If he were to die—she pushed that thought away, unwilling to face it.

"Listen," Chase Mago said suddenly.

She listened, glad of the interruption, but could hear nothing except the same continuous low hum of the harmonium, maintaining power aboard the transport.

"What—?" she began, and Chase Mago waved at her to be quiet.

"Shh."

After a moment, she heard it, too. The noise of the harmonium was changing slightly, inching toward a pitch that would take it out of parking orbit toward the twelfth of heaven. And where beyond that? she wondered, then tensed in anticipation of agony. To her surprise, there was nothing, not even the warning pulse, and she warily pursued the thought. Their destination was almost certainly a depot world, where the prisoners—conscripts, she amended hastily, as a thread of pain worked its way from her belly up and around her spine—could be assigned to their new ships. But which was the nearest? She went through the possibilities quickly. Adaba, Iolcos, Sapriportus, maybe Kison or Peiria—those were the easiest roads. She reached half-heartedly for her starbooks, then stopped. There was no point in trying to second-guess the transport's pilot.

"We've left orbit," Chase Mago said.

Silence listened obediently, but her ear was not sharp enough to detect the subtle changes in pitch. The compartment was buried in the center of the ship and the Tincture-impregnated bulkheads distorted the sound; she remained unsure of their exact position until the twelfth of heaven. The keelsong changed—even here she could hear the new notes—and the material objects in the compartment began to take on the peculiar translucence of purgatory. The padding was the first to fade, becoming a little more than a disturbingly unfocused haze floating above the solid metal of the bulkheads and deck. Silence looked away, wincing. It was like trying to look at the greenish shadows left in her eyes when she had stared too long at a sun. She looked down at her own hands, trying to shut out the double images, and saw bones and muscle, ghostly shadows beneath equally ghostly skin.

They were deep into purgatory now, and she longed to be able to see the voidmarks, but they were blocked by the Philosopher's Tincture in the bulkheads. The familiar symbols would be a distraction from, a protection against, the nebulous, unstable world that suddenly surrounded her. She closed her eyes, but that merely dimmed the scene without hiding it; she set her palms against her eyelids, and saw the bulkhead floating behind a screen of intertwined bone and laced blood vessels. In spite of herself, she whimpered, and heard the noise echoed by someone across the compartment.

She turned to look, but something tugged at her elbow. Her carryall, affected at last by purgatory, was trying to climb her arm, to take its usual place on her shoulder. She jerked the strap into place, then drew the bag into her lap, and rocked back and forth holding it, trying to remain rational. She had been warned of pseudo-animation before, but had always sailed on ships too well managed to permit it; she had been warned, too, of the dangers of a blind passage, cut off from the voidmarks that gave purgatory shape and purpose, but she could not remember the remedies. Oh, there were drugs, elixirs to make one sleep and to give good dreams, easing the passage that way, but that was hardly practical now. She suppressed a hysterical laugh, and clutched the carryall more tightly. It was twitching slightly in her grasp, trying to position itself against her hip where it was usually carried. There were other ways, though, but she could not force her mind to focus on them. She closed her eyes again, resting her head on her bent knees, tried to concentrate. Her thoughts skittered away, refusing to become coherent; her eyes were still filled with a confusion of blood and bone and the haze of the decking. In desperation, she reached for the first lesson she had learned as a pilot's apprentice, seven words on the seven significant notes.

In hydraulis quondam Pythagora adinvenit musae qualitates. She had spoken the words a thousand times, had coaxed the correct sequence of notes from child's flute or beaten monochord nearly as often, though her voice was not pure enough to reproduce the tones accurately. The words and music swelled in her memory, shutting out the distorted vision of the ship—and then, too late, she remembered the one warning the teachers had attached to what had been merely a mnemonic for the seven tones. It must never be spoken in purgatory, they had said—it was the magi's there. The words were bound up in the integral connection of ideal and reality, with the manipulation of matter and of the transmaterial. . . .

The words thundered in her brain, and she cowered beneath their assault. *At the organ once, Pythagoras discovered the natures of the muse. . . .* There was too much power behind those words for that to be their only meaning. She couched still lower, her ears ringing with the memory of sound, and suddenly the universe seemed to turn inside out.

She floated suspended in the voidmarks for the Path Between Willows, most familiar of all the star-roads—no, she realized, the marks were within her, she encompassed them, the sinuous path and the drooping trees, the bridge that was a perfect semicircle, curving up over a stream whose depths no pilot could guess, light like fog shrouding it. Around that vision, compressed to a tiny sphere like the image in a display globe, was the transport's hull, and the gleaming iridescent line of its keel. The ship's decks enclosed the hull, and the compartment where she lay swallowed the rest of the ship, and she herself contained it all, and was contained by something she could not recognize. She wailed aloud, and heard the sound echo harmoniously up and down the scale, bouncing from the walls that suddenly sprang up to surround her.

She was seeing by metaphor, she realized, and that thought ordered the chaos still further. It was the only way an untrained mind could cope with a vision of purgatory usually granted only to the magi. Around her, the image of walls grew more solid, coalescing from formlessness into a vision more solid than the voidmarks. It was the reflection of her own mind, she knew suddenly, with an absolute certainty that banished all fear. She turned her attention away from the translucent compartment and its distractions, pushing it away easily now that it was controlled and contained within herself, and studied the illusion around her. Corridors led off in all directions; she was eager to explore them, but she did not know how to move about in this strange new world.

Experimentally, she tried to stand. Her body did not move, but her point of view changed within the vision. She took a step, then another; her body still did not move, but she floated forward along one of the corridors. She took two more steps, peered into a room that seemed to open off the corridor—and looked into a scene she remembered from her childhood. The beach at Olenos stretched before her, oddly elongated, the low waves lacing the dark sand with foam. Seabirds soared in a sky fading toward evening. The perspective was wrong, she realized suddenly, because she was seeing things as she had seen them then, lying on her stomach on the warm sand. Even as she thought that, a new room opened, showing her ten-year-old self sprawled on a towel.

She jerked back, disoriented, and the room disappeared. Do I want to see more memories? she wondered dubiously. There were bad as well as good, nightmares hidden away that she had managed to forget over time. . . . A gap suddenly opened, directly in front of her, running forward as if it would swallow her. She caught a single glimpse of a face in its depths, felt an old humiliation, and then leaped desperately for the far side.

She found herself hanging in mid-air, looking down at a set of concentric circles that resembled nothing so much as one of the ancient forts on Halesa, central keep surrounded by wall after wall, each with its own gatehouse and turrets. The central tower, however, was shadowed, obscured by too many images—the shape of her own body, the voidmarks, the ship—and she looked away quickly, her head spinning. She concentrated instead on the near palisades that surrounded that core. It was more like a garden than a fort, she thought, the stern walls sheltering a luxuriant variety of images. She stared in wonder for a moment longer, and then she saw the destruction to one side.

On the upper quadrant, to her left as she looked down on the image, the outer wall was breached, debris crumbling into the garden behind it. The next wall was breached as well, and the others further in were cracked, shored up with battered timbers and hastily chosen stones that did not match the orderly arrangement of the rest of the castle. Where the walls had fallen, the profusion of images had been replaced by broken things, mere scraps like torn paper. The colors were faded, or ran with blood. Even where the walls had not been broken, the images were misshapen, pale in comparison to others in the other parts of the garden.

The geas, she thought, and was suddenly filled with cold anger. Those are my thoughts, this is my mind. How dare they injure this? She raised a hand, commanded the walls to rise, the color to return to the creatures that lay broken beneath the shattered stones, but nothing happened. Again she ordered it—and felt, far back in the central keep, a wave of agony contort her body. She fell back, spent and shaking. All right, she thought, I can't free myself this way. But I will—I must do something. She studied the plan of the citadel again, and then, slowly and painfully, began to move pieces of the debris, salvaging what she could to build a wall around the damaged parts, protecting the rest of her mind from the alien intrusion. It was not much of a wall, and each stone was set in place with greater effort, but it was there at least. She hung in the sky staring down at her crude handiwork, and suddenly a black whirlpool rose from the keep. She screamed, and it caught her up, sucking her back down into herself as reality asserted itself again.

She was lying on the padded decking, the strap of the carryall twisted painfully around her left arm and shoulder. Someone was holding her other hand. Realizing that, she tried to sit up, but new pain caught at her muscles. She would have fallen, but someone caught her, lowering her gently back to the padding.

"Are you all right, Silence?"

"Julie?" Silence tried again to sit up, and the engineer helped her ease forward. "God, I hurt!"

"I'm not surprised," Chase Mago said dryly. "You had quite a fit."

Silence frowned. Every muscle in her body felt abused—some stretched beyond recovery, others knotted so tight that the smallest movement threatened to snap them. It must have happened while she was trying to rebuild her dream-citadel, she thought. Though how I did that—and exactly what happened—I don't know. She shied away from further probing, more than ever afraid of the pain of the geas.

"We thought we'd lost you," the engineer went on, his voice softening a little. He nodded toward the sealed hatch. "You came through better than some."

Silence turned to look, wincing as the muscles of shoulder and neck dragged against bone, and shuddered. Piled beside the hatchway were bodies, five in all. Only one lay peacefully; the other four were twisted as though they had died in great pain. She shivered again, recognizing three of them as pilots.

"What happened?" she whispered.

"To you, or to them?" Chase Mago asked in return.

"To both," Silence said.

"We were hoping maybe you could tell us," a new voice said.

Silence looked up, saw Verney of *Grenadier* standing over her. She hesitated again, constrained by more than the geas. What she had done—and she was not even sure what name to give it—was something totally new, something for which she knew no precedent, but however she had done it, she had acted in a small way against the geas. And I was successful, she added, hardly daring to acknowledge the thought. Or was I? She waited, tensed, for the geas to strike her down, but the pain was bearable even in her weakened state. Then I did succeed—I weakened it, I think—but I don't dare say so. The soldiers will kill me if they suspect the geas won't hold, just like they did on Arganthonios. But I have to say something. . . .

"Well?" Verney said.

"Give her a minute, Audan, she's still recovering," Chase Mago said angrily.

"No, I'm all right," Silence said quickly. "I'm just not too sure myself. Tell me what happened here, maybe that'll help."

"Fair enough," Verney said.

Chase Mago glared briefly at him, and said, "When we got deep into purgatory, things got pretty bad—this cow only makes about a sixth of heaven, and that means a subjectively long flight. People started acting strangely. You huddled up, kept curling tighter, until all of a sudden you gave a scream and went into convulsions. It took three of us to hold you. And then, once we started to fall out of purgatory, you calmed down a little, and sort of drifted off to sleep."

Silence shook her head. "Where are we now?"

"Parking orbit, don't know where," Verney answered shortly. "What happened to you?"

"What about the others?" Silence asked in return.

Chase Mago shrugged, ignoring Verney's scowl. "More or less the same thing. People started hunching over, and then, one by one, they fell into fits. And then they just died. I don't know why, maybe they just wore themselves out, or their hearts stopped, or something. . . ." His voice trailed off, and he sat still, shaking his head.

Verney leaned forward, and Silence said quickly, "I told you, I'm not really sure what happened." Her stomach tightened in warning—the geas still censored what she said, though her thoughts were freer—and she hesitated, picking her words carefully. She would not be able to tell precisely what she had done, but she could at least explain the vision, and what had led to it. "I remembered the *In Hydraulis*, subvocalized it, and—" she paused again, choosing the phrase with caution "—things turned inside out." Despite her care, she felt sick, already aching muscles tightening painfully along her rib cage. She gasped, "I can't tell you any more."

Verney whistled softly. "The magi use that to preface a lot of their work. Don't you know you're not supposed to use that in purgatory?"

Silence nodded, the pain receding. "It was the first thing that came to mind. It's the first thing a pilot learns."

Verney was looking at her with new respect. "You're lucky it didn't tear you apart." He glanced toward the hatchway. "If that's what happened to them—"

"It wasn't that bad," Silence protested. "If it's so dangerous a cantrip, it should've killed me too." *I know that's not the answer,* she added to herself, though the geas kept her from speaking. *I was able to* use *it.*

Verney shrugged, and Chase Mago said, "Everybody was looking for something to distract him—I was, and Silence says that's what she did. Maybe they stumbled on something else. Something more dangerous, or more powerful."

"That makes sense," Verney admitted. "And maybe being a woman helped her."

Silence nodded thoughtfully. Women were traditionally passive vessels in the realms of power— that was why no woman could become a magus. She had not fought the vision; perhaps that was why it had not harmed her. Verney stood up, wincing, and Silence turned her attention to the engineer.

"How's Denis?"

Chase Mago shook his head. "I can't tell. Still sleeping, I think."

Silence pulled herself to her feet, glad of the engineer's helping hand. Chase Mago had thought Balthasar was sleeping earlier, and the captain had been caught in some strange trance. But when she dropped to her knees at Balthasar's side, the captain stirred slightly, then opened his eyes.

"Denis?" she asked, and reached frantically for a water bubble. Chase Mago set one in her hand, and she broke the corner seal, offering it to Balthasar. The captain sucked greedily at it, then was sick. Patiently Chase Mago wiped up the mess, and then Silence offered the bubble again, ready to snatch it away. But this time Balthasar sipped gently, and set it aside.

"God, that tasted good," he murmured.

"How do you feel?" Silence asked.

Balthasar managed a wry smile, "Terrible."

"How terrible? Do you want anything?" Silence knew she was babbling in her relief, but could not seem to stop.

Balthasar's face twisted. "No, nothing, please. He closed his eyes again, one hand longingly caressing the water bubble.

Silence and Chase Mago exchanged glances, but before either could say anything, the hatch sprang open. Silence started to her feet, ignoring the protests of her body. A detail of troopers entered, two taking up sentry positions on either side of the hatch, the rest, their sonic pistols holstered, reaching for the bodies that lay beside the hatch. They hauled them out into the corridor, handling them as casually as they would their own baggage, and then the sergeant who seemed to be in charge of the group stepped back through the hatch.

"Any more?" he shouted.

There was a murmur of distaste, of tired anger, but then someone, more quick-witted than the rest, called, "Where are we?"

That's the wrong question, Silence thought, and shouted, "Where are we going?"

The sergeant's head went up at the sound of a woman's voice. "You're at Kison. As to where you're going—" His face split into a grin. "Favor for favor, girl. Step out, and I'll tell you."

There was an angry rumble from the crowd, and Silence shook her head stubbornly. "No favor, man. Where are we going?"

"Nothing's free—" the sergeant began, and the young lieutenant, Marcinik, stepped through the hatch behind him.

"That will be all, Dekel," he said. "You are going to Sapriportus, Sieura Leigh, and will be assigned from the depot there." He glanced up and down the ranks of prisoners, then said, "Hasin Viy?" After a moment, the boy from the warship stepped warily out of the crowd. Marcinik nodded at him. "You will be assigned here. Come with me."

For a moment, it seemed as though Viy would protest, but then his head fell, and he walked blindly through the hatch in the lieutenant's wake. The two guards saluted smartly, and vanished after them. The hatch slammed shut again behind them.

The transport remained in orbit around Kison for a little more than three of Wrath-of-God's days, according to Verney's timepiece. Silence spent some of that time prodding cautiously at the edges of the geas, working obliquely toward the forbidden topics, and shying away quickly when she felt the first pangs. Without purgatory to help her, she was unable to attain her earlier vision, but by trial and painful error she stumbled on a way of thought that she could only picture as somehow withdrawing behind the walls she had rebuilt in that dream. Six times out of ten it worked; she could bring her thoughts to the edge of the forbidden topic, and then pull away quickly, with no more ill effect than a momentary disorientation. It was an oddly familiar feeling, almost like a dream of falling, in which she woke before hitting the ground.

But most of her time was spent watching Balthasar. The geas still weighed heavily on him; though his conscious mind had given up resistance long before, from sheer exhaustion, his subconscious still fought doggedly against the restraints. Almost anything, no matter how innocent, could set off a train of thought leading too close to the forbidden subjects, and set off another round of convulsions. He was unable to eat more than an occasional bite of his rations, though his system was fractionally more tolerant of water, but Silence grew more and more afraid for him. If something was not done soon, it was certain he would die—but she had no idea of what could be done, and she did not dare ask the soldiers who appeared at irregular intervals to check on the prisoners.

By the end of the third day, Balthasar had fallen back into a sort of sleep that gave him some protection from the convulsions.

"Maybe this is the turning point," Chase Mago said for what seemed to be the thousandth time.

"Maybe," Silence agreed, but the captain's quick, panting breath and chill skin told another story. Already, she realized, the other star-travellers were avoiding them, much as they had avoided Minda'a and the other men from *Freya's Witch* while Arne Brodny lay dying. She reached for Balthasar's wrist, but let her hand fall back helplessly. There was nothing she could do.

She almost welcomed the sound of the hatch being opened, and the dull thudding of troopers' boots on the padded deck, and turned to face the newcomers. Instead of the usual pair of soldiers, who would make a cursory inspection and disappear, it was a full squad, and Marcinik was with it. He was looking directly at her, and Silence rose slowly to her feet, waiting warily to see what would happen. Marcinik beckoned to two of the troopers, then crossed the compartment, the sound of his footsteps very loud in the sudden quiet.

"What do you want?" Chase Mago asked abruptly, and Silence jumped. The big engineer took a single step forward to stand at her shoulder, his face tense with the effort of holding back the geas.

Marcinik stopped well out of Chase Mago's reach and said, "That man's dying. Do you want to put him through another trip through purgatory?" His voice was very reasonable, but Chase Mago shook his head violently.

"He is not."

"He's still alive now," Silence said quickly; "He may not die."

The lieutenant looked at her oddly. "I doubt there's much chance of him living," he began, and Chase Mago cut in.

"He is our captain."

Marcinik started to shake his head, and Silence added, "And my husband." She held her breath but, as she had hoped, that was an unanswerable argument. Marcinik shrugged.

"As you wish. We lift in an hour."

Despite Marcinik's apparent surrender, Silence remained standing until the hatch had closed behind the squad. Then she sank to her knees at

Balthasar's side. Chase Mago dropped to the deck beside her, his face very pale.

"Are you all right?" Silence asked.

The engineer shook his head impatiently. "I'm fine. What do we do for Denis?"

"I wish I knew."

After a time, Silence felt the first thrum of the harmonium deep in the core of the transport. She welcomed the familiar sound—for all that it would soon reach the twelfth of heaven, and bring them all into purgatory again, it made her feel somehow competent again. She sighed, staring down at Balthasar's unmoving body. If only the illness were physical, there were techniques even she could use to help him. They weren't proper healing arts, of course; those were the magi's province. But, like all star-travellers, she had learned mirroring, the technique of helping another body recover its health. All it required was one healthy body and some training in the simplest meditative techniques; healer and healed established a rapport, and the sick or injured body inevitably sought to reach the state of the other. It was a pity minds could not be cured so easily.

And then again, why not? she asked herself suddenly. Mirroring couldn't heal the illnesses of the mind, but the geas was hardly an illness. Surely Balthasar's mind would seek to copy her accommodations. . . . If it still could, she reminded herself firmly, ruthlessly choking all hope—but he will die anyway, something whispered within her. It may not help, but he's beyond harm.

It was that thought that galvanized her. She wrapped the strap of her carryall more firmly around her upper arm and shoulder, so that the pseudo-animation, when it came, would not distract her. She looked around then for Chase Mago, but the engineer was already huddled against the bulkhead, head down and eyes closed, braced for the trip through purgatory. She opened her mouth to call to him, but realized suddenly that she could not—did not dare explain what she would attempt. If he told her it was impossible, and he could only tell her that, because there was no other answer, she would never have the courage to make the attempt. She let her mouth fall shut, twisted her hands together in her lap to try and still her fear.

"Denis," she whispered, "if I hurt you, I'm sorry." She knew he didn't hear, and she was suddenly struck by the memory of the twisted bodies flung against the bulkheads. If Balthasar died now, it would be in pain, and at her hands.

She shivered, then put aside the thought, forcing the calm that was the first stage of mirroring. She loosened her hands, laid them flat against her thighs, slowed her breathing until she reached the drugged rhythm of sleep. They were approaching purgatory, the first shadows appearing in solid objects, and she fought new fear. She did not know how purgatory would affect mirroring—so the rapport will be established before we reach the twelfth, she told herself. Already she was in the semi-trance; now all that remained was to gather Balthasar to her. She took his hand, held it lightly between her palms. The captain did not stir, but she had not expected it. There were words that would reach even an unconscious man, when spoken on the proper note and when the speaker held the proper symbols in mind. She said them now, pitching her voice low and clear, and felt the pins and needles tingling along her limbs. The rapport of the body had been reached, but she could not sense his mind. She opened her eyes cautiously—they were into purgatory now, she saw without understanding— and saw Balthasar's face blocked by shadow.

The geas? she wondered. No, not that ... but I don't know what it is.

She spoke the words again, but nothing happened. Balthasar's mind, the part she had hoped to reach, remained remote. She took a deep breath, then had to work to recover the even rhythm that would reinforce her semi-trance. There was only one thing to do, and she had known from the beginning that it would come to this. Marshalling her strength, she recalled the *In Hydraulis*.

The seven words and seven tones echoed in her thoughts, but the sudden reversal of reality was less disturbing this time. Once again, she seemed to encompass everything—voidmarks, ship, compartment—and herself to be enclosed within the citadel of her mind. But there was something else, not within her, but linked, a second being that also surrounded the cosmos, and yet did not contain her. Near the center of herself, she saw Balthasar's body stir in pain, and felt that pain reflected in a shadowed cloud that loomed at the periphery of her vision. Somewhere within that was her captain, or some metaphor of his self that would give her a key to saving him, but she could not bring herself to probe deeply. The shadows loomed ominously; it was all she could do to look at them.

But I have to do something, she thought. Remembering her own vision of the fortress, she thought of leaping, and once again found herself floating above the vision of her own mind. A quick glance showed her repairs holding, some of the broken images slowly creeping about again, showing a pale flush of new color. There was comfort in the sight, and she turned her attention outward. Somehow she had to break through the dark barrier, but when she willed herself into it, nothing happened. She tried the words again, trying to create the mirroring from within, but they fell worthless, less than nothing.

For an eternity she hung there, even the broken citadel of her own mind a mockery of the dark shrouded mind beyond her reach. Then at last, because she had to say something, having come this far, she groped for words, not knowing his fears, but drawing on her own.

"Denis," she said, "acceptance is deception is resistance."

It sounded feeble even as she spoke, but shockingly, the clouds beyond were ripped away as though by a hurricane wind. She caught a sudden glimpse of an iron tower rising from a sea of flame, and a tiny, twisted figure falling, always falling toward the leaping tongues of fire, and then she was swept away, back toward the center of her fortress and through that to reality. But as the double vision faded, she thought she saw clouds open and a torrent of rain.

Chapter 7

This time, her waking was not so painful. She had fallen forward onto the padded deck, arms and legs crumpled beneath her, but her muscles did not refuse to function as she pulled herself to her knees. She had been dragged or pushed away from the spot where Balthasar lay, and a crowd of men surrounded him. Her throat tightened painfully, and it was all she could do to force herself to look at the frieze of backs.

"Julie?" she said, and hoped he wouldn't hear.

"Silence?" To her surprise, the engineer detached himself from the group and knelt beside her. "Are you all right?"

Silence felt hope stir again. "I'm fine," she said. "What happened?"

Chase Mago grimaced. "I'm not sure, exactly. Denis—we were about halfway through purgatory, I guess, when all of a sudden he screamed. He went off into a fit I was sure would kill him, but

then it stopped. He opened his eyes for a minute—
Silence, I'm sure he was all right then, sane and
well—and then he went to sleep." He added, with
an accusing glance at her, "You had passed out
long before this started."

Silence ignored the accusation. With the engineer's help, she pushed her way through the group
and knelt at Balthasar's side. He looked a little
better than he had—no longer quite so pale, the
harsh lines eased a little—but he still lay disturbingly still.

"Denis?" she said softly, and to her amazement,
the captain stirred a little. "Denis," she said again,
oblivious to the stares of the other star-travellers.

Slowly, Balthasar opened his eyes. Chase Mago
was right, Silence realized, the captain was freed
of whatever compulsion had driven him to throw
himself against the geas. She felt tears on her
cheeks and smiled through them, suddenly afraid
that Balthasar would see and misunderstand. "Are
you all right, then?" she whispered.

The captain's gaze was fixed on her, an odd
expression, half curious and half ashamed, on his
face. "Tired," he managed after a moment. "Very
tired." Even as he spoke, his eyelids flickered. Silence touched his hand, then looked up at the ring
of suspicious faces. Yes, she thought, damn you, I
did this for him, and not for you or yours—but I
didn't know how, not until I did it, and I doubt I
could do it again. To her horror, she found herself
crying again, the sobs choking her as she fought to
keep from wailing aloud.

"Leave her alone," Chase Mago said angrily, and
Silence reached blindly for him. The engineer folded
her in his arms, settling her head against his
shoulder. "It's all right," he murmured. "Shh, now."
Dimly, Silence felt the movement of his beard along

her head as he glared up at the others who surrounded them. "Later, all of you. She's dead tired."

Huddled against the coarse cloth of Chase Mago's
jacket, Silence heard Verney mumble something
and move away. Then, for the first time since she
had left Secasia, she gave herself up to weeping.

Chase Mago shook her awake a few hours later,
stifling her automatic protest with a quick, "We're
landing."

Silence rubbed her swollen eyes. Landing meant
Sapriportus and the depot, meant that they would
all be made a part of the Hegemon's Navy. She
fought back her rebellion, her guts twisting with
the geas's warning, and tried to picture what was
waiting for them on the planet's surface. Her grandfather had traded primarily within the Rusadir,
only occasionally with worlds on the outskirts of
the Hegemony. Despite all the stories she had heard
in apprenticeship, she could not imagine an entire
world given over to docks and fleets of starships.

The sound of the harmonium, unnoticed until
now, wailed with sudden dissonance, then stopped
abruptly. The transport settled with a jolt into its
cradle. Silence winced, thinking, I could do better
than that. And I may have to. Slowly, she pulled
her carryall to her, wrapping the shoulder strap
painfully tight around her forearm, her free hand
tracing the shape of the starbooks. The deck jerked
lightly beneath her feet: they were being towed to
a hangar.

The towing seemed to take forever, but at last
the gentle rocking stopped. A stillness almost tangible fell on the compartment, each man staring at
the hatch as if mesmerized by its rounded surface.
The quiet deepened, and then was broken by a
faint scuffling. Silence turned with a gasp, and
saw Balthasar on his feet, leaning heavily against
Chase Mago. She moved to take his other arm, and

the engineer seemed glad enough to shift some of the burden to her. Balthasar was more awake than he had been; he glanced apologetically at her as she settled his arm across her shoulder.

The hatch popped open, admitting a fresh detachment of guards. Most of them wore the brilliant blue uniforms of garrison troops, and carried sonic weapons and heylin, rather than the standard shipboard pellet or dart throwers, but there were a few of the familiar crimson coats of the Thousand. Dekel was among them, and Silence looked away quickly, hoping he would not notice her. Aside from one raking glance that concentrated on her unveiled face, Dekel ignored her completely.

The officer in command of the garrison detachment—a lieutenant, Silence guessed, but she was not familiar with the sleeve and collar symbols— said something, but he spoke in the Asteriona dialect. At the blank looks, he sighed ostentatiously and said, in coine, "All right, move along. You're headed by processing, so you're better be feeling cooperative."

The pompous bastard, Silence thought. There was an edge to his use of the High Speech—the Asteriona dialect that was the official language of the Hegemon's court—that betrayed his unfamiliarity with it. I'd bet he grew up speaking coine like the rest of us. Oddly, the thought steadied her; she stolidly ignored the stares of the garrison troops, and concentrated on helping Balthasar down the corridor.

The transport's cradle had been drawn up to a raised structure that looked rather like an airlock. However, both the inner and outer leaves of the hatchway were folded back, and the short ramp that stretched between the side of the cradle and the lock itself was open. Despite filters, the air smelled strangely of a mixture of spices. Verney sniffed at it, frowning, and sneezed convulsively. The escorting troopers laughed and exchanged sly remarks. Like their officer, they used the High Speech, but it was coarsened and interspersed with coine. Silence listened impassively, hiding the reassurance it gave her.

Marcinik and another, older, lieutenant were waiting at the hatchway. Marcinik looked oddly at Balthasar, and Silence braced herself for an awkward question, but the lieutenant said nothing at all. He and the older man exchanged salutes with the leader of the escort, spoke a few phrases in High Speech—Silence guessed they were relinquishing control of the conscripts—and stepped back into the ship. Dekel and the pair of troopers who belonged to the ship saluted also, and the garrison officer nodded to his people.

"Kestel ai," he said, and swore at the lack of understanding. "Move along, damn you."

The troopers led them across the short catwalk and into a corridor where the walls and ceilings curved away as though they were walking through a giant pipe. Strips of glass filled with filaments of prisoned fire cast globes of cool light that met only at the edges, like beads on a string. Silence shivered in spite of herself, and shifted Balthasar's arms on her shoulder. Already the captain had grown heavier, his steps less steady; she glanced warily at his face and saw that his eyes were half closed.

"How're you doing, Denis?" Chase Mago asked softly, then grunted as the nearest guard prodded him in the ribs with the muzzle of his heylin.

"No talking."

The corridor ended abruptly in a round doorway that gave onto a glassed-in catwalk that disappeared into a fierce sun glare. Silence winced, wishing she could spare a hand to shield her eyes, then stepped through the linking hatch onto the foottarnished bridge. For a brief moment, the light blinded her, and then the glass overhead darkened slightly and she caught her first glimpse of Sapriportus.

To her left the landing fields, multiple tables over multiple field harmonia, stretched to the horizon, capable of handling perhaps half a dozen ships simultaneously, a small fleet every hour. On either side the tables were bounded by the low shapes of hangars and tuning sheds. To her right rose a tangle of buildings, some towering thirty stories or higher, some no taller than the hangar they had left, all linked by a maze of glass tubes similar to the one in which she stood. All the buildings were patterned along the same dull lines, however, a drab brown facade pierced at regular intervals by small square windows. The glass was mirrored so that no one could see in from the catwalks. Above the tops of the buildings, the sky was unpleasant, a pale yet dirty yellow, veiled by a faint haze. The air smelled even more strongly of spices.

"Kestel ai!"

She had slowed without realizing it, caught despite her situation by her first sight of an unfamiliar world. The guard did not touch her, but glared and shook his heylin, and she quickened her pace obediently.

The catwalk ended in a square doorway that looked almost exactly like the windows she had seen in the other buildings. Two more troopers in the blue garrison uniforms were stationed just inside; as the last of the conscripts passed through, a massive door slid shut behind them, and the corridor darkened. There were muffled exclamations from the conscripts, and laughter from the

gaurds, followed by a demand for quiet. The guards
formed them into a ragged line, cursing in the
High Speech. Silence stumbled against the wall,
and was shoved away by a trooper.

"It's all right," Chase Mago said. "I'll take care
of Denis."

"I can walk," Balthasar snapped and, shrugging,
Silence slipped his arm from her shoulders. The
engineer did the same, but kept a wary eye on the
other man.

The hallway took a sudden turn to the left, and
broadened into a long room, brightly lit, with a
counter at the far end. A gnomish man stood behind it. As the conscripts approached the counter,
he tossed each one a khaki-colored bundle. Silence's
mouth thinned, but she took the folded uniform,
trying to ignore the man's sour glare. A guard
pointed to an open door to the left of the counter,
and Silence followed the other conscripts into a
room filled with desks. Behind each desk sat a
man in garrison uniform, hands busy with complicated machinery. A second guard caught her arm
and shoved her toward the nearest desk.

"Position?" the man behind the machinery said,
not looking up.

"Pilot," Silence said.

The man—a captain, she saw by the sleeve
marks—started and held onto the square of plastic extruded by one of the smaller machines. "A
woman?" he said. "Ozul!"

The lieutenant who had led the escort group
pushed past the line of conscripts that filled the
doorway, and came up, frowning. The captain asked
a question in the High Speech, and the lieutenant,
Ozul, answered quickly. He spoke for a long time,
and Silence guessed he was explaining the circumstances of her capture. The captain sighed and
turned back to his machines.

"All right, girl. Where were you trained?"

"I'm married," Silence said. She had not intended to play her only trump card so soon, so clumsily, but the thought of being separated from the others panicked her.

"Married?" the captain said. "Where is your husband, then?"

"There," Silence said, and pointed to where Balthasar and Chase Mago stood. "Those two."

"Both of them?" The captain stared, appalled, then turned to Ozul. "Get the colonel, lieutenant."

Ozul saluted and disappeared; a moment later he was back, accompanied by an older man with a weary expression that suggested many years of service on Sapriportus. The captain began to speak, using the High Speech, and the colonel cut him off.

"Coine, please, Viotto."

The captain made a face, but complied. "Beg pardon, colonel, but this woman claims she's married, to those two men." He gestured vaguely toward the doorway, and the colonel nodded. "What should I do about assigning her?"

The colonel frowned. "What are you, girl?"

"A pilot," Silence said, and added, "sir."

The colonel frowned even more deeply. "Can you prove your marriage?"

Silence rummaged in the bottom of her carryall, hoping she had not lost the slim card she had been given on Delos. She found it beneath the starbooks, and handed it to the colonel. He scanned the tiny numbers and tossed it back at her.

"Assign them together," the colonel said. "There are enough small ships."

"But—" Viotto began.

"The law states that marriage, even peculiar ones, have to be recognized," the colonel snapped. "Besides, one of the men is probably a pilot, and he can back her up. God only knows what they were thinking when they drafted her, but we have to suffer their mistakes. Make use of her." He turned and stalked away.

Viotto sighed and slipped the square of plastic into a larger machine, then consulted a tattered sheet of paper. "Where were you trained?" he asked again.

"Cap Bel," Silence answered.

Viotto punched buttons on his machine, and went on to the next question on his list, covering everything from the number of years Silence had spent in space to the details of her training. Each answer was recorded on the square of plastic. When at last he had finished, he handed the plastic to her, and beckoned to one of the guards. He caught at Silence's shoulder and shoved her toward the far door. It opened onto a narrow room, where a black-gowned magus waited, hands half-hidden beneath his full sleeves. He beckoned her closer, still keeping his hands beneath the fold of cloth, and she came forward slowly.

"The material," he said, and Silence handed him the square of plastic, not sure if that was what he wanted.

"Sit."

The magus had spoken to the geas; Silence sat, feeling the mental bonds tighten fractionally. The magus turned away from her, muttering over the plastic she had given him. There was a stirring in the air that raised the hair on her neck, and cut through the haze that surrounded her. The magus was reaching into hell, Silence realized, and she shivered in spite of herself. Then he turned back to her, his hands held perhaps a foot apart, a glowing blob floating between them. The air around it was warped, as though it was not air at all but a pocket of something utterly other, a window into the submaterial. But it was his hands Silence saw first. They were brightly colored, clown-like, as though some part of the materials with which he worked had been fused to his flesh.

The magus made a complex gesture, and the roiling mass quieted, took on a semblance of form and color. He reached through the invisible barrier into chaos—as his hands passed through, their form wavered momentarily, as though seen through imperfect glass—and gently plucked at the hovering shape. Obediently, it spun out into a glittering wire, coiling into a double circle. Its color remained undefined, all colors, a mix of all the spectrum that was neither any one shade nor the black that should result from such a mixing. The magus drew his hands away and murmured another phrase, this time using a language Silence could not recognize. The patch of hell contracted to a point the size of a man's thumbnail, and the piece of plastic, now drawn out into a long strand, seemed to spiral out from it. Its color returned to a normal blue, except at the very end. The magus lifted it carefully, and in the same motion looped it around the pilot's neck, beneath the soiled collar of her shirt. The motion, and the touch of the plastic, unpleasantly warm, woke Silence from her daze, but both the geas and the tiny spot of hell dancing at her throat kept her from moving. The magus spoke a final word, and the force of it was like the slamming of a door. The loose ends of the plastic snapped together, and in the same moment the opening into hell winked out. Silence reached automatically for the collar and tugged at it, but the plastic was solid. She could not even find the seam with her fingernail. It hung loosely enough to be comfortable, but the circle was far too small to be pulled over her head. It was the visible sign of the geas, marking her throughout the known galaxy as a bondwoman.

From the processing hall, the conscripts were herded through a series of tunnels to a casually guarded barracks. There, for the first time, Silence, Balthasar, and Chase Mago were separated from the rest of the conscripts, and taken not to the halls but to the upper levels of the building, where a single door stood open on a featureless corridor. Silence looked warily at the little room with its single wide bed and tiny shower compartment, wondering what its usual function was. She jumped when their escort cleared his throat.

"You'll stay here until the Routing Officer finds you a ship. You have the freedom of the buildings, but if you're not here when the assignment comes, you'll miss your chance. Meal train comes three times a day. All clear?" He looked at them and, seeing no response, stepped back into the corridor. The door slammed shut behind him.

Balthasar dropped heavily onto the bed, and let himself fall backward onto the mattress, the bundle of clothes still clutched to his chest. Without bothering to sit up, he unfolded the package, frowning at the many-pocketed coveralls and the equally drab shirt and trousers.

"I'd rather wear my own," he said, and winced as the geas caught an unvoiced rebellion.

"I wouldn't," Silence said shortly. She checked the shower compartment, saw that there was no way to clean her own things even had she wanted to keep wearing the uncomfortable cold-weather gear. "I refuse to deal with anything else until I'm clean."

Chase Mago growled agreement, then looked quickly away as Silence began to unfasten her shirt. Balthasar did not move, and the pilot turned her back to the bed to give herself at least the illusion of privacy. The hot water felt almost obscenely good, after the days on the transport, and she ran the machine through its cycle twice before she felt really clean. At last she unlatched the door and groped awkwardly for the piled uniform. She discarded the coveralls as impractical, but the shirt and trousers fit surprisingly well, if loosely. But that was all right, she decided. The fullness of the material would obscure her sex, and she might be able to pass unnoticed, at least in the Hegemony.

The sun was setting beyond the narrow window, the poisonous yellow clouds deepened to the color of curry. Silence settled herself at the head of the bed, staring out over the low buildings to the landing field, where the strict lines of hangars and sheds were blurred by haze. A ship rose from a table halfway down the runway, but the glow of its keel was quickly lost against the vivid sky. Chase Mago showered, then Balthasar did the same, and both men grudgingly pulled on the conscript uniforms. Silence continued to stare out the window, watching the haze-dulled disk of the sun sink below the horizon.

The arrival of the meal train broke her trance, and she looked around with a start. Chase Mago accepted their ration trays from the homunculus, which was even more crudely formed than usual and, as the door slid shut in his face, ran his hand across the light sensor. The single panel, set high in the exact center of the ceiling, did little to cut the sudden gloom. Silence accepted her tray without speaking, and forced herself to finish the tasteless stew it contained. As she ate, she watched the others. Chase Mago ate with a sort of detachment, as though it was his own immense patience rather than the geas that kept him in check. Balthasar ate cautiously, as though afraid of choking. More than once he raised a hand to his throat, worrying at the collar beneath his tunic. He had fastened the shirt's high collar fully, so that the stiff band of fabric completely covered the circle of plastic. Case Mago had not bothered to hide his, Silence saw. She tugged idly at her own collar, wondering how it could be removed. To her surprise, the geas did not immediately censor the thought.

"Where do we sleep?" Chase Mago asked at last. The emptied trays had been placed outside the door for the homunculi to collect, and night had fallen.

"In the bed, I should think," Silence said. She stared longingly at the landing field, now outlined in strings of multi-colored lights. The vibrant keel of a lifting starship cast a brief pool of rainbowed light across the concrete before it lifted and was lost among the hazy stars.

"All of us?" Chase Mago asked.

"We are married, Julie," Balthasar said. He was still sprawled on the bed, and now he raised one hand to his ear in warning.

The engineer snorted. "Not likely," he said. "Denis, we're under geas. Why would they bother—why would they waste money and men—keeping watch on us?"

That made sense, Silence thought, and waited to see what Balthasar would say. But the captain remained silent and, after a moment, Chase Mago shrugged away the discussion.

"I'm tired," he said. "Call it a day?"

"Let's," Silence agreed. After a short search, she found the window controls and darkened the glass.

It was like and yet unlike the nights they had spent on Arganthonios, Silence thought later, after the lights were out and the three had settled gingerly into the broad bed. Then there had been something of her childhood and adventure in it;

now there was only necessity. She stretched cautiously, trying to avoid the lumps in the thin foam pad that served as a mattress, and heard Balthasar stir beside her.

"Silence?"

"Hmm?" She turned on her side to face him, trying not to steal too much of the sheet.

"What the hell did you do back there, on the ship?"

Silence hesitated, trying to marshal her thoughts. "I don't really know," she said at last. "It was like the first time, like I told Julie."

In the darkness, she could see only the movement as Balthasar shook his head.

Silence lowered her voice even further, tensing against the geas. Its restrictions tightened now in warning, forcing her to choose her words with care. "The first passage through purgatory, from Arganthonios. I couldn't handle it, not without work to do, and— I don't know why, it was the first thing that came to mind, but I said the *In Hydraulis*. And—" The geas tightened painfully; she gasped and finished, "The world seemed to turn inside out, like everything was inside of me."

There was no sound from either man, both waiting patiently for her to continue her story—Balthasar trying to understand what she had said and Chase Mago, who had heard it before, waiting for the next installment. Suddenly it was very important to fight the geas, to tell them everything she had seen and done, to hear their interpretation of it, so that she, too, could understand her own new abilities. The pain in her abdomen grew stronger; she dug both fists against it, nails biting into her palms, breathing hard to master it.

"It was like another place," Silence went on, "like being inside my own mind." The geas twisted through her, and she bit her lip against the pain, glad the darkness hid her face. It eased; she gasped and continued, "I could see what the geas had done. I couldn't get rid of it, no matter what I did, so I tried—" She faltered again, less from the pain of the geas, now fully roused against her, than from uncertainty. "I tried to shore things up, to make repairs. That worked, a little, so then, when Denis was so bad, I thought of mirroring, and tried to do the same for him." She stopped, breathing heavily, while the pain receded. At her side, she heard Chase Mago shift uneasily.

"It shouldn't be possible," he said at last.

Balthasar snorted. "I'm here, aren't I?"

"That's not what I meant," the engineer snapped. "Silence, I don't know how much theory they teach pilots, but when I was an apprentice, I learned that the seven pure tones, the *In Hydraulis*, if you like, control the first seven processes; that the reason you can't call those up in purgatory is that there they're a shortcut to a magus's power."

Silence said nothing, still curled in on herself as the pain eased. Balthasar touched her shoulder gently, then said to the engineer, "So?"

"So it should have blasted her, and you."

Even in the darkness, Silence could hear the engineer's anger—directed less at her, she thought, than at the universe for permitting its rules to be broken.

"And it didn't," Balthasar said, "and I'm grateful."

"Why didn't it?" Chase Mago demanded. "How could it not?"

Silence sighed. I wish I knew, she thought. If I did know—she choked off that thought before it could trigger the geas again. I suppose I should've been blasted by the sight, not been able to control it, make sense of it, the way I did. The other pilots couldn't—Denis couldn't've done it without my help, I'm sure of that. But why me? Why not them?

Because I'm a woman? Maybe—even probably. I'm the only woman they captured, but not the only pilot, not unique in any other way. But why does that make a difference? Or am I just missing something equally obvious?

"Silence?" Chase Mago said.

"What?"

"You're sure—" Chase Mago began, and Silence cut him off.

"Yes. I did what I said I did, and there's no chance I was mistaken about it. I know exactly what I did." She sighed again, anger vanishing as quickly as it had appeared. "I just don't know how, or why."

It was over a week before they were assigned to a ship, and there was little they could do with that time. Balthasar recovered his strength, and at his insistence, they explored a part of the barracks complex. They learned nothing useful, however; most of the others captured at Arganthonios had already been assigned to ships, and the other inhabitants of the barracks seemed to be petty criminals shipped to the Navy in lieu of a jail sentence. Wandering through the empty corridors made Silence uneasy—she was certain that a magus had shaped the corridors, the patterns of rooms, and the proportions of the building to create that nervousness—but she could not dispel it, and even Balthasar was willing to give it up as useless.

The assignment came unexpectedly, toward mid-afternoon on the eighth day. The door snapped back without the preliminary rumble of the wheeled carts that meant the meal train, revealing a stocky man with a bored, babyish face. He was accompanied by a pair of equally uninterested guards, who had not bothered to unsling their sonic rifles.

"Well?" Silence asked.

The stocky man started, and gave her an inquiring glance that turned to recognition. It was a reaction she was getting used to; in the Hegemony, it seemed, clothing really did make the man.

"You've been assigned to the mailship *Bruja*," the stocky man said, and hesitated so long over a title for her that he decided to leave it off entirely. "Come along."

There were no preparations to make. Silence picked up her carryall, which now contained, along with her starbooks, their spare clothes, and the three followed the stocky man from the room. At the door that led to the outside, they were issued cheap filter-masks—Silence saw that the door itself was doubled-celled, like an airlock—but even with the rigid plastic encircling nose and mouth, Silence choked on the heavy smell of the air. The man in charge of the escort gave her another curious glance, but said nothing, gesturing instead for them to enter the waiting groundcar. The passenger area and driver's well were enclosed, and Silence could see the grey disks of heavy-duty filters across the air ducts, but even so, the escort troops did not remove their masks. Silence, the spices bitter on her tongue, was glad to follow their example.

The mailship was docked in a hangar more than halfway down the field, one that could only be reached by turning off the main track onto a narrower access road. That was an excellent indication of the status of the ship to which they'd been assigned, Silence thought, and wondered what sort of supervision would be given them. Then the groundcar passed through the tunnel-like entrance to the hangar, and she put those thoughts aside. She would find out soon enough.

The mailship itself was a miniature version of a Dervish-class naval three, and Silence sensed Balthasar's grudging interest. It was a handsome ship, even more sleekly built than *Sun-Treader*, a long, narrow hull balancing on a massive keel. That remained shrouded beneath its baffles, but she had no doubt it would show the peacock mottling, like oil on water, that was characteristic of the keels cast in the Hegemony. As they went up the ladder at the side of the cradle, their footsteps set off sympathetic vibrations even through the baffling, and Silence could hear the perfection of the tuning.

The hatch stood open for them, and the stocky man paused briefly before beckoning them inside. The hatch opened directly into what passed for the common area, and a man was waiting for them. No, not a man, Silence thought as her eyes adjusted to the ship's dim light, a boy, maybe seventeen or eighteen. At first glance, he was handsome enough, in the overbred way of the Hegemony's inner planets, but a closer look showed the marks of a perpetual frown, and prim lines bracketing his too-thin mouth.

"What the hell are you staring at?" the boy demanded abruptly. He had the voice to match his looks, high-pitched and querulous, with the trace of an aristocratic stammer.

"Nothing," Silence said, and added, as the boy's eyes narrowed, "I beg your pardon."

At the sound of her voice, the boy's face changed. His expression went from anger to surprise, and then to recognition as he looked more closely. "Take off that filter."

Silence had not realized she was still wearing it. She snapped free the strap and lifted off the stiff cup, bracing herself for the comments. I should have brought a veil, she thought, or at least a scarf. Or even been a little coy about taking the damned filter off, at least in front of an inner systems boy. This is a bad way to start out.

The boy looked her up and down again, recognition fading into a contempt that he did not bother to hide. Silence flushed, and the boy sneered. "A woman, Makai?" he demanded, turning to the escorting officer. "I take this as a personal insult."

Makai took a deep breath, but answered mildly enough. "They are a married triple, sir. Legally, they can't be broken up."

"And what earthly good is she?" The boy glared at both of them. "Well, girl?"

I'm at least ten years older than you are, boy, Silence thought. She said, "I'm a certified pilot. I hold papers from the Rusadir and the Hegemonic examiners."

"Ha." The boy scowled at her, daring her to say more.

Makai said, "That's correct, sir. They were the crew of one of the pirate couriers, captured at Arganthonios. They're an experienced crew, according to Processing; they should be a great resource."

For an inexperienced officer, Silence thought. She could feel the effort it had taken for Makai not to say those words.

The boy made a face. "Let me see the records."

Makai prodded Silence—the nearest of the conscripts—forward, and the boy caught at her shoulder, pulling open the collar of her shirt. Silence flinched, but forced herself to stand still as the boy pulled a small box from his pocket. He fitted the slotted end over the ring of plastic and ran it rapidly along the lengths of the circle. A minute screen lit, but the boy was not looking at the words that flashed across it. Silence ignored the direction of his gaze and, after a moment, the boy looked back to the screen. He repeated the process with Balthasar and Chase Mago, running the reader along the collar to get a quick summary of their records.

"It would be a pity to miss the job they've lined up for you, sir," Makai said, after a moment.

The boy's head snapped up. "You think I won't do my duty? But I won't forget this insult."

"Very good, sir." Makai's voice was a little ragged, and his color had deepened. "Acting Lieutenant the Right Worthy Esege Druta, this is your crew, conscripts under his Most Serene Majesty's law and mercy. Treat them accordingly." He snapped a salute that was a little too precise to be sincere, turned on his heel, and was gone, his troopers clattering at his heels.

Acting Lieutenant the Right Worthy Esege Druta, Silence thought. She did not dare glance at either of the others for fear she would laugh. He was no more than a midshipman, for all his title, and as for that, Right Worthies were dirt common. Even planetary governors ranked higher than that.

Druta's lips were thinned. Clearly, he had wanted to make something more of the ceremony, or at least of the recitation of his titles. "Very well. We'll begin by assigning you cabins—separate cabins. I'll have none of these Fringe World perversities on this ship."

Balthasar made a strangled noise, turned it into a convincing cough.

Druta glared at him. "You'll have the first three compartments, the first two, and then the one on the right side of the corridor. Engineer, take that one. It's closer to your work."

Silence glanced in the direction of the boy's grand gesture, trying to picture the plan of the ship. *Bruja* had a long, narrow hull that widened toward the stern, and it looked as though the commons ran the width of the ship. A single corridor ran aft from the commons, and she thought she could see, at the end of it, the lighted hatch of the engine room. Which meant that the cabins were arranged to either side of the corridor, and that in turn meant that Druta was giving them the smallest and least comfortable cabins on the ship.

"And one more thing," Druta said. "I want to observe the decencies as much as possible. You, pilot—Leigh, is it? Don't address me directly unless it's an emergency, or ship's business. Anything else should go through your husband—husbands." He turned away before Silence could think of a response.

It was almost funny, Silence thought that night, after Druta had finally given them permission to retire together to Chase Mago's cabin to read over the ship's various manuals. The boy was a horror, and she dreaded spending even another hour on this ship, but at the same time his malice was so comprehensively juvenile that it was robbed of some of its force. She had worried about being the only woman on an otherwise all-male ship, but she had not expected this low-comedy harassment. She glanced involuntarily at the open door—Druta had insisted on that, before going to his own cabin, one of the two large compartments at the far end of the corridor—and Balthasar snorted.

"Keep the door open—what the hell does he think we're going to do, anyway?"

Silence shut her mouth on the obvious answer. She did not want to bring up the subject. "What worries me is what's going to happen when we have to start giving him orders."

"When you have to give orders, you mean," Balthasar said. "You'd think he never saw a woman before."

Chase Mago looked up from a dog-eared engineering text. "He probably hasn't, at least not unveiled." At Balthasar's exclamation of disgust, the engineer closed the book and leaned forward, lowering his voice. "Look, this Druta's not highest caste, but one rank under—not of the Thousand, but the Ten Thousand. And those people raise their children even more strictly than the Hegemon does, just in case they can move up in rank. I've seen a lot of them, when I was younger. They've got strange ideas of what's due to their rank, and of the places of women and commoners, and we'd better remember that."

"And he's a bad one to start with," Balthasar muttered.

"Right. So you'd better watch your step, Denis." Chase Mago's expression changed, was slightly embarrassed. "But it's you I'm really worried about, Silence."

Silence sighed. "He's what? Sixteen, seventeen? He's a child. I can handle him."

Silence had expected it to be several weeks before their cargo arrived. The next morning, however, as she tossed the last of the breakfast dishes down the disposal chute, the buzzer sounded and, at the same moment the hatch slid back. A tall man stood framed against the yellowed sunlight that filled the hangar, his face in shadow.

"Captain Druta, girl."

Well, I suppose this counts as ship's business, Silence thought, and was not sorry to have an excuse to irritate the boy. "Yes, sir," she said, and crossed to the intercom plate. "Captain?" she said, and cut off his outraged answer. "An officer to see you."

Druta's face, when he emerged from his cabin, was thunderous, but he did not address Silence. "Welcome aboard, colonel."

"Thank you." Now that the man was no longer silhouetted against the light, Silence could read the insignia, silver against the black of his uniform. He was a colonel of the Left Hand, almost a magus, one of the men who did most to enforce the Hegemon's will. They were not quite spies, not quite police, not quite soldiers, but a little of all those, and something else besides.

"I am Colonel Gyasi, as you no doubt know," the man went on, and his smile did not quite take the edge off his words. "I assume you are ready to transport me and my equipment to Castax as soon as possible?"

"Yes, sir," Druta said.

"When will that be?"

For the first time, the midshipman faltered. "I'm not sure, sir."

"Well, where's your pilot?" the colonel asked.

Druta made a face when he thought Guasi wasn't looking. "Here she is, sir."

For the first time, Gyasi seemed to see Silence, and she flushed under his gaze.

"Well, pilot?" Gyasi prodded.

Silence gathered her thoughts hastily. She had not had to plot the first leg of a course since joining *Sun-Treader*, but she was not willing to admit that she was out of practice. "To Castax? That's always a tricky run, from this angle. I'd have to consult the astrologers to be sure."

"Do so," Druta snapped.

Silence retreated to the control room, closing the hatch behind her. For once the astrologers were not busy; one worked out the optimum time for departure, when the other planets in Sapriportus's system would create the least interference. Silence keyed the information into *Bruja*'s unfamiliar console, setting up the Ficinan models. They could lift that day, but the line of departure was clouded by the swift-moving innermost planet. The next good time was two days later, when the innermost world would have moved far enough along its orbit to free *Bruja*'s course of most of the interference. The other planets would be in favorable positions then, too. That was the optimum time to lift, and they would need to file notice of their departure immediately. Unless, of course, a Colonel of the Left Hand had high enough priority to win them a space regardless. There would be plenty of common traffic trying to get to a world like Castax. She sighed and returned to the commons, interrupting a low-voiced discussion between Gyasi and Druta. Ignoring the colonel's smile, she explained the situation.

"I don't think you need to worry about competing traffic," Gyasi said. "Castax is under siege."

Under siege. For a moment, the phrase did not register, and then Silence looked up with a gasp. Castax, the most important center for manufacture and the arts on the Fringe, second only to Delos in wealth and influence, was under attack. But Castax was controlled by a merchant dynasty, she thought. How could they have managed to anger the Hegemon enough for him to declare war, when Delos and Athos Maria and all the other opposition worlds haven't done it? Or has the Hegemon decided to start his attack on the Fringe?

Gyasi said, "You might be interested to know that Wrath-of-God is the cause of this war—indirectly, of course, but a number of your ships, driven off at Arganthonios, fled to Castax. When the governor refused to surrender them, the Hegemon had no choice." He turned to Druta. "May we begin loading, captain?"

The rest of the day was spent in stowing the colonel's equipment. At least he had not said it was light, Silence thought bitterly, rubbing her back with bruised fingers. The homunculi had done most of the work of bringing it aboard, but *Bruja*'s cargo space was strictly limited, and Gyasi warned them that seven of the dozen crates contained cargo unusually sensitive to harmonics. Chase Mago had had to shift the heavy crates from one compartment to another, then back again, balancing various materials against each other before he thought the ship was in tune. Silence left the engineer staring dubiously at the last set of crates, stowed now in the empty midships cabin in hopes that the extra baffling in the cabin partitions would help shield the contents, and headed for the common area. Balthasar had quit some hours before; she glanced into his cabin in passing, and saw him sprawled asleep, still recovering from the geas.

In the commons, Silence chose packets of bulk rations from the storage cells above the galley console and fed them into the machine. She switched on the machinery and began to drag the folding table and benches out of the deck recesses. From things Chase Mago had said, she gathered it was a matter of high status to have a woman doing the menial labor, and low status to be forced to let a woman do a man's job. She smiled wryly. At least her piloting was an insult to the midshipman.

The console beeped to let her know that the food was properly reconstituted, and she switched it over to a holding mode. Druta appeared almost instantly, then Balthasar and Gyasi. For a moment, it seemed as though Druta would insist that she wait on the table, but at the last moment Gyasi's raised eyebrow and hint of a smile stopped him. The two Hegemonic officers took their place at one end of the table; Silence and Balthasar sat at the other.

"Julie's still settling those crates," Balthasar said quietly. "He asked me to keep dinner warm."

Druta was frowning down the length of the table. Silence contented herself with a brief nod in response. Balthasar made a face, but said nothing.

"Surely you can't afford to keep to the strict rule

on a ship this small," Gyasi said. There was an indefinable edge to his voice, partly malice and partly condescension, that made Druta wince.

"I'd like to observe the decencies as long as possible."

"A pity. I dare say the sieura would be a fascinating conversationalist."

Silence was suddenly aware of the colonel's eyes on her, and it took an effort of will not to return the stare. Gyasi's thoughts were as clear as if he had spoken aloud: a magus's trick. *Interesting, not pretty. But you'll do.*

Gyasi had not bothered to hide his thoughts from the others. Druta was blushing, and Balthasar's expression was furious. It's odd, Silence thought, tensed against his next words. Not five minutes ago I was prepared to appeal to the colonel against the boy. Now I'll have to play the boy against the colonel.

"I hope I can persuade you to rescind your ban, captain," Gyasi went on. "As a personal favor."

Druta shrugged, attempting to recover his dignity. "If you wish it, colonel, of course. Leigh, you may speak when you want."

"Thank you," Silence said, and could not keep the bitterness out of her voice.

Gyasi smiled as though her anger pleased him. "Are you a Misthian, Silence?"

"No." Silence turned her attention to the uninteresting food, forcing herself to eat.

"Have you been married long?" Gyasi adopted the falsely interested tone of an oligarch making conversation with the child of a client.

"I suppose."

"That's hardly an answer," Gyasi said, and there was steel beneath his smile.

"Three years," Silence lied, and immediately wished she hadn't. Gyasi would know her record.

"So long?" The tone made the colonel's disbelief clear, and Balthasar stirred restlessly. Silence kicked him beneath the table, and the Delian subsided.

"It must be—" Gyasi hesitated with mocking delicacy over his choice of words "—interesting to be married to two men at once."

Suddenly, Silence had to stifle a laugh. Interesting, indeed, but not in the way Gyasi thought. But she could not reveal that truth.

Balthasar said, his voice under tight control, "Captain, will you allow him to ask a married woman questions like that?"

It was a good try, Silence thought, but not good enough. Druta was not going to be strong enough to stand up to Gyasi—how could he be, she thought, a mere acting lieutenant in his first command, opposing a colonel of the Left Hand? She felt momentarily sorry for him.

"Excuse me, please," she said, before either Balthasar or Gyasi could speak.

"Oh, don't go yet, sieura," Gyasi said. His eyes were fixed on Balthasar, and Silence saw the Delian pale. "Your—husband—has just warmed to your defense. Don't you want to stay and see the outcome?"

"No." Silence shoved her plate viciously into the disposal slot and turned to leave.

"Very wise of you," Gyasi went on, raising his voice slightly to be sure she heard. The pitch changed slightly, and there was something in it that stopped Silence in her tracks. "When you consider this one's past, you're wise not to rely on him."

He had not spoken to the geas, Silence realized, but to something else, the shameful curiosity that lurked in every human being, the desire to know the worst about others. He had used some magus's trick to evoke that, and Silence found herself rooted to the spot, listening against her will. Bleak with anger, she fought for enough freedom to turn to face him, if she could not turn away.

"You would expect at least courage in a pirate, sieura," Gyasi said. "But what's this I see? Twice, now, you've surrendered, when a better man might have fought."

"And died," Balthasar whispered.

"Once, I grant you," Gyasi said, with easy magnanimity. "On Arganthonios. But off Wrath-of-God, after your ship blew apart? You were the only survivor, I see—and why were you in a spacesuit, when none of the others were? The only survivor . . . but I don't see you summoning aid. No, you cowered in your pilot's bubble until the salvage teams found you. You would have let yourself die, simply because you were too afraid of death to go down one ladder and send the message that would save your life. It's no wonder you've never set foot on a warship since, you who were in line for command—but is that shame, or more fear?"

"Stop!" Silence fought free with a gasp; her voice shattered the colonel's spell.

"But of course," Gyasi said. His voice was tuned differently now, conceding temporary defeat. "I merely thought you should know the kind of man you've bound yourself to—and what I said is true, isn't it, Balthasar?" His voice held a sudden echo of the earlier, commanding tone. Balthasar winced, but said nothing. He did not need to; his answer was plain.

"Excuse me," Silence said again, her voice tight with anger. She spoke to the boy, not to Gyasi, and after a moment Druta nodded dismissal. She stalked from the common area, and Balthasar followed.

At the door of her cabin, she hesitated. Balthasar

was there, his face wintery. He made a wry face and said, with a painful attempt at a normal voice, "I suppose I should explain. I guess I don't have to say it's true."

"No," Silence said. "You don't have to tell me anything." Balthasar remained standing there, and she held out her arms awkwardly. As awkwardly, Balthasar came into the embrace, resting his head finally against her shoulder. Silence held him for a long moment, until the thought of Gyasi prompted her to edge back into the cabin, freeing one hand to touch the door latch. The motion made Balthasar start and pull away. Silence sighed and settled herself on the bunk, the only piece of furniture in the cabin.

"Sit down," she said.

Balthasar shook his head. "I owe you an explanation."

"You don't," Silence said again.

"He's right, of course," Balthasar went on, as if she hadn't spoken. "That's the worst part—everything he said is true. But that's not the whole of it, Silence, I swear. I admit, I couldn't make myself go down to the control room, and it was because I couldn't stand seeing what was left of my friends. We'd already lost so many, there'd been so much death, that I couldn't take any more." He stopped, managed a dry chuckle. "But you'd probably rather just hear what he left out."

"I didn't say that," Silence began, and Balthasar continued heedlessly.

"What happened was I was chief pilot on one of the warships—I was co-opted by Wrath-of-God when I was sixteen, off a freighter they took. And I was next in line for command. Off Athlit, a squad of Navy ships jumped us, two threes and a five to our four. We got lucky and managed to make it into purgatory ahead of them, and there's nobody who knows how to use purgatory like a pilot trained by Wrath-of-God. We got away, but I'd taken us pretty far afield. I brought us out of purgatory on the far side of the station, under the wave itself. The harmonium blew and the hull cracked. Everybody else was killed."

He sighed. "I was in a spacesuit because I couldn't stand to look at one more maimed or dying man. The helmet was a good blinder. The rest he told you. I couldn't bring myself to go down to the control room and call for help, so the salvage tugs took their time coming for the ship. They spent five and three-quarters hours; I had air for six when the hull went."

"They took away your command?" Silence asked, when it became clear something was expected of her.

Balthasar shook his head. "They offered me a ship, a three. I turned them down."

Silence sighed, not knowing what to say. She touched the cover of the bunk tentatively, and Balthasar came to sit beside her. After a moment, she slid an arm around his shoulders, and the Delian leaned against her, less awkwardly than before.

After a while, Silence said, "We're still here. That's something." There was more she wanted to say, but she feared the geas would stop her. She was surprised that it had not already censored her.

Balthasar looked at her in surprise. "That was what you said, back on the transport. Or something like it." He winced in anticipation, a look of pain that turned rapidly to puzzlement. It was oddly comic, and Silence smothered a smile.

"That didn't hurt," he said slowly. "It should be forbidden by the geas, right? But it didn't hurt."

"I don't know," Silence said. Suddenly, all the

frustration of the past weeks rose to the surface. "If I knew why it didn't, or how I'd done whatever it was, I'd be free by now—" The knifing pain caught her unawares. She doubled over, moaning, then had to fight to keep from being sick on the decking. Balthasar eased her to the toilet compartment, held her shoulders until she was done, then smoothed her hair gently.

"Take it easy," he said.

"Oh, I'm all right now." Silence straightened impatiently, then grimaced as the muscles along her ribs protested the movement.

"You should lie down." Despite her protests, Balthasar eased her to the bunk, pushed her down onto the hard mattress. He hesitated at the door, as though he wanted to say more, but then ducked out.

Silence leaned back against her pillow, closing her eyes. She felt distinctly lightheaded, from being sick and from the aftereffects of the colonel's tricks. And, she admitted to herself, from Balthasar's admitting to Gyasi's accusations. Unbidden, the image she had seen at the very end of the transport's second journey through purgatory rose in her mind, the tower and sea of flame, the clouds and the falling man. This time, it was familiar, an image from the Tarot, one of the oldest, and least systematic, symbolic languages. Her teacher had venerated it because it was old, and had drilled the seventy-eight scenes into her memory. She pictured herself turning the cards, past Magician and Hermit and Death to the sixteenth: the Tower, the House of God.

Set side by side, the images were not as alike as she had thought. The card showed the tower lightning-struck, the turrets in the instant of being blasted away, a pair of figures thrown from its heights. The vision had been different—the tower unbroken but rising instead from fire. Only a single figure fell and, on reflection, she thought she recognized Balthasar's image. The meanings she had been forced to learn did not quite seem to fit, either. The Tower was disaster, catastrophe, occasionally catastrophic enlightenment, not the sort of story Balthasar had told. So that meaning must run somehow parallel to the true significance of the vision. She frowned to herself, and dismissed the remembered card.

She sighed. It was not, perhaps, an important thing, but she could not seem to free herself from this passion for first causes. She let her mind drift, patient in the tangential pursuit of revelation, and let the possibilities wash over her. Flame and guilt were a common enough equation, she was certain first of that. And the tower, like her own picture of concentric walls, would be a metaphor for mind. The falling figure was harder to interpret, unless it merely indicated that Balthasar had never forgiven himself for his fear. You're going far afield, she told herself sternly. There's no way for you to know. But the image spoke of old suffering, and she could not forgive Gyasi for evoking it. Nor will I, she vowed. This is to the death, colonel. She tensed, waiting for the geas to strike, but there was only a fleeting pain.

The thought of vows and undying hates evoked other memories, stories she had heard while an apprentice. She could not remember the plots of the tales that had been whispered among the half-trained pilots, though she thought they had all been much the same, but she could remember the curses. The words were dark, with the gusts of winter behind them, and their shape was hard and bitter in the mouth. She whispered one, savoring the taste.

"Oh, Chaos, Charon, make of him carrion. Gyasi accursed, stands now accused, judge him to die."

The words seemed to echo, for all that she had spoken softly, to gather strength and substance. She could almost see them rebounding from the cabin walls, growing in soundless vigor until they burst through the cabin door and sped down the corridor to strike Gyasi as he sat frowning at his work. The colonel stirred, looked up with a face half alarmed and half surprised. His lips seemed to move in counterspell, and the picture vanished.

Shaken, Silence swung herself off the bunk and went to the door herself. She peered nervously out into the corridor, but there was no outcry from Gyasi's cabin. The safety lights burned unchanged at the door of the engine room; the empty cabins remained sealed up, locks glowing. From the common area came the familiar clatter of a cup held to the spout of the coffee urn. Everything seemed normal. But she had unleashed something, of that she felt certain. She had seen her curse, and felt its power, and the memory of it was cold on her neck. The curse had been real, and the colonel knew she had called it. And, worst of all, she could not know the consequences.

Chapter 8

Silence woke the next morning with a slight ache behind her temples, and a sense of thunder in the air. She sniffed automatically for the smell of ozone and the chill that had always meant a storm in her childhood, before she realized what it was: nothing physical, nothing real, but rather the influence of the curse. She dressed slowly, wondering if the others would feel it, too.

Both officers were in the common area when she finally forced herself to leave her cabin, and Chase Mago brooded over a cup of coffee by the galley console, pointedly not sitting with the others. Silence went to join him, drawing herself a cup of coffee. She wondered where Balthasar was, but refused to ask in front of the colonel.

"Good morning, Sieura Leigh," Gyasi said.

Silence looked up, deliberately matched his stare and held it for a long moment before answering. "Good morning."

"Sieur Chase Mago, you should be proud of your wife," Gyasi said. The engineer gave no sign that he had heard. "She's very loyal—or at least she's loyal to your fellow husband. You'll never guess what she did last night, Druta."

The midshipman looked up unhappily. "No, sir."

"Guess." The word was an order.

"Slapped you," the boy offered desperately.

"Not precisely, though you're right about the general idea," Gyasi said. "The—lady—tried to curse me. Unsuccessfully, I might add."

You're lying, Silence thought, feeling the thunderous air thicken about them. And I know you're lying. My curse is working, and beneath that off-hand pose you're frightened. She fought to keep from showing her terrible elation.

"But how could she?" Druta asked. "She's bound."

"Oh, yes," Gyasi answered, "but curses fall through the gaps in a geas." Druta still looked confused, and the colonel gave a theatrical sigh. "You understand that a geas essentially enjoins obedience and forbids escape?" He waited for Druta to nod before continuing. "Because a certain freedom of action is required, that is all a geas does—it doesn't forbid thoughts of harming an officer of the Hegemon, for example, or even the Hegemon himself. It's assumed that the constraint of obedience will cover any such eventuality. And, after all, in the hands of an untrained person, particularly an untrained woman, a curse is nothing but a malevolent wish, without power."

Silence could almost taste the terrible copper scent of the air, the waiting curse, and she held her breath, sure that something would happen. Then she saw the colonel's hand move surreptitiously, warding off the threat. The tension eased, and she looked around to see if the others had felt it. Chase Mago was frowning slightly, one hand at his temples as though he had a headache, but the midshipman seemed completely unaffected. Silence could not repress a slight, satisfied smile. Then the smile faded. Gyasi might not be willing to admit to Druta that the curse was real, but he would have no cause to conceal that when they reached Castax. What would happen then?

"Leigh," Druta snapped, and Silence looked up quickly. "I think you have duties to see to?"

"Yes, captain," Silence said, glad to make her escape.

Chase Mago followed her to the head of the corridor. "Stay out of his way," he whispered as she passed, and Silence nodded.

That was easier said than done on a ship as small as *Bruja*, but Silence did her best to follow the other's advice. Fortunately, the departure for Castax was only a day away, and she was able to spend most of her time in her own cabin, pretending to be busy with her starbooks. It took her less than an hour to learn the marks for the passage through purgatory—once *Bruja* left the Sapriportus system, the Road of the Travelling Stranger was uncomplicated—and she spent the rest of the time flipping through her books, wondering if she would ever take a ship through some of those paths again. Her eyes turned longingly to the *Gilded Stairs*, and the path to Earth that lay within. Those were ones she wanted badly to fly, if only to defeat her uncle. . . . And will I ever get the chance? Probably not, she thought savagely. And I want to.

There was another warning pain in her belly, and lights seemed to flash before her eyes, wiping out the page in front of her. No, she thought, I won't give in. Instead of retreating from the thought, she held to it defiantly, pushing hard against the limits of the geas. The pain mounted, became unendurable, and she ducked away, fighting to

keep from being sick again. She had a sudden
sense of rushing wind, of falling into her body
again, and then the pain was gone.

She shivered violently, more in anticipation of
pain than anything else. When nothing more
happened, she raised her head, then sat up cautiously. Her mind felt different, and she shook her
head hard, trying to rid herself of the odd tingling.
Carefully, controlling and focusing her thoughts,
she envisioned freedom, thought of carrying a
starship from Sapriportus to Delos, then from Delos to Athos Maria, all at her own desire. The geas
tightened, but it was a remote pain, controllable.
So what have I done this time? she wondered. The
geas felt looser, less powerful, but still very much
present. Once again, she was overwhelmed by
frustration. So close, she thought, and if I only
knew what I was doing—how I was doing it—I
might well be free by now. But all I know is that
it's supposed to be impossible— She put those
thoughts aside with an effort, and was surprised to
find her body tired, as though she had been lifting
crates in the hold. She made a face and stretched
out on her bunk, making her mind a blank, knowing that she would need to be relaxed for the
voyage to Castax.

The passage itself was even less complicated than
she had anticipated. Balthasar handled the tricky
maneuvering required to take *Bruja* out of Sapriportus's system, avoiding the interference set up
by other ships and the other planets. Silence handled only the transition and the passage through
purgatory, manipulating the mailship easily against
the images of sweeping mountains and distorted
shapes that might have been welcoming inns. The
geas made less difference to her perceptions than
she might have expected, though in part she guessed
that this was due to the gains she had made against

it. It was perhaps a little harder to make the images coalesce, but she put that down more to the awkwardness of an unfamiliar ship than to the effects of the geas.

Bruja came out of purgatory easily enough, falling down a toboggan run studded with illusory rocks, and Silence took time to stretch thoroughly before climbing down to the control room. Balthasar and Druta occupied the two couches; rather than risk the boy's reprimand, Silence went on into the common area, intending to watch their approach on the small screen set into the bulkhead there. But Gyasi was already there, and she did not pause, but continued through the common area to her own cabin. She made herself wait, trying to gauge their progress from the slight changes in pitch as Balthasar worked them closer to the planet. She could not judge precisely, but at last the harmonium eased off into the muted, sustained chord that chimed gently with and against the harmonies around it. We've arrived, she thought—she recognized the sound as holding the ship in a parking orbit, working against the harmonies of the planet's core—but she made no move to leave her cabin. After a while, she heard and felt the scraping of a boot against the hull, and then the cabin door slid open.

"Come on then, before Druta comes looking," Balthasar said without preamble. "We're off-loading that colonel."

Silence followed him unwillingly, not wanting to remind Gyasi of her existence, but she could see why help was needed. The air crawled with music, just under and just above the threshold of hearing. The homunculi, sent from the tug to help with Gyasi's belongings, were sluggish, their rudimentary nervous system badly scrambled by the continual unseen presence. It took not only her and

Balthasar, but Druta and finally the colonel himself to get the homunculi to drag the crates to the hatch. Chase Mago was still busy in the engine room, monitoring the harmonium, unavailable. Silence envied him even his job of adjusting the tuning to match not only the nuances of Castax's core but the echos from the other ships maintaining the siege.

"Silence!"

That was Balthasar again, and the pilot collected her thoughts hastily, stepping around piled crates and motionless homunculi to the hatch itself.

"They're setting up a walk-ramp for the homunculi, but they'll still have to cross through an unshielded tube. It seems the locks won't mate properly."

Silence nodded. "Locks rarely do. How're we going to keep the homunculi from shorting out completely?"

"Take this." Balthasar tossed her a control wand, its tip glowing bright red, indicating it was putting out its maximum power. "If you stand about halfway up the tube, and Druta stands at the boat's hatchway, the combined fields ought to override most of the interference. Especially if we send them one at a time."

"Where's Gyasi?"

Balthasar smiled. "Already gone aboard, and waiting impatiently for his stuff."

"Hey!" Druta stuck his head in the hatch, bending forward against the steep slope of the ramp. "Get a move on, Leigh. Surely this isn't beyond a pilot's capacity."

Silence swallowed her answer, and said to Balthasar, "About halfway, you said?"

"I'll show you," Druta snapped. "Come along."

Shrugging, Silence followed him, levering herself through the hatch onto the springy surface of the ramp. To either side and overhead she could see the stars through the transparent material of the transfer tube. She gulped and looked at her feet, but she could still see stars glimmering through the plastic to either side of the ramp.

"Right there," Druta said. "Just keep your wand aligned with ours, and everything will be fine."

I know how to handle homunculi, Silence thought wearily, even if I don't like them, but said nothing. She stepped gingerly off the ramp, settling her feet carefully as the material sagged slightly beneath her.

"Coming out," Balthasar called, and the first homunculus set its ponderous foot onto the ramp. Silence looked up for the first time.

Beyond the transparent tube lay Castax, glimmering blue striped with brilliant cloud. However, in places the blue was dimmed fractionally, the clouds tarnished with shadow. The cause of those shadows floated serenely just within the circle of the fleet's orbit, massive glittering globes the size of small moons. Strange installations and immense bell-shaped projectors rose from their surfaces, marring the smooth perfection, and waves of color washed occasionally across the silver metal: siege engines. Unbidden, lines of song rose in her mind. "The dead shall live, the living die, and music shall untune the sky." There would be a whole ring of those engines around the planet, like beads on a necklace. And on the surface, under a constant barrage of music calculated to disrupt the harmony of the planetary core, to shatter rocks and send seas crashing onto the land, the Castagi somehow survived. And survive they must, Silence thought, or there would be no need either for this siege or for Gyasi's presence, whatever his mission might be.

Somewhat heartened, she tore her eyes from the

engines and looked above and beyond the squat shape of the tug. A line of warships fanned out from the planet, attended by a horde of smaller vessels. The line vanished behind the circle of the siege engines, hidden by the distortion thrown off by the massive constructions. Most of the ships were sixes or sevens, the biggest ships in the Hegemonic Navy, and Silence wondered what made this one attack so important. Castax had never been known to care about anything except its profits; it could hardly be considered a worthwhile object lesson.

The first homunculus lurched past her, crate rocking on its back, and Silence flinched back, almost falling against the soft fabric of the transfer tube. Druta swore at her, but did not dare leave his place. Cheeks burning, Silence pulled herself upright, concentrating on the job at hand. Finally, the last of the crates was transferred to the tug, and the homunculi returned to their place somewhere within the little ship's hold. Druta, still waiting at the tug's hatch, drew himself up importantly.

"I'll be going across to the flagship," he announced. "Balthasar, see that the engineer stabilizes *Bruja* in her orbit."

"Right—yes, captain," Balthasar answered.

Silence made her way back down the ramp, then waited patiently while the hatch was sealed and the transfer tube retracted. The tug detached itself from *Bruja*'s hull with painful scraping, and then the starship was silent, except for the faint thrumming of the harmonium.

"Little bastard," Balthasar said.

"Is there anything we can do to help Julie?" Silence asked.

Balthasar made a face. "I doubt it. I think this is the best it's going to get."

That best was not very good. Over the next few days, Silence spent hours in the engine room, monitoring the harmonium while Chase Mago snatched much-needed sleep. *Bruja* refused to keep to a tuning that would hold her in a stable orbit. Without constant correction, she tended to fall inward, toward Castax and the ring of siege engines. Only Chase Mago had the training to bring the ship back into something approaching stability. Silence and Balthasar could do little more than watch the various gauges, and summon the engineer when the ship had drifted too far toward the danger zone. There was some sort of affinity, Chase Mago said over coffee, one night when he was too tired to sleep, between either the ship's tuning and the harmonies of Castax's core, or else between the metal itself and the destructive music of the siege engines.

The drifting was not the worst of the situation, either. The faint dissonance they had sensed when *Bruja* had first taken up her station grew worse the longer they remined in orbit—the keel, Chase Mago said, was being stressed from its original tuning by the conflicting harmonies around it. Under normal circumstances, Silence knew, they could shroud the keel in baffling, but that would make it impossible to keep station. They could only endure the fitful, almost inaudible discord. Druta began to spend most of his time aboard the flagship—the larger ships were protected by their more powerful harmonia and thicker baffling, as well as being tuned to a slightly different scale—and with him gone Chase Mago was able to unearth some extra baffling among the ship's stores. Balthasar used his spare time to rig extra protection for the cabins, and a second layer of the felt at least damped out some of the dissonance. But the disharmony had served for Silence only to mask the hovering sense of unfinished business that was the curse, and the new baffles brought her little peace.

On the sixth day in orbit, Druta signalled from the flagship. Balthasar disappeared into the control room, and though he kept the hatch open, Silence could make little sense of the words. When he returned to the common room, his expression was grim, and he slapped the intercom on without answering Silence's inquiring look.

"Julie? Will this cow stay put for a minute?"

"For a little bit," Chase Mago answered. "What's up?"

"Come on forward," Balthasar said. "Our latest mission's come through."

"Right." A moment later, Chase Mago appeared at the head of the corridor, flexing his fingers. He pulled a seat out of the decking and settled himself comfortably, still rubbing his knuckles.

"So what is it?" Silence asked.

"We've got another passenger run," Balthasar said. "Only if you thought the last one was something. . . ." He let his voice trail off, and Silence felt a chill run up her spine. But I'll be damned if I'll ask, she thought. I won't play his little games, either.

"Who is it?" Chase Mago asked, patiently, and to Silence's surprise, the Delian looked somewhat ashamed.

"Sorry, that's what the little bastard was doing to me. We're supposed to carry one of the magi from the siege team back to Solitudo Hermae—I guess he forgot something." Balthasar looked up. "Have you ever made that run, Silence?"

The pilot shook her head. "I've heard it's a difficult one."

"That's an understatement," Balthasar said dryly.

"I take it you've made it?" Silence said, more sharply than she had intended.

"Twice." Balthasar seemed unaffected by her tone.

"Is there anything special I need to do?" Chase Mago asked, glancing nervously over his shoulder. "Or is that all you wanted?" Already they could hear the first shift in tone that indicated that *Bruja* was slipping from her place in the line.

"Oh, yes, there's more." Balthasar looked positively pleased to be the bearer of bad news. "We'll be carrying a sensitive cargo on the return run. Druta wants new baffling in the cargo space."

Chase Mago sighed deeply. "I think there's probably enough left. We shouldn't have to tear out too much of the work you did, Denis. When do we leave?"

"Eighteen hours."

Silence whistled softly to herself. "That's not much notice."

"It's a rush job," Balthasar said.

"All right." Silence stood up, already planning her course. "I'll make some preliminary plots while you take a look at the cargo space, and then I'd be glad of any help you can give me, if the roads are that bad."

Chase Mago looked a little startled by her sudden assumption of command, but Balthasar nodded calmly. "Sounds good," he said, and headed off toward the hold.

Silence retreated to her own cabin, pulling out all of her starbooks. As she had half feared, only the *Speculum Astronomi* listed Solitudo Hermae in its tables—but it was only to be expected, she reminded herself. That book was printed by the magi on Solitudo, and of course they would reserve the secret of the road for a book from which they would profit. She turned to the tables, began to cross-reference planets, but to her surprise, there was only one road listed, the Ascending Path. She was not familiar with it, and made a face at the thought of the extra work involved in learning an entirely new set of voidmarks. Then she turned to the description of the road, and her heart sank.

Instead of the usual half-page of obscure text and half-page drawing, the entire page was filled with an elaborately colored and grotesquely detailed illustration. It showed a bearded soldier in the glowing, archaic armored spacesuit of a prewar marine, standing over a naked, dismembered body. He held a stained sword in one hand, and the head of the dead man in the other, blood-darkened fingers twisted in its bright hair. Behind the two figures rose a domed and columned palace that seemed to glow from within, and beside the palace ran a river whose surface glowed white hot. Indeed, all the colors were several shades lighter than usual, as though each object was lit from within by the white-hot light of a young star. Only the soldier's unshielded face, his bloodied hands and weapon, and the pool of blood that spread across the foreground of the picture were dark, almost unnaturally so in comparison to the brilliance of the background. Silence shivered, then got a grip on herself. This was a version of the symbol for calcination, the first step in the alchemical process that created the Philosopher's Stone. It was only to be expected, she thought again. Solitudo Hermae—Solitudo Hermae Trismegisti, the solitude of thrice-great Hermes—was entirely the creation of the magi, a sunless, barren world provided by them with fertile earth, a sphere of air, and above that a thin sphere of fire for light and heat. Of course the magi who defined the voidmarks for transition to Solitudo Hermae would use the opportunity to expound a section of their Art. But what this meant in terms of the actual passage, she could not imagine.

She sighed and leaned back in her chair, pushing away the starbook. Balthasar was right, this would be a difficult run. It was fortunate he'd made the trip before.

Around her, the air lightened suddenly, and she thought she caught a faint scent of rain. The slight sense of headache that had pursued her since she had spoken the curse lifted, and she rubbed her temples gratefully. Then she understood what had happened, and she shivered again violently. Gyasi was dead, the curse fulfilled, and soon the Navy was going to come looking for the culprit. Druta knew she had tried to curse the colonel, and he would lose no time in telling his superiors. And they would lose no time ridding themselves of her. Her eyes burned, picturing the casual killing on Arganthonios. Stop it, she told herself fiercely, think calmly. *Bruja* was due to leave orbit almost immediately, within hours. Perhaps they would be able to get away before the news of Gyasi's death became widely known, before Druta could make the connection. But that would only be a temporary respite. The news would spread, and would inevitably come to Druta. And then it would only be a matter of time until he made the connection. I wish I could think he was stupid enough to forget what Gyasi said, she thought, but I don't dare count on it.

She stood up, one hand tugging fretfully at the blue collar around her neck. The only solution was an impossibility: escape. She winced at the pain when the geas struck and ducked away, as she had learned to do. There was the familiar sense of falling, and she staggered, but the pain faded immediately. Then, defiantly, she turned back to the thought of escape. I will be free, she thought, or I'll kill myself trying—better that than waiting for the Hegemon's people to kill me. Pain washed through her, but she refused to release the thought. Instead, she clung to the idea of freedom, of taking her own ship between worlds of her own choosing. The pain mounted, bringing her to her knees on the bare decking.

"I won't give up," she muttered through clenched teeth. She dug her short nails into her palms, clawed frantically at her own arms, trying to distract herself from pain if she could not ease it. It did no good. She was caught in coils, unable to free herself directly without tearing herself apart. Sobbing now, she flung herself once again against the bonds of the geas, wrenching at the collar as though it was the geas itself. Her hands felt as if they were bathed in flame, her joints were pierced with hot needles. She whimpered, thought she cried out in agony, but her senses were closed to everything but the fact of pain.

Then abruptly the pain dropped away with her body. She felt a part of herself projected above the writhing thing on the decking, saw through those eyes her body wound with threads of fire, each tongue of flame slicing her flesh like a knife. It did not seem to hurt anymore, though she was distantly aware of agony as a thing that was happening to someone else. From this vantage point, she could see not only the geas, but as she looked more closely, she could see the points of stress, like knots in the fiery cord. Cautiously, she tugged at them, then put her whole imagined strength behind it. They gave with frightening suddenness, as though they were already weakened and just waiting for the right pressure to fall apart. She saw the threads break and fall away, and then she was kneeling again on the decking, her face wet with tears.

The collar lay broken in her hands. She raised her head slowly, hardly daring to breathe, uncertain if she could trust her senses. I'm free? she thought, and braced herself for a fresh onslaught. Nothing happened, not even an echo of pain, and she straightened.

It was true, then, she thought, the geas is broken. And, by God, I can do it again. The memory of it, the exact pattern of the threads and the points at which she had broken them, was etched in her memory, only the pain fading to a mere whisper of what it had been. The only thing that remained was somehow to free the others. Rising—she was surprised to find that her body was not sore this time, merely a little stiff—she unlatched her door and peered out into the corridor. Neither Balthasar nor Chase Mago was in evidence—of course they wouldn't be, she thought. It had been less than an hour since she had settled down to learn the road to Solitudo Hermae.

Down the corridor, Balthasar emerged from the cargo space, scowling, his hands swathed in massive, clumsy gloves for handling the coarse baffling felt. He stopped when he saw her. "You want to go over it now?" he asked irritably.

"No, not now," Silence said. Even to herself, her voice sounded peculiar; Balthasar regarded her nervously. "Get Julie, and meet me in the commons. We need to talk."

She did not wait for his answer, but went on into the common area, concentrating on the memory of how the geas was broken. There, she thought, seeing again the pattern of lines, and again there, and there. That's how— She broke off as the others entered, and had to smile at their worried expressions.

"Are you all right, Silence?" Chase Mago asked.

She smiled, in spite of the seriousness of the moment, in spite of her fear that if she laughed she would not be able to stop again. "Never better.

Listen to me, now. The curse has worked, Gyasi's dead. And I'm free, and I can free you, too."

Balthasar grimaced at the words, holding his side as if he had been struck there. A fleeting expression of pain crossed Chase Mago's face, but he said only, "How do you know he's gone?"

"I felt the curse lift," Silence said impatiently. It had not occurred to her to question that; she had known it with too great a certainty. "Do you want my help?"

"Of course," Balthasar said, but she could sense their disbelief.

"Then be quiet." Remotely, she regretted her abruptness, but the knowledge of the geas was driving her. The two men sat on the benches by the table, still staring dubiously at her. She stared at them, ordering her thoughts, and then she summoned the full memory of pain. It was enough; she felt herself rise from her body, and saw, remotely, the body crumple to the decking. She saw, too, the two men's startled movements, half rising from the bench. Then Chase Mago gestured for them to wait, and Silence allowed herself to relax a little, studying them. The marks of the geas were clear— dark, twining vines across the engineer's body, following the course of his veins. The geas had left scars on Balthasar, still seemed to cut deeply into his flesh. But despite those differences, the pattern of the geas remained the same. Silence extended her right hand to Chase Mago, her left hand to Balthasar, took hold of the key point of the bindings. The geas was tougher than she had expected, not weakened as hers had been, but then she found the trick of it. The bonds snapped and, gasping, she released her control and fell, slamming back into her own body.

She looked up and saw her own fatigue, mixed with a sort of wary amazement, mirrored in the others' faces. Slowly, Balthasar put a hand to his neck and pulled away the broken collar; Chase Mago's lay in pieces at his feet.

"My God," the engineer managed, "you really did it."

Silence nodded, then smothered a laugh, almost unable to believe it herself. She was completely exhausted, trembling from head to foot, but at the same time she had to stifle the urge to crow in triumph. I did it, she thought—I freed myself and them. I beat the magi at their own game. That thought, articulated, shattered her elation. If I can defeat a magus, break a geas—me, a woman, a mere pilot—what does that make me? She had no answer, and that emptiness terrified her.

Stop it, she told herself, there's no time for that now. You're not out of trouble yet. We still have to get away from Castax. She could feel herself shaking, and knew her face must be drained of color. Chase Mago rose and extended a hand to pull her to her feet. Silence stumbled up, swaying on legs gone abruptly unreliable, and Balthasar hastily pulled a chair up from the decking. The engineer lowered Silence into it, then pulled out another for himself. Meanwhile, Balthasar busied himself at the galley console, prying open a tin of the pudding-thick soup that was the Hegemony's emergency ration. He stuck the opened tin into one of the heating elements and rummaged in the various storage cells until he found a bottle half full of an amber liquid. He poured most of it into the heating soup—Chase Mago, perhaps recognizing the brandy, made an inarticulate noise of protest—then decanted the hot mixture into mugs, which he handed around with something of a flourish.

The liquor had diluted the soup to a drinkable consistency. Silence sipped cautiously at it, letting the brandy relax her while the soup provided sooth-ing herbs and a vital restorative. The combination banished her trembling, replaced the wild mixture of fear and triumph with a calmer determination. As she drained the last swallows, she felt almost ready to plan what to do next.

Balthasar dropped his own mug into the clean-ing slot, and it fell with a startling clatter. "I don't know how you did it, Silence, but thanks."

Silence tensed, wishing they would not ask the inevitable, logical question, would not make her give the answer she did not want to face again, but Chase Mago waved for them both to be quiet.

"We must be drifting—" he began, then broke off to listen again, his expression puzzled. "No, it still sounds fine. I wonder if this curse of yours, Silence, did something to our tuning?"

"I don't know," Silence said, intensely grateful for the change of subject. "I've been feeling it for days, hanging over the ship, so maybe it did."

"Never mind that," Balthasar growled. "What now?"

Silence sighed. "I'm not entirely sure," she admitted. "Obviously, we've got to go along with this mission or we'll be destroyed. There's no way we can sneak out of the blockade line, and no chance of breaking out, either."

Balthasar grunted his agreement.

"What about the collars?" Chase Mago asked. "Once Druta gets back, he'll notice that they're gone."

"Surely you can rig some kind of glue, hold them together enough to look good," Balthasar said.

"Good enough to fool a magus?" the engineer said dubiously.

Balthasar sighed. "Look, if they spot us now, we're dead. It'll just have to be good enough, right?"

"Yes," Silence said slowly. "We'll have to take the ship. When we reach purgatory, instead of setting the road for Solitudo Hermae, I'll set another. It would mean a slightly different departure route—"

"Druta's no pilot," Balthasar interjected. "He'd never notice a minor deviation from course."

"So we can work within those limits," Silence said. "There must be enough planets along that general line where we could claim sanctuary."

Chase Mago shook his head. "Even if all of them fell within the limits—which they won't—I doubt there's a planet in the Fringe that would risk war with the Hegemon. Especially now. We'll have to kill them."

"If we can," Silence muttered. She did not relish the idea of arriving in the outskirts of a solar system, trying to treat with the local authorities while a battle raged aboard.

Balthasar snapped his fingers. "The dead roads," he said. "Damn, it's a pity I can't take the ship through purgatory. Silence, I'd have to teach you."

"What are dead roads?" Silence asked.

"They're roads that don't lead anywhere anymore—the worlds were destroyed in the war," Balthasar said. "The voidmarks are a little weird, but not too bad." He smiled, remembering something. "Wrath-of-God used them a lot. The only thing I'm worried about is trying to teach them to you without a book."

Silence hesitated. There was no reason, now, not to share the book, but it took an effort to overcome her strange reluctance. "I've a prewar *Gilded Stairs*. That would have them, wouldn't it?"

Balthasar looked at her oddly. "Yes."

Silence rose. "I'll get it, then."

When she returned, the others had pulled the table from its well and Balthasar was spreading scratch paper liberally across its surface, muttering to himself. As Silence came closer, she saw that it was not scratch paper, but printouts from the Navy astrologers, standard projections of local planetary positions. Ideally, of course, they would provide the departure course as well—and probably had provided one, for Solitudo Hermae, Silence realized—but Balthasar was bent over the thickly printed tables, occasionally circling a cluster of figures. Silence opened the *Gilded Stairs* to the tables she had read on Wrath-of-God, copying down symbols she did not recognize, and then turned to the supplement, comparing each world's positional formulae with the numbers Balthasar was scribbling.

"These are the outside limits," the Delian said, after a while. "Oh, you've already found them. Let me see what you've got."

Silence slid the scrap of paper across the table and Balthasar studied it briefly, before circling one symbol.

"That's the one we used," he said, tossing the pad back to the pilot. "I've flown it several times, so I can tell you how the marks have changed. I wasn't sure how it would fit in with the official course."

Silence nodded—the lines of departure were almost congruent—then flipped back through the book to the description of the unfamiliar route. But at least the markings for the Path of Light Darkening were clear enough. Balthasar leaned over her shoulder, staring at the picture.

"That's it," he said again. "It's funny, though, when you try to pilot through it, you can tell the end planet's gone. You have to keep your concentration to hold the marks at all, and everything's just a little off—colors, positioning, everything."

Silence nodded again absently, studying the

image. The delicate miniature showed an oddly disturbing scene, a beach at evening beneath a sky streaked with clouds, a single star showing through the wrack. A bird, a point of light against the dull sky, swung over the low and sullen waves, but there was a heaviness about it that made her think it was falling rather than rising to the sky. The colors were very dark, as though each shade had been prepared and then mixed with jet black ink; the sea itself was so dark that she could not discern the original color, though she did not think it was blue. The commentary was not much help, either: *The subject may fly, but with drooping wings. With firm correctness, one ascends, but all go into the earth.*

Silence sighed heavily. This was bad enough, but Balthasar said the marks had changed. She tried to picture the scene as Balthasar had described it, colors changed or faded, the various components slightly askew, but she could not yet imagine it.

"It's almost garish," Balthasar said quietly, as though he'd read her thoughts. "Like a bad painting—or as though the whole thing was floodlit from behind with a yellowish light."

Silence shook her head. "I can't see it," she said flatly. "Can I get through just knowing these marks?"

"I did, the first time."

"Then that'll have to do."

Chase Mago cleared his throat. "Druta'll be back soon," he warned. "I think I've got some glue that'll hold these together." He held up the fragments of the collars. "But we'd better get to work."

"Damn." Balthasar swept his papers together— Silence hastily snatched the *Gilded Stairs* back out of his way—and fed all but a single sheet into the disposal chute. "You go ahead," he went on. "I want to set this course now, before anyone can ask questions."

"Hurry, then," Chase Mago said.

The engineer's glue, a compound of elemental earth, was just strong enough to hold the shattered pieces of the collars together, though the repairs would not pass a close examination. With luck, Silence thought, there won't be any inspection. She made a quick sign to ward off misfortune, and retired to her cabin to memorize the Path of Light Darkening.

Druta did not return for several hours, despite Chase Mago's warning. Silence lost herself in the contemplation of the *Gilded Stairs*, translating the cryptic sentences and elaborate drawing into a pilot's reality. The buzzing of the intercom broke that concentration, and she looked up startled, before remembering both where she was and what she was doing.

"Leigh!" Druta's voice was sharp, too sharp. She guessed the magus had come aboard with him. "Get out here."

The pilot did not bother answering. It was quicker to go to him. Settling her face into its most impassive mask—for the first time in her life, she wished for a veil—she headed for the common area. The others were there ahead of her, and she could sense in them the same deep-buried excitement. And if I can see it, she thought, won't this magus? She forced herself to look at him but he showed no signs of recognizing the tension. The magus was an older man, as she had expected, but not tall, and so gaunt that he almost seemed unhealthy. His hair and neatly trimmed beard had gone white already, and almost shone in contrast to the dull black of his academic robes. Bands of scarlet gleamed at neck and cuffs, but she did not know how to read the magi's symbols of rank. The magus returned her scrutiny calmly, seeming not to bother with a more searching examination.

"You are fortunate, Captain Druta," he said, after a moment. "A female pilot must provide you with many opportunities for learning that craft. You must introduce me."

The almost courtly courtesy of his tone seemed to quell the midshipman. "As you wish, Doctor. Doctor Isambard, may I present Silence Leigh, first pilot?"

Isambard inclined his head graciously. "I am delighted, sieura. I hope I will have an opportunity to talk to you while we are in transit. I am sure I could learn much from you."

"Thank you, Doctor," Silence stammered, completely taken aback by the old man's politeness. Then Druta cleared his throat and brought her back to reality.

"Excuse me, Doctor, but that talk will have to be delayed. Leigh, have you learned the voidmarks yet?"

Silence shook herself, frightened that she could have lost sight of the deadly chance they were taking. Isambard might be courteous enough, but that could not stand in the way— She suppressed that thought, afraid the magus would in some way recognize it, and said, "Yes, captain."

"Then get up to your post. We leave immediately." Druta turned and made a half-bow in the magus's direction. "Doctor, if you'll follow me, I'll show you to your cabin."

"You're too kind," Isambard murmured, and allowed himself to be ushered down the corridor. Chase Mago followed them, heading for the engine room.

Left to themselves, Silence and Balthasar went on into the lower control room, Balthasar pulling the hatch closed behind them. He made a wry face, and threw the lock.

"Are you really ready?" he asked quietly.

Silence took a deep breath, quoting to herself the first lines of the relaxation exercises, and felt the tightness ease a little from her muscles. "I know the voidmarks," she said, her voice grim. "What happens when we get there?"

Balthasar touched her shoulder reassuringly. "I'll take care of Druta. You just get us there—and be ready to come down and help stabilize—" He broke off as a light flashed above the hatch, and reached to unlock it. "Captain? I'm sorry, I must've hit that by mistake."

Druta glared at him, but seemed unable to think of a suitable retort. "Are you ready to take us out of orbit, Balthasar? And I don't think this is your station, Leigh."

"No, sir," Silence said meekly, and pulled herself up the ladder to the pilot's bridge.

It was a cramped, inconvenient space, especially in comparison to *Sun-Treader*, but at least it was equipped with a couch as well as a wheel platform. Silence settled herself gratefully into it, pulling the webbing across lap and chest, then readied herself to wait as the music of the harmonium built far below her. This is not a good situation, she thought suddenly, not good at all. Here I am, about to take a ship I've flown once on a path I've never heard of to a place that doesn't exist anymore. And when I get us there, we've got to kill Druta and this magus, and then find some world where we'll be relatively welcome. And I haven't begun to think about what happens after that. It's all wildly improbable—we'll be lucky if we get out of the system without someone stopping us.

She shook her head, though there was no one to see. You're being ridiculous, she told herself firmly.

No one can know what we're planning—if Isambard didn't spot it when he came aboard, no one else will know. And for the rest, well, this is a better chance than waiting for someone to connect Gyasi's death with my curse. If we fail, we'll go down fighting. It was not much comfort, after all, and she was glad when the music surged suddenly through the keel, carrying them away from Castax.

Bruja handled well, and far more quickly than the ships to which she had been accustomed. Long before they reached purgatory, she felt compelled to take her station at the wheel, uncertain just how long it would take the fast little mailship to make the transition into purgatory. It seemed that one moment the grey bulkheads took on a tinge of opalescence, and then they vanished utterly.

"You have control," Balthasar said, but Silence had no time to respond. The lock went off, released from below, and she fought to steady the ship against the chaos around her.

The old voidmarks of the *Gilded Stairs* were there, sea and clouds and shadowed sands, but the images were skewed, sand and clouds touching while the bloody sea ran uphill into the sky. She gasped and tried to order the signs, imposing her own vision on the images. Slowly, the scene righted itself, the voidmarks reluctantly taking on a more normal shape and position, but the colors remained strange. The blackened colors of the original were now overlaid by a haze of orange light, like the light of a sunset that was not there. *Bruja* felt heavy in her hands, heavy as a freighter.

That at least was a good sign: she had not let the ship fall too far out of its proper road. She edged the wheel over, uncertain how quickly the mainship would respond. The ship's weight increased rapidly as she maneuvered to align the distant stair and the bird-shape that hung motionless beyond, easing *Bruja* onto the correct path. The harmonium pulsed strongly as the ship settled into its road, and the sensation of weight became almost unbearable. It felt as though the ship itself were falling inward on its keel, as though Silence's flesh were running down her bones to pool at her feet; it took all her strength to remain upright, though she knew the sensation was unreal. Druta will know, she thought suddenly, he'll know this isn't the Ascending Path—even he can't be that much a fool. Can Denis handle him? With an effort, she put the thought from her mind. Balthasar would have to handle it: she had the ship to pilot.

The bird-shape was looming before her, its once-white feathers now stained and drooping. Several small pieces of the image were missing, a wingtip, an eye, a clump of feather from the spreading tail, and she could not seem to make them reappear. Then, with the suddenness of purgatory, *Bruja* was on the image. She barely had time to brace herself, and they were through.

Instantly, the sensation of weight was gone, replaced with nauseating suddenness by a paradoxical lightness. Silence fought to keep her hands motionless of the wheel, despite the temptation to push the ship's nose down in compensation for the new weightlessness. Her feet seemed about to lose their grip on the platform, but she kept the ship pointed steadily at the star that now seemed very remote. There was a rush of speed and the colors grew muddy as *Bruja* fell from purgatory, and then the hull above her clouded and grew solid. Automatically, she locked her wheel, turning control back to the lower bridge.

"Silence, get down here."

That was Balthasar, sounding strained and breathless. Hastily, Silence freed herself from the platform, shaking away the fog that always seemed to surround her after the effort of piloting. She dropped down the ladder to the lower bridge, and only as her feet touched the decking did she realize she was unarmed. It didn't seem to matter.

"Steady her," Balthasar snapped. He was out of his couch, precariously straddling the Ficinan display, tugging at the straps that held Druta's body in its place. The midshipman was dead, that much was unmistakable. Silence swallowed hard and looked away from the smoking hole in his chest. Her eyes fell on a three-shot heylin, tossed in a corner: Balthasar must have broken into the arms locker.

"Steady her!" Balthasar said again. "There's sun-flux here, you've got to catch her."

That was enough to snap Silence out of her daze. She pushed her way between the bank of secondary consoles and Balthasar's couch, not caring if she tripped half the environmental switches in the process. Systems could be turned back on once the ship was stabilized against the discordant music of the broken system. Already she could hear the first signs of the strain, a new note that rose and fell through the roar of the harmonium, unsettling its steady song. She set hands on keys and yaw lever, checking the Ficinan model and musonar displays, but the controls refused to respond. She shoved at the lever again, harder, stabbed the pitch keys a second time, putting the full weight of her hand behind them, and they moved sluggishly.

"What the hell?"

"The bastard tripped the override," Balthasar panted. "And I can't get at it. Do what you can."

Silence nodded, already absorbed in the problem. The Ficinan display was usually more use than the musonar, but Balthasar was blocking her view of it. She concentrated on the screen above her controls, urging the ship away from the remnants of the planet, toward a zone of comparative calm. The musonar showed the pulsing sun, surrounded by ragged waves of music; those waves clashed against the void that was the echo of the energies that had destroyed a planet. The meeting point of those two antithetical harmonies flashed red and orange on the screen, faded to darker eddies and whirlpools that were still dangerously dissonant. *Bruja* was already perilously close to the outermost ring of disturbance, and Silence struck viciously at the pitch keys, trying to change the harmonium's note enough to push them free. Either the keys responded better than the lever or Chase Mago sensed their danger himself: the pitch eased a little, shutting out the new note. Silence leaned on the lever, forcing the ship onto a new line. Interference sang, but she held the course.

There was a thud behind her, and Balthasar was no longer standing on the couch. She sat, checking their position against the Ficinan model, and was shocked to see how far inward they'd fallen.

"Mind your hands," Balthasar said. "I'm killing the override."

Silence relaxed her hold on the controls, and a second later saw an orange light die above her console. She touched the keys again, and this time felt the ship respond easily. Slowly, letting *Bruja* make her own way against the dissonance around, Silence eased the ship onto a safe course. When the last of the interference lights faded from yellow to green, numbers dropping below one, she used the pilot's override to set the harmonium on a note that would hold *Bruja* stable for several hours, then looked around for Balthasar. The Delian was gone—as of course he would be, Silence thought. There was still Isambard to deal with.

She pushed herself out of the couch and pulled open the hatch, then paused long enough to scoop up the discarded heylin. The touchplate was barely warm under her thumb, indicating that the charge had only partly regenerated, but she could not bring herself to search Druta's body, discarded against the bulkhead, for a better weapon. Besides, she told herself, Balthasar would already have taken it. With a deep breath, she eased open the hatch.

In the common area, Balthasar had flattened himself against the bulkhead beside the entrance to the corridor, a sonic rifle propped against his shoulder. The metal lid of the arms locker lay on the deck, completely ripped from its hinges. At the far end of the corridor, Chase Mago peered cautiously around the edge of the engine room hatchway, the warning orange lights giving a strange glow to his beard, and throwing his features into ghoulish shadow. He saw her first, and brought up his heylin on reflex. Then he recognized her, and waved to Balthasar. The Delian turned, beckoned to her, pointing first to the plundered locker and then to the opposite side of the corridor. Silence obeyed, crossing to the arms locker and grabbing the first weapon she saw—it was a heylin, the touchplate hot in her hand—then took up the station opposite Balthasar. "Isambard's still in his cabin," Balthasar whispered. "Hit the intercom, will you? And for God's sake, turn down the power on that thing."

Silence glanced in surprise at the indicator light, and saw that it was glowing bright red, indicating the heylin's bolts would be strong enough to shatter everything but Tincture-cast metal. She swallowed and adjusted it to a more normal, man-killing setting, watching the light fade to yellow, then hit the intercom button.

"Isambard!" Balthasar raised his voice to carry to the pickup. "We've taken the ship. Give parole, and you'll not be harmed."

"That does not seem probable." Isambard's voice was perfectly calm and reasonable, as though he were debating some theoretical problem before a class of admiring apprentices.

"Give us your word not to resist," Balthasar called again, "and you won't be hurt."

There was a long moment of quiet, and then Isambard sighed gently. "No, I do not think I may hamper myself so, particularly when I can see no reason for you to keep your word."

Balthasar made a face. "Have it your way. Come out now, or we'll come after you."

The intercom suddenly spat painful static. Isambard's voice came only faintly through that noise: "I do not think you can."

Nevertheless, the cabin door opened slowly. Silence tensed, and saw Balthasar take careful aim with the sonic rifle. Chase Mago, only slightly out of the line of fire, eased back behind the bulkhead. Silence could guess their plan: Balthasar would fire first, the sonic blast intended to stun and disorient even the strongest magus, and then the engineer would finish the job.

For fifty heartbeats, nothing happened. Then the air just beyond the doorway began to ripple and bulge, like ill-formed glass. The disturbance spread until it reached from the door to the far bulkhead, and then Isambard himself stepped carefully into the corridor. Balthasar fired. Silence winced at the pressure of the backlash, a sound too low and bone-rattling for hearing. The sound died, too unnatural to be prolonged, and Chase Mago appeared in the entrance to the engine room, heylin in hand. He, too, fired, but the ball of fixed fire disintegrated harmlessly a meter from the magus.

"Get back, Julie!" Balthasar shouted, and raised his rifle again. This time he kept his finger on the firing stud, sending wave after wave of sound rolling down the corridor, and Silence flinched back, hardly daring to look. The magus stood motionless, watching, a quizzical expression on his face. Balthasar did not dare keep firing, for fear the sound would disrupt the ship's turning. Swearing, he threw the rifle aside, reached for the heylin he stuck in his belt.

Into the sudden, thick stillness, the magus said, "I warned you." His left hand rose in the beginning of a gesture and the ship quivered as a tiny patch of chaos opened before him.

Chapter 9

"Wait!" Silence cried.

"Why should I?" Isambard asked. Nevertheless, though he lifted one hand, it hung suspended, the gesture incomplete.

Silence tossed her heylin aside, stepped into the head of the corridor. She held out her empty hands, forcing herself to stay calm even though her skin crawled with anticipation of the magus's attack. "We've acted only to defend ourselves," she said rapidly. "You weren't attacked until you refused to promise our safety."

The magus considered that, then nodded. "True enough. But that is no reason to trust you now."

"You wouldn't want to have to pilot this ship yourself—if you could," Silence said at random. She did not know how to reach him, what strings to pluck to make him agree to at least neutrality. Only . . . he could not be loyal to the Hegemon—no magus was loyal to anything but his art, just as the magi on Arganthonios had been. But she had nothing to offer him in return for neutrality, beyond her mere existence as a woman and a pilot, and she could not imagine that that would be enough.

"I might not have to," Isambard said. "You could be compelled." He waved his hand, dismissing the patch of chaos, then made another, too-familiar gesture, this one of binding.

"No!" Silence flung up her arm to ward off that power, and to her surprise, only the ghost of it brushed against her. "I will not be bound again— none of us will. We'll die first."

Isambard was regarding her speculatively. "You have been underestimated, sieura, I suspect," he murmured.

"Are you the Hegemon's man, his loyal servant?" Silence plunged on, not daring to hesitate long enough to work out some coherent strategy. "If you are, then there's no hope of agreement. We can fight, and see who dies."

Isambard smiled faintly at the empty threat, but said, "The Hegemon has been a good patron."

"Then if you're a free scholar, perhaps some bargain can be made," Silence said.

"What can you offer me that's of comparable value?" Isambard asked. "You are indeed an interesting anomaly, sieura, and potentially an object worthy of some study, but I cannot see that such study is worth losing all credit and privileges with the Hegemon."

Silence smiled, suddenly calm, knowing that she held the answer to the one question that would fascinate Isambard and save them all. "I know the road to Earth, Isambard. I will take you there."

She was aware that Balthasar was staring open-mouthed at her, and then she heard him mutter, "That old book. Of course," but she could not spare the time to nod to him. She kept her attention on Isambard, saw the magus nod slowly. His face changed fractionally, was touched by the same desire that had marked the magi on Arganthonios.

"You would not make such a claim if you could not substantiate it," he said, half to himself, "nor are you strong enough to hide a lie from me, now that I am aware of the possibility of deception. Very well, we'll make a bargain, sieura. You will find Earth for me, and I will not betray you to the Hegemon or his men."

"Is that agreed, Denis, Julie?" Silence asked.

"Yes," Chase Mago said from the engine room.

"Are you crazy?" Balthasar demanded. "Take him to Earth? Why didn't you tell me you knew the road?"

"I didn't know I knew until we were already on Wrath-of-God," Silence said impatiently. "Denis, there's no other choice."

Balthasar muttered something, but then nodded. "All right."

"Good." Silence faced the magus again. "You hear, Isambard? We'll find Earth, and you won't betray us."

"Very well," Isambard said. He gestured dismissal, and the protective wall of air that had surrounded him dissolved. "Now, show me this road, sieura, if you please." As he spoke, he came forward along the corridor, walking past Balthasar's still-leveled heylin as though it did not exist. Balthasar shook his head, and Silence suppressed a nervous giggle. In the common area, Isambard seated himself at the table and looked expectantly toward the pilot. Silence hesitated, and the magus smiled.

"You need not worry, sieura," he said. "Your first guess was right: I can't pilot this ship myself."

Silence felt her cheeks redden and turned away, embarrassed. The *Gilded Stairs* was still in her cabin. She paused there, checking the tables, and then turned to the single short road listed for Earth. Her heart fell. She did not recognize the notation at all—it certainly wasn't the Cor Tauri symbology used in the rest of the *Gilded Stairs*—and the commentary was even more cryptic than usual. How am I going to read this and learn the road, much less explain it to Isambard? she wondered, frantically searching her shelves for a starbook with a hieroglyphical index. I don't dare go out there without having some idea of what it means. And I can't fake it, either; he'll be watching for that. She flipped hastily through the appendices of the *New Aquarius* and the *Topoi*, then settled on the *Topoi* as the more thorough. She slipped a marker ribbon in the *Gilded Stairs* and closed it gently. Isambard would just have to put up with her uncertainty, she decided. He has no choice. Somehow, that thought was not very reassuring; her hands were shaking as she returned to the common area.

Isambard looked up at her approach, and beckoned for her to come and sit beside him. Frowning, Silence obeyed, wondering where the others had gone. Before she could ask, however, the hatch to the lower bridge was shouldered open. Chase Mago stepped awkwardly out and Balthasar followed more gracefully, Druta's body slung between them. Silence looked away, and saw the magus nod.

"A young man of limited understanding," he pronounced. "And yet in some sense his death is wasteful. Let me see the starbook."

Trying to ignore the muttered curses as the two men maneuvered Druta's body toward the stern disposal lock, Silence settled herself at the head of the table and open the *Gilded Stairs* to the marked drawing. Isambard studied it avidly, then, with an effort, tore his gaze away.

"Are you familiar with the I-ku-u notation?" he asked.

Silence hesitated, but did not dare lie. "No. But the *Topoi* has a fairly good hieroglyphica."

"I have a better." Isambard rose slowly, one hand lightly touching the page of the *Gilded Stairs* as though he would have liked to take it with him. Silence glared, and reluctantly Isambard lifted his hand. "Wait."

And where would I go? Silence thought, but said nothing. Instead, she turned the book to get a better look at the design. It was a plain, uncolored line drawing, showing a man in an old-fashioned long coat standing before a battered wall, brick covered with peeling plaster. In his hand he held a gigantic pair of calipers, with which he was inscribing the final circle of a very familiar symbolic figure. Within the largest, outer circle was a triangle, its three points touching the circle that enclosed it; within the triangle was a square, and within the square was a second circle, which enclosed two naked figures, one male, one female. It was a fairly common representation of the process for making the Philosopher's Stone, the figures standing for the stone's "parents", the square for the four elements, and so on, but she could not understand how that should translate into voidmarks.

The commentary was no help, either. It was a deliberate misquotation from *Atalanta Flying*, one of the basic alchemical tests: "Make a circle out of a man and a woman, out of this a square, out of this a triangle. Make a circle, and you will have Earth." Silence glared at the neat printing. What should that mean to a pilot? Grumbling, she turned to the *Topoi*'s hieroglyphica, and began to look up the components of the picture. She found the battered, peeling wall—"this indicates a heavily travelled road," the entry said, "and that care should be taken not to be dragged along in another's wake"—and the man with the calipers—"a road often taken by a specialist; also, a warning to be precise"—but the central figure was unlisted.

"Here, try this." Isambard seated himself again at the table and set a crudely bound volume in front of Silence. The pilot lifted the unmarked cover cautiously, not wanting to rip the already strained stitching. The inner pages were coarse and had the greyish sheen of photoflash paper. The title page had an elaborate border of twining snakes and spidery, distorted figures that Silence almost recognized, but could not remember fully. The block letters of the title were in an archaic style, but were easy enough to read: *The System of I-ku-u, or Leading Star of Stars.* The date was N.A. 609—the original book had been nearly two hundred years older than her own *Gilded Stairs*, and she touched the copy's pages with involuntary respect.

"The I-ku-u was originally designed for practitioners of the Art," Isambard observed, "but the pilots borrowed it. It was used until the Cor Tauri guild developed their own system."

"I see." Silence shook away the sudden sense of being back in her apprenticeship, began to puzzle out the I-ku-u's index. Isambard watched her work, maddeningly quiet. He could tell me how this is set up, Silence thought, but this is a test. and I'll be damned if I'll admit I know it. She scanned the first page, remembering her training, and soon began to pick out the pattern, image clusters arranged according to some key sentence. After a couple of false starts, she found the proper cluster. Isambard nodded his approval, but she ignored him and began looking up each section of the drawing.

"How's it going?" Balthasar asked suddenly.

Silence looked up, startled. "I'm getting it," she said grimly. She closed the I-ku-u, shut her eyes, and tried to picture the symbols, and their meanings, knitted together in the seamless image of the starbook's drawing. It was almost there, the separate meanings clear, and she handed the copied book back to Isambard. "It'll take me another three, four hours to learn the road," she went on. "Denis, can you work out a departure course in that time?"

"Yes." Balthasar glanced over her shoulder at the *Gilded Stairs*. "Do you have the number for me?"

Silence flipped back to the first section of the starbook, and Balthasar copied out the appropriate formula. "Thanks," he said, and disappeared into the lower control room.

"If you'll excuse me, Isambard," Silence said, and picked up her own book. The magus kept a hand on the *I-ku-u*, but he gazed covetously after the *Gilded Stairs*. Silence repressed the urge to clutch it more tightly, and went on into her own cabin, where she could work in peace.

But when the door closed behind her, she found it hard to recover her earlier concentration. The memory of Druta's body sprawled in the pilot's couch, then carried lolling through the common area, kept breaking through her guard. She closed her eyes again, pressed her fingers against her eyelids until she saw flashes of colored lights, then sighed and, barely whispering, recited the first three cantrips of the simplest meditation exercise she knew. The picture receded, and she opened the *Gilded Stairs* for what she hoped was the last time. She stared at the drawing, fitting the meanings she had so recently learned to the picture before her, until at last understanding came.

The Earth-road was like an intricate maze, she

thought, although the object was not to reach the center but to find an exit point along the rim of the outer circle. The center itself was perilous, the royal couple standing not for the alchemical "parents" of the Tincture, but for the necessary twinned configuration of unstable stars that shaped this road. She would have to bring the ship as close as possible to them without falling into the reflection of their almost-elemental fire, and then work outward again, past the signs for the four elements. They would be taken in order, earth and air, fire and water, and then brought in to alignment. And when they were aligned, the road would end in a glorious display, the four elements becoming three principles, and the three principles becoming the mundane universe. *Bruja* would be carried from purgatory on that wave of understanding, and they would reach Earth.

Silence sighed and closed her eyes on unexpected tears. Pulling back from that vision, she had caught a brief glimpse of what Earth had been to humanity in the years before the War. Then men that had been able to see their world as a center of the human cosmos despite its insignificant position on the edge of a galaxy itself far from the center of the universe. The road to Earth was beautiful; merely reading it brought a sense of fulfillment. She could understand why the *Gilded Stairs* suggested—in the I-ku-u the figure of the man with calipers had a far stronger meaning than in the Cor Tauri system—that a specialist pilot take this road. It might be all too easy never to pilot again, once the Earth-road had been taken.

She shook herself, angry at the wasted fantasy. The Path of Light Darkening had been distorted, ruined by the destruction of Decelea. It was more than possible that Earth had suffered the same fate, that she would never see the Earth-road in its perfection. The thought was painful, and she put it aside as well, forced herself to concentrate on the physical meaning of the signs.

There was a tapping at the door, and she looked up, frowning at the time display above her tiny workbench. Three hours had passed since she last looked at it; Isambard was probably coming to demand that she get on with her part of the bargain.

"Come in."

The door slid back, but it was Chase Mago who looked in. "I've made—lunch? dinner? a meal, anyway. Shall I bring you a tray?"

"No," Silence answered, surprised to feel just how hungry she was. "I'll come out. I'm done here, anyway."

Chase Mago nodded. "Denis's got his plot worked out, too."

"Good."

The engineer had done little more than open packages and punch a few buttons on the galley console, but the results smelled and tasted delicious. Isambard was nowhere to be seen; the other three ate without speaking until they had emptied their plates. Then Silence pushed aside her empty tray and said, "Where's Isambard?"

"In his cabin." Chase Mago paused, reaching for the last piece of canned bread, and when no one said anything, took it. "I took him a tray already."

"Oh." Silence sighed. "How does the departure look?"

Balthasar gave her a tight smile. "Not great. I had forgotten how awkward this system is—sun's strange, a planet's missing, and the echo of the siege engines is still sounding. . . ." He broke off and shrugged. "I'll manage."

"Right." Silence looked at both men, smiled in spite of herself. "I suppose there's no point in putting it off any longer?"

Chase Mago smiled back. "I'm ready whenever you are. And the harmonium's ready, which is more to the point."

"Let's get it over with," Balthasar agreed.

"I suppose someone should tell Isambard," Chase Mago said dubiously.

"Not me," Balthasar said at once. "I've got to set the final course."

"I'll do it." Silence rose, tossed her plate into the disposal slot, and headed down the corridor. She took a deep breath at the magus's door, then knocked hard. The door swung open almost immediately, and Isambard looked out.

"Yes, sieura?"

"We're ready to leave the system," Silence said. She could not bring herself to invite him to watch from the lower bridge, and compromised on, "I thought you'd want to know."

"Yes, thank you," Isambard said. "I will remain here, I think. I should be able to follow affairs from here."

"Will you want sleep drugs?" Silence asked, and kicked herself for having forgotten them before. Most passengers on starships preferred to sleep through the passage through purgatory rather than try to cope with the distortions it produced; she did not even know if *Bruja* carried the proper drugs.

"No, thank you," Isambard said, with a slight smile. "I'd prefer to remain awake."

"Of course," Silence said, and felt herself flush. It had been a stupid thought, and one likely to arouse the magus's suspicions all over again. "I'll be getting up the bridge, then," she added, and beat a hasty retreat. Isambard's tolerant smile seemed to follow her up the corridor.

Balthasar was already waiting for her on the lower bridge, strapped into his couch before the main controls. Silence hesitated beside the second couch—the cushions were stained with Druta's blood—but then the harmonium's note strengthened, and she forced herself to sit. The Ficinan model showed the ragged flare of music around the central sun, and the flashing interference where that collided with the dissonant remnants of Decelea. *Bruja*'s course wove between and around those pools of interference, hugging the shadow of a second, apparently undamaged world in the seeming hope that its more friendly music would damp out the more dangerous harmonies from the other bodies in the system.

"Ready?" Balthasar asked.

"Whenever," Silence answered.

"Julie?" Balthasar adjusted the headpiece irritably, bringing the microphone into a more convenient position. "All clear. We can pull out on your word."

"Everything's ready here," Chase Mago answered, his voice reassuringly strong in Silence's ears.

"Then do it," Balthasar said.

"First sequence," Chase Mago said. Almost before he finished speaking, the harmonium sang strongly, new notes pulsing through the stable pattern that had held *Bruja* balanced against the conflicting stresses of Decelea's system. In the single viewscreen, the faint light of the starfield flickered faintly as the ship began to move. Silence followed their course on the Ficinan model, frowning to herself as *Bruja* moved from the relative safety of its current position to the snaking line of harmony that skirted the worst of the coil of interference. The music of their own keel seemed suddenly forced, laboring against something more powerful than itself. Chase Mago swore, half to himself, and the harmonium surged, its song overriding the dissonance. But there was a ragged edge to its chords and Silence glanced uneasily at the repeating scale set into her control panel. The needle flickered near the red. Chase Mago was using very close to maximum power.

"How long can you hold this?" she asked into her microphone, and Balthasar nodded his approval of the question, unable to take his attention from his own screens.

"As long as you need," Chase Mago answered. "And there's some in reserve, I think."

"Right." Silence leaned back against her cushions, only a little reassured by the engineer's words. Of course there was always some safety factor built into these ships. The strain gauges always showed red long before they began to break up, but she hated coming even this close to the ship's limits.

"This should ease it," Balthasar muttered. "We're moving onto a better line. Watch the distortion for me, Silence."

"All right." Silence fixed her eyes on the glowing scale, watched the double needles flickering close to the red lines that marked correct pitch.

"Second sequence, Julie," Balthasar ordered, and the harmonium shifted pitch to drive the ship onto its new course. For a moment, the music held steady, blaring triumphant over the surrounding dissonance, and then a note rose from the song, breaking the harmony.

"Off by five," Silence exclaimed. "Seven . . . ten. Julie, bring her back."

The harmonium surged; there was not much power to spare. Balthasar tugged at his controls, muttering to himself, fingering the pitch controls delicately to urge the ship onto a more harmonious course. The ship strained, and then, with a suddenness that made the harmonium lurch and waver, despite Chase Mago's instant attention, *Bruja* reached her proper course. The harmonium sank to more reasonable levels.

"What happened?" Silence asked.

Balthasar shook his head. "I'm not sure. This is sticky space, a difficult progression, but this ship ought to be able to handle it." He shrugged, dismissing the subject. "Anyway, we're out of it now."

"Mmm." Silence could not feel so sure of that, thinking of the road ahead, but there was no point in saying it. She glanced at the indicators, saw that they were still well below the twelfth of heaven, but unfastened the couch's straps anyway. "I'm going on up, Denis. I want to think things out again."

"Go ahead." Balthasar barely looked up from his controls as she left.

Silence pulled herself up the ladder, her feet sticking to the rungs, and stepped out onto the pilot's bridge. She was too tense, waiting to fly the unfamiliar road, to seat herself in the couch; instead, she wriggled her feet into the clingfoam of the platform and set her hands on the dead, unmoving wheel. Closing her eyes, she pictured the voidmarks once again.

A subtle shifting of the harmonium's music warned her that they were close to the twelfth of heaven. She opened her eyes, noting the fading hull above and around her, and began to switch on the wheel systems. Lights sprang up, flicked from red or orange to green, and she felt a faint vibration in the palms of her hands.

"We're coming up on it, Silence," Balthasar announced.

"I'm ready," the pilot answered. Carefully, she rested one hand on the lock.

"Ready to switch to the higher register," Chase Mago said.

"Go ahead," Silence said, and Balthasar echoed her.

"Switching." On the engineer's word, the harmonium split, the music broadening into related chords, massive and glorious. The last hint of solidity faded from the hull, and Silence flipped off the lock.

Ahead of her, and to either side, rose walls of apparently solid greenery—the reflection, she realized instantly, of her own perception of this path as a sort of maze. She adjusted the course fractionally, keeping the ship steady between the two walls to either side, and studied the scene before her. The corridor along which *Bruja* travelled appeared to end abruptly in a solid hedge, but she knew there would be passages to either side. She would turn *Bruja* to her left, there to travel clockwise around the central suns.

As *Bruja* drew closer to the green wall, gaps began to appear in its apparent solidity, light shining out between the leaves. Silence frowned, not knowing if that indicated that she was drawing too close, and her hands tightened on the wheel. Then with a conscious effort, she relaxed. She could only fly the road according to the voidmarks she had been given, and they had indicated she should come much closer to the royal couple before making the abrupt turn.

Bruja drew closer still, and the light began to pour into the pilot's bridge, half blinding her. As her eyes adjusted, she thought she could see through the gaps in the central garden into the domain of the royal couple itself. She winced at the light, trying to shake away the greenish shadows that clogged vision. They faded for an instant, and in the moment before new clouds formed, she saw quite clearly what lay beyond the wall. In a garden that was entirely light, the alchemical king, shaped of the same light that formed his domain, embraced his queen, who was composed entirely of darkness. Her features were invisible, the absolute blackness incapable of contrasting, shaping shadow. She embraced her consort fiercely, her lips fastened on his in a greedy, devouring kiss.

"Silence!" That was Balthasar's voice, and Silence looked away with a gasp. "Pull out!"

The pilot was still half blinded by the light beyond the patchy wall but she could see that the ship was falling dangerously close to the central images. Swearing, she hauled on the wheel, pulling the ship around in a tight turn to her left. As soon as she looked away from the light, the green shadows blocked her sight utterly, and for a terrifying moment she had only memory and her sense of harmonies to guide her onto the proper course. Then her sight cleared, and she breathed a sigh of relief to find *Bruja* steady between the curving walls of the maze.

She did not have long to relax, however. As the ship swung around, the core light still flared within it, more muted now, by distance and her own inattention. It seemed to pick up speed, and the harmonium changed, various harmonies cancelling each other until there was but a single tone. It was not quite a single note, Silence realized, but so close to it that a human ear could not hear the differences. Something leaped within her chest, as though her heart fought to loosen itself from its place.

"God," Balthasar said, "we're halfway to heaven."

"Seven-twelfths," Chase Mago corrected automatically, and then, as though he had just realized what he had said, repeated, "Seven-twelfths of heaven. . . ."

With an effort, Silence put their words out of her mind, and ignored the strange sensations within her own body. The next signs, the elemental symbols, would be coming up soon, and each one marked a change of course; she had to be ready for them.

Already the first, a world that glimmered sullenly, like pitted iron, swam into view around the curve of her path. Silence tensed. It should not look quite like that, time-damaged and metallic, though metals were merely a shaping of elemental earth. It should be oily brown, smoother . . . she frowned at the image, tried to force it into its proper form, but it remained stubbornly as it was. Was Earth itself damaged, then? she wondered, even as she eased the wheel, working cautiously against the ship's apparent speed. What did it mean?

Then she had made the adjustment, and the image retreated to the periphery of her vision, apparently moving with the ship. She shook her head, unaccountably disturbed, and waited for the next image to appear. The path seemed to curve momentarily sharply and there it was, squat and ugly bands of brown and green gasses whipping across its surface. Silence swore, tried to change it and failed again. She made the course change and waited grimly for whatever was to come.

The last two signs appeared in quick succession, an aged sun, swollen and red, and a frozen world unpleasantly like Arganthonios, for all that its surface was faintly tinged with yellow. She did not even try to change them, but adjusted *Bruja*'s course. Then, with a deep breath, she brought the ship up sharply, describing a great loop that took *Bruja* out of its present position, static relative to the powerful elemental symbols, and brought it down so that the symbols had changed position relative to the ship. She could feel the sudden surge of harmony in the ship's keel as it struck the resonant path. Then everything burst apart. The harmonies vanished, were replaced with howling dissonance. The elemental symbols, corrupted though they already were, lost form and ran together into bizarre, unnatural compounds. Fire burned on the surface of the water world, and earth and air combined in an impossibly solid whirlwind. The red sun swelled further and burst with a spray of dead fire, like pus breaking from an infected wound. Silence cried out as she felt her bones stretching, bending under their own weight. The ship shivered violently around her, shaking itself to bits.

That roused her from her fear. The ship needed harmony, a song to order the chaos around her, a note like the one that had sounded as they approached seven-twelfths of heaven. She called out again, trying to tell Chase Mago what was needed, but her headpiece was dead. The deck trembled beneath her feet, tearing free from its moorings. She sang to it, frantically chanting a tuner's scale, and it snapped back into place, but she could tell that would not hold for long. She needed the sound of heaven to save the ship.

Knowing that, a cold calm closed down around her. That note had vibrated within herself, the spiritual substance present within all matter responding to celestial harmony. She reached for that part of her being, touched it surely, and sang the memory of heaven. It caught up the note, and that spread outward, until her entire self, like a sounding keel, gave back the note of heaven in the face of chaos.

Fear faded, and in its place came glory.

There was a hand on her arm, and a soft, insistent pressure within her singing. She opened her eyes, and found she could do so without disturbing the harmonies that spoke through her. Isambard stood before her, the same power reflected behind the fence of his bones.

"You must take us home now," he said, though Silence was not sure how she heard him over the great diapason within. "You know the ways here, as I don't. What are the signs?"

"The signs are broken, corrupted," Silence said, but even as she spoke, she saw, behind that chaos, a wilderness choked with every symbol that had ever been charted. She recoiled from it, and Isambard touched her arm again, steadying her.

"There are signs," he said again. "You must find them."

She looked again, given strength by the power within herself. This time, amid the chaotic undergrowth of symbols, three stood out. Without bothering to point them out to Isambard, she reached for them, brought the ship to them and then past them. Isambard nodded, and spoke a word that was the negation of all music. Silence cried out as that word stilled even the memory of song, and then at last the ship's harmonium reasserted itself. Screeching and strained almost beyond endurance, it nevertheless functioned, falling from purgatory along the ragged edge of the harmonies. They dropped below the twelfth of heaven, and Silence slid to her knees, weeping.

"There's no time for that, girl," Isambard said impatiently. "Get up. There's work to be done below."

Silence barely heard the magus's words through the stifling deadness that still seemed to fill the core of her being, but the audible strain in the harmonium and the shivering of the deck told their own story. She pulled herself to her feet, not even looking to see if she had locked her wheel, and staggered to the ladder. She had to hold hard to it for several seconds before mustering the strength to slide down to the lower bridge.

The lower compartment was lit flashing red by the disaster lights blinking on and off on every console. The sight was enough to clear Silence's head; she pushed her way to her couch, and began shutting down nonessential systems even before she sat down. Balthasar darted her a grateful look, but was too busy trying to bring everything back to a stable harmony to speak. Silence finished shutting down everything that could be spared—already she could feel an easing in the harmonium—and began to copy Balthasar's adjustments to the system. That was less successful, and finally the Delian shook his head.

"Find me a null spot, quick."

Silence reached for the musonar and Ficinan display, switching them on again. *Bruja* had ended up in a system that seemed vaguely familiar, but she could not spare the time to work out precisely which system it was. Instead, she located the ship's position, then looked quickly for the nearest spot where conflicting harmonies cancelled each other. *Bruja* could lie dead there, using just enough power to maintain the harmonium's protective field.

"Here," she said, and read off the relative coordinates. Balthasar glanced quickly at the Ficinan model, but then looked back to his own gauges.

"Talk me in," he said. "I've got to watch the stress."

"All right." Silence took a deep breath, the sense of power she had felt in purgatory already receding, drowned by her new responsibilities. "Come left two degrees, and hold it."

Slowly, tacking the damaged ship against the music of the system, they brought *Bruja* into the dead space, and Chase Mago stopped down the harmonium, the music fading to a whisper that would just maintain the ship's structure.

"How long do we have?" Balthasar whispered. Silence could see his hands shaking.

The engineer gave a ghost of a laugh. "Until I turn her off, I think. Don't worry, Denis, she'll hold as long as we need. Where are we? Did we make it?"

My God, Silence thought, I don't even know that. She turned to the Ficinan display, but Balthasar was there before her, punching inquiries into the locater.

"Mersaa Maia," he said at last. "Interesting. Why're we here when we were supposed to go to Earth?" He glanced quickly at Silence. "And what the hell happened?"

"The marks were changed," Silence answered readily. "I'm not sure by what, but they were badly distorted—the underlying harmonies were, I mean. And when I tried to bring everything together, I was really setting up an incredible dissonance."

"Then what?" Balthasar demanded.

Silence spread her hands. "I—found the harmony. I don't know how." Now that the immediate danger was past, the sense of having lost some great power threatened to overwhelm her. Her eyes filled with tears. "Denis, what am I?"

Balthasar leaned awkwardly across the Ficinan display, pulled her head against his shoulder. Silence clung to him, while he smoothed her hair and murmured softly to her. Footsteps on the ladder made her pull away, wiping impatiently at her eyes.

"I think, Captain Balthasar," Isambard said, "you had better try to call help from—is that Mersaa Maia?"

"Yes," Balthasar said.

"Interesting." The magus stroked at his beard, showing no signs of leaving the control room. Balthasar glared at him, and swung back to his controls.

"Julie? Is there power for the transmitter?"

"Yes." Chase Mago spoke from the hatchway,

and Silence jumped. "I left enough for a couple of hours' conversation."

"That should be enough," Balthasar said grimly, and keyed on the transmitter. Before he could speak, the machine crackled to life.

"Attention, unidentified ship. Attention, unidentified ship. You are approaching Mersaan space without prior authorization. Identify yourself immediately. Repeating, identify—"

Balthasar said, "This is—" and stopped, taking his finger off the key. "How the hell are we going to explain ourselves, anyway?" he asked, of no one in particular.

The others did not answer. Balthasar made a face, and turned back to the console. "This is Hegemonic mailship *Bruja*, requesting emergency assistance. We have been badly damaged in transit, and we need immediate help."

"We have no prior notice of your arrival, *Bruja*." That was a different voice from the unfeeling drone that had asked for their identification, a sharper voice. Unaccountably, Silence felt chill, and saw Isambard frowning.

"What's your point of origin?" the Mersaan continued.

Balthasar looked at the others again. "What do I tell them?"

"Don't tell them you were coming from Decelea," Isambard said quickly. "Say Solitudo. They cannot question that easily."

Balthasar made a face, but answered, "Solitudo Hermae."

There was a long pause, and then the voice said, "We still have no record of your request to put down here. Can you reach Nisibis or Anxur? They are worlds of your own sphere—"

"No," Balthasar cut in. "I told you, we're badly

damaged. We can't even make it in-system, much less go through purgatory. We need a tug."

"Unauthorized ships are not allowed to land on Mersaa Maia," the voice repeated. "You will have to be cleared first."

"This is an emergency," Balthasar said. "What's your authority?"

"I am Port Master of Mersaa Maia," the voice answered primly.

Balthasar cut the transmission. "What the hell's the Port Master doing talking to us now?" he demanded. "And what's the fuss over an emergency? They've got to bring us down."

Isambard smiled bitterly. "Captain Balthasar, Mersaa Maia is the gate to the Rose Worlds. And the Rose Worlds are blocking the road to Earth."

"You can't block purgatory," Silence began, and Balthasar said, "What's that got to do with us?"

"If they don't let us land," Chase Mago said slowly, "there's a chance we might die here. Then anything we might have found out would be lost. Am I correct, Isambard?"

The magus nodded. "Essentially. And, sieura, it is quite possible to block purgatory. Siege engines already do that, in a crude way. Clearly, the Rose Worlders have developed a more efficient method."

Balthasar snorted. "By God, I'll make them bring us down." He touched controls again. "Port Master, I repeat, this is an emergency. I evoke the rights of humanity—and Mersaa Maia is your depot, an open planet. Will you close out an official ship?"

There was a long pause, and then the Port Master said, "Please wait."

Balthasar made a face, but the Mersaan was back in a remarkably short time. "Captain, all our tugs are in use right now. You will be picked up as soon as one is free. You are at the top of our priority list."

Balthasar snarled at the machine, but before he could frame a suitably blistering reply, a new voice cut into the conversation.

"*Bruja*, this is the freighter *Samisen*, out of Misthia." The woman's voice made the last bit of identification unnecessary. "We are within tow range, and can pick you up. There doesn't look like there's much to salvage, if you're worried about the rights. Is that agreeable to you, captain? And to you, Port Master?"

Balthasar laughed soundlessly. "That's got him," he said, and switched on his transmitter again. "Thank you, *Samisen*, your help is much appreciated."

Silence could almost hear the sigh in the Port Master's voice. "Go ahead, *Samisen*, and thanks for your assistance."

Chapter 10

It took nearly two hours for *Samisen* to reach *Bruja*'s position, and Chase Mago used that time to forge log entries for the fictitious passage from Solitudo Hermae. He was good at it, Silence thought, but she doubted the story would hold up for very long.

"We'll have to appeal for sanctuary," she said, closing the starbooks from which they had culled a plausible route.

Chase Mago, splicing record tapes, grunted dubiously, and Balthasar said, "She's right, you know. They're never going to believe we're a regular mailship—where's the officer, for one thing?"

"Isambard," the engineer said, and adjusted his magnifying lens.

"A magus in command of a starship?" Balthasar asked.

"It isn't so improbable," Isambard said mildly, and the Delian glared at him.

"And what are you going to do? Sit back and watch while the Mersaans take us apart? Turn us in, even?"

The magus smiled and shook his head.

Silence turned on him, evoking the one threat she thought might move him. "If you turn us in, we'll get word out somehow—you know we can—and make sure everyone knows you broke your given word. If one magus could, so could any—your own kind will kill you first, just to keep themselves safe, or who'd ever trust a magus again?"

"I have no intention of breaking our agreements, sieura," Isambard began, and was cut off by a beeping noise from the lower bridge.

"*Samisen*," Balthasar announced, and rose from his seat at the table.

Silence followed him into the control room and seated herself in the second couch. "We're stuck with this, aren't we?" she asked. "We're an official Navy ship, bound from Solitudo to Mersaa Maia, whose routing orders never made it into the Mersaan records, and who just happened to stray away from that path and hit a frequency common in the Earth road. It's awfully thin, Denis."

Balthasar nodded, his eyes fixed on the Ficinan display. "Do you really want to tell the Rose Worlders we're escaped conscripts? Or that we were looking for Earth, and we know they're blocking the road?"

"How the hell do we know they're blocking it?" Silence demanded.

"I'd trust Isambard that far," Balthasar said. "And I don't trust the Rose Worlders." He reached for the controls, thumbed on the transmitter as the image of *Samisen* crossed the almost invisible border into the dead zone. "*Samisen*, this is *Bruja*. We're glad to see you."

Balthasar was right, Silence thought, as she settled herself to monitor both ships' keelsong. Isambard had no reason to lie about the interference they had felt, and he would certainly know what had caused it. So she had no choice but to believe him, at least until someone provided a better explanation. And Balthasar was right about the Rose Worlders, too. They were too exclusive, too secretive, to be trusted.

A flash of yellow brought her attention back to the board—the inevitable dissonance had reached an unacceptable level—and automatically she read out the correction. *Samisen*'s pilot made the adjustment deftly, and the Misthian ship settled slowly alongside *Bruja*, the two fields merging almost without interference. Balthasar sighed.

"That's it," he said. "If there's anything you want from this cow, you'd better pack your bags." He left the control room without a backward glance.

By the time Silence had collected her starbooks and packed them into a carryall, the transfer tube was already set up between the two ships, and the Misthian captain had come aboard. She was a tall, angular woman—Balthasar introduced her as Fava n'Ia—of higher caste than Tasarla had been, but with the same contempt for her homeworld's ways. She raised an eyebrow at the details of their story, and politely said nothing.

Samisen's crew, five younger, fairer versions of Fava, helped them transfer two of Isambard's crates, all the magus deemed worth saving, to the Misthian ship, and then the second pilot, who introduced herself as Sirkka neMafalda, took them into *Samisen*'s common area while her crewmates disconnected the transfer tube and made ready for the landing on Mersaa Maia. In the common area, Sirkka offered food and cups of a smoky tea, but after the first sip, Silence leaned back against the chair webbing, hardly able to keep her eyes open.

The strain of the passage, first from Castax to Decelea, and then the abortive attempt to reach Earth, was finally catching up with her. Her head hurt, with a stiff pain that was like the ache of strained muscles, but she was too exhausted to do anything about it. She closed her eyes and let herself drift with *Samisen*'s keelsong.

Balthasar woke her some time later, and for a second, Silence was alarmed by the quiet. Then she realized that she had slept through the landing— God, she thought, I must've been tired, if the change of pitch didn't wake me. She blinked, trying to wake up.

"Customs is coming aboard," Balthasar was saying urgently. "Keep looking dazed; Julie and I will do the talking. Silence, are you listening?" He shook her again, not gently, and dragged her to her feet. "Lean on me, and look dizzy. Understand?"

"Yes," Silence said. She clung to him as she had clung to Chase Mago the night of their marriage party, and felt the Delian shift his position to take her weight. His arm around her waist was comfortingly strong, and she was not sorry for the pretense. Balthasar maneuvered her out of the ship and down the sloping ramp of the cradle. Chase Mago was waiting there, standing quietly beside one of Isambard's crates. Silence let them ease her down onto the crate's lid, and closed her eyes, listening to Balthasar arguing with someone who was out of her line of sight. After a moment, she risked looking around more alertly. The Mersaan Customs men were there, as Balthasar had said, and in force: there were three uniformed technicians, each with a different set of scanning machines; a laborant and an apprentice, carrying diviner's rods; and two men whom she guessed were port officials.

"Could we go through your statement again, Captain Balthsaar?" the older of the two said, and Silence recognized the voice of the Port Master.

"Sure, as many times as you want," Balthasar answered. "But you won't hear anything new."

"For the record," the other port official said patiently, and Balthasar glared at him.

"You say you're a regular mailship, part of the auxiliary forces of the Hegemonic Navy," the Port Master said. "Is that correct?"

"Yes," Balthasar answered.

"You're obviously not nobility or gentry," the Port Master continued. "Are you conscripts?"

Balthasar hesitated, and Silence willed him to remember that they no longer wore the collars that would mark them as geas-bound slaves. "Volunteers," he said, after a moment.

"Since when has the Hegemony relied on volunteers for its ships?" the younger man demanded. "Sir, these—people—are clearly just another group of adventurers. I suggest they be treated as such."

The Port Master nodded. "I'm afraid, Captain Balthasar, that unless you can come up with a more plausible story, I have no alternative but to follow Gearalt's suggestion." His smile belied the gravity of his tone.

There was a heavy sigh from behind Silence, and Isambard stepped forward to stand beside Balthasar.

"I am afraid," he said, "that I must make a fuller explanation."

Silence held her breath, wishing she could draw on that power she had found to gag the magus before he could betray them. Something thrummed deep within her, but before she could pursue it, Isambard spoke.

"I understand your sense of duty, Captain, and appreciate what you have tried to do for me," he said. "However, I must remind you that I have final say over this mission."

"But—" Balthasar said slowly, and Isambard interrupted him quickly, though Silence thought she saw him give an almost imperceptible nod.

"I do not think his Majesty would hold you to your oath, and in any case, I may speak when you must be silent."

Balthasar bowed, his face a mask, and stepped back, away from the Port Master.

"Now, Port Master," Isambard began. "You know that there are a number of magi employed on the siege of Castax?" He waited until the Mersaan nodded warily. "I have been involved in that project for some time, as it coincides with my own field of interest, and the Hegemon very kindly sponsored my researches, to the extent of loaning me this ship and crew. As you so astutely observe, they are neither noble nor gentry; however, they are oath-bound—of their own free will—to serve his Most Serene Majesty, and have done many useful services for him. You will understand why I may not say more—I fear I've said too much already."

He glanced at Balthasar and, as if in answer to a cue, the Delian gestured despairingly. "You've ruined us."

"I doubt that," Isambard said. "In any case, we were indeed travelling from Solitudo Hermae—and I cannot explain your lack of records, unless a rival of mine. . . . No matter. However, I was carrying some—instruments which I had created, which I felt would be of some use at Castax, and they seem to have been insufficiently shielded. While in purgatory, they picked up a sympathetic harmony, and dragged the ship toward the source of the disturbance. We were fortunate to escape."

The Port Master had gone pale. "What is your speciality, Doctor Isambard?"

"At the moment, siege engines," Isambard answered blandly. "And related phenomena. I am still completely unable to explain what happened. I would appreciate a chance to speak to any of your own magi, who would be more familiar with local disturbances than am I."

"Perhaps that can be arranged," the Port Master said hastily. His colleague, Gearalt, leaned close to him, murmuring something Silence could not hear. "Excuse me a moment, Doctor, Captain." He retreated to the baffles separating *Samisen*'s cradle from the next berth, and the two men conferred hastily.

I think we're going to get out of this, Silence thought, and stared at the baffled floor to keep her delight from showing too clearly. It's just plausible enough, and it's a magus who's telling it. They don't dare disbelieve a magus—the magi are too powerful, and the only thing they agree on is the need to preserve their status. If the Mersaans challenged Isambard without positive proof he lied, they risked having the other magi turn on them. And even the Rose World's can't survive without magi.

"Doctor Isambard," the Port Master said abruptly. "You realize, of course, that your story must be verified, but at the moment, I see no reason to hold you."

"Thank you," Isambard said. "Tell me, is there a Hostel in the port?"

"A magi's shelter?" The Port Master looked to Gearalt, who nodded. "Yes, Doctor, all the cabs would know it."

"Then you may find us all there, if you need to question us further." Isambard turned to the Misthian captain, who had been listening with frank curiosity. "I am sorry to impose further, Captain Fava, but may we have the use of your homunculi to move what remains of my baggage?"

"What did happen to your special cargo, Doctor?" Gearalt asked suddenly.

"I was forced to destroy it," Isambard answered. "In purgatory."

"You're welcome to whatever help I can offer," Fava said, "if you can do it now."

"If these gentlemen would permit us . . ." Isambard began, and the Port Master waved his hand.

"Go ahead, Doctor. But I will want to see you later."

"Of course," Isambard murmured, and waited until they were out of sight. When they heard, faintly, the sound of the docking shed's doors closing behind the Customs vehicle, Balthasar said, "I don't know what you're up to, magus—"

"Nothing," Isambard snapped. "We'll talk at the Hostel."

By the time Isambard's crates had been loaded into a cab, Silence was yawning uncontrollably, the pretense of exhaustion turning into fact. She saw very little of Mersaa Maia's main port during the ride from the shed to the Hostel, drowsing instead with her head on Balthasar's shoulder. Only the fear of being supported by one of the exquisitely formed homunculi who staffed the Hostel gave her the strength to follow the others to the rooms Isambard claimed for them. Once there, not even her curiosity could keep her awake. She collapsed onto a couch and fell instantly asleep.

When she woke at last, the time/date projection on the far wall told her she had slept through a complete local day. She sat up, and the lights came on, triggered by her movements. The others had moved her while she slept, she realized after a moment. This was not the room she remembered, but a smaller, more heavily decorated bedroom. The walls glimmered in the dim light. They were covered with tiny paintings, the colors bright as enamels, and with equally tiny mirrors positioned to reflect the pictures, so that she could not be completely sure which was which. Dizzied, she reached for the light controls. With the lights turned all the way on, the illusion faded, and she saw clothes folded on a rack at the foot of the bed. She threw back the covers, wondering just who had undressed her, and got up. She showered quickly, then dressed. The clothes left for her were a one-size-fits-all version of the tunic and hose she had worn on Delos, topped with a light, knee-length coat. There was a palm-sized two-shot heylin in a wrist clip, too, and after a moment's hesitation, she strapped that on as well. Beneath the heylin was a pad of credit slips, and she pocketed them without compunction. How long ago was Delos, really? she wondered. Only a month? It seemed years ago. Shaking her head, she slid back the bedroom door.

She found herself not in the room she remembered from the day before, but in a dimly lit corridor, the watered silk of the wall covering broken at intervals by unmarked doors. Halfway between each door was an elaborate sort of candelabra, a winged metal dancer holding a cool globe of light in its cupped hands. Entranced, she moved closer, and the door slid shut behind her. She gasped, but stood her ground. Denis is here somewhere, and the others, she told herself sternly. You can always find your way to the lobby and ask for directions there, if you have time. They'll probably be along any minute now. And in the meantime, you might as well look at the statue.

She advanced on it, marvelling at the perfection

of the work, wondering how the fire-compound had been fixed in a bubble barely the size of her fist. Then the statue turned its head and looked at her.

This time, she did cry out, taking a quick step backward. It's just a Watcher, she told herself, like the one at the terminal on Delos. Nothing else. And if it's a Watcher, it may at least be able to point to the lobby. Feeling slightly foolish, she smiled up at the statue.

"Excuse me," she began.

"Pardon, sieura, but perhaps I can be of help?"

Silence turned quickly, and found herself facing a handsome young man—or was it a man, she wondered. The person wore a man's coat and trousers, but his cheek was very smooth. She frowned, trying to see more clearly, but the other was standing in the shadow between two pools of light. "Yes, I think you can," she said. "I'm trying to find my—husbands. They've gone on without me."

The young man appeared to consider. 'Yes," he said, after a moment. "Sieura Leigh?"

"Yes."

"They are dining on the roof, if you would like to join them." The other extended a hand in a gesture that was oddly old-fashioned for someone so young. "If you would come with me?"

Silence froze, staring at the hand, lying now just inside the pool of light. The skin had an odd, greyish tint beneath the delicate pallor, and the fine lines and the bone shadows were altogether too regular to be real: a homunculus, better formed even than the ones she had seen before. Silence shivered, then fought back her revulsion. With an effort, she put out her own hand, and rested it lightly on the homunculus's wrist. The pseudo-flesh was cool and paper-smooth, totally non-human.

The homunculus bowed and escorted her grace-fully down the length of the corridor, to a stairwalk that spiralled up out of sight. It helped her aboard—Silence shivered, but submitted to the programmed courtesy—then waited unspeaking for the stairs to carry them to their destination. The stairs swept past several floors of rooms, all decorated with the same silken hangings and Watcher-lampholders, then past three more floors that were sealed off by heavy doors, wood over earth compounds, before coming to an end in an octagonal pavilion. The pavilion's walls were trellised, and a dozen differ-ent species of flowering vines had been woven through the wooden slats. Looking more closely, Silence recognized a camisado vine, and then the narrow black flowers of an adderwort. She did not doubt that the others were just as poisonous.

The homunculus held out his hand again, and Silence let him lead her from the pavilion into a warmly sunlit path winding between two hedges. She glanced dubiously at those, but when she saw no poisonous vines lurking in the foliage, she re-laxed a little and let herself enjoy the illusion of space. The homunculus escorted her through the twisting passages, apparently following a faint sound of running water that grew stronger as they went farther, and finally brushed aside a curtain of cascading vines.

"Your husbands are waiting, sieura."

Silence ducked under the trailing flower—she did not recognize it, and wanted to take no chances —and stepped into a tiny enclosure, bounded on three sides by the same hedges that shaped the paths. The fourth side was a wall of uncolored glass, broken only at waist height by a polished bronze rail. Through the glass she could see Mersaa Maia's port city, a carpet of stubby, scabrous build-ings lining empty, rutted streets. All the streets converged on the single highway that ringed the landing field, but the squat massy tower, like a prison, of the main port building blocked her view of the field itself. The sound of water faded and died.

"Good day, sieura," Isambard said.

The magus was sitting to one side of the enclosure, a book open on his lap. Balthasar and Chase Mago were sitting together against the opposite hedge, staring morosely at the cityscape. The Delian looked up at Isambard's greeting.

"Good. Now you can talk."

Silence looked at him, puzzled, but then Isambard put aside his book, and she realized that Balthasar had been talking to the magus. "What's going on?" she asked.

"Have some coffee," Chase Mago growled. "I think you're going to want it."

There was a massive gold-chased pot on the table, even more elaborate than the one she had seen in the magi's quarters on Arganthonios. She poured herself a cup and seated herself on the bench beside Balthasar.

"Well?" she asked again.

Balthasar snorted. "That's what we're about to find out," he said. "He wouldn't tell us anything until you woke up."

Silence looked at the magus. "What is it?"

Isambard rose and walked slowly across the enclosure. At a gesture, his chair followed him. He stopped it opposite their bench and sat, folding his hands in his lap.

"I know that you have many questions," he began. His mouth twitched as Balthasar muttered something. "And, yes, Captain, I do intend to answer them. In my own time."

Balthasar started to say something more, but Silence put her hand on his knee and squeezed hard. The Delian jerked, and gave her a startled look. Silence ignored him.

"As you please," she said, and sipped at her cooling coffee.

The magus laughed. "I didn't think I was wrong about you, sieura. What is your most important question?"

Silence hesitated, a sudden feeling of power sweeping over her, like the memory of the harmony she had felt on the Earth road. She was very aware of the way the others were looking at her, Balthasar and Chase Mago each willing her to ask the questions they wanted answered. Isambard, too, wanted her to ask a particular question, and she smiled, hugging a new sense of strength to herself.

"Very well, Doctor," she said, and knew he recognized her new awareness. "What am I?"

The magus smiled again, this time with a sort of relieved pleasure. "So. You are—or rather, you have the potential to become—a magus."

There was a moment of stunned quiet. Then Chase Mago said, "How can she be? She's female—"

"That would explain the transport, wouldn't it?" Balthasar said savagely. "Shut up."

Silence nodded to herself. Once it had been spoken, she felt almost as though she had always known. Even Chase Mago's objection, and everything she had learned about the Art throughout her life, could not shake her certainty. She stared out over the ugly city, considering new possibilities. With training—she would have to be trained, but there were enough magi who would teach her simply because she was an oddity—she could do whatever she wanted. There would always be work for a magus, work that paid well enough for her to spend years doing only what pleased her. Travel, study, even the life of an oligarch, if she wanted it. . . . Then her gaze faltered, and she saw again the dirty port city spread out before her. There was not much room for piloting, for her own Art, in that future. At the very least, she would not be able to fly while she was apprenticed to some magus—and what would that do to her partnership, her marriage? *I don't want to leave them, either,* she thought.

"Do you doubt me?" Isambard snapped.

Silence turned quickly. "I don't doubt your power," she said.

"Good. Then hear me out." Isambard steepled his fingers, staring thoughtfully at her. "On board your *Bruja*—"

"Not ours," Balthasar interjected, as though it were very important.

The magus nodded, accepting the correction. "On board *Bruja*, then. We made a bargain, sieura, you and I. You agreed to find Earth for me, and I agreed not to turn you over to the authorities as pirates and murderers. Is that correct?"

"Yes," Silence said.

"I call your attention to the phrasing of the agreement. You have not yet found Earth for me, sieura. I suggest you are still bound, and I intend to hold you to it."

"The hell—" Balthasar began, and Silence said, "Shut up. Go on, Isambard."

"I would point out that continuing our association might prove highly profitable for all three of you," Isambard went on. "You, sieura, could enter into an apprenticeship with me; your husbands could share in the profits of the voyage to Earth, and in anything else we undertake. Is this agreeable?"

"I'd like time to think," Silence said. *There's no need to worry yet,* she told herself. *If I don't agree, there are other options—friends call at Mersaa Maia* occasionally. We can buy a ride off-planet with them, live underground until we reach the Fringe. Even Isambard won't waste time chasing us that far.

"Before you make any decision, sieura," Isambard said, "I ought to point out that you cannot remain on Mersaa for very long. The Rose Worlders are almost certain that you tried to reach Earth, and the longer you remain, the less probable your story becomes."

I'm well aware of that, Silence thought, but bit back her angry response. "I don't think it will take me that long to decide, Isambard," she said aloud.

"Certainly, sieura," the magus said, rising. "I'll leave you to talk things over with your husbands. When you're ready to leave, summon one of the homunculi to escort you." He gestured to a bell-pull, artfully woven into the hedge among the other vines. "I will be waiting for your answer." Pushing aside the curtain of flowers, he disappeared from sight.

Silence waited until the faint crunching of his footsteps had faded from hearing, and said, "Is it safe to talk?"

Balthasar shrugged irritably, and glared at the flourishing greenery as though every leaf hid a listening device.

"I imagine so," Chase Mago said. "The magi go in for live listeners—you remember that monkey-thing Nnamdi's man had?"

"Does it really matter?" Balthasar asked. "We've got trouble, Silence."

"What sort of trouble?" the pilot asked.

"Fava, for a start. She won't help us get off-world—says the authorities here would lift her landing permits if it was even so much as hinted she was involved in such a thing." Balthasar grimaced. "I talked to a couple of other people down in the port—you slept the clock around, Silence. Not that I have particular friends who land here, but I thought my connections could get us off. But it's no go. Everybody says the same thing: the authorities want to keep us here, until they get answers to their questions. I was followed halfway to the port before I shook them."

"Why are they so concerned?" Silence asked. "A lot of people have tried to get to Earth before."

"Not magi," Chase Mago said. "At least that's what Isambard said."

"I can name three," Balthasar muttered.

"Not magi who are pilots," Silence said. "Like me."

"Even so, other ships have survived attempts, and nobody's ever said Mersaa treated them this badly," Chase Mago protested half-heartedly.

"We came close," Silence said. "I know what went wrong. If I had more control...." She let her words trail off, not quite daring to finish the sentence. Next time, though, she thought. Another time, I could make it. "What I'd like to know," she went on, "is why the Rose Worlds are blocking Earth."

"You'd have to go there to find that out," Balthasar said.

"Are you telling me to go along with Isambard?" Silence asked.

"Hell, no. We'll get off-planet somehow—"

"How?" Silence demanded.

"There are ships through here almost daily," Balthasar shot back. "If we can't hitch a ride, we can get a message out, get someone to come get us. I've friends I can call on...."

"Wrath-of-God is broken for now," Chase Mago said, quietly. "Who else?"

Balthasar shrugged. "And Tasarla's dead, and I don't know how to contact Gregor. All right, it was a bad idea. But I think working for the magus is worse."

A smoldering anger had been rising in Silence all through the conversation. "And what about me?" she asked. It was a cold anger; her tone was level and her thoughts were extraordinarily clear, focused through the lens of new realization. "I am, I will be, a magus—maga? Someone powerful, someone unique. Isambard's offered me that, and whether or not I do it, it's my choice, not yours. And I'll make it without your help, thank you very much."

Balthasar glared at her. "You trying to tell me this doesn't affect us, too? You're a magus, all right—"

"Shut up, Denis," Chase Mago said. "Silence—"

"Leave me alone, I want to think." Silence buried her head in her hands. Balthasar's last jibe had hit its mark, and she did not have to hear the rest of it. *You're a magus, all right, you don't give a damn about anything but power.* Just like the magi on Arganthonios, she thought, just like the one—what was his name?—who turned his own son into an instrument of his power. I don't want to become like that. And I want to be a pilot. I've fought all my life to be one, and I don't want to give that up. But I want a magus's power. She closed her eyes, savoring the memory of the Earth road and the harmony that had played through her. I want that, too.

"Silence?" Chase Mago said again, and she opened her eyes.

"Go away, both of you." Her anger had faded, to be replaced by weariness. "I know it affects you; I promise I haven't forgotten. But I don't know what I want, and nobody can make any decision until I know that. Do you understand?"

To her surprise, it was Balthasar who answered,

matching her exhausted tone. "Yeah, I know. I'm sorry."

"It's all right," she said. "Just go away."

"Come on, Denis," Chase Mago said, pulling on the bell rope. After a moment, a homunculus, a copy of the one who had escorted Silence to the roof garden, appeared in the doorway. The engineer gave it instructions in a low voice, and the two men followed it into the maze of greenery.

Silence stared out over the port. The sky had clouded over, producing a milky grey light that was shading toward sunset. The faded light softened the ugly lines of the buildings. Somehow, they seemed more inviting—more familiar—than the well-tended gardens around her, and she reached for the bell cord.

"May I serve you, sieura?" The second homunculus was identical in feature to the one who had escorted her, but the fabric of coat and trousers was subtly different.

"Yes. I need some place to think—not my room, and not here. Can you arrange it?"

There was a brief hesitation, and then the homunculus bowed slightly. "I believe so, sieura. If you will come with me?"

Stiffly, Silence rested her hand on its arm, and allowed it to lead her to the stairwalk. This time they rode it all the way down—Silence counted ten full turns before they reached the cage of twisting metal that protected the last stage. The lobby area—and everything Silence could see of the first floor—was decorated far more soberly than the upper levels. The floor was covered in light and dark wood, the blocks arranged in an intricate, engrossing pattern. Silence frowned down at it, trying to trace the basic unit of the design, then jumped as the homunculus cleared its throat.

"I beg your pardon, sieura, but I have just been

informed that there is a message for you, and for the other members of your party. Shall I bring it?"

"Why not?" Silence said. "Please."

The homunculus bowed and stepped away, disappearing behind a screen of painted paper. Silence glanced curiously around, careful not to look at that fascinating floor pattern. It was too fascinating, she realized, too hypnotic. The whole thing was probably part of the magi's security arrangements. Even knowing what it was, she found it hard to keep her eyes from straying to the space before her feet. Shaking herself, she fixed her eyes on the far wall—painted a deliberately uninteresting beige, unbroken by any viewglobes or painted decoration. Even the tiny gathering area, screened by plants as brown as the rest of the lobby, was as unappealing as possible, merely four brown cushionchairs on a paler brown rug.

"Sieura, I have your messages," the homunculus said.

Silence turned and accepted the folded sheets of printer paper, muttering her thanks. The first message was short and to the point: *You are required to present yourself at the Customs Building, Room 13C470.* The date was two days from today. No, she realized, she had slept through a day. The appointment was for the day after tomorrow—and today was nearly over. Well, she thought, Isambard can surely handle that—if they don't push too hard. The second message was longer, more cryptic. *A certain person is inquiring about you, unofficially. I will have details, at the Green Man tonight, 1700 hours.* It was signed with Fava's name, and a complicated hieroglyph that was almost certainly Fava's private seal. Silence bit her lip, wondering who was looking for her, and why.

"When was this left?" she asked.

The homunculus appeared to consider. "At ten this morning, sieura."

Silence glanced at the wall chrono. If she wanted to reach the port in time to keep this appointment, she would have to leave now. And something stronger than curiosity was urging her on. She sighed, and handed the first paper back to the homunculus, stuffing the other into her pocket. "I won't be needing a room after all," she said. "You can show this to my husbands and Doctor Isambard. Tell my husbands—not Isambard—that I'll be back soon."

"Very well, sieura." The homunculus bowed and retreated. This time, she watched him go, and saw him disappear into a wall compartment. Then she found her way to the massive main doors.

The air outside the Hostel was warm and damp, and Silence was glad her coat was made of a light fabric. The dusty streets were almost empty, and she saw no signs of the tracks or wires of public trolleys. I should have asked the homunculus, she thought, but then shrugged. The port looked to be less than two miles away; she could walk that easily.

As she made her way further into the city, the streets grew busier. She began to pass men who were obviously port workers, company or conglomerate insignia prominent on the shoulders of their baggy overalls. There were more women than she had expected, many of them secretaries in neat tunic and coat combinations, their hair covered by tidy hats or elaborately folded scarves. There were also obvious housekeepers, dowdy in unfitted, shift-like dresses, shopping bags piled on little carts. They, too, concealed their hair beneath coarsely woven scarves. I should have found out about local customs before I left the Hostel, Silence thought. Oh, well, it's too late now. She looked around, but no one seemed to be paying any particular attention to her. Nevertheless, she felt conspicuous, and oddly uneasy.

Even in the center of the port, on streets where half a dozen badly decorated storefronts opened onto the broken paving, and men and women moved from building to building with a purposeful air, she felt the same unease. It was growing stronger, too, a nagging uncertainty like hunger or sickness, tugging at that part of her that had resounded with the celestial harmony. She stopped in the recessed doorway of a store selling sheets of some tri-colored food—there were no benches for pedestrians in sight, though she had seen only a single electric wagon—and tried to isolate the cause of her fears. The low buildings, barely four stories tall, upper windows heavily shuttered against the damp heat, seemed to loom ominously over the street, the lower windows reflecting the pale stone of the buildings opposite like steely eyes. The silent pedestrians, avoiding her gaze, seemed more menacing than open enemies.

The whole scene was strangely familiar, she thought, surveying the dusty street. The heat, the midafternoon quiet, the fear. . . . Her memory did a sudden flip-flop, and she was presented with a vivid picture of a street on Cibistra. There had been sun in her eyes as she topped the hill, walking between streets whose upper stories overhung the narrow road. All the doors had been shut and sealed, against midsummer heat and the sun-broken men who stalked the streets during the daylight hours when decent people were in bed. One of them was behind her; she had known without having to hear the faint scuff of boots on dirt. It had been a matter of keeping going, of walking toward the port, not daring to run, and hoping to reach it before the man behind her made up his mind to attack. She had reached the gates of the port, her back tingling in anticipation of the knife or heylin shot, just in time. She could still remember the sense—almost taste, almost smell, but neither—of her pursuer's disappointment.

In the doorway of the shop, Silence laughed aloud. Of course, idiot, Denis even warned you, she told herself. You should've expected to be followed, fool. Still, the uneasiness remained. So what do I do? Try to lose them? Hardly likely—I'm a stranger here, and I don't have Denis's training. Proceed as though I haven't noticed? Probably the best thing . . . certainly the safest, at least until I get to the Pale. I can lose them there.

Bracing herself, she stepped from the doorway, and could not resist sneaking a quick look over her shoulder. She saw no one familiar, no figure she could pick out as one she had seen before, but she knew they—he? no, more than one, her instinct whispered—were there. She looked away again, took her bearing from the Customs complex, and set off for the Pale.

The streets ran perfectly straight until they hit the broad thoroughfare ringing the port, or so she remembered seeing them from the roof of the Hostel. What she had not been able to see was the way that life seemed to drain from the buildings that lined them. She walked three blocks, then, more slowly, a fourth, noting nervously that the streets were empty of pedestrians and that more and more of the narrow windows were bricked up, the buildings disused or converted to warehouse space. Her sense of being followed grew even stronger, until, closing her eyes for a second, she could almost pinpoint them. There were two of them, one on each side of the street. She was as certain of that as if she had seen them, but the temptation to turn and be sure was still almost overwhelming. She held herself rigidly straight,

fixing her eyes on the pavement ahead, and forced
herself to hold a steady pace.

There was a change in the pace of the men behind her, felt rather than heard or seen. They were
moving faster: whatever their original instructions
had been, they were no longer interested in merely
following her. She quickened her own pace, not
wanting to run until she had no choice. What the
hell am I going to do now? she thought. The streets
were laid out in too regular a grid for there to be
any maze of backs alleys for her to hide in; the
cross-streets she had passed before contained only
the same monotonous line of warehouses and abandoned buildings. There had been what appeared to
be alleys, she thought, running between some of
those structures. . . . She frowned, wishing futilely
that she was back on Delos or Achasa or even
Cibistra, where there were half a hundred places
that would shelter a fugitive. Stop it, she told
herself fiercely, there's no time for it. The men
behind her were gaining, slowly but steadily; she
could sense how the one across the street from her
was pulling ahead of his partner to block that road
of escape. There was a cross-street coming up, and
she took a deep breath. They would still be far
enough back as she came even with it. If she kept
her steps even, if she did not let them know she
suspected, or was any more worried than any
woman would be, walking alone in an unfamiliar
city, she should make it . . .

It was forty steps to the corner of the last, blind
building. She did not dare turn to look down the
street, afraid even the most disinterested glance
would warn them. Three more steps brought her
to the intersection. She swallowed hard, then turned
abruptly and fled down the side street. Behind
her, there was a shout, and she exulted in the
sense of confusion she could feel. It was only

momentary, however; faintly, as much felt as heard, she was aware of pursuing footsteps. I had half a block's lead, she thought, I've stretched it to a block— But it was not enough. She turned right at the next corner, knowing that they saw her doubling back, but unable to stop herself without losing too much speed. Left at the next, stumbling painfully against the rough bricks of the building. Her chest was hurting already—no star-traveller had the stamina to outrun a planetsider—and she knew she could not keep up her pace for much longer. An alley opened suddenly in the blank wall of buildings, and she ducked into it, gasping.

The end was clogged with machinery, the tanks and webbed piping of a cheap venting system. She checked, too out of breath to swear, and saw that there was a space between the pipes and the wall of the building. It looked almost large enough for her to squeeze through. She ran toward it, struggling to regain her earlier pace. In the street behind, she could feel the hunters closing in, slowing a little with the certainty of success. Fumbling, she freed her heylin from the wrist clip. If I have to, she thought, I'll fight.

There was just room enough for her to get through, if she bent nearly double and used her free hand to pull herself along. She bent, reaching for the first pipe, and cried out as the metal burned her hand. More delay, she thought, stripping off her coat and wadding it into clumsy protection, but she could go no further without it. She burned her leg on the same pipe, then pushed herself painfully along the brick wall of the nearest building, one palm braced against a globular tank so cold she thought her skin would freeze even through the protecting coat. The system was cheaply made, poorly shielded— A shout from behind crystallized the germ of her plan.

"Hold it, woman!"

She could tell from the voice that they were at the head of the alley, and she redoubled her efforts, ripping her tunic and scraping the skin along her shoulderblades. Then there were only a few more pipes to cross. She wove her way through them, still dragging her battered coat, and ran.

"Stop!" The shout was followed by a curse, and scuffling, and then a mutter of orders. The second man was being sent back to intercept her from the other end. She skidded to a halt, raising her heylin. Let there be enough power in the magazine, she thought, and fired twice. The globes of fixed fire seemed to take forever to float the length of the alley. Then they struck, and the tanks exploded behind her.

Silence picked herself up slowly, wincing at her new bruises, and a second, lighter blow knocked her to her knees. Behind her, what was left of the machinery was hidden in sheets of white and bluish flame, and there were large gaps in the walls of the buildings to either side, from which bricks fell slowly into the fire. One of the men was dead, that was certain, and if the other had not gone back to determine what was left of the first, he was certainly deterred from further pursuit. Already, Silence could hear the faint wailing of alarms, and knew that specially reinforced homunculi were on the way to fight the fire. She pushed herself to her feet, and started walking briskly toward the port.

Chapter 11

The Green Man was low-roofed and ugly, the sort of building that practically shouted the fact that its owners asked no questions. There were no windows in the stuccoed walls, and the only thing that indicated that the bar was open was the fact that the barred safety door had been taken from its hinges and now leaned against the wall. A mannikin, shaggy with leaves, hung from a pole over the doorway, jigging slowly in the first evening breeze. Silence hesitated outside, staring at the curtain of shadow that blackened the entrance, wondering if the place were safe. Then she shook herself. The Green Man was deep into the Pale, no one but star-travellers would go there. And she would get no more than annoyance from them, as long as it was clear she was herself a pilot. Frowning, she pulled off the scarf she had improvised from the scorched skirts of her coat and stuffed it into a pocket, then hastily smoothed her hair. Then, with a deep breath, she stepped through the doorway.

She came out of the blackness of the shadow-curtain into a broad room lit with a dim, amber light. An oval bar filled the middle section, and dwarfed the tables that clustered in the corners. A casually dressed woman, her hair uncovered, was moving in the bar's central workspace, and Silence sighed her relief. No wonder Fava had chosen this for their meeting place. The tables were mostly filled, but there were still a number of empty spaces at the bar. Silence chose one toward the back, where she could watch the door, and waited, fingering the pad of cash slips in her pocket. The bartender glanced curiously at her, but took her time serving a turbaned man, drawing some sort of beer and spilling a calculated amount of foam onto the stone counter. Only then did she move down the length of the bar, wiping her hands in passing on a towel hanging beneath the counter.

"What can I get you?" she asked.

"What's good?" Silence said.

The bartender stared at her, as though trying to determine her status. Silence returned the stare stolidly. "Regular bar," the other woman answered, after a moment, "and a couple of local things. There's a sweet porter some folks like, spring wine, and a fruit brandy that's a killer."

"I'll try the porter," Silence said.

"Right." The bartender wandered away again, went through the rite of wiping out a stone mug and manipulating the polished handles of one of two massive kegs. Silence glanced nervously around, saw only men in the shadows. Where the hell was Fava?"

"You're new here." The bartender set the damp mug in front of Silence and rested her hands lightly on the counter, waiting.

"Yes." Silence hesitated, not knowing how to answer the unspoken question. The woman wanted to know precisely what she was—star-traveller, someone's mistress, or just a hanger-on. She smiled and said awkwardly, "I hope that's strong. I'd never flown that road before."

It was good enough. The bartender relaxed fractionally, and her smile was less professional. "I'm told it's not easy, sieura—pilot, I should say."

"Thanks." Silence sipped carefully at the porter, got mostly foam. "What do I owe you?"

"One-and-a-half, local." The bartender pocketed the two-credit slip deftly, made only a token gesture of giving change. "Thank you, pilot. Are you waiting for someone?"

"Yes, for some friends."

"Then I'll see you're not bothered." The bartender turned away before Silence could answer, in response to a call from the other end of the bar.

The pilot sipped again at the porter, and nearly choked on the sweet, ropy stuff. God, that's vile, she thought. And where's Fava? She glanced at the time projected in the globe that hung suspended above the bar, and saw that the Misthian was already late. Oh, God, she thought, don't tell me that it was all a trick. If I've fallen for that, the absolute oldest trick in the book. . . . And what will you do if you have? an inner voice demanded. And just how are you going to get back to the Hostel, anyway? Stubbornly, she pushed the doubts away. The message had been real, she was sure of it. And she would get back to the Hostel somehow, however she had to.

"Silence!"

The pilot turned quickly, and only just managed to copy Fava's casual wave. There was a second woman at Fava's shoulder, her eyes watchful, her hands deep in the pockets of her loose smock.

"Hello, captain," Silence said, as the two women took seats to either side of her. "What's up?"

Fava made a face, and waited until the bartender had taken their orders before answering. "I'm not sure myself. But I thought you might be interested in knowing that there are questions being asked about you—you in particular, not your men-folk."

"I know that the authorities have been asking questions," Silence said, and Fava waved a hand in dismissal.

"This isn't them—" she began, and broke off as the bartender set a tall glass in front of each Misthian. "I think you met Sirkka before?"

Silence nodded, and as the bartender walked away again, Fava continued, "Not official questions. You wouldn't need me to tell you that. This is some man off a freighter that landed yesterday. There's quite a bit of talk about you in the port— the authorities haven't been subtle. I think half the planet thinks you tried to reach Earth—"

"We—" Silence broke off, smiled grimly. Any denial would only confirm their suspicions. "Go on."

"Well, when this one heard the stories, he started asking questions of his own. Someone steered him to me, and I told him to get out."

"What was his name?" Silence asked.

"There's more," Fava said. "Then he tried to find out from my crew—he talked to Sirkka—and, well, I suppose she'd better tell you."

"He told me his name was Merestun," Sirkka said readily, her voice more accented than her captain's, "but I'm sure he was lying. I didn't tell him anything more than he'd already heard, but it seemed like he was interested in making the same run. He offered me a lot of money if I could tell him where you were—he said I should say he would be of some use to you, could maybe get you off-planet, if you'd help him."

Does this Merestun really think that's a fair exchange? Silence wondered. Well, maybe it is, since I'm not likely to get off-world any other way. But he doesn't mention Denis and Julie—and there's still Isambard's offer. She looked up, and found the others staring expectantly at her. "Why didn't you tell Denis? I know he spoke to you."

"It's you they were asking for," Fava said, "not him."

That was a Misthian for you, Silence thought. But I shouldn't complain. She wouldn't be helping me if I weren't a woman. "What else did Merestun say?" she asked.

"Not much," Sirkka said.

"Do you know anything about him?"

Fava answered, "He works for a Hegemonic merchant, that's all I know. And the merchant keeps himself in the background."

"I know the ship name," Sirkka broke in. "*Black Dolphin.*"

Black Dolphin. Silence took a deliberate grip on the edge of the bar, squeezed until her fingers ached. *Black Dolphin*, and the merchant would be Tohon Champuy, and the questioner. . . . "The man who spoke to you," she said, keeping her voice steady only with an effort. "Was he a short man? Getting fat? Dark-haired like me, but dark-eyed?"

"I don't know about the eyes," Sirkka said, "but the rest fits."

And Uncle Otto. Silence closed her eyes. The court on Secasia seemed a lifetime away, but the memory—and the anger—was still fresh.

"I gather you know him?" Fava asked, after a moment.

"Yes." They were still looking curiously at her, and Silence sighed. "Otto Razil's his real name.

He's my uncle." She could not stop herself from adding, "And that ship's mine."

"Oh?" Fava leaned forward, hiding her empty glass to avoid interruption.

Silence explained what had happened after her grandfather's death, and how she had ended up with Balthasar and Chase Mago. "So obviously I can't accept Otto's offer," she finished. "Not without losing everything."

The other women were nodding sagely. No, you don't know, Silence wanted to shout. You never had to live by any of those rules, you don't know what it's like to lose something that ought to be yours just because you're female. And you don't know what it feels like now, when I thought I had everything under control, just one decision to make. Just choose to be a magus or stay a pilot, and now all of a sudden Otto's back, to spoil my plans again.

"He doesn't have any legal claim, does he?" Sirkka asked, and gestured for the bartender to refill her glass.

Silence swallowed her first angry reply. "He doesn't need one."

"What can he do, then?" Sirkka went on.

"Look—" Silence controlled herself instantly. "He's made an offer no one else has. And we've got to get off-planet, soon."

Sirkka looked away, embarrassed, but Fava said tranquilly, "I've told your Denis why I can't help you. I do too much business here, and while you're a woman, you're not a Misthian. Not family."

So Denis used my name when he made contact with her, Silence thought. I should've known he would.

"There are plenty of other ships that land here," Fava went on. "One of them will surely help."

"We can't wait," Silence snapped. "The authorities are already too curious." She shut her mouth tightly over the rest of her words, knowing that she was not angry with Fava. Damn you, Uncle Otto, she thought, you have a knack for bringing out the worst in me. But coming back like this, with the ship—my ship—that's too much. "Where's he docked?" she asked slowly.

"You're going to go to him?" Fava asked, and Silence shook her head, not daring yet to admit even to herself what she might be thinking.

Sirkka snorted. "His merchant doesn't spend money easily," she said. "They're in one of the cheap sheds, near the field. Why?"

Silence closed her eyes, trying to visualize the port, but she had been too exhausted to see much of it when they landed. "Show me exactly."

Sirkka exchanged glances with her captain, and then, when Fava nodded, dragged a finger through the rings left by the chilled glasses, sketching a crude map. "There's the port, and these are the main sheds. Over there—" her finger scattered a clump of wet squares "—are the support buildings, magi, guilds, tuners. Down here, the third, no, fourth—the fourth shed from the administration complex, that's where *Black Dolphin*'s cradled. The field's just beyond."

Silence stared at the rapidly fading sketch, wondering. The shed was very close to the taxiways, and to at least one of the launch tables. And besides, she thought, it was always possible to lift directly from the taxiway, and make any course corrections later. . . .

"How large is his crew, do you know?"

Fava looked oddly at her. "You're not thinking of trying Wrath-of-God's games here, are you?"

I hadn't thought of it that way, Silence thought. Aloud, she said, "No, of course not. Do you know?"

"I hear it's small," Fava said cautiously. "The merchant only carries one bodyguard."

That would make sense, Silence thought. *Black Dolphin*'s cabin space was limited, more than either *Bruja*'s or *Sun-Treader*'s had been. They'd have to have a pilot aboard, and with Otto and Champuy to accommodate, that would leave only one more cabin, converted back from cargo space. . . . Besides, neither Champuy nor Razil would want to share their profit with any more than the absolute minimum crew. Nor would they want to give up any more cargo space. Four men, then. . . . If they could be decoyed away from the ship, or neutralized aboard; if the local authorities could be tricked into giving them permission to lift, or if a diversion could be managed, it was just possible they might get away with what Fava called Wrath-of-God's games. In spite of herself, Silence grinned. Balthasar, at least, would be pleased.

"You are thinking of stealing it," Fava said. "You're crazy."

"I don't think so," Silence said, hardly hearing her. Considered rationally, she—they—would be taking a very long chance, but they didn't have a better alternative. At least, she didn't know of one, and if Isambard had something up his sleeve, this would make him show it. More than that, she would be getting her ship back. She had forgotten, or put aside, how much it had hurt to give it up. And most of all, it would let her put off the final choice between piloting and life as a magus. "I think I could get Otto off the ship, Champuy too. . . ." Her voice trailed off as she considered a variety of false messages, and then she put that aside. "Look, is there a magus in the port who handles private communications? Someone reliable?"

Fava shook her head. "Yes, I know one, but—"

Silence cut her off. "One thing. If the others agree, will you contact Otto for me? I'm not asking for anything more."

Fava hesitated, then, reluctantly, smiled. "All right. I'll do that, but no more."

"Thank you." Silence stood up. "How do I get to this magus?"

"Sirkka, show her the way." Fava stood also. "I hope you know what you're doing, pilot."

The magus was exactly what Silence had expected, a wizened, elderly man who kept over-furnished offices in a building wedged between two tuning sheds. A ship was being tuned next door; Silence felt the vibration as she entered the magus's office, but heavy felt padding inside kept out the last traces of sound. Despite that, the magus pulled a second baffling curtain into place before settling into a chair and motioning for them to be seated.

"I am Doctor Tahir," he said, folding his hands across his stomach. "What can I do for you, sieura, pilot Sirkka?"

"My name is Leigh," Silence said. "I want to contact the magi's Hostel, without going through regular channels."

Tahir nodded. "Oh, yes, that can be done, but it is expensive. After all, I have to live here, and I can hardly afford to anger the authorities—"

"How much?" Silence asked flatly.

"A hundred local credits," the magus said.

Sirkka stirred. "That's outrageous."

"I'll give fifty," Silence said. After a minimum of haggling, they settled on seventy, and Silence separated forty from her book of credit slips. "The balance when my message is delivered."

"Very well, sieura." The magus rose, and returned with the viewing globe in an elaborately carved stand. The globe itself was made of some

purplish crystal, almost opaque. The magus reset-
tled himself, frowning into the clouded depths.

"Your message?" he asked.

Silence closed her eyes, hastily framing words.
"I want to contact the magus Isambard," she began.
Tahir nodded, bending over his globe. "Tell him—"
she paused again, trying to decide just how much
she could say. "Tell him that I'm at the port, that I
agree to his offer, but all three must meet me here,
right away. Or, no, not here, at the Green Man.
Otherwise it's all off."

"Leigh is here," the magus repeated obediently.
"And you agree to Isambard's offer, but they must
meet you at the Green Man immediately or the
deal is off."

"That's right," Silence said.

Tahir gestured over his viewglobe, and the opaque
crystal seemed to clear slightly, purple shadows
moving stiffly in its depths. After a moment, images began to form in the globe's center, the purple fading to other colors. Slowly, a reflection of
Isambard's face took shape in the crystal, not as
clearly defined as an official system would produce,
but distinct enough.

"Well? What is it?" Tahir's lips moved, but
Isambard spoke through him.

Tahir repeated Silence's message.

"Let me talk to her," Isambard snapped.

Tahir hesitated, but Silence pulled another credit
slip from the pad and laid it on the table in front
of him. Tahir nodded, and made a complicated
gesture. Whatever he did took effort, Silence saw:
his wrinkled face was covered with a thin sheen of
sweat.

"Speak," he said, at last.

Isambard's face shifted in the crystal, as though
he had leaned forward, and his voice came, disem-
bodied, from a point in the air just above the

globe. "Silence, you were foolish to go into the port—"

Silence said, "It had to be done. I'll explain when you get here. But I know how to get off-world."

"We're being watched," Isambard said. "We can't leave the Hostel—" He broke off, staring not at Silence but at Tahir, leaning over his crystal. "You, magus. What degree do you hold?"

"I am a doctor of the Art," Tahir began, huffily, and Isambard cut him off.

"Then together we can open a janus gate."

"But, doctor, I haven't the strength for that," Tahir protested. "I wouldn't be able to work for weeks, perhaps months."

Silence ripped off three more credit slips, then tossed the rest of the book onto the table. Tahir's eyes shifted, and Sirkka laughed. Silence said, "Will that cover it?"

The image in the crystal wavered as Tahir reached hungrily for the book, and Isambard said, "Count it later, doctor. We'll begin the gate."

Obediently, Tahir dropped the book into the pocket of his faded gown, and spread his hands flat in the air over the globe. His eyes closed. In the crystal, Silence could see that Isambard had closed his eyes, too, and she guessed that his hands were positioned identically above his own view-globe. Softly, both men began to speak, chanting words that hissed and flowed, but were part of no language Silence knew. She could feel the leashed power in them, shaping and preparing the common air surrounding them. Tahir was sweating harder as he spoke the last syllable; his hands shook, and he stilled them with an effort. Isambard spoke a single, flat-vowelled trisyllable, and Tahir answered quickly, drawing both hands up and away from the globe. The air above the table began to shiver visibly, and Silence felt her spine crawl with the gathering power.

The globe seemed to split open then, the colors blossoming like some bizarre flower. The swirling non-images poured out, moving now like water, until the colored shadows struck an invisible barrier and fell back, eddies curling into each other. Slowly, the colors steadied and then rearranged themselves into a recognizable image. Silence found herself staring directly into a room of the magi's Hostel. Had she dared, she knew she could reach through and touch the wood of the table where Isambard sat.

She shook herself, throwing off the sense of awe that threatened to overcome her. She had heard of janus gates before, and knew that they resulted from the manipulation of purgatory, a less complex manipulation than her own piloting. Two places on the same planet—on the same land mass of the same planet, she corrected herself—could be temporarily joined through purgatory. The power is strictly limited, spatially and temporally, she told herself. I will not be impressed by it.

"Hurry, now," Isambard said. "We can't hold this open for long."

Hastily, Balthasar stepped into the field of vision, followed by Chase Mago. The engineer carried a bag slung over his shoulder; with a small shock, Silence recognized it as the carryall containing her starbooks. Balthasar hesitated, then stepped gingerly onto the low table in the Hostel room.

"Step through, man," Isambard ordered. "Leave the crates."

Silence could see the Delian's chest move as he took a deep breath and held it, then stepped from one table to the other. She put out a hand to steady him down, and Balthasar took it. He looked almost surprised at the solidity of her touch.

"Silence, what the hell's going on?"

"Later," Silence said, and turned to help the engineer.

Chase Mago misunderstood her outstretched hand, however, and passed the carryall through first. Silence took it, relieved in spite of herself, and then the engineer stepped through the gate. Isambard looked up, and Tahir's eyes flashed open.

"I'm sorry, doctor, but I can't hold it alone. I haven't the strength—"

"I can see that," Isambard said. "Silence—sieura Leigh. You said you'd accepted my offer, did you not?"

"Yes," Silence said.

"Then you'll get your first lesson now." Despite the strain, Isambard's lips curved in the ghost of a smile. "Doctor, the sieura is an untrained talent; you can draw on her for support."

Tahir looked up, startled. "A woman? Impossible."

"Trust me," Isambard said. "Silence, put yourself into a pilot's trance."

Silence could see the strain on his face, and did not argue. She closed her eyes and took a deep breath, focusing her mind. Usually, she sought the learning state in order to memorize difficult voidmarks; the phrase that evoked it best was the ancient riddle of the gate that was not a gate. But this gate is a gate, she thought, a joining of spaces through purgatory. She felt the world fall away around her, and saw the edges of the janus gate shadowed by an image like the door that ended the Lion Road.

"Don't think," Isambard said sharply. "Just sit there. Don't do anything."

Silence closed her eyes, letting herself slide into the self-absorption that was fatal to a pilot's trance but seemed somehow perfect for this. She listened to the soothing rush of blood in her veins, her slowing heartbeat and the steady sigh of breath, the subtle burring of bone on cartilage and, in a core that was not physically central, a whisper of wakened song. Tahir's touch, when it came, was like the touch of cold hands—startling, but not painful. His presence struck echoes from her own power, like notes of a harmonium repeated in a sounding keel. She savored the sense of strength flowing from her, riding the crest of that song. All too soon it was over, and she opened her eyes.

The gate had vanished, and the air no longer smelled of power. Isambard was bending over the other magus, who rested his head on his folded arms.

"If you'd listened to me," Isambard began, then shook his head. "Rest a few days, you'll be all right." He nodded at Sirkka. "Would you, sieura, find the doctor's kitchen and brew tea?"

"I'm a pilot," Sirkka snapped, "nobody's maid."

"I'll do it," Chase Mago said quickly, and disappeared through a curtained doorway. Isambard turned away from Tahir, who now seemed to be asleep.

"What's happened, Silence?"

Silence seated herself on one of the webbing chairs, glad Tahir had not drawn too deeply on her power. "I got a message from Fava," she began. "It seems my uncle Otto is back in my life."

Balthasar muttered something, and Silence was glad she could not make out the words. Hurriedly, she repeated what the two Misthians had told her. "There can't be that many people aboard," she finished. "If we can get the crew away, or even most of them, we could take *Black Dolphin*, and be off-world before the authorities realize what's happened." The others were very quiet when she finished, and she blushed, waiting for one of them to demolish the plan. Then Balthasar laughed delightedly.

"Damn it, Silence, that's good," he said. "Yeah, I think it'll work—but we'll have to do more than just get Champuy off the ship. We'll need a distraction; the port authorities are bound to check every ship before it lifts. . . ." His voice trailed off, then strengthened again. "We need a disaster."

"Fire, famine, flood," Silence said, then stopped. "Fire."

"Yes." Balthasar turned on Isambard. "You said back there you did siege engines. Was it true?"

The magus nodded, waiting.

"Can you make snakefire?" Balthasar went on.

Silence felt a small, bloodthirsty smile steal across her face, and hastily suppressed it. Snakefire was a nasty thing, a toy for the expert saboteurs of the Hegemon's best engineer regiments. Planted around the port, the creeping fires would do little real damage, and be almost impossible to extinguish. The authorities would be busy for hours, and at the first rumor of fire, half the ships in the port would be clamoring for permission to lift. And would lift without permission, if they thought the fire was bad enough. If no one in *Dolphin*'s dock panicked immediately, it would be easy enough to frighten them.

Isambard was nodding again, this time in agreement. "Yes, I can do that. It should work."

"What should work?" Chase Mago asked, returning with a pot of tea in one hand, and two battered cups in the other. As he poured a cup and shook Tahir awake long enough to force the magus to drink about half of it, Balthasar explained the plan. The engineer nodded, pouring a cup for Isambard.

"Sirkka, will you contact this Razil?" Chase Mago asked, when the Delian had finished.

Sirkka hesitated, then shrugged. "I can. But he'll want to talk to you, Silence."

Silence made a face. "Yes, he'll want to gloat, all right. But I'll do it—if we contact him from somewhere nobody can trace."

"Here," Sirkka suggested, and Isambard nodded.

"I'm sure Tahir won't mind," he said, and there was an edge in his voice that made the other magus nod drowsily. "But first I'll have to create the snakefire—you do have a workshop I can use, don't you, doctor?"

"I—" Tahir began, and Isambard laid a second book of credit slips on the table.

"I'll also rig a protected line for your communications system," Isambard went on. "And then you'll forget that we were ever here. This is for the inconvenience."

"I swear," Tahir murmured, and fell asleep again.

"The workshop's the first door on the left," Chase Mago said. "I thought it was the kitchen."

"All right." Isambard looked around, took a volume from the single bookcase. "Make yourselves comfortable."

It took the magus nearly two hours to create enough snakefire to make an effective diversion, and another hour to find the right places to leave the deadly little packages. Silence used that time to plot a course for Tycha. It was a common staging point, with an easy departure and a familiar set of voidmarks. Then the three men were gone, and Silence was left alone with Sirkka and the sleeping magus, to stare nervously at the elaborately inlaid communications unit.

"Half an hour," Sirkka said at last. "Time to call."

Silence nodded, unable to speak.

The Misthian looked oddly at her, and reached for the machine, punching in a series of numbers.

"No picture," Silence said, and Sirkka nodded.

"*Black Dolphin.*" Silence did not recognize the voice.

Sirkka said, "I wish to reach sieur Merestun."

There was a brief hesitation, and then the voice said, "Wait." Static followed.

"Merestun," a new voice said, and Silence shivered.

"This is Sirkka neMafalda. We spoke of a woman pilot? She expressed interest in your terms."

There was muttering in the background, and Razil said, "Put a picture on."

Sirkka looked at Silence, who shook her head. The Misthian said, "I'm sorry, the camera's not working."

"Then find one that does work," Razil said grimly, "or we don't talk."

Sirkka glanced again at Silence, who shrugged and reached across to flip the switch herself. A thin screen unfolded from the back of the machine. and a face began to take shape beneath its creamy surface. As it took on resolution, Silence could see the expression change from worry to a cruel satisfaction. A shadow fell across the bulkhead behind Razil, a shadow too thin to belong to him: Champuy was standing just out of camera range. Silence stiffened.

"Well, Silence," Razil said. "Well, niece. All your fine plans come to nothing?"

"Wait," Sirkka said sharply, and Silence was glad of the interruption. "What about my money?"

For a moment, it seemed as though Razil would not answer, but then Champuy murmured something, and Razil said, "It'll be sent."

"Not good enough," Sirkka said. She switched

on the console beneath the machine, and said, "Transmit it now, or I cut the line."

"All right."

A moment later, the screen flashed white, then displayed numbers and code letters as the fee was transmitted to the Misthian's account. Sirkka nodded. "All yours, Silence," she said, and stepped out of the camera's eye, turning her back on the machine.

"Well, niece," Razil said again. "And what happened to that man of yours? Did he dump you when you wrecked his ship?"

"I—" Silence checked herself. "No."

"Or did they just find a better pilot?"

"Does your offer stand?" Silence asked.

Razil paused a moment, scowling, but another mutter from off-screen prompted him. "I haven't made an offer," he said.

"You told Sirkka you could get me off-world. What's the price?"

"Just you?" Razil leered. "Not your rugged captain?"

This is worse than I expected, Silence thought. "Let me talk to Champuy," she said aloud. "You're useless, Otto."

Razil stiffened, but Champuy stepped into the picture, and the other's angry response died. "Here I am, sieura Leigh," Champuy said. "What do you want?"

"You said you'd get me off-world," Silence said again. Suddenly she was overcome with disgust at this role she had to play, and she only just stopped herself from pressing the disconnect button. "What's it going to cost me?"

Champuy smiled thinly. "I know what you did for your former captain. I want the same thing, and I know you almost made it. I want you to work for me."

"At what pay?" Silence asked.

"The usual rates for a pilot of your experience," Champuy answered. "Plus hazard, of course."

"And a share of the profit."

"We can discuss that when you come aboard," Champuy said.

"No." Silence shook her head. "We'll settle that first. But not now; I've talked too long already." Out of the corner of her eye, she saw Sirkka nod. "You know Lady Maisry's?" Sirkka had given that as the name of one of the larger bars, and Champuy nodded. "Good. I'll be there in half an hour. We'll talk there."

"All right," Champuy said, "but—"

"Be there," Silence said, and pressed the disconnect button. Sirkka turned to face her.

"He'll come," the Misthian said.

"He'd better," Silence answered. She picked up the carryall Chase Mago had left for her, its weight comfortably familiar. "Point me toward the right shed, will you?"

Sirkka smiled. "I can do better than that," she said. "Come on."

Sirkka led her from the magus's office to a narrow street running between the tuning sheds, and then to a second street that ran behind the outer row of buildings. She hesitated at the main entrance of the docking shed, but Silence waved her on. The watchman, ensconced comfortably in his glassed-in booth, barely blinked at them; nothing else moved in the long corridor between the two rows of curtained starships.

"Your *Dolphin*'s the eighth down," Sirkka murmured.

Silence nodded, and started as confidently as she could down the main corridor. After a fractional hesitation, Sirkka followed her. At the third baffled cradle, Silence pushed aside the curtain and slipped into the dock space. Behind her, she heard a muffled protest, but ignored the Misthian. She walked the length of the compartment, hardly daring to breathe for fear she would wake someone on the cradled freighter. But nothing moved above her. At the rear curtain, she stooped and lifted the weighted cloth. Sirkka slid under on her knees, then held the curtain while Silence crawled out. Together, they eased it back to its original folds. When it was down, Sirkka caught the other woman's arm.

"Are you crazy? Maybe this cow doesn't put bells on the curtain, but that merchant will. You'll never get in this way."

Silence shook her off. "I haven't seen a bell yet. And the others are waiting here."

The Misthian shrugged, plainly not convinced. Silence ignored her. They stood in a narrow corridor running between the walls of the shed itself and the long row of baffle curtains that soaked up every sound. She stared up at the maze of ceiling wires that held the baffles in place, tracing out the divisions between the spaces. She had just found the eighth place when someone stepped out of the curtain in front of her.

"Denis!" The baffles absorbed her exclamation, but Balthasar set a finger to his lips.

"Hello," he said. "I thought you'd never get here."

"Is everything set?" Silence asked.

"Absolutely." Balthasar was grinning, elated.

"When do they go off?" Sirkka asked. "I've got to get back to the ship, warn my captain."

"I spoke to Fava," Chase Mago said. "This way—we kicked out an emergency panel. You've got about twenty minutes before the first one goes, so you'd better hurry."

Silence watched as Chase Mago led the Misthian

toward an almost invisible hole in the wall panels, then turned back to Balthasar. "And Champuy?"

"We saw him leave in a hurry with his bodyguard. Your uncle's still aboard, as best we can tell."

"So it's just him and their pilot?" Silence asked.

"No." Isambard stepped from the curtain, holding up a metal oval like a tuner's egg. "There's only one person aboard that ship."

Silence looked to Balthasar, who shrugged. "Maybe they fired their pilot, or he quit, or something. It doesn't matter." He rummaged in a carryall with shiny sides that betrayed its newness, and produced an army-issue heylin. Silence took it awkwardly, the weight dragging at her shoulder.

"Sorry it's not a rifle," Balthasar said, "but that was all I could get on short notice. Julie?"

The engineer finished replacing the emergency panel and looked up. "What?"

"How long?"

Chase Mago consulted his chrono. "Sixteen minutes."

"Then we'd better get on with it." Balthasar took a deep breath, obviously trying for calm. His face was still twisted in a maniac's grin, and Silence felt the same expression on her own face. "All right," Balthasar continued. "Julie and I'll go first—you two hold the curtain, and come right behind. The lock's a standard model, isn't it, Silence?"

"It was."

"The device I gave you will open everything but a magus's personal lock," Isambard said.

"Let's hope so," Balthasar said. "When we get aboard, Silence, you head straight for the control room. Lock yourself in, and don't open up until you hear from me. We'll deal with your uncle. And once I get rid of him, Julie, you start warming the engines—the first capsule should've blown by then. I'll grab a tug. Is that clear?"

Silence nodded once, and Isambard said, "Yes."

Chase Mago looked thoughtful, then shrugged. "Clear enough. Let's go."

Silence glanced up at the edge of the curtain, where the baffle was fastened to the support wires. She saw no alarm bells, but could not be entirely sure they weren't sewn onto the inner side of the fabric. She stooped and, slowly and carefully, lifted the edge of the curtain. The upper half of the curtain didn't move as she eased it up about a foot. Isambard took hold of it as well, taking some of the weight, and Balthasar said softly, "O.K., that's enough."

He dropped to his knees, then to his stomach, and pulled himself through. Chase Mago followed more slowly, easing his greater bulk through the gap. Silence exchanged glances with the magus, and Isambard nodded.

"After you, sieura."

Silence released the greasy fabric and stretched herself out flat on the dirty tiles. She wriggled through, felt one edge, unsupported on that side, scrape down her body from shoulder to knees. There was no sound from the alarm bells, if indeed there had been any. Then she was through, and scrambled to her feet to hold the curtain for Isambard. The magus crawled through quickly, and Silence lowered the curtain after him. Only then did she turn to face her ship.

They've changed her utterly, she thought. There was a gun turret, gleaming with fresh, raw paint, and the top of the hull was welded with new seams. The stubby wings showed signs of the same sort of tampering, a pair of cannon poking from beneath sampling pods. Then Balthasar beckoned urgently from the top of the cradle stairs, and Silence hur-

ried to join him, putting aside her anger. Balthasar
had already applied the magus's device to the hum-
ming lock as Silence came up the stairs. As she
flattened herself against the hull, Balthasar pushed
buttons on the machine's top and flinched back,
breathing quickly. Silence tensed, waiting for
alarms or an explosion, but nothing happened.
Then a tiny light set in one corner of the device
went from red to green, Balthasar's tense shoulders relaxed; he reached forward and uncoupled
the device, then gestured for Chase Mago to open
the hatch. Very carefully, the big engineer twisted
the lock wheel, then tugged it backward. The hatch
swung free without a sound.

Instantly, Balthasar was through the opening
and into the lock area, heylin held ready. A moment later, he leaned out again, motioning them
in.

"No one in sight," he whispered. "Julie, come
with me. Silence, take the control room, and you,
Isambard, mind the hatch."

The others nodded, and Isambard let the hatch
close again with a gentle thud. Balthasar winced,
but gestured for Chase Mago to follow him forward,
toward the common area. Silence hesitated, then
took a deep breath and followed them, cradling
her heylin in both hands. The common area was
empty, and she reached for the ladder to the bridge,
but Balthasar caught her shoulder.

"Which is your uncle's cabin?"

Silence glanced back, trying to ignore the gap-
ing door that led to the cabin that had been hers.
"Back down, on the left across from the engine
room."

"Right. Now get on up." Balthasar touched her
shoulder and turned away, taking the engineer
with him. Silence hesitated momentarily at the
bottom of the ladder, the heylin heavier than ever

in her hands. There was no sound from the control room, and she started to climb.

The lower bridge was empty, as she had expected, and she glanced at the monitor lights. They glowed steady orange: the systems were on standby. Frowning, she started to set the heylin aside to tend to them, and then she heard a tiny scuffling sound from above her. She whirled, bringing up the heylin and firing in a reflex motion. She missed, but Razil's shot went wild, shattering a square of deck tile. He was on the upper bridge, with the upper hand. . . . Silence edged around the base of the ladder, waiting for her one clear shot. She knew she should call Balthasar and Chase Mago, let them handle this, but Razil was her kin, her enemy. He was her affair.

Something moved above, the hint of a shadow crossed her path. She stepped back, suddenly sure of herself as she had never been before. She fired once, and knew before Razil's heylin clattered to the deck that she had hit him. Then the shadow lengthened on the decking, and her uncle fell past her, the ladder guiding his fall. She raised her heylin to shoot again, but there was no need. She kicked the fallen heylin into a corner, then knelt beside the body. There was no wound to be seen, and she felt for his pulse. Her own heart was beating so strongly it was hard to tell just what she felt, but after a moment she felt his pulse beneath her fingers. Appalled, she looked down at her heylin, and saw that the selector pointed to the lowest, non-lethal setting. Slowly, she released her uncle's throat and twisted the dial, turning up the power to a setting that would surely kill. She lowered the heylin until the muzzle touched Tazil's chest. Then the heylin wavered and fell, and she looked away. The anger that had fueled her, that would have let her kill him, was gone, and she could not call it back. She lifted the heylin again, but the gesture was half-hearted, pointless, and she stuffed the heavy gun into the pocket of her coat. If I had killed him in the fight, she thought, pulling herself to her feet, that would have been one thing. I could have done that, and not lost any sleep over it. But to kill him now, in cold blood. . . . I won't do it. Sighing, she leaned out the hatch and shouted for Balthasar.

To her surprise, the Delian did not argue for long about killing Razil. With only a token protest, he agreed to dump the fat man's unconscious body into the corridor behind the baffle curtain.

"Then I've got to get us a tug," Balthasar went on, already dragging Razil's body toward the door. "The first charges have gone, and it sounds like everything's going according to plan." Then he was gone, and Silence turned her attention to the controls. She settled herself in her grandfather's couch and began to activate the systems. From the sprinkling of green lights across the board, Chase Mago was doing the same thing in the engine room; Silence grinned tightly and concentrated on her own panels.

Very faintly, through the layers of hull and baffling and shed walls, she heard a wail that might be a fire alarm or the yowling of an ill-tuned lift-off. She left the Ficinan model half programmed and reached for the communications board, switching it to the police frequency. There was trouble at every checkpoint, either fire or panic; the emergency channel was not much clearer, two different voices trying to direct fire-fighting homunculi to the widely scattered fires. But it was the third channel, the direct line to the control tower, that told her what she wanted. A dozen voices were snapping at the port authority, demanding instant clearance to lift off.

"—fire threatening—"

"—cargo is valuable, can't risk it—"

"—leaving right now, like it or not—"

That was what she had been waiting to hear, and she thumbed on her own transmitter, moving the needle slightly away from the frequency line to garble the message. "Port Master, this is *Black Dolphin*. I request clearance for an immediate lift-off—"

The machine emitted a burst of static that made her jump back in her couch and, in the sudden quiet that followed, the port master's voice said strongly, "Ships will be evacuated according to their proximity to dangerous fire sites, beginning with docks 7a and c. Those ships have permission to leave immediately. Ships in docks 3 and 4 should prepare to follow."

For a moment, Silence was afraid the Port Master would quell the panic, and she hesitated, hand hovering over the transmitter switch. Then a new voice broke in. "Not likely. I've got a cargo of flammables, and I'm not waiting for anybody. Either you give me permission now, or the rest of you look out, because I'm going."

That set the others off. The Port Master tried vainly to shout over the noise, to calm the other captains, but it did no good. Silence could hear the rising notes of half a dozen harmonia behind the frantic voices.

"Silence."

Balthasar's voice sounded in her earphones, and she reached guiltily to activate the exterior cameras.

"How's it going? Can I hook up?"

The screens showed a triple image of Balthasar sitting on the edge of a tug's turret, his heylin ready on his lap. A single homunculus was poised to connect the tug to the cradle. In the background, Silence could see other tugs moving at reckless speeds, and other ships preparing for a hurried liftoff.

"Go ahead," she said. "I'll lift when we hit the taxiway."

"Right," Balthasar answered, and Silence turned her attention to the Ficinan model, only half aware of the homunculus's movements in the screen. By the time she had finished with the model, the cradle was attached to the tug, and Chase Mago had signalled from the engine room that everything was ready there. She signalled Balthasar and the cradle lurched forward into the towpath. As Balthasar awkwardly turned the linked machines toward the half-open doors, a man ran out from one of the other dock areas, waving his hands wildly. He caught at the low platform where the tug's homunculi sat, and Balthasar shifted his grip on the heylin. The man shouted something, but the selective headset did not pick up his words. Silence heard only Balthasar's response.

"First come, first served, man. Get your own."

The man said something more, but Balthasar raised his heylin, taking deliberate aim, and the other fell back, cursing. Silence looked away from the screen, chilled. The fires were no real danger, but still. . . . She forced herself to concentrate instead on the instruments in front of her. The distortion readings were jumping already, and the interference would be worse once they left the protection of the docking shed.

Then the cradle lumbered out of the massive doors, and the gauges went crazy. Numbers flickered, changed wildly; the warning lights flared red, and the needle of the strain gauge snapped to the top of the scale, well into the danger zone. Chase Mago swore violently, his voice tinny in the earphones, and Silence saw Balthasar drop his heylin and press both hands to his ears.

"Denis!" Silence's hands moved frantically over her boards, trying to block the worst of the interference, or to set up a counterfield. Then the noise fell away somewhat, and she saw in the screens the sliver of a rising keel. "It's no good, we'll have to get down the taxiway. I can't lift in this soup...." Balthasar was shaking himself, straightened slowly to adjust the controls of the tug. The homunculus lay sprawled, half falling from its platform, its delicately balanced existence completely disrupted by the music of the other ship's harmonium. "Denis, do you hear me? Get farther down the taxiway."

Balthasar lifted a hand in shaky acknowledgement. Silence nodded at the image and focused one of the screens on the port itself. The orderly pattern of pale blue warning lights and darkened streets, topped by the bright gold windows of the Customs Building, was broken by the flashing red of the firefighters' lights, by searchlights and the glow of flames and, nearer still, the rainbow gleams of lifting keels. She switched a second screen to the portside camera, trying to keep tabs on the ships around them, but it was clear she would have to rely on the musonar to avoid collisions.

"Julie," she said, "how's our tuning? How far out do we have to be?"

There was a long pause before Chase Mago answered. "We're still not in good position. Another hundred yards, maybe, if there's no more distortion...."

His words were drowned by another roar from outside. Silence saw Balthasar double up in agony, then slip down into the body of the tug. Had he fallen, or decided to risk not being able to see?

"Denis?" she said again.

"I'm all right," Balthasar answered, "but we've got to get off soon."

Silence glanced at the distortion readings, fall-

ing with every meter they travelled down the
taxiway. "Just a few more minutes," she said. In
the screen that showed the port, she saw new lights,
blue-white flashes like lightning: the port authorities had brought their defense cannon into action,
and were firing on the fleeing ships.

"Stop everything," she ordered. "We're going."

In the screen, she saw Balthasar wrestle briefly
with the coupling that connected tug and cradle,
then throw up his hands in disgust and disappear
from camera range, heading for the hatch. A few
moments later, the hatch indicator flared red, and
its alarm sounded as Balthasar came aboard. Then
the light went out, and Silence concentrated on
the readings in front of her. The interference was
still high, but Chase Mago would have to handle
that. Her concern was the fleet of ships that filled
the sky around them, twenty or more pinpoints of
light on the musonar screen. Then the harmonium
surged, and Chase Mago said, "First sequence."

"Go ahead," Silence answered, and before the
words were out of her mouth felt the sudden roar
of song. The darkened field fell away in the screens,
but the ship was shaking badly, caught in some
other ship's distorting wake. Silence glanced from
musonar to the screens to the distortion gauges,
trying to find the interfering starship. The musonar
was too large-scale, she realized with a surge of
fear. The screens were nearly useless in the dark.
Only the strain gauges were of much use in locat-
ing another ship. She banked away from her departure path, feeling new strain build in the keel until
Chase Mago realized what she was doing, and adjusted the pitch of the harmonium, and sought a
new line that was free of other ships. She found
one, then saw the same flickering interference build
on her indicators. She turned the ship away again,
but the other pilot had turned toward her, the

strain needles shooting to the far side of the gauge. Too frightened to swear, she pushed *Dolphin*'s nose down and saw, in one screen, the reflected light of the other ship's keel. A moment later, the ship was shaken by a wave of disharmony that wracked bones and flesh as well as metal. Silence clung to her controls, blinded by the sudden pain.

Then that noise faded, and she pulled the ship back into line, ignoring the new dissonance in the harmonium's song. The strain gauges stayed steady, however, showing only background interference, and the musonar seemed to indicate no other ships in the vicinity. Silence stayed hunched over her keyboard, not daring to relax until *Black Dolphin* was free of the clinging planetary influence.

They passed the boundary at last. Leaning back in her couch, Silence twisted her hands together, loosening cramped muscles. In the musonar screen, she could see dozens of other ships rising from the planet, points of light like seeds thrown off by a puffball, exploding from the surface. The Ficinan model showed her course clearly, free of other ships, and she let *Black Dolphin* take itself into that sympathetic harmony. The readings were green; even the dissonance she had heard on liftoff smoothed from the harmonium's song, and she let herself relax completely. The keel would carry the ship to the twelfth of heaven with or without her.

"Beautiful," Balthasar said quietly.

She turned, and found him standing behind her, supporting himself against the ladder from the common area. He looked tired, his face shadowed by a memory of pain, but he was smiling. Silence smiled back, triumph rising within her.

"Beautiful, darling, a lovely job." Balthasar released his hold on the ladder, came toward her with arms outstretched. Silence rose to meet the embrace, and held him tightly against her.

In her headphones, Chase Mago was saying, over and over, "My God, we made it. We made it."

Silence's smile grew broader, then faded slightly as the impossibility of it all hit her. I'm still a pilot, she thought, and a damned good one; I'm to be a magus; and I'm a ship's master. . . . It's not real. I'll wake up in my old bunk with Otto yelling for me to get out and do my job. She took a deep breath, willing herself to accept the truth. Otto was stranded on Mersaa Maia—and thinking of that humiliation, she was glad she had not killed him—the *Dolphin* was hers, and a magus's power was to be hers as well.

A light was flashing on the control board, demanding her attention, but she ignored it for just a moment longer, savoring her victory.

Coming in May 1985 from Baen Books—Poul Anderson's
first Terran Empire/Polesotechnic League novel in years!

THE GAME OF EMPIRE

Dominic Flandry has fought the good fight—but now
he is of an age more suited to deciding the fate of
empires from behind the throne. Others must take up
the challenge of courting danger on strange planets
filled with creatures stranger still . . . and such a one is
Diana Flandry, heir to all her father's adventures! Here
is an excerpt from THE GAME OF EMPIRE:

She sat on the tower of St. Barbara, kicking her heels
from the parapet, and looked across immensity. Overhead,
heaven was clear, deep blue save where the sun Patricius
stood small and fierce at midmorning. Two moons were
wanly aloft. A breeze blew cool. It would have been
deadly cold before Diana's people came to Imhotep; the
peak of Mt. Horn lifts a full twelve kilometers above sea
level.

"Who holds St. Barbara's holds the planet." That saying
was centuries obsolete, but the memory kept alive a
certain respect. Though ice bull herds no longer threatened to stampede through the original exploration base;
though the Troubles which left hostile bands marooned
and desperate, turning marauder, had ended when the
hand of the Terran Empire reached this far; though the
early defensive works would be useless in such upheav-
als as threatened the present age, and had long since
been demolished: still, one relic of them remained in
Olga's Landing, at the middle of what had become a
market square. Its guns had been taken away for scrap,
its chambers echoed hollow, sunseeker vine clambered
over the crumbling yellow stone of it, but St. Barbara's
stood yet; and it was a little audacious for a hoyden to
perch herself on top.

Diana often did. The neighborhood had stopped
minding—after all, she was everybody's friend—and to

strangers it meant nothing, except that human males were apt to shout and wave at the pretty girl. She grinned and waved back when she felt in the mood, but had learned to decline the invitations. Her aim was not always simply to enjoy the ever-shifting scenes. Sometimes she spied a chance to earn a credit or two, as when a newcomer seemed in want of a guide to the sights and amusements. At present she had no home of her own, unless you counted a ruinous temple where she kept hidden her meager possessions and, when nothing better was available, spread her sleeping bag.

Life spilled from narrow streets and surged between the walls enclosing the plaza. Pioneer buildings had run to brick, and never gone higher than three or four stories, under Imhotepan gravity. Booths huddled everywhere else against them. The wares were as multifarious as the sellers, anything from hinterland fruits and grains to ironware out of the smithies that made the air clangorous, from velvyl fabric and miniature computers of the inner Empire to jewels and skins and carvings off a hundred different worlds. A gundealer offered primitive home-produced chemical rifles, stunners of military type, and—illegally—several blasters, doubtless found in wrecked spacecraft after the Merseian onslaught was beaten back.

Folk were mainly human, but it was unlikely that many had seen Mother Terra. The planets where they were born and bred had marked them. Residents of Imhotep were necessarily muscular and never fat. Those whose families had lived here for generations, since Olga's Landing was a scientific base, and had thus melded into a type, tended to be dark-skinned and aquiline-featured.

A Navy man and a marine passed close by the tower. They were too intent on their talk to notice Diana, which was extraordinary. The harshness reached her: "—yeh, sure, they've grown it back for me." The spaceman waved his right arm. A short-sleeved undress shirt revealed it pallid and thin; regenerated tissue needs exercise to attain normal fitness. "But they said the budget doesn't allow repairing DNA throughout my body, after the radiation I took. I'll be dependent on biosupport the rest of my life, and I'll never dare father any kids."

"Merseian bastards," growled the marine. "I could damn near wish they had broken through and landed.

My unit had a warm welcome ready for 'em, I can tell you."

"Be glad they didn't," said his companion. "Did you really want nukes tearing up our planets? Wounds and all, I'll thank Admiral Magnusson every day I've got left to me, for turning them back the way he did, with that skeleton force the pinchfists on Terra allowed us." Bitterly: "*He* wouldn't begrudge the cost of fixing up entire a man that fought under him."

They disappeared into the throng. Diana shivered a bit and looked around for something cheerier than such a reminder of last year's events.

Nonhumans were on hand in fair number. Most were Tigeries, come from the lowlands on various business, their orange-black-white pelts vivid around skimpy garments. Generally they wore air helmets, with pressure pumps strapped to their backs, but on some, oxygills rose out of the shoulders, behind the heads, like elegant ruffs. Diana cried greetings to those she recognized. Otherwise she spied a centauroid Donarrian; the shiny integuments of three Irumclagians; a couple of tailed, green-skinned Shalmuans; and—and—

"What the flippin' fury!" She got to her feet—they were bare, and the stone felt warm beneath them—and stood precariously balanced, peering.

Around the corner of a Winged Smoke house had come a giant.

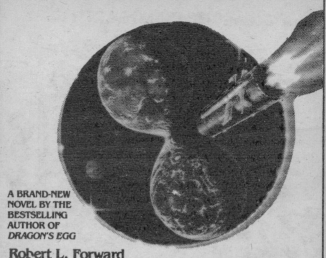

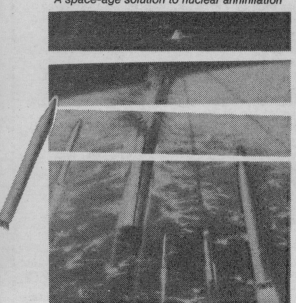